CALL OF THE DRAGON

PENGUIN BOOKS

Also by
NATASHA BOWEN

Skin of the Sea
Soul of the Deep

CALL OF THE DRAGON

NATASHA BOWEN

PENGUIN BOOKS

PENGUIN BOOKS

UK | USA | Canada | Ireland | Australia
India | New Zealand | South Africa

Penguin Books is part of the Penguin Random House group of companies
whose addresses can be found at global.penguinrandomhouse.com

www.penguin.co.uk   www.puffin.co.uk   www.ladybird.co.uk

First published in the USA by Random House Books,
and in Great Britain by Penguin Books 2026
001

Text copyright © Natasha Bowen, 2026
Jacket art copyright © Stonenexus, 2026

The moral right of the author has been asserted

Penguin Random House values and supports copyright.
Copyright fuels creativity, encourages diverse voices, promotes freedom
of expression and supports a vibrant culture. Thank you for purchasing
an authorized edition of this book and for respecting intellectual property
laws by not reproducing, scanning or distributing any part of it by any
means without permission. You are supporting authors and enabling
Penguin Random House to continue to publish books for everyone.
No part of this book may be used or reproduced in any manner for the
purpose of training artificial intelligence technologies or systems. In accordance
with Article 4(3) of the DSM Directive 2019/790, Penguin Random House
expressly reserves this work from the text and data mining exception.

Printed and bound in Great Britain by Clays Ltd, Elcograf S.p.A.

The authorized representative in the EEA is Penguin Random House Ireland,
Morrison Chambers, 32 Nassau Street, Dublin D02 YH68

A CIP catalogue record for this book is available from the British Library

ISBN: 978-0-241-70686-2

All correspondence to:
Penguin Books
Penguin Random House Children's
One Embassy Gardens, 8 Viaduct Gardens, London SW11 7BW

Penguin Random House is committed to a
sustainable future for our business, our readers
and our planet. This book is made from Forest
Stewardship Council® certified paper.

To Emmanuel.
For always listening to me, even when I don't make sense . . .
especially when I don't make sense.

PROLOGUE

The goddess twists deep in the earth, as her husband soars among clouds that crown the sky. There is regret, and the sigh that escapes her is teeth and fire and magic that eat at her burrow.

Yida closes her eyes in long blinks, remembers skimming newborn stars and drifting in the tails of comets. This was the time before they tired of the cold deep and banished the shadow spirits to make this world their own. A time before the creation of the seven kingdoms and the people's expectations.

She pictures her husband among the glitter of gases, warming himself under the sun they always coveted. With a growl, Yida shifts, scales rubbing against the cool rock. The goddess thinks of their reunion, one chosen by stones and stars and the spin of the earth. She turns again, hissing as her nostrils flare at the thought of waiting.

It will soon be time. Yida senses the pull of the heavens, the prayers of the people, and the thunder of their feet as they express their hopes and demands. She shivers despite the heat of the earth, her crimson body trembling as her talons scrape at the rock.

The people are calling.

And the gods will answer.

CHAPTER ONE

When I lift my gaze, it is to scales that shimmer in scarlet and gold.

The dragon balances on her enormous coils, wings folded tightly against her sides. Great claws grip the altar, each talon thicker than my wrist. Her mouth is open, teeth studded with diamonds that sparkle in the flickering light of the temple's torches. The statue of Yida rises before me, as tall as the subterranean chamber that stretches around us, dark rock glittering with veins of gold. Her head touches the stalactites of the cavern, eyes of black pearls gleaming as I hold a hand to my heart and bow before the goddess.

"Please," I whisper. "Grant me your blessings this day."

The prayer hall fills quickly, swarming with priestesses wearing wrappers in the browns of the earth, their hair rivers of black braids. I flush when I see Iya standing with Kakra and Panyin, scanning the crowd of women and girls, looking for me. I was hoping to stay unnoticed, but from the curl of my mother's beckoning gesture, I know I will have no such luck. My back is slick with sweat as I ease my way through the crowd.

"There you are." The lines around my mother's mouth loosen as she seizes my wrist. "Come now, take a place at the front where I can see you. And try not to look as if you are about to pass out. Remember, you are my daughter."

Not your father's. The unsaid words hover between us. She thinks that if everything is perfect, then it will make up for his shame. The years have not softened the ache of his absence, and I force myself not to blink so that the sudden glaze of tears doesn't fall.

Iya glides up the short steps hewn from gray rock, the last priestesses enter the hall, and the doors are closed as my mother steps forward. She waits for absolute silence, glittering in swaths of golden fabric. Thin chains drape across her forehead, loop around the long column of her neck, and lie across her chest. Wide bands of gold encircle her wrists. Her hair snakes down to her waist, and when she raises her head, the brown skin of shaved undersides gleams between braids.

As the principal iyalawo, she lights the amber candles and replaces a bowl of old rice with a new one, setting it on the altar next to the crystal she keeps there, which shines in the colors of a fresh dawn I so rarely get to see. Said to be one of Yida's tears, shed when the dragon goddess decided she was missing her husband, it's always on display. Carefully, Iya scoops out twists of gold from a pouch that hangs next to the crystal, adding to the growing pile that glints in the torchlight. With each full moon, she takes the gold down to the inner sanctum, deep inside the mountain, offering it to the goddess herself. When I was very small, I'd wait by the door, terrified the dragon would devour her, even though I knew better.

"Yida, Mother of the Earth, we send you our gratitude for the world you helped create with Dam, for the weight you bear as you coil deep beneath us. We give our prayers to you through the layers of this world, with gold to show you the wealth of our love, and food to return the nurture you provide. Please feel our gratitude for sharing your idan with us, and for keeping our kingdom pure." Iya surveys the hall full of girls and women with flashing eyes. "We give thanks that tonight Dam's stars will hover over your holy stones, signaling the next Dírágónì ceremony, a decade since the last. We give thanks that some of the pious will be chosen and that the gods will imbue them with their idan. And we give thanks that Yida and Dam will use their idan to cleanse the lands, keeping the emi buburu at bay and ensuring that the shadow spirits cannot return to destroy our world."

My mother holds up her hands, and the hem of her wrapper lifts high enough to show the red dragon that coils around her ankle. No one utters a word as she raises her right foot and brings it down on the floor in a stamp that slaps hard in the quiet. She does the same with her left, and then the hundreds of women and girls copy her, filling the hall with the pounding of their feet.

I point my toes to begin the prayer, and frowning slightly, I try to relax and bring my sole down. The stone floor is rough against the skin of my feet, but I relish the sting, letting it hone my focus. Beside me, a girl who only reaches my shoulders whirls along to my mother's moves, and I spin with her, breathing hard as I try my best to count the steps between each movement.

"We send our prayers into the very earth!" Iya shouts as she stands before us, thick plaits cascading over one shoulder.

"Only when we are barefoot can we connect with the land. Connect with Yida. To look forward to welcoming her. And to remind the goddess of our eternal thanks for the blessings and power she bestows on the Kingdom of Kwa."

A group of girls press closer to my mother, seeking her praise. Like that will help them. Yida will choose whom she pleases.

There's only a little time left before I am needed. I clamber to my feet, patting the bag that bumps against my hip, taking comfort in the crush of wild ginger and lavender inside. It's time to check on my batch of alligator pepper infusion and collect the henna paste, but I know I'll need to slip out to avoid having to help with temple preparations.

I hurry through the prayer hall doors just as a temple nundá slinks through my legs, nearly tripping me. The feline yowls in annoyance, only stopping when I reach down to rub her triangular head. The scriptures say that hundreds of years ago, nundás were bigger and could fly, but now time and breeding have rendered their feathers more decorative than functional.

"Hello, little one," I croon, letting my fingers sink into her plush red fur. The nundás are often desperate for attention, and they steal food but are tolerated by iyalawos because they keep down the population of cloud rats that invade the temple in winter.

The nundá nudges against me before lifting her head, sniffing at the waft of chicken stew coming from the kitchens. She slinks off with another meow, tiny wings fluttering as she pads quickly toward the service tunnel.

I raise my eyebrows. "It's good to see where your priorities lie."

"And what about yours, Moremi?"

Startled, I look down, pointing my toes in respect, my shoulder-length skinny braids creating a curtain between me and Iya. My bag slips and lands on the floor, spilling some of the herbs.

I snatch them up and stuff them back inside. "I'm just going to get the henna to decorate the initiates," I say to Iya. It's not a total lie. I've been perfecting the consistency of the henna for a while, and I can't wait to try it out. But the truth is, I want some air, to escape the crush of the mountain above us.

"Look at me properly, daughter," Iya says.

With a small sigh, I do, eyes lifting from the broadness of her hips and the brown satin of her shoulders.

"Am I that terrible to behold?" asks Iya as she reaches for my hand. Beads of sweat slide through the gold scattered over her round face. She smiles up at me, although the expression does not quite meet her eyes. And there it is. The tiny flicker of disappointment that is always there.

I stoop, painfully aware of how abnormally tall I've grown in the last year, much taller than any of the other girls and women in the temple. Awkward long limbs and the clumsiness of a guiamala foal. I couldn't be more different from my mother. "Of course not, Iya."

"Is there anything you need for later?"

I shake my head. "I just went to find some more herbs while the henna paste was thickening."

"And you added the sanctified golden dust to it?"

"Yes, Iya. The scripture on initiation helped." As did the others on healing herbs and prayers that I managed to slip into my bag. I smile now, a curl of pride catching in me. "The color is exactly what you asked for."

"Good. With Yida's grace, tonight will go well." Iya

tightens her grip on me, her eyes skating over my face as she sucks in her bottom lip for a moment. "And are you sure you don't want to offer yourself to—"

I pull my hand away, scuffing my feet on the rock beneath us. "I told you, I'm happy being an iyalawo of this temple. I'm *proud* of being an iyalawo of this temple. The scriptures speak of so much, and just today I learned that—"

"Yes, yes, we all know how much time you spend in the archives." Iya frowns up at me. "Knowledge is power, but if you were one of the chosen, then you'd be able to channel the goddess's idan. If you just *tried*."

We hold each other's gaze as Iya realizes what she has said. My prayers are not exceptional enough for me to be considered one of the pious, let alone to be chosen by Yida, and they never will be. Of all the priestesses, I have been the slowest to learn the steps, and the most unnatural in my movements. And of all the priestesses, I am the only daughter of the principal iyalawo.

My face flames with heat as I look down at my large feet. Temple prayers have always been hard for me, the rhythm slippery. I've mastered the basics, but that's all it will ever be.

Iya sighs. "Moremi, I just want what is best for you."

I don't respond as I hook the bag back on my shoulder, stomach clenching in that familiar manner. When it comes to my mother, I feel like I am a constant disappointment.

"I need to get the henna for the ceremony," I finally say.

"Of course," says my mother quietly. She looks at me for a small moment before turning her back and heading for the prayer hall.

I open the door of the temple and plunge into a cool afternoon breeze. Free of the press of the earth and the expectations of my mother, I sigh. Warm idan flickers beneath my feet, and I smile at the feel of the goddess's magic.

I tip my face to Dam's temple, perched on the top of Mandara Mountain, where the first babalawos sought to be as near to the sky as possible, all the easier for their prayers to reach Dam. There is a slight chill in the air, and I push my shoulders back, uncurling my spine to stand straight.

The path hugs the mountain, and as I head down, I spot Yida's henge, sprawled at Mandara's base. The stones are tall, but not so tall that a girl cannot climb one. I pause, taking in the shape of their arrangement, one that mimics the goddess's image. Above the henge, carved high into the sheer rock, are the niches the priests will aim for, set out in the same pattern as Dam's constellation. I shiver, thinking of those who will attempt to seek the gods' idan.

"Rather you than me," I mutter as the guiamala compound comes into view, nestled against the side of the rocky slopes. I'd heard the rumors that idan can change a person's mind, not just make them more devout. But they were mostly whisperings of less pious people. *Like me*, I think gloomily.

As I get closer, I spot the creatures' black horns, which sprout tawny hair and are so tall that they top the wattle walls of the enclosure. I have no doubt the guiamalas could crush the pen with their bulky bodies if they wanted to, but they're too docile to do anything but stamp their hooves for food.

"Sorry," I call softly as I duck into the round building that crouches next to their enclosure. I should fetch some hay for them, but if I don't get back to the prayer hall soon, I won't have time to decorate the priestesses.

The smell of honey blooms, nutmeg, and garlic pears greets me as I enter my tiny sanctuary, and I sigh. *Home.* Well, almost. If I could move my bedding roll here, then I'd be truly content. The curved walls hold shelves full of jars with everything from clover, blue basil, and the gowé seed the temple burns to the myrrh I have managed to barter for at the night market.

I slip the scriptures from my bag and add the scrolls to the growing collection on a high shelf. While I'm not really supposed to remove any from the archives, I know that the histories of plants that help treat stomach complaints will not exactly be missed. I stand and look at the dark wooden spines with golden Ajami. Besides, just having them around me makes me happy.

"Let's get to work," I say, knotting a brown length of fabric over my wrapper so I don't stain it.

A large shallow glass dish with a domed lid sits in the center of my workbench, gold swirling through the mixture inside. I've been testing the henna for weeks, wanting a consistency that can hold the glimmer of Yida's gold without being too dense for me to draw ceremonial designs on the iyalawos. And now it is perfect.

I lift the lid and stir it one last time with the small copper spoon next to it. Creamy thick but not entirely solid, it is my best to date. I check the shape I drew on my arm this morning, pleased to see that the henna has retained its color.

"Mo?"

I jump, knocking the bench slightly. I turn around with a scowl to see none other than Nox.

"I told you to knock next time! You're always doing this!"

"Sorry," he says as he ducks through the entranceway, his short curls frosted white.

I huff, taking in hips swathed in a sky-blue wrapper and a

bare chest grown broader this summer. Nox looms over me, wide-set, heavy-lashed eyes crinkled with concern. "I didn't make you ruin anything, did I?"

A wash of marula oil and vanilla rushes over me, the body oil I made for his birthday. His lean muscles gleam with it, skin glowing in the low light. Now I regret making it smell so good. Heat creeps up my neck as I turn my back to him and stir the henna vigorously. "Shouldn't you be helping your father?" I grumble, settling the lid back carefully before I wrap it in cloths.

"I needed some space." Nox waves his large hands dismissively, dancing away, his limbs gangly but coordinated. "Besides, they've been praying for hours now to shift the rains to the southern farms of Kwa. I'm bored. There's not much else I can do until I'm chosen."

"Hmm. Prayers are just as important. Not everyone is chosen, but we all do our part," I chastise, sneaking a look around at the brews and tonics I have made. I might not channel the gods' magic to influence the earth like other iyalawos, or the sky like the priests, but I can still help people.

"Of course, of course."

He watches me as I bustle about and check the alligator pepper infusion I've been working on to help some of the older priestesses' joint pain. As I stir the reddish-brown tonic, I find myself wondering if Nox has noticed that my feet are now nearly as big as his and that my hips are still as narrow as my shoulders. And then I tell myself to stop being so silly.

When we were smaller, as the principal iyalawo's daughter and the babalawo's son, we'd always gravitated toward one another, playing in the meadow beside the mountain, escaping the incense and rituals that marked our home lives. Back then, it had been forts built with branches and small meals of stolen rice in bowls woven from leaves. But last summer, it shifted to discussions of our initiations and the expectations placed on us by our parents. While Nox had shown excitement, I'd fought the crush of pressure to be better. Ever since, I felt both closer to and farther away from him.

"Are you ready for the ceremony?" I ask, adjusting the cloth around the jar of henna so it's tightly swaddled.

"Of course." He lifts an arm and flexes it, his dark brown skin rippling. "I was born ready."

"Why are you showing me your muscles?" I frown, but I can't help my smile. "They might make it easier to climb the mountain, but they don't have anything to do with whether you can sense your god."

"Of course, but they do make me look good, don't you think?" Nox leans closer so our arms touch and winks at me.

I snort with laughter and try to ignore the heat that flushes across my chest. These nerves, the ones around Nox sometimes, are new. And I do what I've been doing for weeks now: I push them away.

"Be careful, though. I've heard the climb to the niches can be treacherous."

Nox flashes a grin and bounces on the balls of his feet. "You know you don't have to worry about me. With this body, I could do it in my sleep."

"Since you're so physically *advanced*," I tease, "you can help me carry all of this to the temple. It's on your way."

I grab a bag of kola nuts for the iyalawos to chew as a way for them to stay awake later. Nox lifts the glass dish carefully, then nudges the door open and starts back up the mountain.

I follow, trying to remind myself to be happy for him. We all respect both gods, but the dragon we worship is the one who used their idan to give life to our ancestors when they created the world. And all Nox has ever wanted is to follow in his baba's footsteps and channel Dam's magic, but when he is chosen—and I have no doubt that he will be—it means we will barely see each other.

And I will still be here.

Nox watches me fiddle with my bag and then bumps me with his hip. "You know I'll still be coming back and barging in on you. And you'll still be getting annoyed with me."

But it won't be the same, I think. I huff a laugh. "I know," I say instead, tipping up my chin and trying to hold his gaze. I push him and force myself to roll my eyes. "Hurry up, stupid."

Once we reach the path that splits, one way to the sky temple and the other to the earth, we pause. The Dírágónì ceremony is only hours away, and those who are chosen will use the gods' idan to aid the kingdom, whether it is priestesses coaxing life into ailing people and crops or priests helping to manage the weather and water sources. For once, Nox looks almost nervous. I take the henna from him and reach up to flick his ear.

"You'll be fine."

"I know," he answers. His eyes are bright. "There's no more time to prepare, so I had better be."

───

My mother waits at the temple entrance amid a throng of young iyalawos, each in a brown wrapper and with a small golden nose piercing. Nerves and smiles ripple through them.

Zaye slinks next to me. I raise a hand to my own nose stud as the knot in my stomach tightens. Although her stature is petite, she is as vicious as a feral nundá. Her wrapper is taut, its folds immaculate. Fine plaits graze her waist as she pushes her shoulders back, her posture perfectly straight. The glow from the torches illuminates her cheekbones as she keeps a half smile on her heart-shaped face.

She looks me up and down, lip curling. "Are you not going to seek the goddess?"

I don't respond. She already knows the answer.

"I can see why you won't," Zaye hisses so only I can hear. "I mean, you don't even have the rhythm to get her prayers right most of the time, *omiran.*"

I am no giant, but the word shames me anyway. I always do my best to ignore her, although I feel my shoulders roll forward as I instinctively try to make myself smaller. Zaye arrived in the temple when we were both ten, fierce and ready to show her love for Yida. Orphans were common new initiates, given a home and a purpose, and the iyalawos didn't speak about her appearance, only that she had a strong feel for the dragon's idan. I'd tried to befriend Zaye by showing her my small metal statue of the goddess. But she'd slapped it out of my hands and called me a baby and that had been that. Zaye opens her mouth to say something else, but I am saved by my mother.

"You have all been selected because you have shown an aptitude for sensing Yida's power, her idan, in the earth, and your prayers are devout. But whether you will be chosen to channel the goddess's magic is yet to be decided."

Iya walks down the steps, followed by her two favored priestesses, carving a path through the crowd. Dark brown wrappers with red-and-gold trim drape the women's muscled bodies. A chain links their nose stud to a large earring in their right ear, marking them as higher-ranking priestesses, but while the women share the same face and frame, their similarities end there.

Kakra offers me a quiet smile as she and her twin sister hold cloths of red in their arms. Panyin does not look at me, but I see her sneer, the scar on the left side of her face pulling at the brown of her full top lip. She sees nothing but my father's mistakes when she looks at me.

She's not the only one.

"If your sense of Yida's idan is truly strong enough, you will be able to make it to her sacred stones when she has been summoned," Iya continues. "Those of you who do will be considered by the goddess."

There are murmurs of excitement now as the girls line the path shadowed by twilight.

"Moremi will anoint each of you before we leave, a blessed sign that you are willing to face Yida and be judged worthy or not."

I stumble over to the stool Kakra places on the ground, nearly tripping, only saved by the priestess, who grasps my shoulder, stopping my fall. I flash her a grateful smile.

One by one, the young iyalawos stand before me while I use the henna to mark their right ankles with a woven filigree of gold. If they are chosen, Yida will replace it with her own mark, but for now it shows their intent, and they all wear it as a badge of honor.

I relax into keeping a steady hand and applying the marks in perfect swirls. When the final girl offers her ankle to me, I squeeze the last of the golden paste and grasp her leg.

"Make sure you do it properly, hey? Not like the lazy prayers you offer to Yida." Zaye grins down at me, lowering her voice. "I'm surprised you've kept your place here. But then, I guess your little potions do come in handy."

I take a sharp breath and force myself to think of the purple of the lavender I found today. It will be used well in the temple washhouse, and I know Kakra and Ayo will be particularly pleased with the scent. With some calm found, I ready the henna.

"Hold still, please."

And she does for one moment, then jerks, breaking the perfect line I began.

"Look at what you've done. You've ruined my anointment!"

I look up at Zaye's large eyes and her small mouth contorted into a faked pout. She shakes her head, long thin braids rippling like grass snakes. "Perhaps you have taken on more than you can handle. Perhaps . . ." She leans forward, her voice coiling between us like smoke. "Perhaps you're just as useless as your father."

At the mention of Baba, I drop the henna. My fingers curl as anger sparks and jumps, heating my blood.

"Speak those words again." My voice is low and hoarse, drawn tight. I open my mouth, but any other words are strangled by the grief that never leaves.

"I don't need to," Zaye says. "Everyone already knows that it was his lunacy that caused Ọba Ojaja to banish him. Worshipping Yida and Dam *separately* is in our blood. It's madness to pray to both." She leans closer to me now, still smiling, baring a small chip on her right canine. "Some say the shadow spirits possessed him and ate all his senses."

"Baba was not evil." I blink hard, imagining fighting back. *I could,* I think. *I should.* My right hand twitches, palm closing to form a loose fist.

"Go on," Zaye sneers. "I dare you. Or are you just like your father, cowardly as well as crazy?"

Baba would have told me to walk away, and Iya would have told me to remember my place as her daughter. But all I can think of is the venom in Zaye's words. My vision wavers. My fingers flex but my hand doesn't pick the henna back up. Instead, it cuts through the air, catching Zaye on the side of her face.

At the smacking sound of flesh on flesh, my head clears, leaving me with a brief sense of satisfaction. The girl's full mouth hangs open in shock, her hand pressed to the cheek I have just slapped. Violence is not the way of Yida's temple or Dam's, and I swallow, the guilt instant.

Zaye doesn't leave me any space to apologize, though. She lunges, her clawed fingers grabbing a handful of my braids. There's a stinging across my scalp as she tugs, and I swing wildly, feeling my hands graze her shoulders, scraping her wrapper. I scrabble at the thick fabric and push her away from me so that she stumbles backward against the rocks, and for a moment, I don't even care when I hear something crack.

But then I look down at the girl who lies sprawled against the mountain, her leg hanging at an unnatural angle.

"What is going on?!" barks Panyin, her mouth pulled down as she runs over to us.

Zaye whimpers on the floor as Kakra steps forward, her gaze sweeping over mine as she frowns. "Did you do this?"

The softness of her words brings the guilt crashing back. Panyin reaches for Zaye, trying to lift her. The older woman shifts, her feet moving in the practiced dance of a basic healing prayer, and the hem of her wrapper twists up, the dragon wrapped around her ankle glowing in a sheen of gold as she channels the goddess's idan. Zaye's leg jerks once, twice, and straightens.

"Why, Moremi?" Kakra's eyes flit over mine. "This is not like you. What happened?"

"She . . . She said . . ." But I can't get the words out. I don't even want the shape of them in my mouth.

"Sister, it does not matter what happened." Panyin releases Zaye, her eyes hard as she signals to a few older iyalawos, who rush over to the girl curled on the floor. "Her leg was broken. The bones have been mended, but she will need rest, and there is no way she will be able to take part in the ceremony with the pain."

Iya hurries over to us and I drop my gaze. "What happened here?"

"It was Moremi!" Zaye's voice quivers in a hiss. "She pushed me after she couldn't get the anointed mark right."

"I did *not*—"

My mother holds a hand up, her mouth pressed tight in anger. "The whys and hows do not matter. The goddess will not even consider giving her idan if there are not the same number of girls as there are stones." She looks at me and her face shifts, eyes flashing suddenly. "There are no others who have offered themselves. Moremi, you have caused this . . . and so you will have to take Zaye's place."

CHAPTER TWO

I open my mouth, protests ready to spill from my tongue, when two small girls burst through the doors. Both have large dark eyes and chunky plaits that barely skim their small shoulders.

"Iya Nana, please accept our apologies for this interruption—" The girl on the left wrings her hands, her eyes flickering over us nervously.

"—but we have a message." Her friend is more composed, although she still doesn't look my mother in the eye.

"Ọba Ojaja has arrived with a guest—"

"—and has requested an immediate audience before the Dírágónì ceremony—"

Their matching voices are cut off with one raised hand from my mother, her heavy bracelets clinking together. Thin chains drape across her forehead and ripple over the sudden lines of her frown.

"Always something. What has he come to criticize us about

now?" she mutters, her mouth twisting. "I will be there shortly. Please tell Ọba Ojaja I am sorry to keep His Majesty waiting."

The girls turn and sprint back in the direction they came from.

"Kakra, Panyin," Iya says, "make sure Zaye is taken to the healing quarters, and lead the iyalawos back into the prayer hall."

The two women nod simultaneously, and we watch as the priestesses follow them through the doors.

"Iya, I can't offer myself to Yida," I burst out as soon as they are gone. "This is lunacy!"

"It is not." My mother's voice is calm. "Your prayers may be . . . lacking, but you've always been able to sense her idan. It is an opportunity for you to redeem yourself."

From what? I think. *Or for whom?* "The goddess will never choose me."

"Then you have nothing to worry about. Think of it as a way to honor her. Now wait here while I speak with Ojaja. In fact, you can apply the henna to your ankle right now." Iya takes a moment to compose herself and then plunges back into the temple.

Beneath my feet, the earth is damp from dew, and I inhale the fresh scent as I try to calm myself. My mother will never allow me to back out. And if I'm not going to be chosen anyway . . . does it matter so much?

I suck in another deep breath. I'll take part and keep her happy. The Dírágónì ceremony will be fulfilled, we'll all celebrate, and I'll be able to get back to my plants.

I pick up the wooden stool, overturned in the fracas, and feel a wash of guilt again. *Look what you have done to yourself*, I think, huffing as I retrieve the henna and slowly begin to squeeze. Golden paste oozes from the tight funnel as I concentrate, patterning my bony ankle with the swirls of the offered. *Not my choice, not my choice* rattles through my mind. So why is a small part of me feeling excitement?

"Your ego, you silly girl," I mutter as I finish the loops on my skin.

The quiet sound of a stone being kicked makes me pause. I put the henna down and stand up. There's the shadow of someone off to the side. The flames from the entrance sconces eat up the dark, but the silhouette is still not clear.

"Good evening." The voice is low, and I can make out the arch of a foot as the person greets me while moving from the shade of the mountain.

I flinch as I spot the gold and silver that gleam on the ends of two plaits, while the curls on top are a frosted white. Jagun, the ọba's son, steps forward.

Not as tall as the babalawos, the ọmọ ọba is still bigger than me, his chest solid and broad. His agbada is a riot of colors that match both the heavens and the land; strands of gold are wound around his neck, and thicker ropes of silver hang from his wrists.

Jagun stops with some distance still between us, his eyes on me, brows drawn together. I bend to touch the floor in front of him, but I can't help sneaking a look at the prince as he stands with his hands by his sides, arms knotted thick with muscle in a way that speaks of rigorous training. His sword is strapped to his back, a bulbous ruby sparkling just over his right shoulder.

Jagun catches my eye and his mouth lifts in a smile. I twist my fingers together and find myself wishing I'd neatened my braids.

"I'm sorry for startling you," he says. He points to the sky. "I was looking for Dam's sign while I wait for my father."

Picked out in stars that are just appearing, the shape of a dragon glitters in the sky. The symbol of Dam stretches across the dark blue, his tail a long smear of light that casts its glow over us. His shape mirrors the one the stones depict at the mountain's base.

Two dragons.

One beneath—Yida, who holds up the earth.

One above—Dam, who arches across the heavens.

"They are magnificent," I whisper.

"They are." Jagun turns to me, his eyes hooded by shadows. "I also wanted to offer my apology."

Looking up at him, I feel a small frown forming. "What for?" I ask, dipping my tone and my head.

He's silent for a moment, and I wonder if he has heard me. I can smell the oils used on his skin and hair, delicate hints of sandalwood and vanilla that now lace the air.

"My father can be dismissive of your temple, and I know he has been . . . abrupt in the past. But my mother . . ." His voice trails off, and he rubs a hand over his eyes. "Iya was a loyal follower of Yida. And if it weren't for the priestesses who healed her, she wouldn't have had as many years as she had. I hope to be the leader she dreamed of me becoming."

It is well known that Jagun's mother favored the goddess. I remember seeing her visit often when I was little, the swirl of her wrapper and the rubies and diamonds that dripped from her neck and fingers. She came to bask in the goddess's idan channeled by my mother. It has long been said that with each year that passed, the ọba's wife became sicker, until not even Yida's magic could save her.

Jagun leans forward, close enough that I can see the vivid ring of hazel that brightens his eyes. "I will forever be grateful to all you do here. Not just for the use of Yida's idan to heal, but for your medicinal infusions also."

My mouth hangs open. No one ever comments on my potions. I lower my eyes to the stones underneath our feet. Jagun's are even larger than mine. "We are blessed to worship the goddess," I say.

"Well, the relief your medicines bring is famous." Jagun stares at me for a beat more, the moon flashing in his eyes. "Will you be at the Dírágóní ceremony later? Perhaps—"

Before he has a chance to finish, the doors of the temple fly open, and a man with salt-white skin and hair the color of flames strides out. It is his eyes that catch me, though—one blue and one brown, his gaze sharp as it rakes over me.

"Addaf," says Jagun, bobbing his head and bending at the waist but not quite touching the floor, as befits his station. "An ambassador from the Kingdom of Carew," the prince says quietly to me.

I frown. No outsiders have ever been permitted to visit the temples before. At the rustling robes, I kneel and bow, as is fitting, and when I stand again, Iya and Ọba Ojaja are framed in the doorway behind Addaf.

The king's agbada is a vivid swirl of land and cloud, earth and sky, and when he lifts his chin, the fat silver knot of his necklace glints among folds of dark brown skin. With the torches shining behind the king's head, the golden circlet perched on his silver curls looks like a tiny sun. The ọba's guards fan out behind him, each clutching a sword the length of my leg, leather straps with daggers crisscrossing their chests. I swallow and bow again, stomach churning with nerves at so many important people.

Addaf steps forward, his gray tunic hanging in folds on his frame, and I wonder what god he is aligned with. And then he smiles, revealing the scarlet gleam of his teeth.

So, it's true. Kakra always described how the people of Carew display their allegiance to their ancestral dragon god, but it's another thing to see it.

"Your temple is as beautiful as I had imagined it to be." Addaf's voice is low and thick, his Ajami perfect.

"Not something you are used to seeing, I imagine," says Ojaja behind him, the gloat in the curve of his mouth.

Addaf turns away from the king, gazing at the gold-flecked rock and down at his feet, no doubt imagining the goddess coiled deep in the earth beneath us.

"It is not. Kwa is blessed over all others to be the kingdom the gods call home." The ambassador's frown is a small wrinkle that he instantly smooths away, but I catch it. "And I am honored to visit. My wife was a devoted Yida follower. She would have been overcome with joy if she were here."

His words are sad but sweet as Aziza honey, and although he smiles at the ọba, his eyes darken.

Ojaja spreads his arms wide and gestures to my mother. "The dragon gods decided on all of this. We are but their thankful children. Come, it will soon be time for the ceremony, and the palace bakers have been at work since dawn. Their puff-puff is like no other."

The ọba sweeps down the path where his royal palanquin has appeared, ready to take him to the gathering place. Addaf assumes his place beside him, head bent attentively as the king prattles on. Jagun pauses, but on sensing my mother watching, he holds my gaze for a few moments more and then nods, following his father and the guards.

"The ọba is allowing him to witness the Dírágónì ceremony?" I can't help the incredulous tone that lifts my question. "Iya, surely he can't permit that."

"He is. And I do not agree, but it is not my place to say." Night has stolen the light from day fully now, and Iya stands, her profile sharp in the flicker of the torches. "Addaf also wanted to see Yida's tear, but of course I couldn't permit that. Favored ambassador or not, the prayer hall is sacred."

I blink. "Why would Ojaja allow him all this?"

"Oh, the ọba values power, and such men are always greedy for more. It is the way of the world, and something our gods keep balanced. We all have a purpose." She pauses now, her brown eyes narrowing. "And I am wondering what purpose this *Addaf* has."

"Is he not an ambassador? I remember seeing some from the Kingdom of Alkebulan a few years ago. Didn't they come to trade?"

Iya taps her front teeth with a long nail. "That may well be, but why has Ojaja brought Addaf *here*? I have not heard any news of what he has agreed to trade. And the ọba responds to only two things: flattery and an increase in wealth and power."

"Is that not three things?"

"Wealth and power are one and the same, Moremi. You would do well to remember that."

Kakra and Panyin lead the priestesses out onto the path just as the babalawos arrive. The top of Mandara Mountain is wreathed in clouds, so when Dam's priests descend the winding path, it is as if they are walking down from the sky itself.

Most are tall, almost impossibly so, said to be chosen so they can reach higher than any other person, all the better to give their prayers to Dam. With their wrappers in the blues of the sea and the purple of storms slung low around their hips, they show off the sweeping ivory designs that spiral on their brown skin like clouds. Thick twists of silver encircle their throats, and the tips of each man's tight curls are an icy white.

At their presence, my stomach starts to churn. Despite accepting both gods, the people of Kwa pledge allegiance to whichever of the dragons was said to give life to their first ancestors, and rivalries can sometimes cause rifts between the fervent. Not today, though. Everything feels more real now, and instead of stuffing my face with stew at the ceremony, I'll be *part* of it.

As the babalawos move closer, the man in the lead holds up a hand, pearlescent rings glowing on every finger. Twice the height of my mother, the principal priest looks down at her with hooded eyes, lowering his hand.

"Iya Nana." Bannu says her name in a voice that rumbles like thunder. The mark of a dragon curls tightly around his right wrist, tail flicked up toward the light brown crook of his arm. "We are honored by your presence for the Dírágónì ceremony."

My mother bows her head briefly. "Baba Bannu, we are honored by yours."

"It is time," says the babalawo, and now he is smiling at Iya with large, even teeth, the corners of his eyes crinkling.

He turns to me and winks as I greet him in Dam's way, clasping my wrist in respect. Nox stands by Bannu, almost as tall as his father. He adjusts his blue wrapper and touches a hand to his tight curls, which are neat with freshly frosted tips. When he catches sight of me with the iyalawos, a frown rips across his forehead.

"What are you doing?" he whispers, looking down to see the henna on my ankle. "You're pledging yourself to Yida? How did this even happen?"

"I'll explain later," I mutter, eyes on my mother as she laughs with Bannu.

"But—" Nox's mouth hangs open, his eyes wide.

"Let us make our way," interrupts Iya, pursing her lips at Nox, causing him to bow his head.

"I'll be expecting the whole story later," he manages. And then he is swept along with the rest of the priests.

Once we reach the bottom of the winding path, the people of Kwa are waiting and ready, drinking in the sight of the priests and priestesses greedily. They press against the side of Mandara Mountain, spilling across the cleared gathering space, smiling as they point their toes and clasp their wrists in respect. Guiamalas with packs of produce strapped between their three humps are led through the throng by traders from the west coast, and merchants finish setting up their stalls for the night market.

Right by the main path, a small boy sits on the shoulders of his father, a chubby hand clutching a carved likeness of Dam. Next to them, a girl a few years younger than me buys a statue of Yida, her face alight.

The space quickly fills as hot food is shared, some worshippers scooping balls of rice into their mouths as others press around them with wrapped slices of mango and salted pancakes. There are even Aziza sweets, which two small girls are drooling over: precious honeycombs, glittering in pinks and oranges, with ewebe, a sweet herb only found in secret places of the Sambisa Forest. One of the tiny beings hovers over the delicacies, her wings a delicate gossamer blue and her tight curls giving her a perfect halo. Small nundás in shades of silver gray and orange slink about on the edges of the crowds, their claws and teeth thin and sharp, batting their tiny wings as they fight over scraps.

Then comes the beat. A hush falls over the crowd as the boom grows louder. Every face turns up, mouths open, eyes wide, waiting. I wipe my hands on my thighs, a tangle of expectation thrumming through me as the king's musician strides up the mountain pathway. Nearly as tall as Bannu and twice as wide, the man pauses, hands resting on a mother drum the size of two people. He surveys the crowd with a grin, and then he is pummeling the iya ilu, slapping out a complicated rhythm that speaks of power and strength.

When Ọba Ojaja steps forward, swaying in perfect time to the beat, the crowd surges, their voices raised as one in a cheer that splits the air. The guards keep them at bay with copper-tipped spears, creating room for the king to make his way into the center of the gathering space.

The ọba lifts one bejeweled finger, commanding silence.

"Kingdom of Kwa, last night the stars of Dam were spotted directly above the stones of Yida, signaling the alignment of the two dragon gods."

The ọba pauses, casting his gaze over the swell of people, his eyes black in the moonlight. He lifts his long plait over his shoulder, stroking it. Behind him, I see the thin figure of Addaf. Even from here it's obvious the man is struggling with the heat, his skin a pale red despite the large palm fronds being used to fan him.

"I welcome you to the Dírágónì ceremony, where Yida and Dam will choose who will channel their idan, and then cleanse the lands." Ojaja raises his hands, and there are claps and the stamping of feet. "Your worship keeps us in their blessings, and today will be a celebration of that and the gods."

From behind him, Jagun walks up to join the leader of Kwa. The boy stands tall, plaits gleaming, broad shoulders thrown back as he takes his place by his father's side.

"Today, we worship and celebrate as one kingdom and one people." The ọba walks backward, clasping Jagun's arm. "There is balance in the two!"

"There is balance in the two!" the crowd roars back. All eyes swivel to the gathering place as a dozen iyalawos stalk through, their brown feet skimming the ground in practiced steps.

But I keep my gaze on Ojaja. As the ọba watches the women match the pounding of the giant drum, his eyes narrowed, Addaf sidles up to him. The ambassador's hair burns in the bright torchlight, making him look as if he wears a hat of fire as he bends down to whisper into the ọba's ear. A look of glee passes across Ojaja's face—something I am not alone in noticing—and Jagun draws closer to his father at his reaction.

The two older men split apart, and Ojaja claps his son on the back, gesturing to the iyalawos, as Jagun flushes and looks down at his feet. I don't envy his position, and I suddenly wish I could somehow offer him the words of comfort he gave me earlier. I know all too well what it feels like to have the weight of expectation piled on you, the panic that swells within when the pressure builds, threatening to make you crack with the force of it.

The dancers, chosen by my mother for the perfection

of their prayers, grow more frenetic. The priestesses move in a matching rhythm as they make a large circle, their bodies spinning with the beat, their braids flying, their skin and gold and smiles gleaming. Their soles graze the ground, and envy twinges at my admiration. I am jostled by the crowd as we watch the performance and people murmur in excitement. Nox catches my eye and grins, hands swinging in wild claps, eyes alight.

We wait only a moment before the women are joined by a selection of tall babalawos, their claps loud in the pale slant of the moon. Once they are all inside the circle of iyalawos, the largest of the priests stands in the center, his torso as wide as a baobab tree. Four others, almost as heavyset, brace themselves next to him, arms linked. The remaining babalawos wait, in descending order, largest to smallest. One by one they deftly climb atop the row of priests, using tight clasps and corded muscles. The last man left scales the human tower, skittering over footholds of flesh as he climbs aboard the shoulders of the highest.

The babalawo pauses for a moment as we all gaze up at him, the light burning our eyes as the priests stand firm, stacked up beneath the scald of the torches. The smallest man teeters before holding out both of his arms and bringing them together in a series of short cracks, a prayer released directly into the sky and to the dragon god himself. Clouds slide away instantly and the naked moon beams down in a shaft that highlights the men.

The crowd laughs in delight as the iyalawos begin their invocation dance in earnest, the slap of their soles hard against the ground, sending their adoration through the earth. Small flowers with purple blooms rise out of the dirt, their scent filling the air with honey as the crowd cheers. I join in the calls, pride in my temple swelling in my chest.

Bannu and Iya weave through the dancers and the bottom pillars of the prayer tower, shining in their ceremonial robes of silver-blue and red-gold, each one tailored to look like the scales of the dragon gods. Iya stops just inside the ring of priestesses, and Bannu moves past them, his jewelry the silver of a full sharp moon.

As she begins to dance, he begins to climb.

The brown flesh of my mother's feet is a blur as she stamps and whirls, her dragon glinting gold with the power of her summoning. My feet begin to form the basic prayers all Yida worshippers offer. This, I can do at least, and I take comfort in the simple steps, letting my hips sway with the movement, moonlight glowing on my shoulders.

And I relish the feeling. Here, there is some sense of belonging. Here, I am nothing more than a worshipper of the goddess.

Bannu reaches the top of the prayer tower quickly. Opening his arms to the sky, he throws out his fingers, showing his giant palms to the devotees of Dam, who in turn show him theirs. With his large frame supported by the babalawos beneath him, Bannu is offered to the bright burn of the god's stars, and when he brings his hands together in a loud smack, thunder crackles and echoes all around the gathering place. He begins to clap in a pattern and rhythm only used by the principal priest, the dragon on his wrist gleaming silver with his prayer. And all the while, my mother dances, her feet syncing to the rhythm of Bannu's slaps.

The crowd roars, their stamps and handclaps blending in a

harmony. Only when my mother and Bannu complete their call to the gods, with the dance ending and the men climbing down from their prayer tower, do the people of Kwa fall silent. The principal priest and priestess stand apart from everyone else, waiting. I let the quiet settle me, blood hot in my veins, as I watch the returning clouds swirl together, whipped grays and whites. There's a tightness in the air, as if everyone is holding their breath at once, and even the sky seems brittle now, ready to shatter at any moment.

The screech is distant, but we all hear it. Strands of green and purple thread through the clouds as if preparing them for a storm. The shimmer of colors transforms again, this time shifting to spiderlike threads of yellow and pink that mimic an unnatural dawn, heralding Dam's arrival.

A sudden tremor runs through the earth, jerking everyone to the right, the crowd rippling like a wave. They part like the tides, leaving a wide-open space in the center, where Iya and Bannu wait. I'm pushed against the mountain, my feet digging into the ground that grows warmer beneath us, and a frisson of excitement snakes through me.

The gods are coming.

CHAPTER THREE

I close my eyes and take a deep breath, remembering the first time I saw Yida and Dam, ten years ago. When I was seven, they'd seemed like a fresh and beautiful terror. Both dream and nightmare, our destiny and our end.

My mother stands still, the mark on her ankle shining bright gold as a beating thump fills the air. Beside her, Bannu holds up his hands, the dragon on his wrist now a luminous silver. A breeze flutters through the meeting place.

I scan the skies again and catch a glimpse of a magnificent wing that cuts through the clouds. A thunderous roar echoes around us, and I flinch, eyes on the heavens.

Then a god tears open the sky with his arrival.

The dragon swoops down, another drawn-out screech accompanying a long, winding body, snow-white scales, and a silver belly. Dam skims over the rocky crags to land just beyond the gathering space, his coils spreading out. He throws back a giant head with spikes that run down the curve of his skull, each as sharp and glittering as ice. The dragon looms above, iron-colored eyes raking over us. His jaws open, and he produces a shriek so loud that I clap my hands over my ears. Fingers wrap around my arm, and I look up to see Nox next to me, his eyebrows raised. I nod my head at him and lift my chin, forcing myself to put aside the small prickles of fear at the sight of such a god.

The devotees of Dam grin. They stand as tall as they can, with some hoisting one another on their shoulders.

Then the ground shakes again, and the rocky slopes tilt as something burrows up from deep within, and I can't help smiling. My feet welcome the burn of the earth, absorbing the thick slow heat that is our goddess. Her idan seeps through my soles as always, hot and spreading, my limbs feeling heavier as the ground continues to shake. Some people fall to their knees, but I plant my feet apart, letting the fieriness race through my veins as Yida bursts from the earth just beyond the base of the mountain, her scarlet wings unfurling, chunks of dirt falling from her rotund coils. She hangs heavy in the air, blotting out the moon for a moment, a scattering of gold peppering her stomach, before plummeting down and crashing into the earth next to Dam. Under the light of the stars, Yida's body shines in scales of crimson, her face flecked with dark gold, framing the ink of her eyes. Spines sprout from each side of her head, radiating in a crown the color of blazing flames.

The sound of worship fills the air as the dragons stand, towering over us all. For a moment, they do nothing but glare. And then the gods roar together, their great heads scraping the clouds that gather above them, wisps of crowns that speak of power we only glimpse.

Iya and Bannu face Yida and Dam with their hands placed one on top of the other and pressed close to their hearts. There is a stretched-out moment of silence before Baba Bannu claps once again and Iya stamps. Our sign, as those who seek to be chosen by the gods, to begin.

Immediately, the young priests flock to the low crags of the mountain that overlook the gathering space, and the priestesses rush to follow my mother to the meadow at its base. I hurry after them, my hands shaking as I take each step down the path to join the line that forms among the swaying grass. My heart kicks painfully as Kakra and Panyin move among us, tying blindfolds over our eyes.

"Make your way to Yida's sacred stones using only the sense of her idan, and prepare to face her benevolent judgment," crows Iya as she paces up and down, adjusting knots and touching arms.

When she reaches me, she whispers in my ear: "This is your chance to redeem our family. You will do well, Moremi. This I know."

My throat clicks as I try to swallow, wishing for black tea with cardamom. *Later,* I tell myself as Iya ties my blindfold herself and the world disappears.

The sudden dark is satin black, clinging to me like a second skin. I know the other girls are spread out around me, longing for the goddess's magic, but all I can think of is Iya's face. The hope. I know that every time she looks at me, she sees my father and his choices. It doesn't seem to matter to her that with my herbs I can cure coughs and aches and bring fevers down. It is not enough for her.

I was five when Baba was forced to leave, and I can only really remember his dark brown eyes and large hands. The way he could hoist me into the air, and the softness of his gaze when we would sit underneath the sky. He would tell me the stories of the stars and how they could be used to plan the planting of crops and to navigate the lands. His mistake was believing that iyalawos and babalawos should share temples, to celebrate the dragons together and try to combine their idan, the way the gods had when they'd created the world. Madness to most because we are pledged to either Yida or Dam, unless royal—never both. And a belief that proved ruinous when revealed to the ọba, who exiled him immediately for lunacy and treason. There are rumors that the idan consumed him, curdling his mind. Since he was banished, my mother can't even speak his name.

And now, as I make my way to our goddess, I ask myself if being an iyalawo is really enough for *me*. What if I *could* channel Yida's idan? What if I could heal with the goddess's power as well as using my herbs and tinctures? The thought yanks at me.

I hold my hands out in the soft press of darkness, my movements uneasy. I just need to get to Yida's henge in one piece. I can at least do that for Iya, and maybe . . .

I shake my head. Taking even breaths to force the panic down, I step forward, dew from the grass seeping between my toes. *Slow your heart and idan will come.* I breathe again and let my shoulders drop, waiting.

It will come.

And then there it is, the crackle of heat that pulses beneath my feet. I smile in relief and walk forward, following the slow burn of the dragon's essence. I think of Kakra's advice to call and pluck at the magic but not force it. The more you grasp, the more it will resist.

Grass tickles against my legs as I move through the meadow, guided by the idan I can feel streaming up from the earth. When the ground cools, I change direction, taking tiny steps until I feel the warm ribbon of power once again. I let it guide me, wondering if the other girls have found it too. I take another, larger leap, following the current of idan that weaves between small stones and the tangle of roots. *Trust yourself,* I think as I feel the magic surge beneath the soles of my feet, the thick scorch of it as it grows.

I'm so sure in my path, I don't sense the rock that sends me sprawling. It's only as I lie in the dirt that I feel the throb of pain in my right ankle, smell the sharpness of blood in the air. Panic begins to bloom, and I force myself to even out my breathing. Rolling onto all fours, I swing my head around as if I can see, not caring about the scrapes on my hands or the raw skin of my knees.

I clamber to my feet and spin around, unsure now of what direction I'm going in, unable to find the hot coils of idan from the earth. All I can feel is the ache in my ankle. I hear the pad of other girls running close by, and I turn again, grasping to find any hint of power, my fingers raking at the air, desperate to snag someone's wrapper, anything to tell me I'm going the right way.

The footsteps recede.

A howl catches in the soft parts of my throat as I struggle to swallow it, letting only a small keen escape my lips. Now that I've begun, I don't want to let Iya down.

Now that I've begun, I wonder if I can be more.

Stamping my feet against the ground despite the sting of my injury, I reach for Yida's essence. Nothing happens, so I grind my soles against the loose earth, envisioning the glitter of idan just as my mother taught me, sucking in a mouthful of night air, heart thudding against my ribs.

But still, there is nothing.

My shoulders slump as tears burn at the backs of my eyes.

And then I feel it. A delicate pulse, a thread of something that curls deep in my soul. With a sigh, I reach for the idan, eager for it to spread through my body, where it will catch at my heart and settle in my mind.

But it is not where I expect it. Instead, the idan is sharp pricks of ice that needle at the crown of my head, winding through the coils of my hair.

The idan pulls, urging me on.

I begin to run again in a limping lope, hands held out, blocking out the discomfort in my leg. I can't hear anything apart from my own ragged breathing. I ignore the stitch in my side, following the bite of power as it presses down from above.

I'm close, I can feel it. But the relief is mixed up with the stinging in my head as the cold jaggedness of idan burrows deeper until bursts of white and silver shatter against the dark of my eyelids. I don't stop as it guides me, though I can't help crying out in pain, shaking my head back and forth even as I stagger forward.

And then it is gone, and I am standing still, bare feet on warm stone, chest heaving, sweat trickling down my neck and back. The sound of footsteps behind me becomes clearer, mingling with the pants and sobs of the other girls. I scuff my feet on the rough rock just to reassure myself that I am here, wanting to sit down, feeling the sudden shake of my knees.

I made it, is all I can think before my blindfold is yanked away and I'm blinking into the familiar face of my mother.

"What happened?" she hisses, her eyes a hard brown. "Did you cheat?"

The dragons loom over the gathering place, crouched and watching us all. I frown, nails digging into my palms, red crescents rising with the pain. Cheat at . . . *what*? How could I cheat? Why would I? I didn't even want to take part in the ceremony, but I'm here at Yida's stones because I felt her idan.

My mother comes closer, placing her lips against my ear, her familiar scent of musk oil and saffron washing over me. "Kakra and Panyin say that you . . . fell. That you were last at one point." She pauses, her breath tickling my neck. "But you arrived at Yida's stones before anyone else."

At least I arrived at the stones. My throat tightens and I pause, trying to think of what she wants me to say. "I followed what I felt."

"And what did you feel?"

"What? Why would you ask that?" I pull back, my eyes darting over her face and the line scored between her brows. I look away. "I followed Yida's idan. I felt it in my soles. I felt it . . ." My words trail off as I remember the second pulse, the keen pressure from above. The ice of it. I tell myself that doesn't matter. "I felt Yida," I say, keeping my voice even.

Silence stretches between us as the night grows blacker and colder. I can feel the other girls watching, and heat spreads across my chest and up my neck. I may not have been seen as good enough before, but my place is earned. I made it to the stones because I could feel the goddess's power.

My mother grabs my arms, turning me away so we can't be overheard. "Are you *sure*?" she asks.

"Yes, Iya," I whisper, even though doubt is now beginning to pluck at me. I think of the icy barbs I felt in my mind, and my stomach jolts. "Why?"

Her eyes flash, but she slides her hands around my back to hold me, pressing her trembling palms against the blades of my shoulders. "Moremi, I need you to tell me how you were able to reach the stones faster than anyone else."

I hesitate, thinking of the way the earth cooled under my feet, the fading of Yida's idan. And the pressure from above.

"I . . ." My fingers go to my temples, steepled, remembering the flash of pain. I swallow. "I . . . I lost the trail of Yida's power."

"You fell."

My head droops as I blink quickly, trying to stop the burn of shame and confusion. I think of making something up, but Nox always tells me how pathetic I am at lying. "I did. But—"

"You rushed when you didn't need to."

"I fell and then I got up and then I couldn't feel . . . I couldn't feel anything, and I panicked."

My mother's mouth is pulled down, but her eyebrows are raised now, and she tightens her grip.

"I felt idan. I'm telling you." I avoid the heat of her stare as fear dips in me.

My mother stands very still for a moment, her eyes shining. She rolls her lips and lifts her chin. Then she joins the other iyalawos before I have a chance to tell her anything else, and I am left standing alone on the stone that makes up the tip of Yida's tail. I focus on the rock underneath my feet and remind myself that I am here.

I am *here*.

That is all that matters. I take a deep breath.

Never in a million years did I think I would be standing on the goddess's holy stones, offering myself to her. A small laugh bubbles out of me and I chomp it down, fighting the giddiness that fills me.

Once the girls have had their blindfolds removed, we wait in the spreading glow of a yellow moon. I stand tall, my body still thrumming with energy. Most of the iyalawos are crying with joy, weak with their success and the passing of adrenaline and idan. I try to calm the shake in my own legs as my mother stands in front of us, the henge curling around her. Her feet are spread wide apart as she raises her hands, and there are stamps of prayers from the crowd as they watch eagerly.

"You all followed Yida's idan to her anointed henge. Tonight, you have proved you are worthy of your intention." Iya looks up at Mandara Mountain and the flare of fresh torches. "But are you worthy of Yida?"

Slowly, I press my hands against my thighs and try to even out my breaths. *I can do this.*

My mother begins to pray again, and the girls on the stones join her, their movements speaking of respect and joy. I copy them as best as I can, feet tender against the rock, trying to ignore the nerves that writhe in the pit of my stomach. I shouldn't be scared, but I am. I'm not really supposed to be here; how will the goddess find me worthy?

Yida lifts her head, scarlet wings unfurling from her immense body. Her roar splits the night sky, but I don't flinch, not even when I think of jaws cracked wide open, pointed teeth bared in the cold spread of midnight blue. My mother stops. The dragon on her ankle now has a golden sheen that glows in the starlight.

"Do not be frightened," she says, her words fractured with triumph. "Our goddess will choose."

I can't look anywhere but at the dragon that snakes toward

us, even as the people scatter, making space for her. The earth shakes with each sinuous twist that brings Yida closer until she stops at the edge of the stones, giant coils in ripples behind her. The goddess roars and we pause our prayers, feet bruised and cooling against the stones we stand on.

My chest burns as I hold my breath, eyes fixed on the dragon that hovers over us, her tapered claws gouging the ground. Yida is here, right in front of me. This is not the first time I have seen the goddess, but it is the only time I will be judged by her. I press my lips together to stop them trembling. I think back to the idan I had felt sharp against my crown. What if the goddess senses something within me?

Something . . . wrong. Something unnatural.

One of Panyin's favorite criticisms snakes its way in. *You look just like your father. What else is there inside you like him?*

I shake my head to dislodge the thoughts. That doesn't matter. I have worked hard to help take care of the people of Kwa, just like iyalawos have been doing since the beginning of our world. I am the daughter of Iya Nana, principal iyalawo of the temple of Yida. I followed the goddess's idan to the sacred stones, and now I will face her with the grace and courage of my mother. Tipping my chin, I plant my feet wide apart.

Yida shifts, her tail flicking behind her, and my thoughts stop. The dragon rears up, her crown of spines puncturing the sky. I tell myself that I am not afraid, but fear still mingles with the awe I feel. The goddess opens her jaws once again, revealing a molten flow of red and gold that glows in the back of her great throat.

I bite the side of my mouth and watch as the goddess lowers her head, breathing out a blaze of ruby gold that sears the earth, filling the air with the scent of ashes and old bones. The crackle of heat is loud in the still night but dissipates as it sinks into the land, creating fissures of light that spread toward the henge. The strands of magic wind their way closer until each stone is ringed in a sheen of gold. My chest is hitching now, rising and falling fast. Yida stands monstrously tall once again, claws anchored into the ground as she watches us, her eyes an impenetrable black.

The heat beneath my soles grows but I don't lift my feet. Stronger than I've ever felt it, Yida's power flows into me. I gasp, my hands balled into fists at my sides. My heart thumps in time to the spike of my pulse, a deafening beat as the stone grows hotter still. The idan climbs my legs, twisting thick inside me, feeling as if it is searing flesh and bone. I choke on a smoky, bitter taste at the back of my tongue. Yida's idan courses through me, following the flow of blood to my heart.

As my head falls back, I open my eyes wide to the sky. Stars shatter the night above me. A cloud shifts, gliding over the moon so that the world is muted for a moment. And then the burn begins. My fingernails curl deeper into my palms. The stars waver above me, white bursts edging my vision. My hands go slack, and just when I think I might pass out, the scald flares hotly once and then fades.

I close my eyes to the beat of giant wings, the ground rumbling again as I crumple against the stone.

"You are fine, Moremi." Cool fingers wipe the tears that trickle down my cheeks and slide to my shoulders, which are slick with sweat. "Come now, open your eyes."

I'm shaking as I blink into the night, trying to focus. My mother is grinning. She grasps me by my waist and looks down. I follow the line of her gaze to see the tiny dragon that now winds around my ankle.

CHAPTER FOUR

"Yida chose me?" I whisper.

"She did."

"She chose me." My voice cracks as tears gather. I reach down and touch a fingertip to the edge of miniature scales, the skin cold beneath them.

"I told you that you were worthy!" Iya cups my face, kissing my cheek. "You are not just my daughter now, but one of Yida's too. As are two other girls."

I take another look at my ankle, elation soaring through me at the flick of a tiny tail. I had only agreed to take part to make it up to Iya, but now . . . I try to suppress a grin but fail miserably.

But there is no time to ruminate on being chosen, as the air thickens. Yida waits crouching beyond the stones, her eyes on the sky above. It is Dam's turn now, and he takes flight, skimming over us all to land on a crag of the mountain, his tail whipping through the night. The young babalawos begin to climb, each using their sense for Dam's idan to find a carved niche in the side of the mountain. The god watches them and throws back a giant head. His jaws open, his roar reverberating around us.

As the dragon circles above, I scan the dark rocks, looking for Nox. He clings to the thin shelf of a niche higher than the others, and I fight the urge to roll my eyes. He has always had this need to be better than everyone else. Dam swoops toward the boys who have made it to their positions that mimic the shape of his constellation, and even from here I swear that I can see the gleam of Nox's toothy grin. I know how often he has replayed this event, and I want this for him as badly as he does.

The dragon spreads his wings wide and hangs in the air for an impossible moment, riding the currents of the sky before he roars, spewing forth his idan and fire, aiming at the mountainside. They blend together, the white and blue of a pure flame flowing over the bare rock and boys. Each niche fills with the dragon's essence until the god lands before them, closing his great jaws with a crack.

There is silence as the idan dissipates, revealing the babalawos who shiver in wonder against their mountain alcoves. Dam worshippers strain forward, trying to see which young men may have been chosen and marked. But as a scream breaks out, they all freeze. A figure hangs from a delicate ledge, feet scrabbling for purchase against the mountain.

Nox.

I hear the panicked shout of Bannu even as I leap from the stone, shoving my way through the crowds. On my left, I see the priest, his mouth pulled tight because he knows that, per initiation rules, he can't intervene.

But I can.

"Moremi!" Iya screams my name, but I don't stop until I am beneath Nox, looking up at his feet.

"Pull yourself up!" I shout as I try to climb.

Nox doesn't answer, but I catch the gape of his mouth and a flash of his eyes. He's strong; I know he can make it, but if he panics, then his chances of falling are higher.

I don't know if it is my words that reach Nox, or whether he merely manages to be calm enough to drag his body up, but he heaves himself onto a shard of rock, back in the niche. I breathe in shakily, a hand pressed against my heart, until I feel a slice of frost that burns as it slides along my skin.

Turning my head slowly, I am met with the iron talons and Dam's pearlescent scales. His sleek body speaks of the currents in the skies, the soar of the drifts of air he uses to traverse our world.

I stand still, my mouth suddenly dry as my heart rises in my throat. A pounding fills my head, growing stronger as coils of magic seep from the god's jaws, the smell of fresh salt water washing over me. I hold my hands up, showing my palms, and Dam leans forward, sniffing the air above my head before snorting, enveloping me in a cloud of cold breath.

I shouldn't have left the stones.

The iciness winds around me, frost licking at my skin, a slash of breeze throwing my braids up. I tremble, daring to look at the dragon god through the black of my hair. He crowds over me, shielding me from the view of everyone else. His teeth sparkle, razor-like and white. The god opens his jaws, and the night is leeched of any warmth as he roars once, releasing his idan.

The cold is instant and piercing, flaying me like a winter

storm. The force of it pushes me to my knees. All I can see is the shimmer of Dam as I blink away the icy crusts that form on my eyelashes. *Be calm*, I tell myself as panic swells. *He is not Yida, but this is still the god who helped create your world.*

The raw chill grows, invading my mind. I swallow the pain and keep my gaze down under the weight of Dam's idan as the pressure increases, skittering over my skin. I choke on a gasp, the taste of iron on my tongue. My wrist burns cold, a scraping at the bones that makes me cry out. There is no answer, but the pain stops.

I lift my gaze to see the spread of Dam's wings as he turns away, leaving me to cradle my numb hand. My fingers creep over the sting of my skin. I stiffen at the feel of raised scales.

A dragon encircles my right wrist. Each scale is perfect, just like on the dragon around my ankle. A miniature tail flicks toward the sweaty crook of my arm.

I swallow the nausea that rises, questions spiraling. How is this possible? I run the tips of my fingers over the mark, fear swelling.

Yida has marked me.

And so has Dam.

"Moremi!"

Hands clutch at me, pulling me away from the god, as Bannu spins me around to face him. It is not anger that mars his face but concern. He stills when he spots the dragon on my arm, then whips his head around to make sure no one else has seen. He silently rips a strip from his wrapper and ties it over the mark.

"Do not speak of this until I have had a chance to discuss it with your iya." His voice is a tight hiss.

I nod, too numb to say anything, overwhelmed by the dual dragons that now mark my skin when there should only be one, if that. I turn toward Nox, relief spreading through me as he makes his way carefully and safely down.

"Did I give you a scare?" he asks cheekily, but I hear the tremble in his tone, and he quiets as his father shoots him a look.

"We will speak about this later," says Bannu, a thick frown on his smooth face.

Nox nods. Without another word, he holds out his arm, and I see the dragon, tail flicking at the crook of his arm. The boy tilts his head and then grins when he sees scales on my ankle.

"We've both been chosen! This is more than we could have ever wished for."

My throat clicks but no words will come. It doesn't make sense in any way, and right now my mind is spinning.

"What's that?" asks Nox, reaching for the makeshift bandage on my wrist. "Are you hurt?"

"No!" I manage, pulling away just as Iya arrives, clutching at my other arm.

"*What* were you thinking? What were you going to do? Use your body to break his fall? You know that Noxolo would have been all right!" she says, her voice shrill in a way I've never heard it. "Get back to the stones! The gods need the closing Dírágónì prayer before they will cleanse the land."

I let her tug me back, my mind still churning. My hand rests on the scrap of wrapper on my wrist. The skin is warm now, but the memory of biting iciness is still there.

The ọba stands in the middle of the gathering space, his eyes following me as I clamber back onto my stone, ignoring the stares of the other girls, and for a moment I wonder if he saw Dam mark me. Ojaja narrows his eyes but turns away, sweeping his gaze over the dragons and then back to the crowd of people.

"Yida and Dam have come to us, and we give thanks." He glides forward to stand between the gods now, his face solemn. "During the last Dírágónì ceremony, I watched my father oversee the blessings and cleansing bestowed by the dragons."

In the space of his speech, my mother points her toes while Baba Bannu raises his giant hands, both ready to begin the closing Dírágónì ceremonial prayer. "With this in mind, I am faced with important questions. Why should there only be a select few who are conduits?"

Nox looks down at me, the surprise on his face mirroring mine. My mother's hands clench and I see the sudden hunch of Bannu's shoulders. I swallow tightly when I see their confused faces.

"We are all familiar with the coming together of the gods and worshippers every Dírágónì ceremony . . . And we are truly blessed to have our priests and priestesses, assets that are unique to the Kingdom of Kwa. Nowhere else in the seven kingdoms are there babalawos and iyalawos like ours, as powerful as ours!" Ojaja pauses while people cheer. "They heal our people and help grow our crops; they manipulate weather so that each season finds us fortunate. We are truly blessed. But what if the ceremony had a different meaning? What if it was a time to unite both gods' idan, and what if that idan was embodied in just one person? Imagine both gods' magic within reach, to use whenever the chosen individual felt the need, and not just when the temples' chosen decide." Ojaja motions to Addaf, who steps forward. "The Kingdom of Carew has long since chronicled the histories of our world, with Addaf Myrddin garnering an abundance of knowledge during his travels around the seven kingdoms."

What is going on? This sounds so similar to what Baba said years ago, was punished for. And now Ojaja is claiming the same thing? *None of this makes sense,* I think as the ambassador smiles thinly. The ọba brings his hands together even as his palace guards move closer to him.

Dread forms a knot in my stomach at the sight of their swords, their eyes on Iya and Bannu.

"Addaf has shared his knowledge with me, as an act of good faith from Carew and in return for our allyship. To honor him, I have granted his presence at the Dírágóni ceremony." The ọba nods at Addaf and holds a fat hand to his heart. "Knowledge is worth more than gold."

The ambassador steps forward, and my mother's head whips around at him, but Ojaja's guards move closer, discreetly drawing their weapons, the razor points held at Iya's and Bannu's backs. No one else sees; the crowd is fixed on the ọba.

I take a step forward until I see the small shake of Iya's head. Her fingers point briefly, telling me not to move.

"My first ancestor was given idan by *both* dragons, marking them as the leader of Kwa," Ojaja announces, his voice ringing out. "My family are destined not just to be rulers but to command the truest power there is." Ojaja steps closer to the dragons, his onyx eyes glittering with fervor. "Addaf has helped me see the true meaning of the Dírágónì ceremony. A chance for one person to become the single holy conduit for both earth and sky, for Yida and for Dam. A chance for me to embody both gods, to command them and harness their idan."

Iya and Bannu stand frozen in horror. The knot in my stomach grows tighter. How has he come to believe such a thing? And from an outsider, someone who has no true ties to the gods? Dam and Yida choose who will be able to channel their idan and then they chase away the emi buburu when the ceremonial prayer is completed. This is the way it has always been, the way in which the dragon gods have decided.

Yida's idan flows hot, awash with a burnt bitterness that crackles on the back of my tongue. I let it stream through me, trying to keep my eyes open. Fury tinged with scorn, I realize now, frowning as the taste and weight of it keep me in place. My thoughts are sharpened by fear. If Ojaja really thinks he can command our gods and their idan, then he is a fool.

There is a stretched-out silence as the ọba stands before Yida and Dam, a mere speck against their vast beauty. Ojaja holds his hands to the sky and begins to sing. The words have a cadence I recognize as Carew, but not a dialect I know, the intonations guttural and harsh. Behind him, the dragons shift, their scales rippling in the colors of fire and ice. Fear, clawed and cold, winds its way through me.

"It is time for our gods to be here when *I* decide!" shouts the ọba. "To bless me so that I alone can channel their joint idan!"

Now the crowd sees the weapons pointed at Iya and Bannu. The people glance around at one another, eyes widening with alarm, muttering uncertainly. Like Iya, I am frozen in shock. I can scarcely believe what is happening. Ojaja has gone further than even Baba. The scriptures are firm in our hierarchy, in the values and purposes of the pious and the royal family. I know I have never read anything like what the ọba is declaring. He's wrong.

The gods. How will the gods respond to such a slight?

Ojaja raises his arms, face thrown up to the skies as he stands before Yida and Dam, screaming the last of his commands. The dragons dip their great heads, spines curling so they can peer down at him. So sure is the ọba in his words that he kneels before them. He doesn't see them when they open their jaws, teeth long and glittering with a brilliant sharpness. I think for a moment that they will both take giant bites of Ojaja, swallow him and his audacity whole. A small voice inside me whispers of destiny and death, that the ọba deserves this for his arrogance.

Instead, a spiral of rage and indignation echoes in the gods' cries as they tip their heads back up to the dark sky, releasing slivers of idan into the air as groans fill our ears. Heads whip around, searching. I lock eyes with Iya, and the bright terror in hers makes my gut clench. Without the closing prayer and a chance to bask in the people's worship, the gods have not cleansed the land.

Thick shadows ooze from the night, seeping from the ground and the rock around us. The groans turn into ragged yowls as the stink of rotting flesh rises in the air. The shadows flow toward one another, spinning and solidifying as they take shape, elongated limbs and arms that stretch into wicked claws. Red-orange eyes flicker above slashes of mouths as four figures plant themselves in the middle of the gathering space.

"Emi buburu! Emi buburu!" Shrieks rise from the crowd as people begin to back away from them.

Cracked palms and stamped feet echo around me, pleas that

reach the dragons as they arch away from the shadow spirits, the gods' snarls loud in the night. Although there are tales of the emi buburu, they have always been just that: stories to remind us of what the world was before the gods made the seven kingdoms, what could go wrong if they did not bless the world they made. Something that has never happened.

A woman screams as one of the emi buburu swipes at the crowd, black shadowed hands made solid, nails long and serrated. She is not fast enough, though, and the claws catch her throat, holding her there as the darkness oozes from its grip. The woman's eyes roll back as black rot spreads across her skin, and she crumples to the ground.

People peel away, screaming as they push and shove one another. I search for Iya and Bannu, but in the scramble, I can't see them. Ojaja still crouches before the dragons, his face marred by confusion, and I know there and then that the fool truly believed Addaf's lies.

The dragons rear back, scales gleaming in shades of crimson and cream. Their great throats ripple, long teeth slipping past their lips as they snap open their jaws and roar, releasing their idan in a cascade of fire and bright magic. I watch as it flows toward the emi buburu, hope rising at the gods' intervention. But is it too late? The energy rains down, sparks singeing the breeze as the shadow spirits flicker like smoke, avoiding the gods' idan before re-forming. *They're still trying to help,* I think as relief courses through me. *Despite Ojaja's blasphemy.*

With snapping jaws, Dam snakes forward, driving through the earth as he lunges at the closest shadow spirit. The emi buburu spins to the side, staying just out of reach. The god tries to turn, but before he can move, the spirit swipes, dragging its claws along his flank. Dam roars, head shaking from side to side in anger as the three other emi buburu close in, and Yida dives toward her surrounded husband.

I stumble back and look wildly for my mother, but she and Bannu are too far. Ojaja cowers against the mountain as some of the babalawos and iyalawos fight along with the flood of people unwilling to leave Yida and Dam. But what good is channeling idan when the source of it is being attacked in front of our eyes?

In her fury, Yida spews forth golden-red idan, which splashes against the nearest spirit, sizzling the smoke-dark body. The emi buburu screeches as it wavers, unable to re-form. Instead, the scraps that are left drift to the nearest shadow spirit, merging to make it even larger.

This is what the stories in the scriptures warned us against, I think as the spirit opens its mouth and shrieks before diving on Dam. The god screams as silver blood flows from his wounds, and Yida's roar makes the very air vibrate as she rakes at the emi buburu, but they do not falter, and she cannot reach her husband. And even as I open my mouth to scream, to warn them both, a shadow spirit reaches up with its long razor nails to slash at Dam's great belly.

CHAPTER FIVE

Lightning pierces the dark as the dragons keen in a way I have never heard before, a cry echoed by the wails of the priests and priestesses around us. Gold and silver splatters of blood wreathe the rocks as the emi buburu climb the spines of our gods, their claws trying to cut through scales. The dragons' pain quivers through the air, and I feel it in the clench of my heart, tears running over my cheeks.

Iya screams, and there is a shudder as the dragons grapple, crashing into the rocks around them, releasing a shatter of splinters that rain down over my mother and Bannu. I see her double over, clutching at her side, then reach for the principal priest, pulling him down so that he can hear what she's saying. The babalawo nods and takes her hand.

Together, they face the gods and pray. Bannu claps his hands, great cracks rending the air as he is joined by the complicated stamps of my mother. As they pray, the dragons on their ankle and wrist begin to shine. In the chaos around us, the other marked priests and priestesses see this, and their faces calm in understanding. The men slap a beat with their open palms, and the women begin to dance.

Yida raises her head, fiery eyes flashing. She shakes off the emi buburu straddling her great spine. Dam snaps at it, crushing the form between his jaws, letting the shadows bleed out from the sides. Together the gods close their eyes, soaking in the idan that is given back to them by the pious.

When they rear up, it is with fresh roars that shake the mountainside. Their jaws spew forth a molten fire of idan thick with strands of luminous gold and silver. A shimmering mass of their essence, it is released in a wave of fury, flowing over the emi buburu. The spirits shrink away, their forms sizzling under the onslaught of idan.

I watch in frightened awe.

This is how it must have been when the gods first cleansed the shadow spirits from our world. The dragons cut a swath through the black forms that still gnash and lunge, ripping the figures into shreds. But rather than disappear, the torn shadows only withdraw, seeping back into the dimness and gloom of the night. Have the emi buburu been cleansed? Or just forced away?

Finally, the dragons close their jaws and lower their heads to the ground. Steam escapes from the gods' nostrils in glittering plumes as they lie in pools of metallic blood.

They are hurt.

Iya and Bannu stand before them. The priest plaits his fingers in uneasy knots, while my mother places a hand on her side, her face creased with pain. Before they can do any more, the gods growl, nuzzling each other once. Their scaled sides are ripped in places, and Dam's talons twitch, trying to reach the bleeding slash in his stomach. And then the god is launching himself into the velvet night sky, disappearing behind a bank of thick cloud.

Yida stares up at the stars before she roars her rage and pain, her wing fluttering over her side. And then she too is gone, her rotund body skimming the meadow, blotting out the curve of a milky moon that sits low on the horizon.

There are only a few of people left in the gathering place, their tearstained faces aimed at either the sky or the earth. The girl with the small statue of the goddess cries into her arms as she sits, legs curled to her chest, rocking back and forth. Dam's followers have their shining faces tipped to the heavens, cheeks wet.

"The gods are angry!" cries a man, the push of his large stomach making his wrapper a tent of river blue.

"They are hurt! We must pray hard!" says a woman next to him, her round face surrounded with hair wrapped in pale blue cotton, the ends explosions of black puffs. She claps loudly with already red palms, the plump flesh of her arms swinging with each smack.

"Iya, what's happened?" I call out, pushing toward my mother as she and Bannu stagger, the priest catching her as she nearly falls.

"Moremi..." My mother reaches for me, her fingers bright with blood, and my heart quickens. *Blood.* She is injured. But Iya looks over my shoulder, her frown deepening. "Stay where you are—"

"Iya Nana and Baba Bannu, you are accused of interfering in the ọba's rule."

I jerk around to see Addaf with the palace guard at his back. Though they wear the colors of whichever god they worship, they still ready their weapons against the priests and priestesses, the dragons' holy emissaries. Jagun stands among the priests, his hand clutching the hilt of his sword, a tightness in his knuckles and the set of his shoulders. A hand curls into mine as Nox sidles closer to me and pulls me behind him, his gaze shifting between our parents and the ambassador.

Ojaja peels away from where he was cowering against the mountain, striding to Addaf.

"What is this?" Bannu asks, but the oba does not look his way.

"Addaf, we need to speak in private," Ojaja says, his voice low, shaking. "You assured me the invocation would work."

The ambassador's blue and brown eyes rake over us. "It will." He doesn't look at the king but motions to Iya and Bannu. "But these two interfered."

The guards grab at my mother, but she pushes back despite the blood seeping from her side. "You will not desecrate Kwa's rituals. Where is your shame?" She gasps, grabbing at the scrap of red that flutters from the nearest guard's chest. "Are you not a man of Yida?"

The man pulls back, his eyes downcast in shame. But then Addaf lunges forward, moving like a grassland viper, striking her around the face. The crack of flesh on flesh is loud as Iya's head flies backward. She lands on her side, hands splayed against the ground.

The shouts of Bannu and Nox echo around us as I throw myself toward Iya, getting between her and the guard.

"Stop!" I scream, face turned up at the men, who look grim but determined.

My mother looks up at Addaf and Ojaja through her braids and then spits on the ground at their feet. "You have forsaken the gods. They will not forget that."

"Secure them and the rest," says Addaf as he takes hold

of the ọba's elbow, steering him toward the path. "We cannot tolerate any more meddling."

My mother collapses, face against the dark earth. The ọba throws only one look over his shoulder before allowing himself to be guided away from the mountain. The guards fan out, their eyes uneasy but their weapons held steadily.

"Iya?" I cradle her head as it lolls to one side. "It's me, it's Moremi."

Her eyelids flutter as Nox rushes over. I only know I'm crying when I see my tears slip onto my mother's full cheeks, sparkling amid the golden dust still scattered over her skin. When her fingers curl against mine, I smile, tasting salt as tears catch in my teeth. Blood oozes thickly from her torn skin, the muscle exposed. The ragged wound in her side makes me want to retch.

My herbs and tonics wouldn't be much use here. Yida's idan flares warm in my chest, and if I were not a new iyalawo, if I had even a little bit of control over how to use Yida's idan, then I could heal Iya.

But as usual, I can do nothing. Nothing but hold her and pray.

"Moremi?" Iya murmurs.

With a hand under my mother's thick plaits, I lean forward as she opens her eyes. "I'm here."

She shakes her head and winces. "You should not be. Leave now. Please. The guards . . ." Her rings dig into my upper arms as she grabs me. She turns to Nox and her eyes shimmer. "The guards will take us all otherwise. And then there will be no hope."

"She is right." Bannu stands over us now, flanked by Nii and Ade, his favored priests. "Nox, take Iya Nana and Moremi."

"What about you, Baba?"

But there is no time for his answer. With the straggling crowd under control, the entire guard faces us and closes in. I would never have thought they would pledge their allegiance to the king over their gods, especially when the king seems to have gone mad.

Bannu steps away from us to meet the guards. He looks back over his shoulder. "Go. All of you."

I bend down to Iya. My hands hover over her wound once again. I think of my father being forced to leave, of the splinter of sadness that still lies lodged in my mother's heart even though she rarely speaks of him. And I know that I'm not strong enough for that kind of grief.

She can't die.

She can't.

Nox follows my gaze, his mouth tightening when he sees the scarlet bloom. "We need to get her back to the temple. Get you all back. Baba—"

"Go," repeats his father. "We will hold them off."

There are shouts from behind us as the priests clash with the guards. Nox paces next to us, and I know he's fighting with himself even as he relents and bends down, slides his arms beneath my mother, and gently scoops her up.

I clamber to my feet, limbs feeling leaden and useless, just as the point of a sword digs into the small of my back. I see Nox's eyes narrow as he bares his teeth.

"Turn." The voice behind me is low and laced with warning. Instinctively, I hold out my hands and pivot slowly, taking another glance at the shallow rise and fall of my mother's chest.

Brown eyes rimmed with green meet mine. Jagun frowns,

his blade still held out before him, the tip close to my chest. I stare back at him, remembering his kind words at the temple, the dip of his head as he smiled.

"Iya Nana is requested by my father," says the ọmọ ọba, but his words are soft, and his gaze doesn't leave mine.

"She's hurt." My voice cracks and I clear my throat. "We need to get her back to the temple. Please," I add, tears blurring my vision. I blink quickly to try to clear them. "You must see what your father has done, what he's caused."

Jagun's fingers slip on the jewel-and-bone hilt of his weapon, the glow of the ruby strobing across his knuckles, like blood on skin. "It wasn't Baba," he says haltingly, but he sounds uncertain. "The ambassador . . . Addaf. He convinced him somehow. My father would never have displeased the gods intentionally." Jagun looks down at my mother and then back to me. A fight of emotions rips across his face, and I know I can reach him.

"None of this makes sense," I say softly. "I don't know what Addaf would have to gain from this, but we'll find out. First, though, Iya needs help."

Jagun looks down at my mother, at the blood on her wrapper.

"Go." He speaks the command quietly, but the words are sharp. "Your temple healed my mother over and over. She never forgot, and neither have I." The ọba's son holds my gaze. He lets his blade dangle by his side, and I remember the confusion in his eyes when his father had announced he would be leading the ceremonial prayer. "I thought I was spending time with my baba, getting to know the people and the temples so that I could learn how to protect Kwa. How to be a leader." He looks around him at the guards tussling with the priests and a few priestesses. "This is not that at all."

"Moremi. Come on." Nox's low hiss pulls me away from the green-brown gaze of Jagun. I walk backward slowly.

"Quickly," the prince murmurs, his words urgent. "More guards will be coming. Baba has ordered them to find you all."

"Thank you," I say.

Jagun nods. He cocks his head to one side, hand tightening once again on his sword. Watching me, his gaze is steady and weighted.

I turn and run after Nox.

Nox settles into a smooth lope, holding my mother as steady as he can. I jog to keep up with him, trying to focus on the motions and not the fear that pulses with every heartbeat. I keep thinking of what Addaf must have told the ọba to make him believe that he could control the gods. But then, what do you have to say to a man already hungry for power?

When we reach the temple, my lungs are burning. I draw to a stop, panic lapping at my mind. Where the wooden door should be is a crisscross of vines wide and round as my legs. Long spikes jut out, with only a hint of the carved mahogany door underneath them.

"The iyalawos will have tried to secure the temple," croaks Iya. "Get me closer."

Nox shuffles next to the covered door, lifting my mother higher as she reaches out with a hand. Gently, her fingers slip between the thorns, grasping the vines. Her lips move as she murmurs, and the tendrils begin to curl back on themselves, revealing the door underneath.

I turn the handle, pushing my way into the outer chamber of the temple, holding the door so that Nox can duck inside. His eyes dart around, taking in the crystals set in the walls and the way the lit scones create what looks like a wave of fire.

The twin iyalawos rush to us, their eyes identical mirrors of horror when they see Iya.

"We tried to get the people out as soon as we could," says Kakra as her sister seizes Iya from Nox.

"Can you heal her?" I ask. Iya attempts to smile at me, but blood bubbles in the corners of her mouth, and my throat goes dry.

"We will try."

And then they are gone, heading down the passageway that will take them to my mother's room, closer to Yida's inner sanctum, where the dragon god's idan is at its thickest.

"She'll be fine." Nox offers me a crooked smile that droops from his lips. "We both know how stubborn your mother is."

I nod, but all I can think of is the mix of gold and blood.

"Moremi," Nox says softly. "This won't stop Ojaja or Addaf. They'll be coming for her too. We need to prepare. I'm going to see if any of my father's advisers made it back to the temple. Ade or Nii will hopefully have an idea of what to do. The gods . . ."

He doesn't finish, desolation drowning the end of his sentence. Shadowed claws and metallic blood fill my mind. It's not just my mother who needs to be healed. *The dragons were still able to fly,* is all I can think. *Iya's and Bannu's idan will have helped them.* But the worry is slippery like a moss swamp eel.

"I'll ask Kakra and Panyin what they think. When they've finished." I clear my throat, hating how my voice cracks. I should be stronger than this. Better. "I'll come to the sky temple."

"Be quick," is all Nox says as he ducks back through the door.

I lean against the wall, exhaustion washing over me. I am alone for only a moment before footsteps pad into the room, and I look up.

I freeze when I see Zaye's face.

The girl raises her chin as she holds out a steaming cup to me. I hesitate, looking down at her leg, her ankle stained with an ugly-looking bruise. Part of me wants to slap the cup out of her hand, and yet . . .

"Earlier, I shouldn't have . . ." The words are the right ones, but I struggle to get them out.

"Kakra and Panyin will heal her." Zaye's words are loud and firm, her eyes unreadable. "And that is what matters."

I accept the cup. The rooibos tea is hot, kept that way by the goddess's idan woven into the vessel. My eyes skate over the graze on her forehead. "What happened? To everyone else?"

"The iyalawos rounded everyone up. I was here when they arrived. Panyin said that lots of girls were lost to the feel of Yida and her pain . . ." She trails off, eyes gleaming, as if remembering the presence of the gods. "But none of the girls were left behind, even as the guards tried to stop them."

I'm about to ask if she thinks the ọba's prayer was real or just a creation of Addaf's, but Zaye is already turning away from me, heading back toward the kitchens. I eye the tea suspiciously and set it down on the floor just as a loud boom comes from the temple doors.

I back farther into the room as the pounding comes again.

Ojaja's guards.

I spin around, running down the corridor toward my mother's room. When I arrive, I'm out of breath, my heart hammering nearly as loud as the attack on the temple. Layered with copper scales, the door is small, like all in the earth temple. When I place a hand on it, I stoop down, my head almost scraping the archway that peaks into a crest, and I hear a moan from within. I shove my shoulder against the door, pushing my way inside before slamming it shut behind me.

My mother lies in the center of the room on a dais made of satin wood. Kakra and Panyin flank her, hands cupped as they run them over her body; clouds of gold dust billow in the perfumed air. They don't stop when they see me, stamping their feet in a practiced prayer, their dragons flashing.

At my back, I can hear the distant thud of the ọba's men. I draw in a deep breath and step forward as the shimmer of dust settles on my mother's skin.

"Iya?"

When she says nothing, I lean down, looking for the rise and fall of her chest. A wave of fear washes over me as I grab at her limp hand.

"Iya!"

A loud gasp, and my mother sits up, eyes wide open. Her hands fly to the russet smear of her wound as she whips her head around, taking in her surroundings. Kakra and Panyin back away, sweat dripping from their high foreheads. I see Kakra hold her sister's elbow, steadying her, before she flicks the lock of the door.

"Moremi?"

"I'm here, Iya," I say, sinking next to the dais, my knees weak with relief.

"Listen to me. The Dírágónì ceremony was ruined." She pauses to catch her breath, her fingers curling around mine.

A crash and a scream echo down the corridor. I see Kakra's and Panyin's gazes flicker to the door.

"Ojaja has changed everything with his greed. He has invited the emi buburu into our world, allowed them to cross over from their realm. The gods have left us, in pain from Ojaja's betrayal and the attack from the shadow spirits. But they must be brought back together in harmony while Dam's stars are in alignment with Yida's stones. If this does not come to pass, then they will not cleanse the lands and they will never again grace us with their idan." My mother winces. "But it is not just that. What Ojaja claimed about the Dírágònì ceremony... The gods *are* destined to be manifested in one. It was thought that it was one people, one kingdom, the Kingdom of Kwa. Even your baba fought for this in his own way. But I think it might be—"

The shouts are sudden but muffled by the thick door, and Kakra and Panyin jump at the same moment.

"How do we fix this?" I ask, my eyes flicking over my mother. "Perhaps the scriptures—"

"Not all answers are found in the archives, Moremi. Listen to me now. Yida will have taken to the earth and Dam to the sky. You need to bring them together while his stars are still in alignment with her stones. Make sure the Dírágònì ceremony is completed." Her eyes flash. "Join them."

A great hammering begins on the door, and I wince, squeezing my eyes shut as panic bubbles up. I tug at one of my braids. Find the gods? Complete the ceremony? I should be back with my herbs and tonics.

"Moremi, listen to me. You won't fail. You are my daughter, and you are also Yida's. You know what is at stake, and you were chosen. Bannu told me what happened with Dam. You are favored by both." Her eyes dart across my face. "It must mean something."

Leaning into her touch, I blink away tears. "Iya, I don't want to leave you. The guards . . ."

"The guards will take me, but the ọba won't kill me." My mother lifts her chin. "He is not that foolish, despite what this Addaf thinks. The consequences have already begun. He'll keep Bannu and me just in case."

"But—"

"There's no time." Her tone is harsher now. She brings my head closer to hers. "You are worthy. Never doubt that." The pounding turns to the screech of metal on metal. It sounds as if the guards are trying to hack their way in. "Go now, Moremi. And take Yida's tear from the altar. It will bless your journey." My mother presses her lips to my cheek. "Kakra, show her the way."

The iyalawo nudges me toward the back of the sanctum. "All will be well, my sweet one." Kakra squeezes my hand, then pushes against the wall at the end of the room, clicking open a hidden door, its edges indistinguishable from the rock it's set in.

I don't take my eyes from my mother's as she gets to her feet, supported by Panyin. The temple of Yida has never needed weapons, so now they stand with jagged crystals broken from the walls, their shoulders thrown back and eyes shining with anger. Kakra shoves me gently through the doorway before returning to them.

"Bring the dragon gods together, Moremi," my mother says. "Our world depends on it."

CHAPTER SIX

The dark is cold and absolute, smelling of metal and earth. My hands graze rock as I feel my way forward. Behind me, there are shouts and one rough scream that makes me pause in the blackness.

Find the dragons. The thought urges me on, my breathing ragged, chest burning. I splay my hands into the press of darkness until I feel a slight draft, and then there's a crack of light, a warm breeze on my skin.

I spill from the tunnel, falling into the pepper of burning gowé seeds and sweat-soaked prayer. The back of the hall is full of cool shadows, and I emerge unseen as the beat of hundreds of feet fills the air. The women of Yida's temple are gathered in the rock-hewn space, stamping their prayers, their faith palpable in the heat. I scan the crowd, knowing they are waiting for my mother to lead them, to guide them through what Ojaja has caused.

The altar is drenched in the pink glow of Yida's tear. Its glittering facets draw me in, and I scurry toward the raised dais, remembering Iya's words as I wind around the dancing priestesses, their eyes almost closed in concentration. When I get to the altar, I stretch forward, standing on the tips of my toes, using my long reach to grab the crystal orb. I exhale in relief and tuck it into the tight folds of my wrapper, then run back to the shadows.

Slinking along the edges of the cavern, I shuffle toward the doors until shouts filter through the air. I lean into the lightless recesses, close enough to see the bulge of wood. With a loud crack, the panels smash against the rock, the doors framing men, their weapons, and their snarls. Pressing a hand to my mouth, I stifle a gasp, feeling sick as the ọba's guards enter the sacred space of Yida. Hisses fill the air as the women stop, turning to the men who desecrate their place of worship.

"Shame on you! How dare you enter the goddess's scared prayer space?"

Some of the men look down at their feet, regret marring their faces. Most wear scraps of red fabric pinned to their leather chest plates to signal their allegiance to the goddess. This is not how they've been taught to behave, but a few reluctant guards do not change the orders given from the ọba. The men part as another stalks through to the front, his thin shoulders jutting forward.

Addaf.

I close my eyes briefly, remembering the twist of his lips when the ọba began to recite his prayer. Apprehension churns through me as I dip farther into the shadows.

"Ojaja has stated that all places of worship are now under his command." As he speaks, Addaf's eyes rove over the iyalawos and initiates. "Where is your principal iyalawo?"

"The temple of Yida knows no other authority but the

goddess we serve." Zaye steps forward. She folds her arms across her chest, shaking her braids over one shoulder so they writhe like tiny black snakes.

"That might have been the old ways, but not the new." He fixes his startling eyes on the girl. "Tell me, where are Iya Nana and her daughter?"

Zaye's eyes flick to the crevice where I'm concealed. She must have seen me, but she doesn't point me out.

"We recognize no authority but the principal iyalawo and the ọba. And you are neither."

After the cut of her constant comments, the thought that she might be helping me again is almost more shocking than the guards in front of the sacred altar. More iyalawos move to stand behind Zaye, and a swell of pride rises in me as the group grows, their glowers hot.

But Addaf only sweeps his gaze around the prayer hall until it rests on the altar. He pushes Zaye aside, barreling through the other women even as they shout their outrage. The soldiers look unsure as Addaf climbs onto the dais, his thin neck twisting as he searches around the statue of the dragon. When he finds nothing but the bowls of offerings to the goddess, his face tightens.

Iya's words spin through my mind.

Take Yida's tear from the altar. It will bless your journey.

He's not just looking for us.

"Perhaps there needs to be a lesson in compliance in this temple," says Addaf softly as he rises tall underneath the statue of Yida and smiles. His voice is low and tight with anger, the redness of his teeth glowing like bloodied pearls. He lifts his hands up in the air, making small gliding shapes with his fingers, and the shadows thicken, moving like water until they crowd the altar.

I stare, not wanting to believe what I am seeing. Rising in a spiral, the darkness spins like a plume of smoke around Addaf. The man is still visible as he continues to mouth unintelligible words. I press against the rock, a hand to my throat as a chill sweeps over the space. The iyalawos move backward, their rounded eyes fixed on the offerings of food. Black fungus crawls over the rice and red fruit, shriveling each grain and rotting it all within moments.

Addaf lunges to his left, seizing the wrist of an iyalawo only a little older than me. His fingers dig into the brown of her skin as he yanks her to him, and a guttural moan vibrates on the air as the smell of sulfur and spoiled eggs spreads. I watch from the dark as the shadows envelop her, as the gleam of her skin turns dull and she shrivels into dark desiccated folds. As her eyes roll back in her head and her mouth hangs open in a silent scream.

The girl's body slithers to the floor when Addaf lets go, her skin and bones a soft crumple in the silence that has spread throughout the prayer hall.

Just like the woman in the gathering place. The horror of it rolls over me, echoed in the cries of the priestesses around the altar. How has he done this? My breath comes in tight gasps as the black veil fades, the ambassador's hands still, the darkness now just shadows again. I know channeling when I see it, but what Addaf used was not the gods' idan. I'm shaking, thinking of how the emi buburu dispersed, gone but not cleansed. And he's calling on them. Feeding them.

"Tell me where they are."

I clutch the dragon's tear and slink along the curved wall, heading for the open doorway. How many guards did Addaf bring? If there are more in the passage, then I don't stand a chance.

But the hallway is empty. Some of the torches have guttered out, and I jog forward on shaky legs, keeping to the pockets of deeper darkness. The broken temple doors stand open, vines in tatters at their base as a chilled breeze winds its way through. I look back along the corridor that leads to the inner sanctum, but before I can change my mind, I scramble out of the temple entrance. There's a moment to worry if there are more guards . . .

And then a body presses against mine, lean muscle molding to the curve of my back, fingers clamping down hard on my mouth.

"Be quiet!" The words are hissed into my ear as I'm dragged away from the temple doors, my feet slipping on moonlit grass.

Panic runs through me, bright and instant. I thrash, hands clawing at the arm clamped across my chest, a choked scream locked behind the grip. But it does no good and I am hauled off the path. Stars smear across my vision as the smell of musk and damp hay grows. And then the pressure lifts and the night rushes back in.

My legs buckle. I kneel on the straw of the guiamala compound, drawing the welcome air deep into my lungs, and stare up at Nox.

"Sorry. More guards are heading up the path. They would

have seen you." His voice trickles through, edged with panic. "Come on, Mo, I thought you'd know it was me."

He holds out a hand to me, and I grab his fingers, twisting them as hard as I can.

"Ow! Moremi!"

A flare of grim satisfaction warms my chest at his brief pain. I get to my feet, fire racing through my veins. Nox looks down at me, his hand cradled to his chest, dark against the blurs of white body marks.

"I said I'm sorry!" he says.

He leans forward and wraps his arms around me, holding tightly. The warmth of him and the familiar scent of chalk and white lime used to create the swirls on his skin break something inside me. Tears course down my cheeks as I choke back a sob. Nox holds me for a few seconds more until I make myself push him away.

"Sorry. I'm just . . ." I sniff, wiping a palm across my face, scrubbing at my nose. "Addaf came." I tell him what the ambassador did in the prayer hall, my words stilted, breaking at the end when I describe the dead iyalawo.

"What do you think?" whispers Nox, his tone careful. I can hear fear in the clip of his words.

I swallow, wringing my hands. "The only thing I can think of is that he's managing to channel the emi buburu's power."

"Really?" asks Nox. His fingers tremble as he cracks his knuckles lightly. "And how would he even know how to do that? I thought you said he was aligned with Yida?"

I don't say that his red teeth remind me of blood and death rather than the goddess.

"I'm not sure, but I know what I saw."

"But why would he do that?" Nox shakes his head. "It doesn't make sense."

I wipe at the last of my tears, trying to focus on what I do know. Addaf deliberately sabotaged the Dírágónì ceremony, tricking the ọba to summon the shadow spirits, and is using their essence, maybe even embodying them. But how is he doing that? And if he can do that, what will he do next?

I draw in a shaky breath. "What happened at the sky temple?"

I look up at Nox as he lowers his hand, eyebrows raised. He glances down the mountain path, the guiamala compound gates obscuring us from view, and holds a finger to his lips. Voices trickle through the darkness, and we crouch down as a line of guards move into sight, their faces washed with the silver glow of the moon.

My throat clicks as I swallow, sounding impossibly loud in the stillness. We wait, squatting in the scrubby grass as the men file past and trek up the path into the temple. Only when they've gone does Nox turn back to face me.

"Baba Ade was there. And Baba Nii . . . but Nii was hurt. Ade said that they . . ." He looks up at the night clouds that swirl around the sky temple and blinks rapidly. "He said that they fought back, but my father was still arrested."

"He's alive?"

Nox nods, but he blows out his cheeks to stop himself from crying, something he used to do when we were little.

"I'm sorry." I dance my fingers over his shoulders, wanting to comfort him. I give him a moment and wish we had more time. "It's not just Addaf that we have to worry about. Iya told me that we need to find the dragons and unite them while Yida's stones and Dam's stars are in alignment. Otherwise . . ."

My voice trails off. "The gods will no longer grant their blessings through idan or cleanse the lands."

This time it's Nox who pulls away, his face veiled in shadows. "Do you think that's what Addaf wants?"

"I don't know why, but it must be."

A small silence stretches, the weight of my words heavy between us.

"Five days to find the dragons." Nox stares at the ground, his jaw clenched, then looks up at the night stars. "And they're injured . . . Where would they even go?"

A snort comes over my shoulder, and I jump back as something nibbles at one of my braids. Clouds clear the moon, and I can make out the tips of dark horns and humps, the soft thunder of cloven feet. There's a low grunt, and I look up into the sand-colored muzzle of a guiamala. A string of ropelike drool hangs from the animal's thin lips, and when it shakes its head, it splatters me. I wipe the slobber from my cheek, feeling weak with relief at the sight of the gentle animal.

"Do you know where they are? Have you heard anything?" I whisper to the creature as thoughts and memories slowly form.

From what I've read in the temple's archives, all I know is that both dragons would have to be somewhere holy.

"The monasteries?" I say slowly. The Adamawa mountain range stretches along the southeast coastal boundaries of the Kwa Kingdom and is home to the sky and earth monasteries. A place where the holiest scriptures and relics of the gods are kept, overseen by previous principal iyalawos and babalawos. Their exact location is a secret, concealed to protect the most pious and all they look after. "The holiest place for the gods. They must be there."

Nox nods but he doesn't smile. "You're right. But five days isn't long enough to search the whole mountain range."

"And there's no way we can look in the earth temple for the location of Yida's monastery. Not with Addaf there." I take a deep, frustrated breath.

"I wouldn't risk the sky temple either—the guards are crawling all over it. But if we find Dam, then we find the goddess too," says Nox, pacing in a tight circle. "I might have an idea how we can locate his monastery . . . and Yida's is said to be close by. Akyem is a Dam-aligned village in the Sambisa Forest, much like ours in Mandara Mountain."

"Like Osumenyi?" I ask, thinking of the large settlement high on the side of the pass on the way to the south. Some settlements declare themselves Yida- or Dam-only villages, despite the priests and priestesses frowning upon it.

"Kind of. Osumenyi still has some Yida people, though. Akyem . . ." Nox fidgets, pulling at his earlobe with long fingers. "Akyem doesn't allow anyone apart from Dam devotees. They believe that he did most of the work creating the world. That without him, there would not be life at all."

"But Yida holds the world together," I say automatically. "She is the reason we're all here right now."

"And without water there would not be life," answers Nox, one of his eyebrows raised.

I shove my toes into the earth, trying in vain to sense the idan that will comfort me. "That's not the point."

The boy holds his hands up and takes a step back. "This is why the people of Akyem keep to themselves, and we at the temple don't push their beliefs. It's not the way of Dam as we understand it. It's an interpretation, Mo," he says. "But anyway, I mention it because they track signs of the god where they can. Routes he has taken, where he's been. If he is at the monasteries, then Akyem might have a map or directions to them. Something."

I nod. That is a start. "We could make it by dawn," I say.

"I'd say an hour before sunrise, if we take the guiamalas," comes a voice from behind me.

The words still us, and Nox pulls me closer to him. Slowly, I raise my face to the guiamala on my left and meet a familiar gaze, framed by black plaits and sharp cheekbones. Zaye doesn't smirk, but her mouth looks like it's on the verge.

"What? I'm not about to stay in a place that's been desecrated." She walks toward us, her eyes flicking to Nox.

My fingers curl into a fist as I turn away. "You want to come with us?" I ask, my words brittle and tight.

"Well, *want* is a strong word." Zaye shrugs, her thin shoulders high. "I take my vows to Yida seriously. And so, there is no other choice. Not really."

I stare her down, but she doesn't look away. Instead, she comes closer, jabbing her finger against my chest.

"I've worked hard for *years* to take part in the Dírágónì ceremony, to have a chance at being chosen by Yida to channel her magic." Her voice breaks on the goddess's name, but she recovers herself and glares at me. "Something you took away from me. Now I'll have to wait another decade. I . . ." She falters, then pulls her shoulders back. "I need this. I need to prove I'm worthy of the temple."

I soften. Because how often have I felt the same? I remember how Zaye argued with Addaf, drawing his men farther into the prayer hall so I could leave unnoticed.

"If you're coming, then we need to leave now," says Nox as he fusses with the leather straps of the creature closest to him.

The beast gives another faint groan, lips smacking together. The boy attaches two saddlebags, checking to make sure each holds dried fruit, waterskins, and blankets.

"That's settled, then. I've already chosen my guiamala. One of the less smelly ones." Zaye looks at the animal still trying to nuzzle my head. "That one seems attached to you. It wet itself earlier, so I guess it's chosen well."

And just like that, annoyance flares. She turns and climbs nimbly up the bony joints of her guiamala, perching on the cushions and blankets between its humps. If we had more time, I would strongly reconsider letting Zaye join us. But . . . what's important is setting things right.

Only then will our parents be safe.

Only then will Kwa be safe.

I turn to the creature who tried to eat my hair and look up. The saddle is high, and I can already feel the swirl of nausea that being at that height will bring. The guiamala eyes me, coarse lashes blinking around black pupils.

"Shall we ride together?" asks Nox. We once tried to climb the baobab tree and I only managed to climb a quarter of the way before I froze, unable to continue or even slither back down. He had to half drag, half carry me to the ground.

"I'm fine." But the wobble in my voice says it all.

"Don't be so stubborn. Get on."

"I said, I'm fine." I frown at him, stepping closer to the stalk-like legs. The creature bends down and licks my arm with a long pink tongue. I've never actually ridden a guiamala, but it can't be too hard. I pat one of its seven black horns nervously, running my palms over the brown hair that sprouts from the hard points. "You'll take good care of me, I know it," I whisper, and carefully climb on.

Nox leads the way, followed by Zaye. I stretch out the muscles of my neck and try not to think of my mother, the sheen of desperation and anger in her eyes when the door to her inner sanctum was destroyed. And then I wonder why Addaf wanted Yida's tear so badly.

I shiver as I cluck softly, trying to make my guiamala move faster, but the creature merely stops to take a mouthful of corn plant before ambling along. I admire its nonchalance when my own stomach is a pit of writhing nerves. The iyalawos use guiamalas to traverse the kingdom when needed, which means this creature has seen more of Kwa than me. I know from the scriptures that we may encounter creations of Yida and Dam that I have never come across before, those that are the creatures of dreams and those that are the monsters of our nightmares. Not all were made as we were, and the line between good and bad, animal and monster, is often blurred. I take a deep breath and will myself to have more courage.

As the night stretches around us, shadows swallowing the light from a subdued moon, a breeze lifts the edge of my makeshift bandage, and I run a finger just under it, touching the raised edges of the tiny dragon scales. I shudder. So it was real. I'm tempted to lift the scrap of fabric just to look at it again, but I smooth it back down, in case Nox or Zaye sees. I'm not sure how I even feel about it, and I don't want questions that I can't answer.

The trees grow taller as we lumber through them, their long branches reaching for the sky above, roots rippling over the ground, twining around one another. The cloven hooves of the guiamala pick their way through them with ease, and I settle into the gentle swaying motion, tiredness arriving in waves that dampen some of my fears.

I jolt a few times, the yips and calls of painted wolves echoing through the trees and quickening my heart. But their howls move away from us, the creatures on the hunt for prey in the Sambisa Forest that is thankfully not us.

Nox slows his pace to stay close to me, always checking that I'm not feeling sick and even stopping when he finds some wild ginger, asking if it will help with my nausea. I try not to think of my treasures of plants and tonics, missing the fresh and earthy scents that make up the best parts of my day. A few young n'damas help to distract me, their spotted fur bright in the waning moonlight, nubs of silver horns above large eyes. A tiny one watches as we pass by, legs like small stilts, its nose quivering as it scents us.

It is only when night is clawed apart by the dawn that we reach Akyem. The backs of my eyes are gritty as I blink into the pink light that slashes through the trees. The forest has grown to monstrous proportions. Giant trees raise their wide branches, twists of sable wood that are held up to a fading moon. The sky is crowded with leaves, splayed in the open formation of expanding green stars. And beneath it all, cradled in the boughs of the trees, nestles the village of Akyem.

"Wow," I croak, rubbing at my eyes. "I've seen drawings of this in the archives, but . . ."

They do not prepare you for the real thing. The dwellings cleave to the trunks, resting on the thickened parts of the trees, the roofs made of leaves, making them almost impossible to see if you aren't looking for them. I search the trunks, wondering how the villagers climb to their homes, and see that the roots of the trees have been manipulated into living staircases that wind upward. Ropes spread weblike between the dwellings, connecting them all in myriad ways.

"Come, they'll be rising with the dawn for prayers to Dam. When the clouds are clearing and the day is fresh clean," murmurs Nox.

I manage to urge my guiamala slightly faster so that I edge past Zaye, taking my place behind him.

And then a group of giants step from the shadows of the forest and level their spears at us.

CHAPTER SEVEN

"Ẹ káàárò̩," says Nox as he slides down from his guiamala, landing sure on the soft earth of the forest. He holds his wrist in greeting.

The warriors are as tall as the babalawos of Dam's temple, with combed-out curls teased up into high wedges of hair. Their narrow chests gleam, a shining ebony broken only by the purple storm of their wrappers. My breath catches as the men skulk forward, cloaked in shadows as they evade the light of dawn, as if dragging the last of the night with them.

"Do not greet the morning without first greeting Dam," says the tallest of the warriors, his eyes a glittering black.

Nox lifts his hands high above his head, bringing them together three times, sharp cracks in the cooled air, a prayer to the dragon god. He holds his palms up, expression calm, before lowering them and facing the six men who surround him in a loose semicircle.

I look down at the dragon on my ankle and the scrap of fabric concealing the one on my wrist.

Chosen.

I am chosen.

With my heart in my throat, I slide awkwardly from my guiamala. The smell of sweet rot and overripe plums greets me as the men's eyes swing to meet mine. Full beards grace their lean faces, eyebrows knitted together on high foreheads. Even though they grasp their weapons tightly, their muscles speak of readiness, not violent intent.

"Good morning," I add, stopping myself from pointing my toes in greeting, wary of what Nox said about Akyem. Instead, I hold my wrist briefly and awkwardly.

"Moremi . . ."

I lift my chin and ignore the warning in Nox's tone, edging next to him, trying not to look at the spears. And I smile to show that I'm not scared, despite my racing heart. "This is Noxolo, son of Baba Bannu, principal babalawo of the temple of Dam," I say, moving backward to demonstrate his importance, gesturing to the dragon on his wrist.

At my words and the mark of the god, the men's expressions shift and they snap down their spears, bowing their heads briefly. The man in the middle, a touch taller than the rest, steps forward to greet Nox correctly, right hand holding his left wrist. The young priest mimics the gesture.

"Welcome," he says, stepping back and offering the boy a wide smile. "We are not used to guests. I apologize for our lack of acknowledgment. Your father is a man we all respect. Please, forgive our rudeness. Join us as we break our fast."

"All of us?" asks Nox, shoulders straight. I know what he's asking. We are so obviously daughters of Yida that there is no point in trying to pretend otherwise.

The man pauses before he dips his head in a nod. "You and your companions."

I turn to see Zaye climb down from her guiamala. When she reaches the forest floor, she smooths the folds of her wrapper. Even dwarfed by the warriors, the girl stares up at them with a regal authority that I've only seen in the older iyalawos.

"Akyem is impressive," she says, clasping her wrist in greeting, cheeks glowing with the dawn. "We have been told of such places, but to see this village is testament to the skill of your founding ancestors."

The men greet her and puff out their chests at her praise. I suck my teeth at the sweet smile on Zaye's face until Nox nudges me, shaking his head.

One of the warriors secures the guiamalas for us, and I brush a hand over the side of my animal.

"Back soon," I whisper as it rolls its eyes at me. "You'll be fine."

I follow Nox as we are led to the base of the largest tree, the roots winding around one another and the trunk, creating a twisted set of steps. We begin to climb as the sun pierces the canopy, drenching our heads and shoulders in new light.

"This is much worse than the guiamala," I whisper to Nox, one shaking hand trailing the trunk of the tree, the other pressed against the lurch of my stomach.

The boy slows his steps so I can keep up. He holds out a hand, and I take it, gripping his fingers tightly. "Just don't look down," he says.

The stairs spiral up the tree, making me dizzy by the time we pull ourselves through a circular opening. Despite Nox's advice, I can't help peering beneath us. At this height, the enormous guiamalas have become tiny specks. I stand, holding my hands out for balance, and stay close to Nox across a vast platform made of wood.

As we follow the warriors, I take in the large dwelling set flush against the trunk. Made from woven branches, oiled and supple, the green-and-brown walls are topped with enormous dried fronds. My attention slides away when a lone clap shatters the early morning.

From this elevated point, we can see the other platforms and homes of Akyem. The village is spread before us, ensconced in colossal trees, rope bridges creating pathways. The light beams through, shafts of saffron and lemon that make the dwellings glimmer.

I don't see the people until the next clap happens and hands are brought together in response. Gathered in the growing dawn, the old and young stand tall, faces upturned to the flashes of sky that beam through the leaves separating us from the heavens. Most are gathered on the platforms outside their homes, greeting the day with slow smiles and open palms, flocking to the claps that call them to prayer. I spot a group of three boys and two girls on branches to my left, vines looped around their thin ankles for safety. Then one loud, lone clap rings out, and I crane my neck, looking upward until I see who they are all staring at.

The figure is a blur of sun and skin and black hair. All I can really make out is a giant silhouette on a tiny platform higher than any other. The figure gives another sharp clap, which is echoed by the villagers, then leads the people in prayers for Dam. I recognize the cadence and rhythm of blessings for what has passed and thanks to the dragon god for the day to come.

My hands feel conspicuous, hanging by my sides, stiff fingers grazing the swaths of my wrapper. Nox finishes the prayer and gestures to the figure, who is now climbing down, sure in every movement and foothold. When the man lands on our platform, it is with a thud, and the warriors clasp their wrists before gathering close to him, speaking softly.

"Let me do the talking," says Nox, and I frown. He sighs. "Mo, I just don't want anything to happen to us. To you."

I look away, shifting from the intensity of his gaze. And I nod.

The man who led the prayer tips his head to one side, listening carefully, his gaze still on us. A shaft of bright sun falls on his face, and, for a moment, I think it is this that creates the swirls on his body. And then he is stepping forward, out of the morning shade of the tree, and I see that his skin is a blend of dark and light. Full lips are encircled with white skin that spreads up his face to bloom on a high forehead. The marks dip down along his throat, sprawling across his broad chest to each pointed shoulder before they snake down his arms. I'm reminded of lemon balm and the rapid spread of the plant's white flowers. As he holds out his large hands to us, each the color of bone, he smiles, and his eyes gleam amber.

"Welcome, son of Bannu. We are honored to have you and your friends in our village. I am Tayo." His voice wraps around us in low, smooth tones.

I am in awe as my eyes race over the colors of his skin, thinking of the marks the babalawos paint on themselves to show their love for Dam. And here is this man with natural whorls of white on his beautiful brown skin.

"Please accept our hospitality." He holds his open palms to his chest as he smiles first at Nox, then Zaye. His gaze lands on me next, and his mouth opens in surprise, eyes flashing as his fingers curl into claws.

I falter, stepping back.

Tayo blinks. "Forgive me. I thought you were . . . Never mind," he says, rubbing a hand over his face. He smiles again, but the expression doesn't reach his eyes.

I swallow. Who did he think I was? But despite my worries, Tayo makes a sweeping bow, gesturing for us to follow him. I try not to frown, blinking quickly and attempting to quiet my nerves.

The doorway of the dwelling he leads us to is bordered with wooden carvings of Akyem's founders, wound through with the slinking scales of Dam. The men and women depicted have their faces turned toward the sky, smiles on their mouths, their open palms raised high above them. The dragon snakes around the frame so that his head is at the top of the doorway, jaws open wide, giving the illusion of walking into his very mouth. I think of the god who appeared last night, of the spines of his teeth, the mark on my wrist, and I shudder. Do the people here know of their god's pain and anger?

Ahead of us rears a silver statue of Dam, his spine arched and contorted on coils, diamonds for eyes, jaws shut, large teeth overlapping curved lips. At the base are offerings of yams, cracked-open coconuts, and plain white rice. There are silver bowls of water in various sizes placed in the shape of his constellation, all shimmering with pearlescent dust.

"Please, sit." Tayo gestures to a connecting room. The woven panels open to reveal a plethora of silk cushions and a low mahogany table heavy with papaya, akara fritters, and corn pudding.

I eye up the koko, my mouth watering at the sight of the creamy porridge sweetened with ginger. Bannu used to feed this to Nox and me when we were little and went through a phase of insisting on having breakfast outside on chilly mornings. I inhale deeply, letting the memories of warm bowls and wooden spoons filter through. My hunger wanes when I think of Bannu and Iya.

Zaye lowers herself onto the bench, dipping her fingers into the vessel of water to clean them. She flicks the water from her long nails and slides a small look at Nox as he leans toward Tayo.

"What is it that you have come to our village for?"

Straight to business, I think. Nox pauses and I see his mind clicking over what to say next. "We are looking for Dam himself. We are hoping you might help direct us to the sky monastery."

"Dam was spotted flying over Akyem, and Yida was sighted just beyond the forest," says Tayo as he sits opposite us. He takes a sip of water from a small wooden cup. Up close, the swirls of white on his body are even more beautiful, like bursts of clouds on the brown sky of his skin. "As our scriptures plotted on their sacred maps."

"Really?" I ask, swallowing quickly, knocking my bowl as I look around me. "Where are your scriptures? Do they include maps, or are they just directions?" The questions burst out of me in a way that has Nox and Zaye staring in surprise.

Tayo cocks his head to one side, turning his full focus on me. Nox nudges me with his thigh, and I know he wants me to be quiet, but I shift away from him. Before Tayo answers me, I feel a frisson of something, a small tug from behind.

"They are on the other side of you, on the other side of that panel."

I twist around to eye the supple woven branches that look

like the coils of a dragon. Flecked with silver, they flash in the brightening day. I am half out of my seat before I feel the hand on my bandaged wrist, and when I look down, I see the long ivory-white fingers of Tayo.

"You are forgetting your food," he says without a smile as I snatch my hand away. His eyes are darker now, the color of earth after rain.

Slowly, I sit back down, ignoring glares from Zaye and Nox. I had forgotten myself, which is not something that ever happens. "Forgive me," I offer, taking another bite of the porridge so as not to be rude. The food sticks in my throat. "I feel a little sick."

"She has always had a thirst for learning," adds Nox. "And a bad head for heights."

Tayo rises smoothly. "We cannot have one of Yida's daughters suffering on our account. One moment and I'll be back." He leaves the room, and Nox whirls on me.

"Mo!" he says. "What's gotten into you?"

Annoyance floods through me along with a snaking worry. What *has* gotten into me? "We don't have time to sit here having long conversations!" I retort, choosing an easier tone of defensiveness. "We need to find the monasteries. Or have you forgotten that?"

Nox recoils, his lips tightening in a way that makes me instantly sorry. I don't apologize, though. Instead, I take another stubborn mouthful of the koko that tastes of our childhood.

Zaye nibbles at one of the fritters, oil coating the tips of her fingers. "It's fine. Tayo knows who we are. And he's helping anyway. He would never dream of disrespecting Baba Bannu's son."

Nox sighs. "The location of the monasteries could be right

there. *Right there.*" He points to the room just beyond. "If we're polite enough, and I use my father's position, I think Tayo will let us look at the scriptures. And that's what's important."

I deflate at his words, rubbing my eyes. "You're right. I think I'm just tired."

Nox rolls his lips, and I know he's thinking about ignoring me. He releases a sigh and then does something he hasn't in the last year. He punches me on the shoulder, enough to hurt a little, enough to make me smile.

"Just . . . let me talk to him. It's polite to show him the respect that he deserves. It's what Baba would say too."

We are silent a moment, and I think about the difference a day can make. My mind goes back to the temple again, to the determination of my mother as Kakra and Panyin stood by her side. I won't allow myself to think of anything other than her being that way. *If I think it, then it will be,* I tell myself, hand going to the crystal tucked against my chest.

Tayo smiles as he returns and places a steaming cup of rooibos tea in front of me. "This will settle you." He sits down, his knees poking up, not contained by the table at all. "And to answer your questions, and I know you have many, I will let you peruse our archives. However, the sky monastery location is a well-kept secret, and although there are several rumored maps, I have not seen them. I admit, my interest is mainly in prayer. But you are welcome to look."

"That is very kind, I—"

Tayo puts his hand up, closing his eyes until Nox stops speaking. "But you must do something for us. There must be a trade. You cannot seek without the will to give."

Nox sits back. His knee begins to bounce up and down a

little. I see him try not to frown, giving in to just one small line that sits evenly between his eyebrows.

"What would you ask for?" Nox leans forward as he chews his lip, weighing how best to respond, how much to reveal. "The ọba's guards have control of the temples, and our parents have been . . . taken." He pulls at one of his frosted curls. "We only have what you see."

"Oh, I know all of this. It is the reason I allowed your presence here. As well as entertaining the daughters of Yida." Tayo smiles again, but this time he slaps his palms together twice. "We are pure and true followers of Dam. What I ask of you is to be acknowledged as such."

"I don't understand." Nox sits up straighter, his mouth a line.

"He wants Akyem to be declared as a sacred village, an outreach of the sky monastery," says Zaye, her eyes narrowing. "This means a share of Dam's silver."

"Very succinct." Tayo strokes the sides of his beard with both hands, a white smile blooming on his face. "We offer prayers to Dam like no other village. Other worshippers come here to do the same. Everything in Akyem, from our high position to the food we consume, is with the dragon god in mind. *Everything.* Surely it would be no big feat to recognize this?"

And collect a healthy tithe, I think but do not say. Nox smooths his face into a small smile. "What makes you think that I am in a position to offer this?"

"Your father is the principal babalawo." Tayo steeples his fingers together and leans forward. "As his son, you have influence."

Silence thickens in the growing warmth. I know that only the principal babalawo can bestow the honor of a village becoming an official religious settlement. But if Bannu is imprisoned, can his son give that title?

Nox glances my way a moment. "If I agree, it will only be to ask my father. He alone has the power to decide such a thing."

"Of course, of course. That is enough. I'm sure he'll take how we have helped you into consideration, along with our piousness." The leader of Akyem unfolds himself from the table and stretches to his full height, fingertips skimming the roof. He rubs his stomach with his right hand and gestures with his left. "And with that agreed, I can show you all the scriptures and maps we have. Some of them are only available here, scribed by me and babalawos who have traveled onward."

Tayo turns his back to us, arms spread wide as he grasps the woven panels before us. A trail of white climbs from his tapered waist up his spine before exploding across his broad shoulders. The marks look a little like tall mountain peaks with a birthmark sitting to the left. I narrow my eyes and lean closer, taking the marks in, but then Tayo rolls open the doors, and I am staring at more scriptures than I have ever seen. The room revealed is the same size as the main chamber, but the walls are covered with racks of scrolls. Giddy at the sight of so many wooden spines, I raise a hand to my mouth and inhale the scent of parchment. Silver letters flash, each one decorated with the colors of Dam.

We stand, wiping our fingers clean and adjusting our wrappers in haste.

"May I?" I ask, no longer able to keep still, my hands outstretched to the nearest shelf.

Tayo dips his head in assent, backing away through the open doorway. "I will leave you to read."

Surrounded by the scriptures, I feel my excitement peter out when I realize just how many there are, how many we may have to read before we might find a map or directions. I pluck the nearest one to me, fingers tracing the raised Ajami inlaid with silver. Unfurling it reveals drawings of constellations. Yida's temple only contained knowledge on all things to do with the earth dragon, stories of the henge and how the stones came to be, the power they hold and how to access it. Since my father left, his deeper knowledge of Dam as an elder babalawo was out of reach.

"We're looking for the Adamawa Mountains, where the dragons will be sheltering," I remind the others. "Specifically, for the location of Dam's monastery."

Lowering myself to the floor, I see that Zaye is curled up in the corner, a neat stack of parchments next to her. When she looks up at me, I take a few more manuscripts from the shelf, making sure my pile is just that little bit higher than hers. Nox raises an eyebrow, and I turn away, heat rushing up my neck. He shakes his head but then begins pulling out scrolls methodically until he too has an armful.

The day is spent with the scent of old paper, drawings that chronicle Dam and the signs of his powers over the centuries. As the light paints the late afternoon in strokes of dusky mango, Zaye finally stands to return her latest batch of manuscripts to the shelves before stretching with a loud groan. When she twists her hands together, I envy the grace in her movements. Her golden nose stud glints, and I raise a hand to mine, touching the lone similarity between us.

"I am done with my pile," she says, rotating her neck, a hand squeezing her left shoulder. "I'm going to stretch my legs."

I watch her leave and then go back to the scroll I've been scanning, the lone one that even mentions Yida alongside Dam.

FROM THE SCRIPTURES OF BABALAWO AMADIN, FIRST PRINCIPAL PRIEST OF THE KINGDOM OF KWA

In the beginning, the dragon gods flew through the cosmos, skimming newborn stars and twisting in the tails of comets. They stretched their wings across infinity, scales rippling in the light from the newly burning sun, breathing in the glitter of gases. And then, after tiring of the cold deep black, they decided to make their home on a world they found. Somewhere they could rest in the earth and in the sky, in the dark and in the light. But the world was inhabited by the emi buburu, and before they could make it their own, they had to cleanse the shadow spirits with their idan. Once they had done this, Yida let loose her essence, watching as the molten burn cooled into rock and soil, eventually creating mountains and fields, while Dam let his fire turn cold, pouring water from his jaws, forming the seas, rivers, and lakes.

At first, the gods were content to roam the world they had made, Dam soaring through the heavens and Yida burrowing underground when she wanted to be by herself, both reveling in their new creation. It wasn't until a thousand years later that they thought to add any other living creatures.

And when they did, they began with us.

After coiling in the earth for centuries, Yida finally emerged. Unsure if her husband knew where she was, she placed stones on the ground in her shape, a henge, to show her husband where he could find her. When Dam still didn't return from the skies, she despaired of her loneliness, crying tears of immense sorrow. And then Yida began to gather soil together, fashioning it into the shapes of what she hoped would be companions. But each time she created them, they would crumble. When Dam finally returned, guided by the henge, it was to his wife roaring at the piles of earth in grief. When he found out how much his wife had missed him, he blazed a new pattern of stars into the sky, one that showed his form, and promised Yida that every time his stars aligned with her stones, he would visit her. And together they would cleanse the lands of the emi buburu, ensuring the shadow spirits could not return.

But the goddess still wanted companions for when her husband was away, and so Dam used his power to summon water from the air, turning the soil into clay. Both dragons shaped the clay into the first people of the new world, the people of the Kingdom of Kwa. For days they were left to harden in the sun, and on the seventh, they became a permanent form. The gods watched over the beings that they had made, but seeing them inert was a great disappointment.

And so, they set about giving them life.

With Dam's stars glittering above Yida's stones, the dragon gods gathered the forms they had made and released their magic upon them, a show of their love and power. As the fire and ice of their idan flowed over the first people, the gods' essence seeped into each creation, giving them a soul and bringing them to life. Whichever dragon's essence gave the human their spirit determined the god they would worship, passed down from generation to generation.

Only a single being being remained still, and so the dragons came together to breathe their idan as one, bringing him to life. And that was the first ọba, made from Yida and Dam, his royal line worshipping not one but two gods.

More creatures were given life by the gods, providing the world with many different kingdoms and animals, both good and bad. All living creatures worshipped the gods, but Yida and Dam favored their first creations, and so they blessed the Kingdom of Kwa over all others, choosing from the pious. They tested those in Kwa who could sense their magic, and if their devotion was true, they were gifted with the ability to use the dragons' idan, thus protecting the kingdom and ensuring its prosperity in the new world. The deities demanded worship in return for this power, and every time Dam's stars are in alignment with Yida's stones, the people of Kwa come together to celebrate as one, no matter which god they are aligned with, and give thanks.

Only in this way are the blessings and idan of the dragon gods continued.

Only in this way are the emi buburu kept at bay.

I try to take comfort in the universal story of creation, slotting the scripture back into place on its shelf, and then sneak a look at Nox to see him absently picking at the inside of his nose.

"You'll have even less brains if you keep doing that," I say, moving to stand next to him. He rolls his eyes. "Anything?"

"Nothing." Nox taps his parchment against the shelf. "There's a few mentions of the sky monastery and the Adamawa Mountains, but nothing about where the entrance is. And now we've wasted most of a day."

"That's that, then," I say, my voice small as I rub my eyes.

"Is it?" Zaye saunters in, a smile draped over her face, eyes glittering. It is the same look she wore when she'd beaten me in a prayer test set by the iyalawos at the temple.

"What is it?" I say. "What have you found out?"

"What if I told you there was one more scripture? One that Tayo conveniently didn't tell us about?"

"I'd say you might be making things up . . ."

"Or would you be eternally grateful?" She wiggles her eyebrows, adding a sly grin. "Perhaps it's something I should keep to myself. I can imagine how grateful Iya Nana will be when I'm the one who gets us to the monasteries."

I should have expected nothing less from Zaye. "Just tell us. Especially since we've been the ones going through the last of the scrolls."

"Very well. I bumped into one of Akyem's guards outside. She was waiting to offer me some trinket."

"So you've been flirting while we were in here doing all the work?"

"I was getting information." Zaye glares at me now. "Chika was telling me about another secret map—"

"Not so secret if she knows about it."

"If you'll just shut up for a moment and *listen*." The girl sucks in a deep breath, glowering at me.

"Mo, just be quiet. Let her speak."

I purse my lips at Nox's words. I know I'm being unfair, but after a lifetime of Zaye sniping at me, the harsh words just spill out. I bite the inside of my mouth. If Zaye has found out something, then all is not lost.

"It's a set of directions that only Tayo and the elders of Akyem know about. Apparently, it's hidden outside of their village because it also details the location of the earth monastery. Chika only found out because she overheard them talking one time."

"Where is it?" I ask.

"Hidden deeper in the Sambisa Forest. She said we can find it if we can sense Yida's idan."

"But how does that even make sense? I thought Akyem only truly recognized Dam?"

"That's why it's in the forest."

We are silent a moment while we take in Zaye's words.

"Perhaps that's why Tayo was so quick to agree to us looking at all this," says Nox finally . . .

Just as shouts ring through the air.

Nox moves first, standing behind the screen. Slowly, he peers around it, a hand held up. I tilt my head to one side, filtering through the sounds of birds until I hear another shout rising from the ground, followed by cries from the treetops.

We jump as the panel is yanked back and Tayo looms over us.

"The ọba's guard is here." His face is pinched together. "With an interesting guest."

"It's Addaf," I whisper instantly. How did he know where to find us?

I lean out the window, shaped like the dragon's eye in the woven wattle of the room. Men swarm the giant trunks of the trees like ants, apart from one who stands still in their midst. Addaf's red-gold hair is unmistakable even from this height. Pushing down my panic, I dart back in.

The ambassador stands in a tornado of shadows that flickers and morphs into the tall shapes of the emi buburu. My hands fly to Yida's tear, tucked in my wrapper, my heart pounding harder at the sight below us.

I watch as the village scurries into action, retracting ropes, raising platforms and doorways now hidden behind foliage. A well-rehearsed defense procedure, but one I worry will not be enough.

I don't have to wait long for my fears to be proved true. Down below, the sprawling roots of our tree begin to darken, bark cracking loudly as life is slowly leeched from it. The rot spreads, climbing up the trunk until it stops halfway.

He's warning us, taunting us. Or else the reach of the emi buburu only goes so far. Or maybe not. I fight the panic that crawls along my skin as I survey the forest around Akyem. Blackened trunks and rotten leaves pattern the foliage in large swaths as life is taken by the shadow spirits. Stifling a gasp, I make out the tiny, still mounds of a few n'damas, their antlers crumbling horns of ash gray.

"Akyem has no current enemies," says Tayo, eyeing us, his shoulders curled forward.

"They're here for us." I won't lie. "But they'll ruin the whole of Kwa if we can't stop them. We just need to get to the monasteries. Help us. *Please.*"

A villager runs over and murmurs to the leader. Tayo inhales deeply before turning to us. "They're coming from the ground. There are men at the base of every tree."

"Can you get us out of here?" I ask, my tone a high quaver now.

Tayo nods, worry in the clench of his jaw. "Dam teaches us care and duty for others. If we can help, then we should. And from the look of things, if we help you, we help us. The quickest way out for you is the Glide."

He hurries back through the temple, slipping behind the silver dragon of Dam. Behind the statue of the dragon is an oval doorway leading to a small platform. A long line of silver stretches away into the canopy at the back of Akyem.

The Glide. My stomach flips.

"This will take you beyond the outskirts of our village. I'll get someone to bring your guiamalas if we can." Tayo reaches down to a large woven basket containing ropes with metal clips and handles. "We will keep them busy. The forest gives us life. We will fight for it and win, just as we have done before."

I hesitate, remembering the spears held to our faces. The villagers are warriors.

"Moremi, we need to go." Zaye's eyes are wide.

"She's right," says Nox as he holds one palm to his heart. "Our thanks. Come on, Mo."

Tayo mirrors the gesture. "Remember, Akyem is to be pronounced a sacred village and we are even." He clips Nox's rope to the metal wire and steps back.

Nox looks over his shoulder, the muscles in his back rippling. Then he grasps the handles tighter before he swings into the air, his body a slash of dark brown, the silver line taking him toward a ground crowded with bushes. Zaye waits on the lip of the platform as Tayo clips another rope and gives her the handles. She speeds forward without even a glance, her feet neatly together, toes pointed downward.

I wait for a handle to be handed to me . . . and instead look down to see a dagger pointing at my heart.

"You look so very much like your baba." Tayo smiles at me, but his eyes are clouded with tears. "He was here just after he was exiled."

The village leader takes a step closer, and I move backward until one of my heels hangs over the edge. My father's name is never mentioned in the temples. He let us down for his beliefs . . . and now it looks like he may have done even more harm than that.

"I don't know what my baba did to you or your village—"

Tayo shakes his head, but his dagger doesn't waver, and I feel a ripple of fear.

"It is more what he did *for* us. Your father was a visionary." Tayo's smile grows. A tear slips over his right cheek. He flips the dagger over and offers it to me. "His connection to Dam was unlike any other."

The blade glitters in the sun, the color of pure moonlight. I take the bone-white hilt of the weapon offered to me, gasping as a cold crackle encircles my wrist. Beneath the scrap of wrapper, my skin glows as an iciness seeps into my grip and a humming fills my mind. "This is . . ."

"The scale of our dragon god, honed into a blade made only for those worthy. This is a relic of Dam brought here by your father." Tayo looks down at my wrist and taps it once. "He left it with an intent he never explained, but it is clear to me now. It sings to *you*."

My jaw drops, but the village leader shakes his head. "Hurry. There's no more time."

There are thumps behind us in the temple and a strangled shout. Tayo turns me around, clipping my rope to the wire. I tuck the dagger in my wrapper, the blade cold against my chest, settling against Yida's tear.

"Go now." The village leader smiles, his cheeks wet but eyes hard as the sounds of shouting come closer. My trembling fingers curl around the handles. "Remember what you have *seen*."

And then he pushes me off the platform.

CHAPTER EIGHT

My feet skim the air as I struggle not to scream. Leaves spin past me, blurs of green and yellow. I gulp, fighting to breathe as I whip through spirals of fading light. I have never felt like this before, this terrified, this... *alive.* The muscles of my arms are drawn tight as I zip past the giant trees, scraping the topmost branches, the leaves a soft velvet. Akyem is left far behind, and the wind cracks around me in a way that feels as if I am coming home.

And then it all ends as the bushes swallow me when I near the ground, coming to a stop just before the silver wire ends, wrapped around the base of a raffia trunk. I tumble toward Zaye, who neatly steps aside, looking down at me with barely concealed disgust when I land in an ungainly heap next to her. Without a word, the girl sighs and turns from me, pushing her way through the foliage.

"Mo, are you all right?" Nox lifts me up, hands on my waist, dipping so he can look in my eyes.

I nod, unable to speak, my legs still shaking, the roar of an unfamiliar power quickly disappearing, but Nox's gaze is now fixed on the forest floor. The last of the sun flashes on the blade of Dam. It must have fallen out of my wrapper.

I bend forward and snatch it from the ground, but Nox has already seen it.

His brow furrows. "Where did you get that?"

"You know what it is?" I ask, hands curled tight around the ivory hilt.

"It looks like something my father has often spoken of . . . Can I see it?"

Reluctantly, I lift the blade up. A wisp of a smile plays across Nox's lips as the edge glitters sharply.

"Baba spoke of a dagger made from one of Dam's scales. Unbreakable. Dam allowed the first principal babalawo to pluck a scale from his back as a thank-you for building the sky temple. It was said to have been made into a blade that only the pious can wield."

I glance at the fabric tied around my wrist, Iya's warning searing in my mind. What would she say about this?

"Tayo gave it to me. He said . . ." I tighten the folds of my wrapper to secure the weapon, my eyes fluttering at the rush of raw chill. I haven't mentioned my baba to Nox in years. Gradually, I stopped speaking about him, but I was always in despair over whether he was dead or not, so I used to imagine him on a pilgrimage instead. He'd gone somewhere holy, I always thought. And that's why he could never write to me—because he was too busy praying. I run a hand over the dagger now, blinking away a tear when I think of my father leaving this for me. "He said that Baba brought it to Akyem. That he left it there for a reason."

"For you?" Confusion clouds Nox's gaze. "Why?"

But I don't know either. Why me? Why not a fellow priest of Dam? I turn to look back at Akyem, but the village is obscured by the canopy, as if it doesn't even exist.

Still, it won't take long before Addaf and the guard realize that we are not there.

"Let's work it out once we put some more distance between us and Addaf. It's not like I can use the dagger anyway—you know my coordination..."

"Is as good as a newly born guiamala," finishes the boy for me.

For a moment, he stares hard at the weapon, his mouth tightening. I know what he's thinking. If anyone should have the blade, it should be him.

"Come on. We need to move. Tayo and his warriors will only be able to hold them off for so long." Nox turns away from me, his shoulders stiff.

I don't even want to think of how many trees Addaf could kill before that happens. I picture the brilliant green of the canopy and the houses woven into it, and I shiver. They had known peace and prayer, and then we brought them death.

We quickly wind through the forest, one minute bleeding into the next. I hold a hand to my side, a stitch jabbing my ribs. Zaye remains ahead until she deigns to stop next to a tamarind tree, its light brown pods drooping down. I'm so glad her leg has healed that I don't moan about the pace, even though my feet are hurting.

"First, how do your little legs carry you this fast?" Nox pants when we catch up to her. "And more importantly, what did your intended say again?"

Zaye rolls her eyes. "Chika is *not* my intended—despite trying to give me jewelry. As if I would be swayed by a small

small bracelet." She examines her nails before touching a fingertip to the gold in her nose. "All I need is Yida's grace and, when I rise higher in the temple, the matching head chains and ear piercing." I blink, struggling to keep my face neutral. "So she told me the other scroll is a Yida one. And that we should follow her idan."

"Not exactly the best directions," I grumble, scuffing my foot in the crackle of fallen leaves. "Can you even feel anything?"

Zaye shrugs. "Not yet, but Chika said to head northeast, where the forest is light and then dark."

I sigh and look up at the sky. I've had just about enough of vague hints and directions. My heart sinks when I think of the four nights left that Dam's stars are in alignment with Yida's stones. "It's nearly nightfall."

"Let's take it literally and head away from the setting sun," says Nox. He points east, into the forest, which is gilded with the very last of the day's light, palm trees splashed with burnt-orange rays.

We walk into the screeches of golden-faced monkeys, and I catch sight of a female, her fur an iridescent sheen as she scrambles up a tree, baby clutched close. She knows that when darkness draws over the land, the stars and the moon will not save her from being hunted by wild nundás and painted wolves.

"How was Iya Nana before you left the temple?" Zaye's voice is quiet, and I realize that she has slowed her steps so that she can walk next to me.

I stare at her, eyebrows raised.

"What? Is my question so out of the ordinary?" The girl sniffs once. "Iya Nana is the principal priestess. She can teach me a lot. And . . . and I can't imagine the temple without her."

My eyes prickle. I chew my lip, remembering blood on my

mother's wrapper, the red of it in her mouth. But then I think of the prayers of Kakra and Panyin, and the sight of all three of them ready to face the ọba's guards. I know that if I dwell on it, I will sit down and cry, and then I might never get back up again.

"She was mostly healed, I think," I manage. "At least enough to stand and force me to leave."

Zaye nods. I see her hand lift, but she lets it drop, fingers stiff before tucking them into a loose fist. "Good. Ojaja knows he's made a mistake with the gods. It would be stupid of him to believe that demon from Carew and hurt her."

I know she's speaking plainly, but my shoulders curl forward. To send him after us, Ojaja clearly still has faith in him. But at least Addaf is following us and not using the emi buburu to harm my mother and Bannu.

I run a hand over the outline of the blade pressed against my skin, shivering at the chill. Dam's idan sparks against my chest in flashes of stinging cold. My steps falter, and I dart looks at Zaye and Nox. But neither notices. The iciness begins to seep away, and I hate how it's slowly beginning to feel almost as normal as Yida's idan. I still don't know what it means to be chosen by both of the gods, but Iya seemed to think it meant something. I adjust the bandage and try to nurture the hope that she had.

I let myself fall behind as Zaye walks next to Nox, flicking her braids over one shoulder as she asks the boy questions about the sky temple. I roll my eyes and move to examine the plants that are scattered beneath the trunks of the trees: ogbono and moringa sprout in the shade, as well as yarrow. I cup a delicate blade of the leaf. My mother showed it to me, explaining how it would help with my monthly bleeds.

She always says that Yida does not put us through that which we cannot overcome. I hope she is right.

Finally, as I pick my way across the forest floor, night shadows growing, a frisson of idan filters through to my soles.

"Zaye, did you feel that?"

She looks at me sharply and stops, her feet making semicircles in the earth. She shakes her head slightly.

But I can still sense it—a warmth surging against my soles. "This way," I declare, leading us toward two lines of wild black plum trees that converge in a V.

Their leaves are the usual green, but as we get closer, we see that each is edged in a honeyed glow. Yida's idan grows beneath me, the heat of it wrapping round each ankle and climbing my legs in a familiar smolder.

"You're right," murmurs Zaye. Her eyes are half closed with the feeling of the dragon's power.

I walk faster, almost running now as the idan grows, my soles crackling. The trees come together to mark a clearing. I skid to a stop, my breath catching as I step past the last of the hanging fruit to a sudden darkness that gathers in the meadow.

A hole as black as a moonless night.

"Where the forest is light and then dark?" says Nox. He stares down at the blank deep and cracks his knuckles nervously. "Is this what Chika meant?"

"It must be," I whisper, the scorch of the goddess's magic bright in my veins now. I creep closer to the hole in the center of the clearing. "And I can feel Yida's idan."

"Me too." Zaye is at my side now and she slides a look at me. "What do you think?"

"I think that you need to return to your temple," a voice

booms through the near dusk. "Or face an arrow in your heart."

My mind goes immediately to Addaf, but the voice came from in front of us. There's no way he would have had time to catch up, let alone circle around.

"State your business or face the consequences."

I glare as the voice reverberates through the clearing, scanning the bushes and the black plum trees that ring us. A wave of hot anger rolls over me, and for a moment, there is no separating Yida's idan and the sudden rage I feel at being threatened *again*.

"We would if we knew who we were speaking with," I snarl. "Show yourself if you have the authority to make such statements."

There's a moment of silence, and then . . . "Look down."

The forest floor shifts, undulating like a restless ocean. But the ground is not covered with waves of water. Instead, a red flow of large insects makes its way toward us.

Immediately, Zaye, Nox, and I jump back, but the termites stop just short of our feet.

"I am the guardian warrior of this grove," the voice rings out. "If you are requesting access to this part of the Sambisa Forest, then you must state your business."

I peer down, squinting as I catch movement on a termite bigger than the rest. Now I make out the tiny man perched on the back of the insect. He holds a bow as long as his arm, the tip of a miniature arrow aimed at my face.

We have come arcoss an Umutwa, the smallest of fairies.

I hold an arm back to keep Nox from getting too close, not taking my eyes from the tiny man. "Apologies." I bow my head, remembering what Kakra had told me about. Nomadic hunters, with arrows powerful enough to kill large animals. Kakra always said there was a proper way to greet everything created by the dragon gods, whether it be the sun that rises or the predator that stalks you in the night.

I lean back down, my knees in the warm soil, not caring when a few stones stick into my skin. I file through Kakra's stories and those in the temple archives, and just as the Umutwa pulls back his bow, I place my hands palm to palm and nod my head once. The small fairies always need to be flattered in a way that shows someone is wary of them, that shows the importance and implication of their threatening presence. I think furiously.

"I saw you from across the clearing." I wince. Not far enough. The Umutwa lowers his head, patting the arrows in his holder made from a small leaf. He plucks at them, adding another arrow to his bow so that two poisoned tips face me. "I mean, I saw you from across the forest! When I was high in the village of Akyem!"

"Akyem?" He pauses, the string on his bow going slack as he squeezes his legs on the termite's sides, urging the insect closer to me. "That is very high. And very far."

I don't move, and I hope that both Zaye and Nox will hold their tongues.

"What were you doing in Akyem?"

I place my hands on the tops of my thighs now and try to smile, telling myself to relax. "We were looking for something."

"A scroll," adds Zaye as she kneels next to me. She lets her braids fall over one shoulder and smiles prettily down at the tiny man. She just couldn't keep quiet. Only that girl would try to flirt with an Umutwa who could kill us with an arrow each.

"Hmm." The man lowers his bow and gazes up at us. "I am Sanele. And I have been tasked with keeping this area safe. None shall pass or enter."

"Is that because of the scripture?" asks Nox, bending down to join us.

Sanele tightens his grip on his bow but makes do with puffing out his chest. "There is no scroll."

"What's that?" I ask, pointing to the hole in the clearing. Now that I'm closer, it begins to look more familiar. The sides are smooth, and the thickness of the dark suggests it is deep. Very deep. "Is it one of Yida's burrows?" I whisper in awe.

There are only a few that have been found intact in the Kingdom of Kwa, said to be tunnels left from where the goddess first accessed the earth. I've only seen one map in the temple detail these, and that was in the south, the burrow fortified by metal to keep the shape of the dragon goddess. Many have collapsed or have been overtaken by the land around them, but all have the same strong remnants of Yida's idan.

"There is no scroll, I told you. Only Eneh."

I snap my head back in the direction of Sanele.

"Iya Eneh is here?" Zaye squeaks, holding a hand to her mouth.

"She is," answers Sanele. "And none shall pass unless she wills it."

"Iya Eneh?" asks Nox. "The previous principal iyalawo?"

"Yes." I gaze into the black hole, remembering when my

mother took her place years ago. "She declared she was too old and ceded to Iya. We thought that she would go to the earth monastery, but she disappeared. Some said she went back to her home village, but there has been no word of her."

"In her time as principal iyalawo, she traveled all over Kwa," Zaye says. "Not only did she make any crop flourish, but she also healed every person who needed it. Without her, the ọba's son would have died when he was born."

"The way she could feel, summon, and use Yida's idan was legendary. *Is* legendary." I look toward the hole again and something snaps into place. "We need to speak to her."

Sanele snarls and raises his bow once more. "None may enter."

"But—" Nox starts.

"I said none may enter. Eneh said the only people allowed are those who are accompanied by the one chosen by both."

My hand flies to my wrist, clamping down on the bandage instinctively. My head swims.

"Right, well, *that* really makes sense," says Nox quietly, his eyes on the arrows still pointed at us.

"Chosen by whom?" I ask faintly.

The miniature man sits tall on the termite and gestures to the ground and the sky. "By Yida and by Dam."

My stomach drops. I look down at the dragon that loops around my ankle and at the scrap of pale wrapper that is still tied around my wrist. How did Eneh know?

But the jolt of uncertainty is swiftly followed by hope. Maybe Iya Eneh will be able to tell me what it all means. I slide a look at Nox and Zaye. The idea of telling them too . . . My skin itches with nerves.

"What is it to be?" Sanele glares at me, pulling back the string of his tiny bow.

Biting the inside of my mouth, I lift my ankle and turn it, showing the scales, teeth, and tail of Yida. When I touch my bound wrist, I hold my breath. I half hope that when I unwind the fake bandage, I will have imagined the mark of Dam seared into my skin.

I let the scrap of wrapper fall away, blood pounding so hard in my ears that I almost don't hear the gasps of the others. The dragon curls around the bones of my wrist, its tail flicking up toward my elbow. I flex my fingers and the scales ripple.

Sanele lowers his bow and his head. "You may pass."

"Moremi?" Zaye hisses. "How did this happen?"

Before, I would have reveled in being chosen for something over her, but now I hold my wrist, still overwhelmed at the imprint of the scales cool against my palm. There's been no time. My plants and tonics have never felt so far away.

I look to Nox, but he is silent, his dark eyes bright with something I can't quite make out. I'd rather he was angry at me for keeping this from him. His lack of words now makes my stomach swoop more than the Glide did.

"It happened earlier." I trail a hand over the dragon on my wrist, shivering once. "When the babalawos were in the mountain niches. Nox nearly fell and I ran over and Dam . . ."

"Dam marked you?" Nox's voice is quiet. He sits back, his eyes flickering over me.

I squeeze my arm and nod. "I thought he . . ." *Was going to attack me.* But I don't say it. "I felt his idan. It was so . . . *cold.* Like splinters of ice."

The weight of the boy's stare is heavy, and I don't look up

until I can't bear it anymore. "I know there must be a mistake," I whisper. "I know that no one has ever been chosen by both gods before."

None of us moves or speaks, the silence thick and heavy. I cover my wrist when Nox reaches out, his hand enfolding mine. He peels my fingers away carefully and my eyes go to the dragon on his skin. When my matching mark is revealed, he sucks in a breath.

And then he smiles. "The gods don't make mistakes, Mo."

My shoulders loosen at his expression. I hadn't realized how worried I was that he would be disappointed. That he would think that something was wrong with me.

I snatch a look at Zaye, hardening myself for her barbs, but she only sniffs and turns to peer at the hole ahead of us. "I don't really care about what it means, as long as we get to the monasteries. Come, we can't just hang around here."

"You cannot enter until the dark meets the black."

"Nighttime?" I ask, looking again into the hole. *Great, another rule.* "You said we could pass if I was chosen by both."

"You can. But I only relax the protective wards under the cover of night. You never can tell who is watching."

"I know you're taking your role seriously. But that's time we don't have." Zaye has her hands on her hips and is glaring at Sanele.

"You would have Eneh put at risk?" His voice rises now and his hand twitches on his bow. "I already told you, I do not make the rules."

I step smoothly between them and look down at Sanele. "Thank you. We will take this time to rest."

The man bows, urging his termite toward the trunk of a

tree, and the rest follow him. "Do not thank me. Thank Yida and Dam."

Nox and Zaye arrange themselves close together, huffing as they cup their faces in their hands, but I can already see the exhaustion in the droop of their shoulders and the flutter of their eyes. *We all need this short rest*, I think as I gaze down into the endless black hole. *After all, who knows what is down there?*

CHAPTER NINE

After Baba left, I used to wake in the ripest part of the night, bad dreams clinging to me like spiderwebs. I could never remember what they were about, but the lingering dread would stay until the sun fully rose. Sometimes, I'd cry out for Iya, taking comfort in her cradling arms. If I couldn't return to sleep, I'd tell myself Baba's story of the Stars' Path, the tale of a young girl who was lost at night. She panicked when she realized that she could not see beyond the fire she had made to cook her dinner. Worrying about how to find the way home, the girl came up with a clever plan. She threw the burning sparks of fire up into the sky to make a path in the darkness. I'd repeat this over and over, finding my own way through the black night and into another day.

Sanele wakes us up to full dark. I wipe my face. I needed that sleep but not the worries that slip back over me now. I try to brush away thoughts that maybe Sanele has tricked us, that really, we're heading into a lair full of traps. Nox and Zaye rise next to me, their breath steaming in the air. As we climb over the full lip of the hole, I'm reminded that there are things darker than the night. Legs trembling, I lower myself into the viscous blackness, reminding myself of the fact that Iya Eneh is in its folds.

"How will we see?" asks Nox. He runs a hand over his hair.

"We don't need to," murmurs Zaye. She stands next to me, her head only reaching my shoulder. "We'll let the idan guide us since it's brought us this far. If Moremi can keep up."

This girl. I can't believe her audacity, speaking as if I was not the one to lead us here. Does she not realize the importance of being chosen by the gods? I huff, feet skidding on the smooth walls of the tunnel as it dips sharply down. "Just stay close."

Nox holds on to my arm, and I slide my hand into his instead, the rough heat of his palm gentle against mine. I tell myself it's just to guide him, but my heart flutters when he tightens his grip.

The idan feels different once we're inside, burning away the chill of the tunnel and pulling me deeper into the blackness. "Are you feeling this?" I whisper to Zaye.

"Yes," she says, voice taut with nervousness. "Just keep going."

We continue, sliding along the tunnel. It is said that Yida created these burrows when she first explored the deep earth of the mountain, and I can almost imagine the might and strength of her body as she dove through dirt and stone, her scales ripping and smoothing the space she created. I hold out a hand shaking with reverence, touching the slick sides, following the hum and heat that radiates from all around us.

When I see a familiar glow, I pause, and then the light splits and swarms at us in a buzzing rush. Nox's fingers dig into my arm as he tries to ease himself in front of me, but I stretch out my arms to block him. I wish he'd stop thinking of me as needing protection all the time. I'm strong, now more than ever. And the flow of idan only reinforces this feeling.

"It's all right," I say, even though my words quiver. The glow combined with the buzzing of what I think are small wings calms me somewhat. "I think it's the Aziza."

The beads of light come closer until I can make out the blur of wings and the pale luminance in each of the star apple–sized bodies. The only Aziza I have seen before are the ones at the night markets with their rare type of honey.

"Stay still," I murmur as the fairies surround us. They are not aggressive beings, but they have stingers on their feet that can paralyze a human for a good few hours.

I hold my chin tilted up slightly as an Aziza darts close to my face. She's frowning, eyes chips of amber, small lips pursed. I don't speak, my heart knocking, and am rewarded with a beckoning gesture.

We follow the glowing beings, and the temperature begins to change, growing warmer as the tunnel leans upward. Yida's idan is as strong as before until it flares suddenly and then draws away, as if being absorbed.

The tunnel opens into an oval space lit with a blaze of torches, and for a moment, it looks like a dragon is curled around us. Idan crackles, thick and strong. I blink the gloom from my eyes and see that the scales are actual imprints in the rock, from when Yida rested here. At the back of the cave are four tall Aziza hives made from golden sand. Speckled with small holes, they are nearly as tall as Nox.

"Oshwiee."

The evening greeting echoes around us, along with the

gentle slap of bare feet. Iya Eneh moves forward through the shadows, a dark brown wrapper draped around her small frame. I point my toes in greeting as the elderly woman glides closer, arms held out, thick bangles of gold nudging at her hands.

"Come, my children, and sit." Eneh smiles and the wrinkles of her face form in beautiful swoops and grooves, highlighting every grin and frown of her long life. She has three lines scored delicately into each cheek, from the corners of her mouth pointing to her ears, with two more vertical ones beneath both eyes that look like stretched-out teardrops. She adjusts the golden fabric that covers her head, its ends plaited so the tassels hang down over her shoulders.

The Aziza swarm toward the old woman. The one who gestured for me to follow holds a wooden thimble to Eneh's mouth, and she takes a sip.

"The Aziza share their honey with me and they revel in Yida's idan. It makes their nectar sweeter." She presses her palms together. "Thank you, Aminah."

The tiny being swoops away, the rest of the Aziza following her as they fly toward their hives.

Eneh points to a pile of floor cushions in the colors of a furious sunset, settling herself in a rocking chair of mahogany and ash wood overflowing with pillows. Zaye and Nox follow me as I sink among the softness.

"I know all of what has happened," says Iya Eneh. "Just as it has been foretold."

"Then you know what Ọba Ojaja has caused." My back straightens, and I hear the pain tucked among my own words. "He has a man, an ambassador from Carew, who has told him . . . things. He's told him that he is the one person to control the dragons." The words tumble out in a rush. "But he's made the gods furious and they're . . . injured. And he has our parents." My voice shakes on the last word and I know it's not just because of the pain from what has happened. I've placed so much on the priestess telling us where the dragon gods are, but I'm also hoping that she'll be able to tell me what I am now. What I'm supposed to *do* now. How do I even learn how to channel Yida's idan? And what about Dam's? I feel like a failure before I've even begun.

Eneh reaches out for me, and my shoulders round as I bend my head at the woman's touch. A tear spills over my cheek, and I wipe it away.

"He will not kill them," Eneh says. "But what he has unleashed may destroy the entire world."

"You know about the emi buburu?" I ask.

"I sensed their entry to this world, yes. It is not just this. The gods need to be united to complete the Dírágónì ceremony. But they are also destined to be united in one." She looks down at my wrist and then at my ankle before sitting back and folding her hands on her belly. The torches flicker, throwing long shadows as she rocks forward. "We need to speak about the marks you have been given. Both of them."

I had thought the gloom of the tunnel would have made my wrist harder to see, but the old woman's gaze is pinned on it. She holds out her hand and I place my arm in the dry cradle of her palm. Her fingers run gently over the scales that wrap around my wrist. "I find that the answers we seek are often to be found within us."

Eneh looks up at me and my heart stills. I want so badly for her to tell me what my purpose is now.

"Baba Niyi took my words seriously in his own way and held them close," she says quietly, and tears immediately fog my vision. "He wanted the relationship between sky and earth to be deeper. But when he tried to bend others to his belief, it cost him his reputation."

And my mother.

And me.

Eneh strokes her thumb on the side of my hand. "You have embodied what your father tried to force."

"But . . . What does that even *mean*?" My voice shakes, cracking on the question. I can't take any more riddles. I want real answers.

"It means what it shows," Eneh says, and squeezes my hand gently. "You will be able to call on Yida's and Dam's idan. I'm sure you have already felt both kinds."

I look down at the scales on my skin. "This hasn't happened before?"

"It has not." Eneh sits back and massages her hands slowly. "But that doesn't mean it should not."

"Will she be able to do exactly what I can?" asks Nox, his eyes lingering on the dragon on my wrist.

"She will. Great blessings are often unexpected." Eneh leans closer now, her voice dropping to a whisper so that only I can make out her words. "And great blessings come with sacrifices. Idan is powerful, and two types could ruin a mind that is not strong. You must be strong."

Eneh sits back while I digest her warning. My mind spins with the thought of such power, such damage. We've always been taught that dragons imbue the pious with their magic, not destroy them. The old woman squeezes my hand as if to reassure me.

"And what about the gods?" Zaye interjects. "How can we find the monasteries? Surely you know where they are?"

For once, I am glad of Zaye's pettiness, and a weight lifts when she changes the subject. Being strong enough to be able to use the idan of both dragons ... My head pounds just at the thought.

Eneh gives a great sigh. "I knew once upon a time, but I am afraid the years have dulled my memories."

My eyes close as disappointment courses through me. We've already lost a day. There are only four more until Dam's stars fade ...

Eneh grins, her teeth all surprisingly still there.

"But I do have directions."

I exhale loudly and Nox laughs as the old woman stands and curls her forefinger at us. "Come. I can show you, but you will have to read it yourself. It is impossible for me to do so."

Then, of all things, she starts to fumble with the folds and ties of her wrapper. As the fabric begins to slide from her body, I'm reminded of those elders in our communities whose minds are not the same, forgetting names and places and even what they should be wearing. I lurch forward, hand outstretched, ready to pull Eneh's wrapper back up.

"If you want to know the way to the monasteries, then you will not touch me." The old woman's voice is stern and unwavering. She loosens the wrapper so that it slithers from her spine, leaving her back exposed.

Leaving the directions exposed.

Eneh's back is covered in swirls and swoops and lines, creating a beauty like no other.

"They are ... *words*," whispers Zaye fervently.

"Directions," says the elderly iyalawo. "When I had a vision of the gods' holy places, I felt it my duty to record it in a way that it will not get lost. My village reveres scarification as part of our identity. These marks are the stories of our lives and our ancestors', of our joys, our pain, and our beauty. In this way, they are with us always, in life and in death."

I step closer, hand tracing the air close to Eneh. The words that trickle across her skin are in old-fashioned Ajami, like many of the scrolls in the temple. My lips move as I silently read.

When I finish, I step back, my hands shaking.

"What did it say, Mo?" Nox touches my elbow.

I feel lightheaded and hot, my spirit tapping into the idan of the space once again. Eneh hikes her wrapper back up and turns to face us.

"The earth monastery is deep beneath the smallest Adamawa peak," I say, my voice faint.

Zaye claps, but Nox frowns at my expression. "What about the sky monastery?"

"It only speaks of Yida's." I purse my lips as their faces fall. My mind whirls, going to another back, this one covered with white marks and swirls. "But I think I also know where Dam's is."

CHAPTER TEN

Just before Tayo pushed me off the ledge, he told me to remember what I had *seen*. I think of when he stood with his back to us as he opened the panel to show the archives. He did show us the way. We just weren't looking properly. But I remember the white swirls on his brown skin now, and the way they mix with the words on Iya Eneh's back.

"The sky monastery is in the second peak, next to the smaller one." I tell the others of the map on Tayo's back.

"What? How do you know that?" Zaye snaps.

I explain the whorls on the village leader's back and the hint he gave me.

"It is up to you all now." Iya Eneh sits down on her mahogany chair, settling among the pillows. "Moremi cannot do it on her own."

She's right. The thought of facing the gods makes my stomach swoop. I shouldn't even have been part of the Dírágónì ceremony, let alone be here right now. Yida's tear is warm against my skin, close to the frantic beat of my heart. Why would they believe in me when I don't truly believe in myself?

I scrabble at my wrapper and draw out the crystal, choosing its heat over the chill of Dam's blade. My mother always spoke about it being a holy artifact, a physical manifestation of the goddess, but I just liked how it glowed in the same way as a new sunset. Even holding it is a comfort, and I stroke a finger down the side.

"I don't even know how to channel idan," I say tentatively.

Eneh tips her head to one side like a bird, her eyes pebble black. "Is that what I think it is?" She holds out her cupped hands, knuckles thick and swollen.

I lower Yida's tear, letting it slide into the cup of Eneh's fingers. She closes her eyes at the touch of it, rocking back and forth gently. A smile wrinkles her face. "One of Yida's tears... This was always on the altar." The elder turns it over, tapping the hard pink. She nods to herself, showing white teeth as she grins.

"I've never seen it . . . I've never been allowed into the prayer hall," says Nox as he crowds around me, peering down at the crystal. "I've heard it mentioned, though."

"They are said to have been shed when the goddess and her husband separated after creating the world. Dam was exploring the skies, while Yida was connected to the earth," I murmur. "But even though Yida wanted time on her own, after a thousand years she became sad at being apart from Dam and she cried for seven days straight. Her tears were scattered over the world as she searched for him. This was before Dam had made his constellation and they'd agreed that when it was above her stones, he would return to her for the Dírágònì ceremony. A time to be spent together after the cleansing of the lands."

"Is there something about it that can help? Does it channel idan somehow?" asks Nox.

"No," I answer. "They're just said to be incredibly rare."

Eneh tuts loudly as she passes the crystal back to me. "It has power."

"The scriptures—"

"Not everything is in the scriptures, child."

I bristle. Knowledge is something I often use to comfort myself; it never lets me down, and unlike the prayer dances, I never get it wrong. Eneh's face softens at my expression, and she offers me the crystal.

"Yida is stubborn. She's angry and she will no doubt burrow very deep under her sanctum. It will be easier to find Dam first, since he is said to perch on the monastery's highest point. And that tear is the key to getting him to go to the goddess." The old woman leans back, placing her hands in her lap. "The tear is a connection between Yida and Dam. If you offer it to the god, then he will recognize his wife's grief and you will be able to take him to her. She will come when she senses him. Once they are healed and united, there is a better chance they will be able to see past Ojaja's betrayal . . . see our worship and dedication to them. And then you can appeal to them to complete the Dírágónì ceremony."

I look to Nox. "You can speak for us at the sky monastery. The babalawos there will listen to you."

The boy rubs at the flaking swirls of white on the planes of his chest. "I can try. But first, we need to get there."

"Follow the paths in the skies, the paths of Dam," says Eneh. "It will take you on the fastest trail."

"The way through the lowlands will be our start," adds Nox. "Baba spoke of one of the god's traditional routes through the Ghost Ocean."

I clear my throat. "Then that's where we'll head. Hopefully, Tayo will have found a way to get the guiamalas to us." I crouch down in front of Eneh and she takes my hands. The skin on her palms is soft like faded cotton, the veins on the backs of her hands snaking like the dragons we worship. "Thank you."

The old iyalawo presses a kiss against my forehead, and I breathe in the smell of incense and shea, of home. Of my mother.

"Believe in yourself, Daughter of Yida, and now of Dam," Eneh whispers in my ear, her fingertips grazing my jaw.

If only it were that easy.

We follow the tunnel as it slinks back up toward the lip of the hole. I hold a hand against Yida's tear, tucked back tightly in the folds of my wrapper next to the dagger. If we can get Dam to return to his wife, get them to finish the ceremony, then our parents will be safe. We will all be safe. I press my lips together and tip my face to where I imagine the moon is. Faith is something I am familiar with, am strong in, but it feels different to dare having it in myself.

As we creep from the tunnel, a scan of the clearing reveals black plum trees and coarse tufts of grass that push up against the trunks. Tentative moonlight seeps from between the bushes, and much of the forest is still wrapped in the night. The shadows make me uneasy, especially when they shift and dark shapes separate, crushing apart the grass.

The guiamalas are waiting for us in the clearing, their heads almost level with the tree canopy. Mine noses its way through the other two and bends down, smacking its lips together and blowing its hot, stinking breath in my face.

"Tayo must have kept Addaf busy," I murmur, but Nox doesn't answer. He watches the edges of the forest, waiting until Zaye and I are on our guiamalas before swinging up onto his. The scowl on his face doesn't go away, even when we leave the clearing.

I know he's hoping the same as me, that the villagers are unhurt and that the emi buburu have not taken any more of the land.

The moon races alongside us until my stomach rumbles so loudly that Zaye turns and smirks. Nox finally abandons his frown and smiles at me.

"You're always hungry, Mo."

"I can't help it," I say, heat creeping across my cheeks.

"She needs more food than the other iyalawos, though I'm not sure where she puts it." Zaye runs her gaze over me. "She's got hollow legs."

"If hollow legs look like that, then they don't seem so bad to me." Nox grins and gestures to me, and I hide a blooming smile with my hand. "There's a stream up ahead. We'll stop and get some water, and maybe catch a fish or two."

Zaye may have had the other younger iyalawos to turn against me, but there's no way Nox will.

"How can you tell it's there?" I ask, my back to her.

"I can feel it," says Nox, staring into the bushes. He looks over at me. "Can't you?"

I look down at my feet and think about how Yida's idan usually arrives as heat through my soles. Dam's arrived from above, but I can't feel that now. I shake my head.

"I can show you." Nox slows his guiamala so that it is level with mine. "If you'd like."

"Yes," I say as a shiver of nerves ripples through me. Dam chose me, but it wasn't after an initiation. All my life, I've been a disappointment. I can't disappoint in this as well. Not when everything is at stake.

Nox gives me a nod. "Baba always told me that first you need to make space in your mind. When I was younger, I used to hold my hands up." He lifts his palms above his shoulders and tilts his face to the darkening sky. "Sometimes I could sense a little of Dam in the moisture in the air."

Feeling silly, I let go of the guiamala's reins and lift my palms, the sway of the animal beneath me rocking me back and forth. I try to relax, to open myself to what might come. "Like this? What am I trying to feel?"

"The cold, the sharp pull . . ."

I strain, nails pointed to the stars that glint through clouds. The bulbous white moon is slowly edging its way across the sky, and just as I am about to let my hands fall into my lap, I feel the smallest splinter of idan. I reach up higher, the chill needling my hands, spreading to my arms. It's stronger on my left and I point in that direction.

"The stream is that way."

"You can feel it!" Nox's voice is light with a smile.

I lower my hands, studying the dragon on my wrist, its scales iridescent in a splash of new moonlight. "It's so different. Dam's idan."

"I can imagine." A hand touches my shoulder, sliding over my back. Nox gives me a half hug and my face heats up. "You'll get used to it."

I hope so, I think as I hold on to the reins, my guiamala

following Nox's as he leads us in the direction of the water. *No, I know so*, I correct myself. If Iya Eneh can be so confident in me, then I can too. I used Dam's idan to sense water. I'm learning. And I'm doing my best.

The evening is warm and bright with the moon as we slide from the animals. I repeat my affirmations under my breath, only faltering when I twist my ankle climbing down the guiamala's last leg joint. Gritting my teeth, I say them again.

Nox stands on the bank of the stream, and as we reach him, I can see his frown. "The water is low. Lower than it should be at this time of year."

We don't speak for a moment, but I know both of us are thinking the same thing. Have the dragons taken their blessings already? I reach for the boy's hand and squeeze once.

Zaye breaks us from our thoughts, looking carefully around for any signs of ikaki. Despite their appearance as turtles, the ikaki are tricksters, stronger than they seem and capable of dragging a person and drowning them in even the shallowest of waters.

She creeps to the stream's edge and cups a handful of water. My thirst feels sudden, my throat dry as sand. I follow her, kneeling by her side as we both drink from our hands.

Nox stands a stride away from the stream, his eyes closed, lips parted. His hands tremble as he holds them toward the water, muscles rippling under his skin.

"Come and drink," Zaye calls to him.

I stay silent. I know what he's doing. After our initiations, we should have been taught how to wield the gods' idan. Now it is up to us to learn on our own.

Nox bends his hands in a beckoning gesture, fingers curled to palms, and waits. Nothing happens for a long moment.

Finally, a small ribbon of blue floats over Zaye's head. Her eyes widen and she opens her mouth, then thinks better of it, lifting her hands so they cover her hair. The water quivers once, before continuing to float its way to Nox, hovering above him as he cups his hands. I see his little finger twitch and his eyes flash just as the water falls on his head, with only a small splash making it into the curve of his fingers. He shakes his head, droplets spraying as he licks his palm and sighs.

Zaye laughs and I clap my hands together in excitement. "That was—"

"Not good enough," the boy finishes, scowling at the stream as he bends down next to us, scooping water out with his hands instead.

"It was something. We're going to have to start somewhere." My voice is soft as he finishes drinking and lowers himself onto the grass next to me. "How did you do it?"

He tugs at his damp curls, forcing the frustration away and smiling. He's always been able to let things go in a way I have never been able to. "I'm not entirely sure. But I can maybe show you?"

Something inside me tenses at the idea. I can't even pray to the gods right. How am *I* meant to wield their idan? Sensing their magic is completely different from using it. I need more time to understand it all.

"Let's eat first," I say, ignoring the thought that I'm just delaying the inevitable.

Nox wades into the shallows, trying to manipulate the current so that he can scoop out fish like a nundá, but after half an hour of this, he gives up.

"There's no fish," he says, voice rough. "There's never not been any fish in a river."

I swallow, thinking of the broken ceremony and the way the land feels as if it is changing already bit by bit.

"How about these?" I suggest, grabbing at some yellow stars close to a bush, digging the root vegetables up with a stick.

"These would be better roasted," mutters Zaye as she nibbles.

I don't answer, gnawing at the tuber until it is a nub in my hands. There is nothing to be gained by complaining. Or reacting. Instead, I retreat to the bank of the stream again, drinking as much as I can to wipe away the earthy taste of the yellow stars. I think of my jars of turmeric, cinnamon, and bitter leaf, wishing I could use some to add flavor to the tubers. I just found some bee balm a few days ago and the lemon-scented mint plant drenched the space with a bright tang. I wonder if it's all still there, and then I shudder at the thought of everything black and rotten, its essence eaten by the emi buburu. I take some deep, calming breaths and focus on the water. I am here. We are alive. And in a way I could not have imagined, I am getting to explore what lies beyond the temple's boundaries for the first time. A rush of excitement floods through me even as I remind myself to focus on the now.

As my hands dip into the cool water, my fingertips tingle, and at first, I nearly rip them out of the stream. Addaf flashes through my mind, then the emi buburu snaking through my home. The broken roars of Yida and Dam echo in my ears. What will happen to them if we fail? The forest around Akyem has already been decimated, and now my mind spirals, thinking about the crumpled form of the young priestess at the temple and the n'damas in the forest. I look to the sky, worrying now when I see thickened clouds clustered toward the coast. Should it be stormy yet? We're not in the rainy season.

I take a deep breath to try to calm myself, keeping my fingers submerged in the water, my nails shimmering in a rush of moonlight as the prickle grows. I focus on the bite of idan, lifting my hand from the stream, holding in a gasp as water rises with them in glittering arcs. There's pressure from above, cold against my scalp as it burrows into my skull. I narrow my eyes, the sting becoming more and more familiar.

"I knew you could do it."

The voice makes me jump, the water falling from my fingertips. Nox is at my side, a smile slicing across his lips. I grin back at him, cradling my freezing hand.

"It's not like I did that much," I say, but inside, I can scarcely believe it. My heart races at the feeling of using Dam's idan.

Nox steps closer to me, and I look up into his dark eyes, his face in a serious expression. "It's not nothing, Mo."

"Let's rest." I turn back to the guiamalas, not wanting him to see the pathetic relief in the sheen of my tears. Zaye has taken her saddle blankets off her guiamala and is tucking them in the curl of her creature as it settles down to sleep.

"Thank you for your permission," Zaye mutters as she pulls the blankets over the blade of her shoulder. "I might be able to get some sleep when you finally stop stomping around on your big feet."

I roll my eyes and leave Nox behind me as I begin to haul my own blankets off my mount. I feel his gaze pinned between my shoulder blades, and I can't remember if he always used to look at me like this. I frown and try to concentrate on folding the blanket.

"I'll take the first watch," he murmurs, veering toward a large stone perched higher than the bank, giving him a good view of the edges of the forest.

Slumping to the ground, I lean against my guiamala. I tip my head back to the glitter of stars and catch the Crux constellation. My father taught me that the four brightest are a herd of female guiamalas, with the two pointer stars thought to be guiamala bulls chasing them. I pat the side of my own guiamala and give thanks to Yida for the creature as the beast's light snores lull me to sleep.

CHAPTER ELEVEN

A cold slip of breeze wakes me as dawn seeps across the land in the same shade as the dragon's tear. Instinctively, I pat at my wrapper, taking comfort from the shape of it and the dagger. From here, I can only see the drape of Zaye's braids that tip over the blankets she has swaddled around her. Nox, on the other hand, has slumped over the rock he perched on last night, and I chuckle. So much for keeping watch.

Then there's the crackle of a twig, and I freeze. Belatedly, I have the sense to drop into a crouch, tucking myself behind my guiamala. Peeping over its ruff of coarse fur, I scan the line of the forest, squinting, until a glimmer of reddish gold catches my eye.

Addaf steps silently into the grass that leads to the bank of the stream, a thin sword gripped tight in both of his huge hands. His gray agbada hangs off the spikes of his back, shoulder blades looking like folded wings. Behind him, more of the ọba's guards slink forward silently, but my eyes fix on the person at the front.

Jagun's braids shimmer in gold and silver as he steps from the trees, and Addaf nods at him. Then the boy creeps toward Nox beneath the dying moon, his blade held high.

"Nox!" His name is ripped from my mouth. Jagun snaps his head in my direction and then runs toward the young priest, the guards sprinting after him.

Nox leaps to his feet, his eyes wide in the dawn gloom. "Go, Moremi!"

I ignore the desperate edge in his words, my feet skimming the earth, crackling with idan. All I can think about is getting to my best friend before Jagun does.

The rock is rough beneath my feet as I leap onto it beside Nox, and the guards fan out, surrounding us.

"I told you to run," he says quietly through a clench of teeth and jaw.

"And I told you I'm not leaving you, stupid." I take his hand, twining my fingers with his.

Nox doesn't have the time or space to complain, just straightens his spine so that he towers over the men beneath us. I find myself doing the same, an unfamiliar feeling washing over me. It feels strange to revel in my height for once.

Jagun keeps his distance, but his eyes linger on me before he lowers his gaze, a frown puckering his forehead. Addaf takes his time, winding through the guards as they unsheathe their swords, his hair like spun rose gold in the weak light of dawn, the peaks and crags of his face in complicated shadows.

"You are wanted by Ọba Ojaja," says Jagun. "Leader of Kwa, chosen of—"

"He's chosen by no dragon god, just his own ego," snarls Nox.

Addaf's head cocks to one side, a curl of a smile on his

skinny lips. His skin looks paper-thin, carved lines framing his mouth. Somehow, he looks more sickly than he did just days ago. "Your words are treasonous, boy."

"My words are only treasonous to those who would disrespect the gods."

I eye the distance between us and the guards around us. Where is Zaye? I shift slightly toward the guiamalas, but I can't see much in the folds of fading night.

"Come down. And give me Yida's tear." Addaf takes another step, his eyes fixed on me. I want to press a hand to the crystal, to check that it's safe, but I don't want to bring attention to it. I remember how he searched the altar. Why does he want it so much? "I do not wish this to be by force."

"Listen to him," says Jagun, his voice low. I see the twitch in his eyes as he tries not to look at me. I think of his words at the temple, his praise and kindness at odds with his father's dismissal. He let us go in the aftermath; surely he's only with Addaf because his father ordered it. "Please. There doesn't need to be any more bloodshed."

Blood. I remember the helpless spread of it on the gold of my mother's dress. "What's happened to my—to the principal priestess?" I say.

Now Jagun has no option but to look at me. "Baba said they are . . . safe." His words are softer, and he holds my gaze, his rimmed pupils locked onto mine. "And so will you be, Moremi. If you just give Addaf what he wants."

Something in the way he says my name catches at me. And then Nox wraps his arm around my shoulders, and I see the prince's eyes flash.

"Please." Jagun lowers his head. "You have no idea what he is capable of. The things—"

"I've seen it," I hiss. I remember the moan of the shadow spirits in the temple, the death in their dark touch. So he knows that the ambassador has been calling on the emi buburu after all. Why is he still with him? Is the king so hungry for power that he would ignore the devastation these spirits have already caused? Ojaja knows what the emi buburu are capable of, that they will decimate the world we know. I can't believe the ọba thinks that he can control such a thing.

I think of my mother, and any fear is quickly replaced by hot anger. Has the ọba put her in the palace prison? I have only seen it once, and the thought of the windowless tower makes me shudder. "Ojaja has no authority over us," I say. "Not anymore, not after what he's done."

"I beg to differ," says Addaf as he positions himself in front of Jagun. Jagun's expression slips to anguish, and the ambassador moves closer still. "You will show him the respect he deserves as the royal leader of these lands." He smiles thinly. "And us, by extension."

Nox spits on the rock in front of Addaf and leans forward, shoulders bunched as he balls his fists. "It is not Ojaja who heals the people of our kingdom. It is not him who brings rain, aids their crops, and gives them comfort when they seek solace. It is not *him* who wields the gods' idan. I will not respect any man who chooses to destroy everything we stand for."

Addaf grins, revealing the expanse of dark red teeth. And the royal guards close in.

Nox steps back, and my hand goes to my wrapper. As soon as my fingertips brush the dagger, I feel a spark of frost, idan needling my palm as I draw it out. I nearly drop the weapon and curse my clumsiness. Hopefully, the guards won't even think that I would use such a blade.

The closest man reaches up, raising his sword as if he means to chop at our ribs—before a loud groan splits the early morning behind him. We all swing around just in time to see a giant lumbering mass. Heavy cloven hooves shake the ground as a guiamala charges toward us, quickly covering the space between us with its huge strides, with Zaye on its back.

Her ululation trills through the air, a fierce battle cry, as the usually docile guiamala kicks at the men, scattering them in seconds. Addaf and Jagun draw back as two of the guards take a hoof to the head, collapsing in the tall grass even as Zaye is tipped from her perch. She gets to her feet and scrambles up beside us.

"Any ideas?" asks Zaye, her eyes flitting over the half dozen men who are beginning to converge on us again. With the stream behind us, they do not need to rush. I look wildly around the clearing before doing the only thing I can think of.

I jump down from the rock and spread my feet among the crinkle of grass, toes splayed in the moist earth. Ignoring Nox's and Zaye's yells, I focus on a pulse of Yida's idan, willing it to come to me. Where Dam's idan was cold and foreign, the goddess's power is something I have felt ever since I could walk.

Jagun's eyes are on me. He holds his hands out, as if to calm a skittish guiamala foal, just as Yida's idan seeps into my soles. I think of how Nox held his hands out to channel the magic, and then I think of my mother's summoning dance. Of how it's taken ten years for me to even be able to do the basic temple prayers.

I swallow past the lump in my throat and begin to move my feet in a way I've seen Kakra do when she uses this prayer to clear the ground of rocks and stones, to make certain swaths of land arable. But my limbs are clumsy, and seeing and doing are two completely different things.

My steps are uneven, but still the idan thickens, growing hotter.

Please let this work. I shove the dagger back in my wrapper.

"Mo—" Nox begins just as the ground shivers once.

Addaf narrows his eyes as the guards pause, their eyes widening at the shift. And then the land groans, another shudder that has them looking down at their feet while holding their arms out for balance. Addaf mouths words silently as his fingers curl. Around him, shadows form quickly, spilling from the ground, a denser mass of black than before. I can make out rudimentary figures now, claws for hands and spiked shoulders.

They're getting stronger.

But so are you, something inside me whispers as the ground continues to rumble after my prayer. I push back so the rock is against my spine, the fire of the goddess in my blood. It's something I have felt ever since I can remember, but never this much, and as my soles burn with it, I let the dragon's magic storm through me. For the first time, my prayer is righteous and true. I gasp, giddy with the feeling of such power even as the guards watch the earth fearfully, freezing when a loud crack fills the air. The ground shakes, and we are all brought to our knees.

But I grin to myself, the fever of Yida still blazing inside me until a black hole opens between us. The prayer was supposed to bring rocks to the surface, to distract Addaf and the guards long enough for us to run, but the hole expands, swallowing the earth in chunks that force the ọba's guards and Jagun to move back to the treeline. The shadow spirits waver as Addaf loses his footing, backing away hastily. There's a strangled shout and gasps from the men as the land shatters.

I stand now, my spine straight, the fiery burn of idan coursing through every part of me. For once, I am powerful. A roar burns in my throat—

But I turn to Nox and Zaye.

"Now we run!" I snarl.

We peel away from the rock and sprint across the meadow. As we race through the grass, Zaye still finds a way to glare at me from between the swinging braids that hang in her face. "Could you not have opened up the earth in the right place to swallow them all?"

Snatching a look behind her, I see Addaf leading the men to the side of the treeline, scouting a way around the gaping hole in the earth, still widening. The emi buburu flock around him, but he doesn't send them just yet. I wonder if they are tethered to him, and if so, how much they rely on him to feed them with prayers and some kind of life force.

A slither of panic winds through me as I watch the expanding blackness I created. What if it doesn't stop? What if I've done the prayer completely wrong and it swallows everything around us? What if I've failed again, but in a different way? For a moment, I am paralyzed by the idea, fingernails digging crescents into my palms.

And then the hole comes to a stop at the edge of a growing patch of sunlight. My shoulders relax and I let out a sigh of relief.

Addaf and his men pick their way carefully around the sides of the chasm as smaller rocks crumble, falling into the blackness. Behind them, Jagun continues to watch me.

I swallow. "Let's get across the stream," I say.

We splash into the water, putting more distance between us

and Addaf, until the stream comes up to lap at our waists and the current begins to tug at us. Nearby, there are large splashes as the guiamalas emerge from the trees, following us across the water. I see my creature's head tilt toward me as it lumbers forward a little faster.

"Be ready to run to your guiamala." Nox is nearly at the opposite bank now, water streaming down the muscled slope of his back.

I push harder against the current, moving faster, the high of escaping bubbling up. It's only as I wipe my hand on my wrapper that I realize Yida's tear is missing.

The water swirls around me as my stomach drops. Frantically, I scan the bottom of the stream as my panic rises, acidic and sharp. I fall to my knees, fumbling among the pebbles.

"Moremi!" hisses Nox from the bank, the guiamalas assembled behind him. "What are you doing? Come on!"

My tongue is thick in my mouth and the words won't come. I stand, swinging my gaze back to the edge of the stream that we just left. Did I drop it earlier? The thought of the tear tumbling into the hole flashes in my mind, but I push it away and try to focus. Scanning the earth where we stood, I see a glint of something as the sun pushes past the canopy, flooding the rest of the area with a golden light. I lean forward, squinting against the sudden brightness.

There it is. Glittering in a tuft of grass just past the lip of the bank. Without a word, I turn from Nox and Zaye, plunging toward the sparkle of Yida's tear.

"Moremi!" Nox's yell doesn't stop me as I thrash through the current, my feet slipping slightly on the moss-slicked stones.

I catch sight of Jagun on the bank. We lock eyes before

Jagun's gaze jumps to where I was looking. He pivots, racing along the water, and I feel the burn of my thighs as I throw myself at the brown strip of land.

Heaving and gasping, I flop onto the bank, hand reached out to snatch up the orb. The thunder of the guards' footsteps vibrates through my chest as I press against the ground, my fingers closing around Yida's tear. Then I slip back into the cool water.

Or try to.

Fingers wrap around my wrist, iron-strong and warm. I look up into the brown-hazel of Jagun's eyes, my breath heavy as I try to pull back.

"Stop fighting," he hisses.

I yank my arm down, my other hand clutching the crystal. "Let *go*—"

But he hauls me out of the stream and to my feet, his eyes burning into mine. My heart thumps wildly as he presses me to him, the leather of his chest plate and the gold and silver wound around the ends of his two plaits scraping against my skin. He spins me around, blade drawn tight against my throat. Fury spills through me, but I go still, blinking against tears as I watch Nox and Zaye make their way back, the stream rushing around them.

"Please, Moremi," Jagun murmurs against my ear. "Listen to him. I promise none of you will be hurt."

"How can you say this when your *dagger* is at my neck?" I spit. "Just like your father promised to protect the kingdom. Like he promised to protect my mother and Bannu as part of his oath." I gasp as the blade scrapes my throat, my eyes closing against the flood of idan bursting at the contact. It crackles through my veins, red and orange stars exploding on the insides of my eyelids. And then Jagun stiffens behind me, easing the weapon away from my skin. The idan cuts off, and I sag against him, my mind spinning with the feeling of it.

"I need to explain. I don't—"

But the boy doesn't finish, his words dying as Nox and Zaye reach the bank.

"Let her go." Nox's hands are in fists, his knuckles skimming the surface of the water.

"You do not get to issue orders," rings out Addaf's voice. He and the guards come into view, and my heart plummets. "I am surprised that in the Kingdom of Kwa, youngsters do not show their elders the proper respect."

I feel Jagun tense behind me as Addaf approaches. The emi buburu are still with him, but as I watch, they move closer, legs and shoulders and heads joining so they are now one monstrously tall shadow figure. It reaches for me with a skeletal hand. I shrink back, but there is nowhere to go, and all noise is muffled as the emi buburu wraps its fingers around my arm.

Searing pain forces a rough scream from me. Bile rises from the back of my throat. My eyes roll as hot white fills my vision, my legs and arms convulsing with the wrongness of the power that invades me. A thick moan seeps from around my bitten tongue, and a screech invades my head, as if a thousand knives are being dragged over steel, and I try to call out as drool spills down my chin. The void gnaws at my soul, and I can do nothing to stop it—

Until I'm being pulled back, and the inhuman grip on my arm is released.

"You said you wouldn't hurt her!" Jagun yells, his whole body shaking as he holds me away from the dark figure.

I gasp, sweat dripping from my head as I struggle to stand.

I feel hollow as I stare blankly at the shadowy figure. The emi buburu stands, bloated and giant, having taken in the opposite ways that idan gives, absorbing my energy and the goddess's power. I shove aside the worry of what I have lost even in those short few moments.

"I am fast running out of patience," Addaf snarls, holding his hand out, gaze fixed greedily on my curled fingers. "Give me the tear or I will let the emi buburu suck you dry of your soul and any other scraps of idan you have."

I'm weak, mind still spinning, but it's then that I realize there is blood on my wrapper, bright red in the early light. Distantly, I feel a sting on my neck from where Jagun must have nicked me.

Gold and red.

I remember my mother and the slackness of her face when she was placed on the dais. The ọba and Addaf caused that. Her pain, her fear.

And I won't allow him to get away with anything else.

I still myself, letting the rage hone me. I try to find words, struggling as the emi buburu looms over me. Addaf can think that we are all weak fools from the temples. It's all anyone has ever thought of me anyway.

"If I give you the tear, will you take us back to our parents?" I ask finally, making my voice small. I glance at the ground. I'm pulled tight against Jagun, toes scraping stones, but if I can get my soles back to the earth, I fully intend on trying to use Yida's idan to rip it apart again. And hopefully this time, all of them will be lost among the rocks and the darkness.

"The tear," is all the ambassador says, his blue eye a cold glimmer while the brown regards me calmly.

Jagun loosens his hold on me, and I turn to face him, feeling my feet sink into the cool soil. A twist of idan flows toward me and I seize it. I think of all the times I endured disappointed looks when I couldn't master prayers, when even my mother turned away embarrassed. But it wasn't just that; I know my face and height are mirrors of my father, reminders of his alleged madness. I used to think the same weakness was in me. That it was the reason I failed when all others succeeded.

The idan scorches inside me and I relish the sear, wishing in that moment I had the power to break the world apart.

But before I can even try, the sound of a bell rings, clear and beautiful.

I pause, cocking my head to one side as the tinkle comes again. Around us, the men do the same thing, turning to the wave of grass at our backs. A chime sounds once more, and I smile into the sun that rises behind the treeline. Letting the idan go, I take a step toward the sound, joy bubbling up in me. Addaf's eyes widen as the bell rings again, a sound so beautiful that I feel a tear trickle down my cheek. Wiping it away, I let out a small laugh.

Next to me, Jagun holds his hands loose at his side, a beatific smile smeared on his face. He laughs as his dagger thuds to the earth, but he doesn't even look down at it, taking a tentative step toward the thicker part of the forest. Nothing matters but finding the source of that sweet chime. I scan the trees, and in the crowded dark spaces between the trunks, I see a shift of shadows.

I take another step as the bell tinkles, louder now. The sound lifts me up, keeps me craving more, as I move in step with Jagun. The guards around him do the same, eyes sparkling and mouths stretched into blissful grins. Even Addaf twitches as he faces the forest.

Ahead of me, the men drift toward the edges of the trees, weapons abandoned. There's another ripple between the slim tree trunks and a shiver of trepidation runs through me.

The bell rings again, and I feel the unease smooth away, replaced with a crystalized happiness as my lips tilt up. I'm still grinning as the men ahead of Jagun get closer to the forest, still smiling as they are yanked down into the tall grass, their fresh screams cutting through the morning air.

CHAPTER TWELVE

The bell chimes again and I keep walking, even as the cries of the guards are reduced to gurgles. The pungent scent of blood rises with the rest of the sun, lacing the air with warm metal. Nox and Zaye are screaming my name.

But none of it matters except reaching the sweet knell.

Jagun and I don't pause, not even when we see the men dragged into the forest, with the last guard lying in the grass, his body thrashing as it is pulled closer to something crouching just within the still-darkened treeline. Addaf jerks along beside us, his mouth open as he raises his hands to his ears and mutters something I can't quite hear.

There's movement at the edge of the forest, and the shadows shift into a creature covered in grass and moss, with a snout cracked open to reveal large canines. The squat monster's jaws split like those of a python as it fits the man's head in its mouth. A moan of revulsion escapes me, and the creature looks up with silver eyes and pinched eyebrows, pausing at the sight of us. With clawed hands, it reaches down to grab the tiny golden bell hanging from its neck, shaking the clapper until once again the horror seeps away, allowing me to stumble toward the creature as it begins to eat the last of the ọba's guards.

And then the cold slap of damp hands cups my ears, and I stop as the sounds of the world are cut off. Turning, I look into Zaye's wide eyes. She has her hands still clamped tightly to the sides of my head, and I can see she has stuffed moss in her own ears. Nox looms behind her, moss sprouting out of his too, a look of terror on his face.

The girl shakes me, and I look down at her, reading her lips as she speaks slowly. "Don't listen to the chimes of the bells, you stupid girl."

I nod, not trusting myself to move while Zaye swaps her fingers for moss, blocking my ears from any sound. I'm shaking, eyes back on the creature as it finishes swallowing the man.

Bile rises in my throat, burning the back of my tongue as I dry retch. The eloko, a creature of the thickest forests that craves the flesh of humans, doesn't bother to look at me as it continues to eat. I think of the rest of the men who have been snatched by the others that lurk in the raffia trees. I sob, the sound muffled and echoed, fear freezing my entire body. No one deserves to die in this way.

Nox places a hand between my shoulder blades. His fingers tremble across my spine as he slides his hand to my arm, slowly pulling me backward. I stumble with him, still unable to look away from the nightmare in front of me, stopping when my foot nudges something hard. A scorch of fire ignites where it touches my skin, and I look down to see Jagun's dropped dagger. Heat bursts across my palm when I snatch it up, like it did when the blade had been pressed against my throat. Holding it closer, I see the familiar curve of the weapon, feel the weight as it sits comfortably in my grip. This blade's iridescence catches on the sun rather than the moon, but it feels strangely familiar.

It's the same, I think, patting the other dagger, the one hidden in the folds of my wrapper. I draw it out and hold the two before me. The twin blades are both dragon scales, and they burn in my hands, one in an arctic chill of Dam's idan, the other the searing crackle of Yida's.

A movement in the corner of my eye makes me look up. The eloko has finished with the guard and has now pulled Jagun to the ground by his leg, claws deep in his thigh. Addaf watches, hands clamped over his ears, his lips still moving. His blue and brown eyes glitter before they turn blank for just a moment. As I watch, an eloko bounds from between the trees, heading straight for Addaf. He is no longer armed, and for a thin moment, hope sweeps in.

Then the cut of cold sweeps past me, ruffling my hair. Addaf's eyes are wide open as a black ripples over the brown and blue. He closes his eyes as ribbons of darkness cloak him in smoke like shadows. The eloko skids to a halt before the man, saliva dripping from its large mouth. It sniffs the air once, twice, the stench of rot suddenly thick, before a whine slips from the back of its throat. Addaf spins a hand, almost lazily, and a tendril of smoke snakes out to lick against the eloko's face. The creature yelps, snapping its jaws before turning and running.

Nox tries to pull me back even more, but I shrug him off, glaring at him. I gesture toward Jagun, still pinned to the ground by the other eloko. I'm not leaving anyone to die like . . . *that.* I can't.

It appears the eloko doesn't bother with his bell, not when he already has a hold on the boy, and awareness trickles back into Jagun's eyes. The prince looks up at me, his eyes round with horror, blood oozing from his thigh. Again, I think of his words of encouragement in the temple, the way he let us take Iya when she was injured.

And of course, Addaf doesn't even attempt to help Jagun. The shadows that were spun around him are gone now, but I see him look at the eloko and make his judgment. Addaf retreats, melting into the opposite treeline, where the sun has blazed through the canopy.

Just then, Jagun is pulled around so that his head is closer to the eloko's mouth. I hold the blades tightly, squeezing both hilts, breath coming in ragged gasps, and I jump over Jagun to slash at the eloko's hand. The bell falls into the loose soil as the creature screeches, its fetid breath rolling over me. Gagging, I wobble as my ankle is kicked out from under me, the eloko's leg longer than I thought, extending from under it like a frog's.

Jagun crawls away from the creature, free of its enchantment, leaving a smear of blood on the leaves of the forest floor. I plant myself between the eloko and the boy, my leg shaking as I try to put weight on it. If I can ground my feet, perhaps I can call on Yida's idan again. But even as I try to access her power, the eloko lunges, eyes pinned on me with a feral hunger that makes me stumble backward.

"Get him out of here!" I shout.

Nox hesitates for a moment and then grabs at Jagun, hauling him to his feet. Zaye gets the other side of the boy, and together they help him hobble back toward the stream. Eloko cannot cross moving water, and the creature opens its great jaws and bellows loudly. Immediately, responding bays come from the forest, and the hair on my arms prickles, standing up.

There are more. And it's calling them.

No wonder Addaf retreated. I back away, not wanting to take my eyes from the creature, even though I can see the ripple of movements in the treeline as its brethren answer its call. The thump of my pulse is all I can hear. It's not a matter of turning and running; there is no space, no time.

There's a sudden growl and a swipe of long claws that catches my leg. I hiss as my skin splits open, blood and terror flowing as I stagger away.

I can't outrun it.

The thought stops my breath, my chest going tight. I'm going to die here, and there will be no one to let down their hair for me, no body for my mother to burn, no ceremony for Yida to mark my passing. A stone digs into the sole of my left foot and it's the only thing I can feel.

The creature barrels toward me, growling as it cuts through the swaths of grass despite the sun, angry—or hungry—enough not to hide in the dark now. I lift the daggers, readying myself to do as much damage as I can, panting as adrenaline pumps through my body. And then my hands spasm, my hold on the weapons changing as my fingers stiffen with a blaze of energy.

I cry out in pain as the sting in my palms spreads to my wrists, changing now, scorching in my left hand, frigid in my right. Looking down, I see the daggers gleaming in the dawn light—Dam's a bright white blue and Yida's a blaze of red and orange.

The idan shoots through me as I lift the two weapons, holding them out as I revel in the magic that straightens my spine and has me planting my feet in the earth. I feel taller, stronger, relishing the burn of my muscles as I tighten my grip and stance, the power of both dragons flowing through me.

And in this moment, I know: The Moremi who stumbled her way through prayers, who wasn't going to take part in the ceremony, whose father was cast out—that wasn't quite Moremi after all. In this moment, I am me, but I am more. And as the idan sinks into every part of me, I open my mouth to roar.

The eloko runs closer, claws raised, and I sweep the daggers down in one sharp slash, Dam's blade hacking its shoulder. Watery amber sap rushes from the wound, and the creature hisses as it swipes one of its claws at me. I jump back, bringing down Yida's dagger, the heat in it matching the singe of eloko flesh as it cuts into the monster's head, severing its large ear.

The eloko screams, a sound that is echoed by its brothers in the forest, and I only have time for a glance quick enough to see the other creatures surging from between the trees. There's no way I'll be able to fight them all at once. I look down at the daggers in my hands and think of what my mother would tell me to do. *Deal with what needs to be done first.*

The blades hum in my hands, the idan crackling in waves of searing energy that pulse through me, and I bring the sparking edges together. Releasing them, I swing the daggers out, wide and smooth, and then chop them together, taking the eloko's head from its body.

Once, I would have vomited at the sight, but now I just burn with a fiery calm. Without wasting another moment, I stow the weapons and move back to cross the stream before the other eloko arrive.

Nox has just helped Zaye to dump Jagun on the opposite bank as I emerge there too, gasping and drawing in deep breaths, clamping a hand to my stinging leg.

An arm grabs mine, and I look up to Nox's warm gaze. "It's all right," he mouths. "I've got you."

I take the moss from my ears, and we settle on the bank in silence, watching the eloko hiss and howl on the opposite side of the stream. Before long, they retreat to the trees, and we are finally left alone in silence.

===

The son of Ojaja is alive but unconscious. Zaye drags him into the shade of a tsamiya tree, its tamarind pods drooping down from thin branches. I sit with my knees to my chest, watching the boy to see if he's still breathing. The daggers are pressed between my thighs and my stomach, Yida's tear a reassuring lump in the wet folds of my wrapper.

"Mo . . ."

I shake my head at Nox's voice, at the questions I know he wants to ask. "Not yet. Just . . . Just let me get my breath back."

He gives me a look but doesn't say more. Squeezing my eyes shut, I try to block out the sounds of teeth crunching bones, the memory echoing louder now that the eloko have gone. I know that I did what I needed to. I know this, but now the slide of the blade against skin, even an eloko's, will not leave my mind.

At the temple, we heal life, encourage it. Never are we supposed to end it. My eyelashes are spider-soft on my skin as I shiver. But once I start shaking, I find that I can't stop.

"Moremi." Nox's voice is low. "Come, sit in the sun. You need to get dry." He curls his arm around my side and tugs at me until I stand on wobbling legs, and then he guides me to a swath of grass in a patch of scalding sunlight. "Here."

I take the waterskin, sipping until I begin to gulp, realizing how thirsty I am.

"What happened back there?" he asks quietly. "The daggers..."

We look over at the blades I've placed next to us. The razor curves of their edges glint, and I remember the power that flew through them both.

For a moment, I crave it again. The want sears me through, hot and blinding.

"It was the gods' idan," says Zaye when I don't answer. I look up to see her watching me.

"Makes sense. Because one is made from the scale of Yida, the other from the scale of Dam." Nox sits down next to me, not touching the weapons. The shimmer of gold and silver dances along the blades and their identical hilts.

"How did Jagun have Yida's?" Zaye asks, moving closer. She's frowning, and I swear she's concerned about me.

"A question I'd like to ask him," Nox mutters. "Among others."

They both turn to glare at the boy, who lies sprawled in the hot grass, but I don't join them. No matter what Jagun's orders were, he hasn't hurt me.

Nox reaches out to kick the prince's leg. "Hey, wake up."

I peer at the gouges in Jagun's thigh. Mine are scratches compared with his, and I instantly begin to think of the mixture of grated bark and honey to seal the wound. "He'll be lucky if it doesn't get infected."

Any of the brief tenderness Zaye just showed me leaves her face as she scowls down at the boy. "And that's our problem? He shows up with Addaf, attacking us, and you're worried about healing him?"

I ignore her. The ragged skin, with its drying blood, already looks puffy.

"We need something to clean it," I say.

Zaye folds her arms and just looks at me, so I rip off a wet strip from Jagun's wrapper, using the cloth to dab at the angry edges of his wound. Despite my queasiness, I focus on wiping and cleaning, taking solace in the repetitive motions.

"You need to tend to your own," says Nox, nostrils flaring. "Here, let me—"

But I twist away from him as annoyance swells, unfamiliar. Just days ago, I would have loved Nox's constant attention, but now . . . "I will. Just . . . stop telling me what to do."

I avoid Nox's stare and finish cleaning Jagun's leg. Once I've removed most of the gore, I'm relieved to see that the gashes are not as deep as I thought. Looking down at the scratches on my leg, I give thanks to Yida that both of us are still in one piece. By the time I'm done cleaning my wounds as well, the sun has dried most of my wrapper, toasting my skin so that I no longer feel the chill of the water.

Nox returns to my side, and he unbuckles Jagun's weapons harness. "Here," he says, swinging it toward me. "You can't keep those daggers stuffed in your wrapper."

I reach over to take the straps of leather from him. As our fingers touch, Nox's face softens, and he tugs one of my plaits.

"Don't do anything like that again," he says. His fingertips graze my cheekbone, and I watch as his hand drops to trace the dragon that winds around my wrist.

"What?" I ask, heart thumping as I pull away. I tug the harness from him and slip my arms through the straps, pulling them across my chest. "I dropped Yida's tear. I had to go back."

"Not without me, you didn't. And you didn't need to save him."

I pick up the daggers, their edges wicked bright. "Priestesses heal, Nox. I had to."

When I finally look properly at Nox, he is gazing at the blades in my hands, his mouth tightening as I slide them into the holster. I scoop up the waterskin and bend down over Jagun, letting a trickle fall onto his face.

The boy splutters, hands wiping at his eyes as he sits up and groans in pain. He opens his eyes.

And he lunges for me.

CHAPTER THIRTEEN

"Don't touch her!"

I jerk away from Jagun's fingers as Nox draws his fist back, knuckles bulky under taut skin.

"Wait!" I say, hands going to the weapon the prince had tried to snatch. "He was going for the dagger, not me."

"You shouldn't have that," gasps Jagun. "It's not for you to wield."

My fingers splay against the leather scabbard and the point of the dagger, a spark of Yida's idan burning my fingertips. I hiss and drop my hand.

"That blade speaks of the goddess," snarls Nox, "and as such, should be in the temple."

Jagun sinks back against the grass, eyes glittering as they fasten on me.

"Where did it come from?" I ask, my voice quiet. He hadn't hurt me earlier, and even now I see the anger fading in his gaze. "How did it come to be yours?"

The boy turns his head away, silent, until he says, "It was

my mother's." He looks up at me, his eyes glassy. "She gave it to me just before she passed. She said it would be needed one day."

I say nothing, but I don't ease the dagger from its harness even though my hand twitches with guilt. There's no way I can give Jagun a weapon when he's sided with his baba and Addaf. But even as I tell myself this, the quieter reason burns beneath.

The way the gods' idan flowed through me was like nothing I have ever experienced.

Even now, I want to feel it all again.

"Why were you with Addaf?" I say. "There was no shock on your face earlier. You know he's been channeling the emi buburu." Just saying the words makes me feel queasy, and for a moment, I am back in the icy grip of the shadow spirit.

Jagun squints at me and doesn't speak. Nox lunges, but I put my arm out, barring him.

"Answer," I command.

"Baba ordered me to go with him."

"Why?" I ask. "Because of what happened at the Dírágónì ceremony? He doesn't trust him anymore, does he?"

Jagun averts his eyes, as if that makes it easier. "He doesn't. But he still thinks he can help him get the power he wants."

"And you? What do you believe?"

"I believe in the gods." The prince looks up now, his brown-and-hazel eyes on mine. "It's why I came. I still want to learn how to be a leader, the leader that Kwa needs. I thought that was with Baba, but . . ." He shakes his head. "It's not. I want to help make amends."

"And you expect us to believe that?" Nox's laugh is a bark.

He kicks at Jagun before I can stop him. "You hunted us down with Addaf and allowed him to attack Moremi. As if imprisoning our parents wasn't enough?"

Jagun hangs his head. "I thought that if I was there, I could stop him from doing anything even worse. And it was the best way to find you."

Nox scoffs, and I blink. In this moment, Jagun looks defeated, more like the kind prince I met at the temple than the attacker at Addaf's back. I find that I believe him . . . but would that make me the fool?

Jagun looks up again. "I think I know why Addaf is calling the emi buburu."

Nox and I both pause. Addaf has shown he is willing to risk the world by endangering the gods and summoning the shadow spirits, but the why has been needling me.

"I've been trying to work him out. He's been here for months, longer than any other emissary. I . . . I can't say that I like him, but I'm not so stupid as to think that liking someone is important when it comes to trade and politics." Jagun tries to sit up and winces, holding the wound in his thigh. "But I have never seen my baba so close to an outside adviser before. I think Addaf has swayed him somehow. Tricked him. Addaf keeps speaking about power that can be gained elsewhere."

"Obviously," snarks Zaye as she comes to stand next to Nox. "He's been calling on the forbidden spirits. I think we can all tell that it's for the sake of power."

"Yes, but why is he so bent on this? Why has he given up on Yida?" I think of the man's red teeth. He was clearly devout at one point. "What changed him?"

"He lost his wife and daughter at the beginning of this

new year," Jagun says. "He told Baba at dinner when he first joined us."

My wife was a devoted Yida follower. She would have been overcome with joy if she were here. His words were laced with a sadness when he first came to the temple with the ọba.

"There was a blight in the Kingdom of Carew. I remember King Beli asking for help, for the iyalawos to at least try and heal some of the people." Jagun pauses, his face slack. "Baba said no."

I think of those who died, the despair and loss of hope. The priestesses of our temple could have helped, I know it. If the ọba had let them.

"But even so, why would Addaf risk a kingdom, an entire world?" asks Nox. "It doesn't make sense."

I remember Baba's big hand taking mine, the songs he would sing about the stars, and the way Iya has tried to shoulder her grief at losing him, for me.

"For his wife and child," I say softly. "The emi buburu were banished by the gods, stuck between this world and the next."

Jagun nods. "I think . . . he believes they can bring his family back."

We fall silent under the burn of the sun, crickets chirping in the grass around us. *People are willing to die for less*, I think. But knowing that Addaf has nothing left to lose if he fails scares me even more. The emi buburu only want to return to the world and claim it as their own, as it was before Yida and Dam. Even if they did bring Addaf's family back, what kind of world would they be brought into?

"He's gone for now, which is all that matters at the moment," says Nox, adjusting the straps on his guiamala. His mouth is a taut line, his movements jerky. "If all of that is true, then it's even more important for us to get to Dam and Yida."

"What about him?" asks Zaye, her face a curdle of annoyance as she gestures to Jagun.

Nox sniffs and looks back toward the forest. "We leave him here."

"No," I say, sharper than I mean to. Immediately, I wish I could gulp my quick reply back down. I look at Jagun's thigh again. He'll never make it back on his own, and if he stays here without us . . . I think of the eloko, and the way its life ended at my hands. There are other creatures, other dangers. Not to mention Addaf, who left him like it was nothing. I pinch the top of my nose and then lick the sweat from my upper lip. "We'll take him with us."

"What?!" explodes Nox.

"I won't have someone's death on my hands. I . . . I can't." I don't look at Nox. His tone is enough to let me know what he thinks, but this is one thing I'm going to be firm on. "And he helped my mother. He comes with us."

Jagun sits up, framed by the tall grass, and winces only slightly. I don't have any of my medicines with me, but I do have Yida's mark. I make a mental note to ask Zaye if she can help teach me a healing prayer. Again, I'm briefly awash with the weight of all I don't know.

With Nox staring at me in shocked silence, I somehow feel more alone than ever. I know he doesn't understand my decision, can't understand what I'm thinking like he used to. But I need to do what is best. What is *right*.

The prince climbs slowly to his feet. "I'll return to the palace. I don't need anyone to look after me."

Nox steps up to him, his greater height giving him a slight edge as he manages to peer down his nose at Jagun. "If Mo says you're coming with us, then you're coming. We're not having you return to get more guards or help your father again."

The two boys stand chest to chest, their fists balled. Nox's sea-blue wrapper is vivid against the swirls of earth and sky of Jagun's. I'm struck by the differences in them, the slim muscled frame of my oldest friend and the broader stance of the prince. Nox spreads his feet wide apart, and I know the exact look he'll have on his face, down to the jut of his chin. He's always been able to appear fierce, even when he doesn't mean it. I can read him like one of the scriptures. Whereas Jagun stands with muscles loose as if unbothered, eyes unreadable. I'm drawn to the relaxed slope of his mouth as he keeps himself calm. He's a curious mixture of confidence and restraint, the promise of violence gilded with the kindness he's already shown. I'm not sure who would win in a fight, and I don't want to find out.

Zaye slips between them, forcing Nox to take a step back and splitting them apart before she stomps over to me. "Are you sure about this? It's just going to make things harder. We'll have to keep an eye on him."

"It's three against one," I answer. Bringing him with us is a risk, but one I'm willing to take if it means avoiding more death. "Besides, it's less of a risk than letting him go and having him come for us again. Maybe with even more men."

Zaye watches Jagun, a frown wreathing her face. "And the palace nundás."

"Exactly. Let's go. The guiamalas are waiting." I head toward mine, and it blinks at me sweetly. A smile comes to my face as I pet its black muzzle.

"I'm not riding with him." Nox folds his arms across his chest, mouth in a scowl.

I take a breath and make a quick decision. "You don't have to." My stomach twists when I face Jagun, his hazel eyes meeting mine in a steady gaze. "He can ride with me." Then I turn my back on them both, not wanting to see either of their reactions.

I climb my guiamala with as much dignity as I can. As I sit on top of the saddle blankets, I look toward the edges of the rolling meadow that stretches in the direction of the Ghost Ocean. The low level of the stream and its lack of fish, the unnatural storm clouds, and the black rot of the forest scroll through my mind again. I wonder how much more is already out of balance, how much more of the land, and its living, has been devoured.

Our time is running out.

My fingers go to Yida's tear, tucked in my wrapper, its smoothness giving me comfort.

I take the reins of my guiamala as Jagun climbs up, his injury slowing him somewhat. It's only when he settles behind me that I breathe properly again. Rather than hold my waist, his hands grip the blanket on either side as he carefully positions himself away from me. I can sense the heat of him, though, and I sneak a look at his thigh to check on his wound again. It's already scabbing, but the edges are slightly puffy. I'll definitely have to do something about it soon.

The creatures amble into the afternoon light, the hours slowly rocking by. I close my eyes as the sun cloaks my skin in heat. Thoughts of my mother and Bannu crowd into my mind, but I push them out, opening my eyes to the green of my surroundings.

"I should be saying thank you."

I hold my breath for a beat, thinking of the shyness I had felt at the temple, now long gone. "Go ahead. I'm waiting."

Jagun is silent a moment and I wave a fly from my face as he finally clears his throat. "Thank you for helping me."

"Saving you," I correct him, a tiny smile creeping up.

The boy waits a beat, and then, "Yes, for saving me."

I don't answer, letting the sun roll over us both.

"How was your iya? When you took her back to the temple, I mean." The prince's words slip through the hot air, and the worry that is now always there pulses in my chest. "Baba won't hurt them, you know."

"If you believe that, then you really are a fool." I think of the blood blooming on her golden dress. How she stood side by side with the priestesses, her spine straight and her eyes flashing. "Kakra and Panyin healed her. But does that matter to your father?" Anger ripples through me, and for a moment, I'm glad I can't see his face.

"He didn't order them to be killed. He wouldn't do that." Jagun still holds himself away from me, but I sense the tension of his body. "My father doesn't want anyone dead." His words are so confident, so sure.

"Your father has allowed himself to be Addaf's pawn. His actions endangered the gods. And everyone else."

"It's not his fault." Jagun adjusts his seat behind me. "The ceremony, what he did, it's not something I knew about." Frustration colors his tone. "It was as much a surprise to me as to you. I told you, it was Addaf."

I tense. "What does Addaf know about Yida's tear?"

Jagun coughs uncomfortably. "I'm not sure. He just claimed that he wanted to compare the relic to the ones he has seen in other kingdoms."

I don't answer. Eneh said the tear is the way for me to unite the gods, but what if Addaf knows this as well? If he stops us from doing this, then nothing will prevent the emi buburu's return.

We carry on in silence while the sun crawls across the sky. I try to keep up with Nox, but he's urging his guiamala to go so fast that I'm always two lengths behind him. By the way his shoulders are drawn up tight, I can tell he's doing it on purpose.

I sigh. He is my oldest friend, yet sometimes he acts like we're still children.

"How far to the Ghost Ocean?" I call to him.

Nox deigns to glance back at me and then nods toward the horizon. "Not far. Maybe a couple of hours."

Zaye pulls up close on my right and I catch her checking Jagun's wound too. When she sees me watching her, she looks away.

"Can you teach me a healing dance?" I seize on her one glimpse of sympathy. "It'll be quicker than finding the right herbs I'd need."

Zaye snorts, cutting her eye at me. Gone is the softness she showed me after the eloko. I know she thinks it should have been her chosen by Yida to channel her magic. And for a moment, I do too; she'd be able to heal Jagun instantly. Instead, he's stuck with me. "I can show you. But who knows if you'll be able to do it?"

I stiffen, trying not to let her words stick. She glances at the dragon on my ankle before looking away. My cheeks burn as I bite back a retort, refusing to be drawn in by one of her barbed comments. I hate that a tiny part of me agrees with her.

The afternoon passes in a hot haze of sun and the lilting gait of the guiamalas as they pick their way through the grasslands.

"We'll rest here," Nox says, back still straight with anger. He dismounts and stalks over to a fallen tree, settling on the rough bark.

Jagun slides from our guiamala, landing on his good leg. He holds a hand out to me, but I climb down carefully on my own.

"Come," Zaye sniffs. "I'll show you the prayer. I don't want to have to deal with the smell of rot if his wound gets infected." Her fingers curve into the crook of my elbow as she tows me toward a space near her resting guiamala. "I've been practicing for years. I'd rather it doesn't go to waste."

I take a deep breath. I have only tried this dance once when I was eight. I'd found a baby owl at the base of Mandara Mountain, its wing shattered. It was so weak that it didn't even attempt to eat any of the mealworms I foraged. I laid it on the ground and danced in a way I'd seen Iya do. I thought that since I could sense Yida's idan, I would be able to use just a tiny bit, chosen or not. But the pounding of my feet was wrong, and most of all, I did not have a dragon curling around my ankle. When the owl died, I cried for days, failure sinking deeper inside me.

Zaye lifts her wrapper so that I can see her tiny feet. "Pay attention."

I wring my hands, fingers twisting at the thought of mimicking her. I watch as Zaye sweeps her right foot through the dirt, mirroring the movement with her left. She then stamps her feet in a pattern that I've seen Kakra do before, toes pushed down, with one heel raised. As I take in shallow breaths, my eyes flick over every twist and flex as panic blooms in the clench of my gut.

"Moremi, just . . . stop." Zaye reaches for me, unlocking my grip and squeezing my hands so hard it hurts. She looks at the dragon around my ankle and is silent for a moment as she thinks. Then she sighs.

"This is a basic healing prayer," she says, her voice not quite soft but lacking the edge I'm used to hearing. "Remember who your blood is. Your mother is the most powerful iyalawo we have seen in centuries. You are her daughter. And you're Yida's."

I yank my hands away and force my shoulders down. Zaye nods at me, frowning seriously, and I find myself mimicking her expression.

"Watch, and then copy."

We break the healing prayer down into simple movements. I twist and stamp, turn my heels out and whirl in a way I have never managed before. The dance flows through me now and I know it is because of the goddess's idan. I can *feel* it. I wipe the sweat from my top lip, relieved when Zaye finally smiles at me. My feet are sore, but I know I have the steps right. I grin, the feeling of perfecting a prayer flooding me with adrenaline.

"You see . . . I'm thinking that perhaps your problem with prayers wasn't your lack of rhythm, but your teacher." The girl flicks her braids back from her face, her cheekbones sharp in the sun. "All you needed was someone as talented as me."

The smile slips from my face when I remember how she used to taunt me. "Or perhaps what I needed was you to leave me alone. Perhaps I could have learned more without the worry of you laughing at me."

Zaye lifts a hand to her brow as she raises her gaze to mine. Her mouth is open as she pauses. "I didn't realize that any of this was important to you . . . You never seemed to care. I—"

"What was I supposed to do? Cry all the time about my failures? Let you know how much it hurt when you made fun of me? Display my shame like some ragged little trophy?" I shake my head, blinking away angry tears.

Zaye looks at me like she's seeing me for the first time and tries a small smile. "If it's worth anything, your dance was very good." She lifts her chin, but her eyes search mine. "Almost as good as mine, if you—"

"It's fine," I say, cutting her off. "Let me help Jagun. Then we can be on our way."

I turn away from her, wiping at my cheek. I hate that I'm crying. *This doesn't change anything*, I tell myself. But for that short space of time when she was teaching me, it felt like having a friend other than Nox.

"I need you to be still, and for your body to be connected to the earth," I say to Jagun, trying to keep my confidence when I catch sight of the puffy wound on his thigh.

"Wait." Nox rushes over, glowering at me. "If he's healed, then he's more of a threat. We should think about that."

I grimace, and I know he sees my disappointment. "It was you who always talked about us becoming priest and priestess, and now you're trying to tell me to ignore what I am supposed to do?"

"Mo—"

"Get out of my way," I say, shoving him aside. "And stay out of my way."

"The wound is already infected," I can hear Zaye hissing at Nox. "If she doesn't heal him, then he will die. And then we'll be as heartless and greedy as the ọba and Addaf."

I don't turn around, but I know Nox will be scowling at the truth of our words.

Jagun stays sitting on the ground, his eyes catching the light as he looks at me. My heart thuds painfully.

I focus on my toes until I feel the smolder of Yida's idan, and I let it curl up within me, welcoming the surge of power. And then I begin to move, pretending that Jagun is not there.

I tell myself that I am alone with no one watching me, that I am moving in the heat of the sun, with the earth and the dragon beneath me. The dance is fresh in my mind and the steps flow into each other, my feet skimming the ground as I move closer to Jagun. Idan crackles against my soles, and when I steal a glance down, I gasp, seeing the mark of Yida glowing gold, the scales of the dragon gleaming.

The goddess chose me.

Me.

The idan is fire in my blood, and I feel a layer of something stronger. Cloves and bitter ashes line my mouth as I stamp out another beat, embracing the flex of power that pours from me. The world around me blurs as my connection to Yida grows. Heat laps at my mind as my fingers form claws, mimicking sharp talons. My legs are burning, a bright kind of sear that pushes me on as my whirling moves lift my braids, and my mind is flooded with images of wings unfurling in the wind, a soaring feeling that I remember from the Glide. The prayer concludes with a twirl and a heel slap that punctuates the end.

I stop, sweat streaming down my neck and back as I collapse onto the ground.

Jagun leans over and grasps my wrist, then stands and lifts me to my feet. I wobble, stars sparkling around his face. Closing my eyes briefly, I take a moment to regain my balance, to ground myself. And then I'm examining his thigh, scanning the muscles and smooth skin where once there was a jagged gouge.

"Thank you." His voice is quieted by gratitude. Jagun's palm is warm as it slides from my wrist. "Again."

"I did it." The words are small and not for him, but he smiles anyway. When I'm finally able to hold his gaze, I blink. The laugh lines transform his face.

"You did."

Nox whoops behind me, and suddenly I am swept up and swung around as I grin in relief. When the boy slows and places me gently on the ground, his hands linger on my waist—but I look to Jagun. There is gratitude in his eyes . . . but there is also something else. Something deeper, like a question. Something that has me turning away.

I'm breathless now, words snatched by the momentous thing I've done.

I've mastered a prayer.

I've healed someone.

"Dam's idan and now Yida's. And look at your own leg." Nox squeezes me hard against him as I smile into his chest. "Well done, Mo."

The deep scratch on my leg is a faint scar now. The dragon curled around my ankle is no longer glowing, but I still feel the pop and burn of its magic linger within me. I wonder if Jagun feels it too. "Thank you."

Zaye is watching, a rare look of open admiration on her face. "To be honest, I didn't think that you'd be able to do it."

The feeling of accomplishment is not eclipsed by her words, but I'm still stunned when she puts a hand to my shoulder and squeezes once. Nox turns to Jagun as he lets go of me, and for a moment, I miss the warmth of his arms, his apology for attempting to tell me what to do.

"Don't think about trying anything now that you're all

healed." Nox narrows his eyes at Jagun. "You'll get home when we're done, and that's only because of the pity Mo feels for you. Me? I would have let that eloko swallow you whole."

"Nox . . ." I warn. I know he's protective of me, but this is a side I haven't seen before. And not one I like.

The boy backs away, holding his palms up and mouthing "What?!"

Jagun says nothing, even as his eyes flash. His mouth tightens as he squeezes the waterskin before drinking. I linger, unsure what to say, until the silence becomes uncomfortable.

Nox sits on a fallen branch with Zaye, watching the prince with a pinched gaze. The soil is rich beneath my soles as I make my way over to join them, the bark rough beneath the backs of my thighs.

"Just so you know, he doesn't agree with what his father has done," I say quietly.

Nox makes a disbelieving noise. "At least he knows what the ọba is responsible for."

We watch as Jagun lifts the hoof of my guiamala, picking stones from between its toes. The creature releases a low sigh and licks the boy's shoulder with its long pink tongue. The ọmọ ọba grimaces, but his expression changes to a smile as he murmurs something and places one hand on the guiamala's jaw, gently easing it away.

"Don't be silly enough to think that we can trust him, Mo." A muscle ticks in Nox's jaw and I swallow.

"I didn't say we should." I think of the screams of the men dragged into the forest by the eloko. "But . . . perhaps Jagun can help."

"If he chooses to," mutters Nox darkly just as the prince looks over at us, at me. Something in his gaze makes me drop mine. I fiddle with the end of one of my plaits and force myself not to look back at him.

"Which way now?"

Zaye stands over us, casting a slim shadow as I hold up a hand, squinting against the sun that blazes behind her. And then I see it. Swirls of pink and green wisps mix with the blue of the sky, twisting around each other. My eyes widen, Nox's and Zaye's voices fading as I stare at the clouds that break apart above us. Strands of purple and faded red spiral around the undulating colors of the heavens. The hairs on my arms stand up.

"That way," I answer, pointing at the part of the sky that ripples with Dam's essence.

CHAPTER FOURTEEN

The babalawos say the colors in the sky are trails of the dragon, that they are a physical manifestation of Dam's idan as he traverses our kingdom. The god's signs are not often seen, but if anyone does catch a glimpse, then they accept the blessings and thank Dam for showing himself. I find myself agreeing with the devotees of the god, because what else could cause such beauty in the skies above us?

Nox's grin is wide, while Zaye lifts her chin, her eyes bright. "Can you feel it, Mo?"

I nod. This time Dam's idan feels like tiny slivers of cold rain. I tilt my face to the rainbow sky. The raw frost of the dragon's magic burns stronger to my left.

"That way?" I point with a shaking finger at the twist of colors that shifts southward.

Nox grins at me, nodding. "At this rate you'll be channeling faster than me."

I try to smile, but being chosen by both gods and the expectation of learning how to use their idan make my stomach twist.

How am I supposed to do something that has never been done before? I swallow, waiting for the spin of nausea to leave me.

Nox hugs me to him, and immediately, I'm taken back to all the times we were this close growing up. I breathe in his familiar scent, feeling calmer as I draw away, only to see him looking down at my mouth.

"Come," he says, voice rough and low as he gently pushes me away. "We need to get going."

I step away from him, hurrying to my guiamala. Jagun is already perched on top, and he holds out a hand to me. "Here, let me help you. I don't think Bisi likes it when you grip her so tightly."

I scowl at him. "Since when does she have a name?" If anyone should be naming the creature, it's me.

Bisi looks down with her doe eyes and blinks once. She snorts, blowing hot air at me before nuzzling my head. I push her away but press my lips together to hide a smile at her obvious affection.

Jagun's hand hovers, and I consider ignoring it before giving in and reaching up to grasp his palm. His fingers wrap around my wrist, and with one smooth movement, he swings me up and through the air. For a moment, I'm surprised at his strength, and I flounder. I manage to clamp my legs around the blanket saddle on Bisi's back, and I fuss with the reins, waiting for the heat in my chest and neck to fade.

"Nox said we're heading across the Ghost Ocean," says Jagun from behind me. As ridiculous as it is, I wonder what the back of my hair looks like and then feel silly, forcing myself not to fuss with it. Eloko killed a group of men only hours ago and I'm fussing with my plaits?

I grip the reins harder. "It's the fastest path." I clear my throat. "And Nox said it's one of Dam's favored routes."

Around us, calls of the yellow-billed turaco shatter the hot day. Bisi's large steps rock me back and forth, and I clamp my legs tighter, not wanting to slide into the boy behind me.

"Have you ever been?" Jagun's voice is light, conversational.

"Have *you*?"

"Once. When I was fourteen." He lets a small silence build and I wipe the sweat that slides down my neck. "Baba thought it would be good for me to get out and see the kingdom. To get to know the lay of the land. And the people I'll one day rule."

"That *you'll* rule?" I can't help the tone of my voice.

"Yes. But not in the same way my father does," Jagun says quickly. Anger bleeds into his tone. "The way Addaf wields the emi buburu? Using power for darkness? I don't know what he's done to my baba, but if I were ọba, I would *never* let Addaf get away with that."

I don't speak for a moment. Again, Jagun seems . . . earnest. Despite Nox's suspicion, I find that I believe him.

Besides. He hasn't attacked us yet. We are his way of making amends, and a way for him to learn more about the people he speaks of serving.

"What were they like? The southern lands?" Curiosity burns at me, hotter than the afternoon heat that sticks my wrapper to my sweaty back and thighs. I have never been farther than the meadows and woods surrounding the temples, but the scrolls I've read always felt like they made up for it, describing the grasslands, the desert to the north, and the wastelands and second range of mountains to the south.

Jagun pauses again and I find I'm already getting used to his silences. When he speaks, his voice is soft. "I can tell you that it is balmy and warm. And there is an intense joy and respect they instinctively have for life and one another, no matter the god they worship."

"Like how everyone is at the Dírágónì ceremony?"

"Exactly." I can hear the small smile in his reply, and I fight to keep one from my lips. "I swear to you, even their mangoes and Aziza honey tasted sweeter!"

As we ride together, Jagun tells me about his tour around the kingdom. From being presented with a nundá cub by a village between the grasslands and the northern Achimota Forest to visiting the clear, cold springs found in the Adamawa Mountains.

"What did you do with the nundá?"

"She was too young to have left her mother so soon, but Baba said I couldn't refuse the gift even if I didn't want it." Jagun's voice hardens. "He told me everything has a price, and if I couldn't look after her, then I should kill her. That her pelt would fetch decent money." He chuckled. "So I took the cub home. I had to wake every two hours to feed her for that first month, but it was worth it to prove him wrong."

I imagine the kind of boy with a small winged feline cuddled on his lap, drip-feeding her milk even as his eyes droop. That Jagun made such a choice shows a different side to him. So very different from his father. My chest warms. "I'm sure it was."

Bisi carries us over the last of the grasslands until the Ghost Ocean stretches before us. We pause at the lip of salt and lava that nudges against the land, gazing down on what looks like something a giant created by pressing a thumb into the earth, shoving the ground down against the core of the world. Steam rises in yellow plumes, pouring through crusts of salt beds that are twice the size of the prayer hall in our temple. In the distance, a wide pink lake shimmers.

I take a swig from the water Nox passes me and sigh. "How are we supposed to get across that?"

"Guiamalas traverse the Ghost Ocean all the time," he says, scanning the terrain. "They're famous for it."

"You're speaking like you've had firsthand experience, when I know for a fact you haven't been anywhere like this." I turn to give the water to Jagun, but Nox grabs it from me, throwing an annoyed look at the prince.

"How would you know?" he retorts.

I say nothing and just stare at him. There's no forgetting how long we've been friends.

"All right, all right." He launches the water at Jagun, who catches it in his right hand. "But Baba said there's a good reason why they're used by both temples. They're not fast, but they're dependable on most kinds of land."

"He's right," adds Zaye, guiding her guiamala up next to ours. "Their long legs keep them away from the worst of the heat. Besides, there's a path you can take that avoids any of the major thermal seeps."

For some reason, anger sears through me at her response. It seems everyone has a clever answer but me. "Let me guess, you've been here too," I snap, hands tightening on Bisi's reins. The animal groans as I tug.

Zaye shrugs, her eyes sliding to Jagun behind me as she flips her braids over one shoulder. "Panyin took me when she was on her healing pilgrimage last year. We visited thirty villages in thirty days."

I take a steady breath and loosen the reins, trying to

remember that my pride doesn't matter, and neither does my need to prove myself. At least not in the way I felt I had to back home. But even when I was at the temple, I didn't usually feel *rage,* not unless someone mentioned Baba. I can't shake the unease at these feelings. Where are they coming from?

I think back to the water moving with my fingertips at the stream, the blades that felt like fire and ice. The healing prayer I performed. Perhaps all I ever needed to do was relax myself.

I purse my lips and blow out some air. "Nox, what are we looking for? Dam's idan led us here, but what route do we take?"

When the dragons created humans, the world was mainly water, and Yida reminded Dam that the people would need more land to live. Dam argued that they could live in the seas, but eventually the goddess persuaded him otherwise. Dam let loose his idan and scorched away the waters, while Yida channeled hers into vapors that became more solid earth.

The Ghost Ocean was all originally sea, but working together, the gods left nothing but the great salt flats and a volcano that lies sleeping underneath. This land looks almost uninhabitable, but I know from the scriptures in the temple archives that the Nefu people have lived here since its creation.

The sun moves closer to the horizon, lighting up the terrain in streaks of yellow, and the thought of another day passing by makes my stomach dip. I find myself looking back at Jagun, at the jut of his jaw as he takes in the Ghost Ocean. His eyes are narrowed, a hand held to his brow, the other fiddling with the golden bead on the end of one of his plaits. "The central pathways are safer."

Nox nudges his guiamala closer to us, taking in the bubbling craters that pepper the way ahead. "Are you sure you're not just trying to get us killed?"

The ọmọ ọba lifts his chin but his eyes flash. "And die myself? How would that make sense?"

"You tell me. Your father wasn't exactly thinking of anyone but himself when he summoned the emi buburu."

Jagun runs a hand over his face and sighs loudly. "I know."

Nox's mouth hangs open at his admission, but he quickly shuts it.

"I told Moremi it's not something I knew he was planning. And it's not something he would have done if my iya was still alive." Jagun looks at me. "She . . . tempered him."

I think back to the shock on his face as Ojaja began to sing. The way he let us take my mother.

"Besides, I won't forget what Moremi did for me earlier. I can't."

And again, I believe him. "We can trust him or not, Nox. But we need to find Dam."

"Everyone just needs to stop arguing so we can get going," announces Zaye. She glares over at us. "Jagun is right. We go the central route. Follow me."

"You heard her," I say to Nox, cutting my eye at him. Not once did I ever think that I'd find myself agreeing with Zaye, but here we are. I sigh and shake Bisi's reins, being careful not to grip them too tightly. "Let's go. We don't have time to waste."

The last of the grass gives way to snow-white salt flats and small lakes so rich with minerals that they glitter in greens and oranges. As our creatures pick their way over the land, it grows even hotter. Now it's not just the searing sun above us but the vicious heat that rises from beneath that has us all instantly sweating. I wipe a hand over my brow, wishing I had something to shade my eyes. We should have been more prepared. I pat the waterskin, knowing it might not be enough, trying to shake off the worry that winds inside me.

Zaye leads the way, with Nox bringing up the rear. I know it's so that he can keep an eye on Jagun behind me, but the more I think about it, the less I think the ọmọ ọba would be so willing to go along with our plan if he didn't believe in what we're trying to do. *He has no choice if he wants to make amends*, I tell myself, trying to find comfort in the thought.

"Stay clear of the smaller pools," shouts Zaye, gesturing to the bubbling surfaces that are a milky blue green. "They can be dangerous." Along the crusted edge of one of the pools, I see a tiny bone, and I shudder.

"I know the Nefu are nomadic, but I'm not sure how any living thing apart from Yida could exist in a place this hot." Jagun's voice is quiet.

But as soon as he speaks, Zaye points at something in the distance. The specks slowly grow until I can make out a chain of much larger guiamalas, some with riders on their backs.

I think of asking what our next move should be, looking to the others, and then I catch myself. I always used to wait to be told what to do, whether by Iya or Kakra or even Nox. Now something unfurls inside me. I straighten my back and clear my throat.

"We can't avoid the Nefu, that would be stupid," I say, my voice loud. "We make our way to them. Perhaps they can confirm we're on the right path."

As we get closer, I see the bend of hunched backs and the spikes of long poles. The Nefu miners are wrapped from head to toe in thin black robes that billow around their ankles, helping them to stay cool in the unflinching glare of the sun. More fabric is wrapped around their mouths and heads, raised forward in peaks that give them shade.

The first group of miners have poles in hand and are prying loose slabs of solid salt from the desiccated land. Another group have large, curved daggers they use to chop up the salt into chunks. The guiamalas behind them are older adults with short gray fur and longer black horns that sprout sun-whitened coarse hair. Their backs are bare, and I can't take my eyes off the scars that crisscross large humps, a reminder of the heavy salt bars they will carry. I stroke a hand over Bisi's head, catching one of her soft velvet ears between my forefinger and thumb.

Behind the miners are homes, on a sea of ash, that are built to be portable. Made from brush, they are light enough to allow heat to escape but dense enough to give cover. Bleached goatskin and woven straw mats lie beside the structures, the sun and air readying them for night. The homes will be packed up and loaded onto guiamalas when it's time to move on to another location, where a fresh bed of salt will be broken down. Kakra told me that Nefu traders take the salt to markets across the Kingdom of Kwa, returning with food and trinkets to sell.

While we wait to be acknowledged, strangled shouts reach us as a group of the men argue, their blades flashing in the sun as others come to calm the row. I wonder if it is in reaction to us, but the Nefu don't even look our way. Instead, they gather around two men who throw fists at each other until another steps in between them. They all quiet at the loud tones of a small old woman who barrels over to them.

"Is this normal?" I ask Jagun.

"No. Just . . . be careful."

I stop, and the others pause behind me as I slide down from Bisi. I bow my head in front of the old woman who calmed the fight as she comes to greet us. She is even smaller than most of the priestesses at the temple, but what she lacks in height she makes up for in width. Tiny black eyes take us all in from underneath a beetled brow as she chews with strong white teeth on pako ijebu, the stick hanging from the corner of her mouth, thin lips twisting and crinkling. Thick beads of blue crystal hang from her neck and drop from her wrists, while large earrings of the same blue stone pull her lobes down, stretching her ears almost to her shoulders.

I stare in awe. The scriptures say the gems are solely located in a mine in the Ghost Ocean, and are only found as long as you're willing to brave the jumping worms that are attracted to human hosts. If one manages to slither inside your ear or mouth, you have just a few hours to get rid of it before it attaches to your lungs or liver. Ọba Ojaja presented his wife with his wife a giant Nefu pendant as a wedding gift that cost ten men their lives.

"What is it you want, young iyalawo?" the woman rasps. She looks behind her to check that there is still peace, her hands shaking. "My apologies. The mood has been changed as of late. Our people are perhaps suffering from the sun today."

I lift my head and nod once at the recognition before speaking. "We're looking for the quickest route across the Ghost Ocean."

The Nefu elder holds her left wrist with her right hand, chunky prayer beads clinking. "You should not be here, wandering around." She looks over at us. "Tell me why you would choose to brave the Ghost Ocean unaccompanied."

The others dismount and I glance back at them as they draw level with us. I know that we're all thinking the same thing: *Should we be telling people that we're on our way to the monasteries?*

Jagun steps forward. "My greatest respects." The ọmọ ọba pats his chest and dips his head in a way that is not royal protocol but is deeply respectful. "But we—"

The ground rumbles beneath us. I throw out my hands for balance, meeting Zaye's gaze. There is no weeping burn of idan, but still a sharp crack fills the air as the earth shakes. Could Yida be close?

A strangled shriek comes from behind the old woman, and she snaps around at the cry. There are panicked shouts as the huddle of Nefu poke at the split salt. I creep forward, eyes on the ground that has opened, my knees weakening as I see what the miners are shouting about.

Fresh blood spews from the hole in the fractured earth, filling the hot air with the unmistakable stench of death.

CHAPTER FIFTEEN

"What is happening?" shouts the Nefu elder, elbowing her way through.

The crowd around the hole grows as more miners gather. A few poles are hoisted in the air, their ends saturated with a thick red that drips, splattering the white salt in crimson. Nox holds me steady as I catch flashes of faces, eyes round and mouths pinched.

"What is it?" I croak as Jagun edges his way forward.

Zaye peers ahead, a frown hardening her eyes as she watches the Nefu throw their poles onto the salt bed. "It's some kind of liquid mineral. It's causing that smell and ruining the salt."

My shoulders sag and Nox leaves me to stand beside Zaye. The miners gather a distance away from us, but their voices cut through the heat, rising and bubbling. I can't hear what the old woman says, but it doesn't calm the Nefu. They pick up the same poles they discarded, hitting at the salt that is pinkening before our eyes.

Jagun and Nox return with grim expressions on their faces. "They're saying it's a curse from the emi buburu."

My stomach flips. I crane my neck. Is Addaf here? But the flat white landscape of the Ghost Ocean stretches around us. "How?"

The miners' voices rise. One spits on the earth as he angrily adjusts the black fabric wrapped around his shoulder-length ringlets.

"They're saying that Dam has forsaken them because we arrived and that the emi buburu are making themselves known."

I remember the first scriptures, where it describes the shadow spirits: *They will make the earth bleed as they tear their way back into their world, taking life and leaving rot in their wake.* First the forest and now this. I swallow, my dry throat clicking. A few of the Nefu take steps toward us, and two men lower their poles, the points wicked sharp. Above the wrap of black fabric, their brown eyes are hard. Black.

Changed.

They hiss and lunge toward us.

My hand goes to the daggers that crisscross my chest, but Jagun steps in the way.

"Stop," he commands, lifting his arms to bar them from me and Zaye. His hand whips up to snatch at the pole shoved at his face, the tip a hair's breadth from his nose.

And then the old woman is there, her words torn away by the hot breeze but still sharp enough to force the miners to turn back to her. There is shock in her eyes as she looks between us and her people.

"They are not themselves." She gestures to the bleeding salt. "Hearts and minds can be infected without the gods."

I stumble backward as more of the Nefu turn on us, the blank look rippling over their faces, spreading like a wildfire.

"We need to leave," I whisper. "Now."

And then there is a sharpness against my spine, and I freeze. The Nefu have us surrounded.

"Mo . . ." Nox takes my hand and eases me closer to him as Zaye and Jagun move to our sides.

I scan the dark umber faces, but only the old woman seems herself, worry splitting the deep lines of her expression. And then she goes still, face tipped up as she raises her hand, pointing into the sky. We follow the line of her arm and finger to see the same ribbons of color we had seen earlier now staining the entire unending blue. As one, the Nefu are lifting their faces to the strands of orange, lilac, and green that swirl above us, dropping their poles on the parched land. I reach for Yida's tear in my wrapper, nails clicking against the facets as my heart races.

Dam.

"Nox . . . ?" My voice rises.

"Some say the dragon god has been known to stop in the Ghost Ocean, that he pays homage to the sea he once created." Nox brings his hands together, clapping in expectant prayer. "Get ready just in case, Mo. If you show him the tear now, then maybe he'll stop and we can explain what the ọba has done, what the emi buburu are doing. It's a reminder of Yida, a reminder that he needs to go to her. And then we can call on them to complete the Dírágónì ceremony."

I press my hands against the twist of fabric that holds the crystal orb. What if Dam already knows what the shadow spirits are doing? What if the gods truly do not care? I shake my head as if to dislodge the thoughts.

The Nefu raise their hands slowly, their eyes no longer glazed. Wrapped around their hands are flat prayer beads in shades of the seas, clinking together as palms smack against palms. A cut of air forms above us, a sharp swoosh of an unnatural breeze. I hold my breath as shards of cold press down on me. As one, we all turn our faces up to the heavens as an ethereal silver wing dips down, eclipsing the sun.

I duck instinctively, hands pressed against my head, gasping when I'm enveloped with an iciness. The glint of silver scales on a giant scarred belly fills the air above us. Dam roars. My mouth floods with the tang of iron as the dragon swoops down, blasting the earth with his frosted idan. I claw at my braids, numbness spreading across my body. The wind spirals into funnels that flatten me to the salt-crusted ground as I struggle to look up at the god.

And then there is stillness.

And the rush of heat that tells me all I need to know.

"He... he's gone." The words slip out as I try to stand, scanning the skies too, hoping that I'm wrong. But the feel of the god's idan is no more and I know that he has left.

I sit up, a hand to my chest. My fingernails scrabble for the tear, even though I know that it's too late to draw it out. I let my hand fall back into my lap. There are moans of praise from the Nefu as they rise to their feet around us, faces aimed at the heavens. All I feel is the scrape of deep disappointment. There was barely any time, and yet...

Anger lines Zaye's face as she kicks at a crumble of salt. "You weren't fast enough," she snaps. "You never are."

I try to swallow around the lump in my throat. All too quickly, I am back at the temple. Clumsy. Not good enough. Zaye's words cut at me, as sharp as they ever were.

"Mo." Nox's voice is steady, his hand dropping onto my shoulder.

"He was on his way to the monastery." Jagun's voice is firm as he turns to me. "Dam was injured, remember? There's no way he was stopping. There wasn't any way you could have offered up Yida's tear."

"We don't know that," counters Zaye. "If he'd just seen it—"

"He was too far away." Nox lifts my chin so that I'm staring into his face. "We carry on as planned."

While part of me agrees with him, the girl from home wants to cower. Wants to return to plants and tonics, things I actually *know*. But too much has happened, too much has changed. And now we are up against gods and monsters. For a moment, my old hesitation returns: How could someone like me ever be enough?

I give Nox a shaky smile, his hand warm underneath my chin before he lets go. Clearing my throat, I gaze across the Ghost Ocean to where the sun bleeds into white, turning the salt shades of blood orange. Nox means well, but we're running out of time.

Zaye scowls. "Let's go." She stalks off, hands crossed over her chest in frustration as she heads away from the Nefu.

The Nefu watch us in silence, and my skin prickles at the memory of their sharp poles and black eyes, the mention of the emi buburu by their elder. The shadow spirits are infecting more than the land.

Zaye has already mounted her guiamala, a hand held up to shade her eyes, and I can practically feel her scowling at me. I turn away, running my fingers over Bisi's coarse warm fur.

Jagun climbs up, and the animal snorts as I follow him,

settling myself in the blanket saddle. Behind me, the prince shifts, and I realize that I'm leaning back and almost resting on him. I ease forward, clearing my throat and pushing away the braid that hangs over my left eye.

"It's not your fault," whispers Jagun, but I ignore him.

It is.

We head toward the edges of the Ghost Ocean, salt flats peppered with the green of tenacious acacia shrubs and the scurry of mud moles searching for tubers that will quench their thirst and hunger. I stay silent, hating the fact that I've let us all down, before I tell myself to remember who I am. I can still feel a faint slither of idan lacing my veins with ice. I latch onto it and remind myself that I've been marked by the dragons. How can I let one thing stop me? I sit up straighter. We'll find the gods.

Nox points to where the salt plains end and the grasslands begin again. "Once we leave the Ghost Ocean, we're in the territories of the Anyoto."

The name sits between us in the warming twilight air. I scour my memories of lessons from the temple, and just as spotted hides and wide jaws come to mind—

"The leopard beings," I say uneasily.

I feel Jagun shift again behind me. "We can go around their lands. If we keep to the outskirts, then we should be safer."

Safer. Not *safe*.

"What do you think, Mo?" asks Nox, holding my gaze.

A story comes back to me now, of their lack of tolerance for outsiders. Of how the Anyoto ambushed a group of iyalawos in Iya Eneh's time. Eleven of the thirteen women were killed.

But we have no other option.

"It doesn't matter what I think." I pull on Bisi's reins gently.

My stomach sinks, but I try to keep my voice even. "It's what we have to do."

We gallop toward the setting sun. As the guiamalas slow to their usual amble, I slump in the blanket saddle, still taking care not to lean against Jagun. The attack this morning in the Sambisa Forest woke us early, and now I'm so exhausted that my eyes feel as if I have rubbed sand in them. I blink, rolling my shoulders back, trying to wake myself.

"You're tired."

"Mm-hmm." I don't turn to the prince.

Nox rides up to us. "We'll take a break." He gestures toward some raffia trees that are giving shade. I all but fall from Bisi, leading her under the canopy and sighing in relief.

From the other end of the shade, Zaye scoffs, and immediately, fury burns in my chest again.

"What?" I retort. "If you have something to say, then just say it."

Zaye's eyes flash. "First, you fail to catch Dam's attention, but apparently that wasn't enough. Now when we have no time to lose, we also stop because of *you*." She marches over and grabs my arm, twisting it painfully so that Dam's mark on my wrist can be seen. "You think that you're worthy of both gods? You couldn't even sense him in time. What's going to happen when we get to the monasteries?" She pokes my chest. "How are *you* going to unite the gods when you can barely pray, barely even walk around without someone having to help you? Without—"

I shove her back, idan flaring at my feet and in my hands. The wild twist of fire and ice that seems to have taken root inside me now explodes, feeding my anger and blazing away the last parts of my hesitation.

"I may be learning, but I can still slap you." The words are out in a fast rush that I can't take back, and raw satisfaction burns in my stomach. Staring at Zaye's sneer, I don't want to take it back.

The girl eyes me, her hands in small fists, her eyes hard.

"Try it," I spit out, and I've never heard my voice so taunting before. But in this moment, idan scorches from my feet and through my chest, and I don't care. I've never felt like this. So . . . righteous.

I try to relax my stance so I can be ready for Zaye, my lip curling. "We're not in the temple now."

She leaps forward, swinging for me, and her knuckles catch the side of my jaw before I can lean away. With anger and idan flowing now, I kick out, my feet hitting her stomach. She doubles up with a grunt and I lunge forward.

"That's enough!" says Nox, pushing in between us.

Zaye pushes him back, her face pinched when he doesn't move. "Get out of the way."

"Enough! I won't watch you speak to Mo like this. And you?" Nox jabs at me. "What are you doing? We don't have time for this!"

I'm panting even as the fight leaves me. As the rage and idan drain away.

He's right. Of course he's right. I feel myself deflating and scuff my big toe in the earth. Zaye scrubs at her face, blinking away tears, and the rest of my anger fades.

"Let's just . . ." I start, and sigh. "We need to get on if we're going to do this." It's not much, but my words are a small gift of peace.

She takes a deep breath, a hand rubbing her stomach. "I agree."

"And I'm sorry." I gesture to her, waving a hand at her leg too. "If I could go back so you could be part of the ceremony, then I'd change it."

Zaye sighs. "No, you wouldn't. And if you did, that would be stupid." She tries a tiny grin. "And I'm beginning to realize that you aren't as stupid as I thought."

I snort just as Nox sighs. He reaches for my hand, fingers loosely linking with mine.

"Come on, let's get some space and try to use that idan in the right way, channel it."

We walk away from Zaye, and Nox points up at the canopy above us. Now that the day is drawing to an end, beams of light only just penetrate the spread of leaves. A shaft spears through and the boy is highlighted in a blaze of dancing gold. His cheekbones are bronzed and his dark eyes glitter when he suddenly smiles at me.

My breath hitches. For a moment, I want to smooth a frosted curl that hangs over his forehead. He lifts his hands in the light and tips back his head. "Together now. Let's work to channel Dam's idan. You already did it earlier."

He leans close to me, and my eyes catch on his mouth. After a whole childhood together, his presence is as familiar as breathing, and there is an ease to his proximity. But since this last summer, there have been several moments like this. Times when I've been paralyzed by the closeness of him.

"There's a small stream over there. Being closer to the water will help our connection, but this time I want us to try something different." He squeezes my hand and tows me toward the bushes and the gurgle of running water, the dragon around his wrist pressed close to mine. *He's right,* I think, studying the perfect scales on the tails that flick to the crooks of our elbows, *we need to try everything.* And who knows what two marks mean in terms of idan? Maybe I'll be able to channel twice as much.

A chill brushes against my mind as a tiny stream comes into view, not more than a trickle of clear water over gleaming pebbles. The smell of crushed honey flowers is strong in the air, reminding me of the sweet cakes that Kakra would often make on the cusp of the new moon.

We sit on the grass, damp from the stream.

Nox still hasn't let go of my hand.

"We will . . ." His voice trails off, and then he points with his free hand. "Look!"

The dragonfly is the biggest I have ever seen, its long body a green that shimmers with blues and yellows. Large translucent wings span larger than Nox's hand, vibrating as the insect hovers above the water. We watch in silence as it finally moves, climbing high into the air before zipping off over the stream in a loud buzz.

"You know what this means, Mo?"

I shake my head, taking care not to move my hand from his.

"Lots of babalawos believe that dragonflies are signs from Dam. And because this one is flying high, it means that so is Dam. A healthy sign. If it had been on the ground, then it would have been a bad omen." Nox turns to me now, a grin on his full lips. "Maybe it was also sent to give us hope . . . a sign that we can access the dragon god's idan properly."

I look at the water, my free hand reaching out. Nox mirrors

me, and I think perhaps our physical connection could act like an anchor or enhance our channeling. Either way, it can't hurt.

Besides, I like the closeness.

"Baba told me to imagine the water as a separate energy. The slip of it. Its coolness. Try."

I close my eyes and let myself feel the pull. The now-familiar needles of cold pepper me like a storm, but this time I don't buckle underneath them. I embrace the chill, letting it sweep away the heat of the day, welcoming the shivers that radiate across my crown.

"Now think of the stream as one long ribbon. Let it curl toward you, feel it bending to your will."

Moving my head from side to side, I try to keep my neck muscles loose. Iya always tells me that tenseness is a block to any emotion and power. Perhaps that has been my downfall for so long. I open one eye, but the stream is still the same.

"Try harder!" says Nox.

"I am!" I huff. "Stop shouting at me. I'm trying." I try to picture the water as a creature that I'm calling, controlling. "And you're just making me more nervous."

"No excuses."

"Shh!" I say, finally feeling a tugging sensation, a cold flow enveloping me. I try to block out Nox's bossy tone.

"Mo," he whispers as the smell of wet earth rolls over us.

"I said shh!"

"Mo, look."

I open my eyes to a sky turned to water, gasping when I realize what we've done.

The stream stretches out in the hot air, bending and twisting, catching spikes of sunlight. It ripples like a hungry snake as it writhes above the bed of gray pebbles.

"We did this?"

The water flexes at my words, shimmering and dropping slightly.

"Don't lose focus," says Nox. He bends his hand, fluttering his fingers, and I laugh when the water responds, spinning and twisting. "Now you try. On your own."

I don't have time to panic, splaying my fingers and then turning my hand over, palm to the sky. The stream spirals and flips. I lean forward, frowning as I concentrate. Letting go of Nox's hand, reaching out with both hands.

My fingertips tingle as if sensing the water. I call it to me in my mind, imagining its fluidity. And then I push out with my hands, watching as the stream bends in the air, bucking like a snared rabbit. I let it shimmer for a moment, a rainbow caught in the loose moving folds, before I toss it left and then right with a flick of my wrist. The water does what I want it to, and the realization sends a pulse of power through me.

I'm doing this.
This is all me.

Laughing again, I yank the thick ribbon of water closer, wrapping it around us as if it is fabric. The boy turns to me as I look about, grinning at what I have done.

"Look, Nox!" I lift a hand and twirl it, delighting in the spin of water that encompasses us now. Droplets spray across our faces, sliding down the slope of our noses and catching in between our lips.

"I am," he answers, but his eyes are on my face.

I stop playing with the water as he reaches for my hand again, threading his fingers through mine. My heart knocks against my ribs.

"I can't look at anything else," he says, bending closer so that our noses touch.

The water stops moving, but it still has us pinned in place. I think of all the times in the last few days that Nox has spoken up for me, checked on me. When he used to make space in his temple duties to come meet me, the hours he spent listening to me talk about anything from moringa to the best uses for aloe.

He's always been there for me. And he is here for me now. I know him inside and out, and that is special all in its own way.

When he presses his warm lips against mine, I stay very still.

And then I shift, kissing him back with just a little pressure. He tastes of sun and the heat of the day. Nox slides his hands around my waist, right hand spread out against my spine, his left resting on the curve of my hip. I lean into him, letting him kiss me harder as the stream begins to churn around us.

It's only as the roar fills our ears that I pull away. Splattered by the water, I laugh as the stream undulates lazily and touch my mouth.

"Moremi . . ." Nox's hands squeeze my waist as he leans back now, not taking his eyes from mine.

And then the water crashes down around us, drenching us in its coolness.

CHAPTER SIXTEEN

I jump, hands held up as the stream flows back to its snaking bed, taking with it the small watery world I had made for us. We stand in the dusk, wet hair plastered to our heads, chests heaving.

And I stare at Nox's lips. Instantly replay the press of them, and how soft they felt. My heart kicks in my chest.

I can't deny imagining this kiss for months, but now that it's happened... Nox is my best friend, my oldest friend. If he becomes something more, then what happens to our friendship?

I take a deep breath. "We should be going," I say slowly.

Nox keeps his eyes on my mouth, and I dip my head and turn away. The heat of shyness simmers now that the water isn't shielding us, and I shake my head. It was just a kiss. *Besides*, I tell myself as I brush down my wrapper, *there will be no chance to explore anything if we fail.*

If I fail.

My face drops. The dragon gods should be my focus. "Come. The others will be wondering where we are."

"But, Mo—"

Nox catches my arm, his fingers sliding to my hand. I pull away and pat my wet braids.

"I thought that you didn't want Jagun left on his own?" My question is sharper than I mean it to be.

"He's with Zaye."

"Who's a third of his size." Even though she's more than vicious enough to make up for it.

Nox says nothing, but his shoulders sag. "Is this you trying to tell me something?"

"It's me trying to remind you what we need to be doing." But at his warm eyes, I soften. I reach out to punch him lightly on his shoulder, wanting to fix things. "Do you really need to make this all about you, bighead?"

Nox rolls his eyes, but he still looks at me in a way that spreads heat across my chest and up my neck. "You think you can punch me now because you've controlled a whole stream?"

I bring up both fists, dancing backward, trying to get some lightness back. "What do you think?" I say—

Just as I trip over a tree root and land hard in the earth. I wince, and Nox laughs.

"I think," he says, his smile broad as he bends down to help me up, "that you are getting ahead of yourself."

I really am, I think. I look up at him and see the slight confusion flickering behind his smile, the want and expectation still there. And I wish I could take it back. Even the kiss. Especially the kiss. The gods are our mission, our focus. Not this . . . feeling that exists. Nox is my friend. My *friend*. If I don't want to lose that, then I need to keep it that way.

When we get back to the guiamalas, Zaye and Jagun are sitting on a log, their heads bent close.

"I don't like the look of this," mutters Nox.

Neither do I, but I imagine it's for different reasons. I try to ignore the small twist of jealousy at how close they're sitting, and the way Zaye has her head tipped so that her braids frame her heart-shaped face.

"He could have overpowered her at any moment," continues Nox, his voice low.

"But he didn't."

I ignore the look he throws at me and walk to Bisi. Zaye joins me, taking the woven red-and-orange blankets and layering them in neat folds.

"So? How did it go?" she asks. "Did he manage to teach you anything?"

My heart leaps at her words. I lick my lips and tighten my wrapper, still damp from the spiraling water. Immediately, the press of Nox against me rushes back, and my cheeks warm.

"She channeled an entire stream. Tossed it about as if it was nothing." He pushes my shoulder lightly before moving to his guiamala. "That's what she did. Her baba would be proud."

Baba. He would be amazed that I can do such a thing. A pang of sharp sadness pierces my heart when I think of how pleased he would be.

"Is that all?" says Zaye. Her eyes widen, and Jagun's gaze flits between Nox and me. For a moment, I wonder if he knows that we kissed, and my stomach folds in on itself. Then I feel silly for it. There's no way he could know. And no reason for him to care.

Or for me to care.

"The guiamalas are ready," says Jagun, and he turns to Bisi, checking the straps of her saddle.

"So you've moved on to whole bodies of water now?" Zaye

nudges me, and for once I don't flinch, but neither do I feel the need to answer. "Perhaps we should move on to something else too."

I don't speak immediately, trying to work out which Zaye I'm talking to. Temple Zaye or Now Zaye.

"Would you teach me more prayers, then?" I ask, careful to keep my tone neutral.

"Why not? I've been preparing these for years now for when . . . well, for when I thought I'd need them. And now you do. So . . ."

"But . . . why?" I don't understand this change in her, even though I find that I want it.

Zaye sighs heavily and then looks over at Jagun. He nods at her and smiles encouragingly. "I shouldn't have been so . . . harsh. We should be helping each other right now."

I can't help the narrowing of my eyes, but something shifts in me when the girl lifts the corner of her lip in a half smile. "Next time we get a chance, I'll show you some more prayers. Try not to be too clumsy, though. I don't like repeating myself over and over, even if the sound of my voice is pleasing."

Who would have thought there would be a day I practiced prayers with Zaye? I fight a smile as I turn away and sit down against Bisi. There's no time for a proper rest, but I manage to close my eyes and force my shoulders to relax. The guiamala's warm fur feels good and I let myself drift.

"Let's move," says Nox after what only seems like half an hour. *Better than nothing*, I think as I clamber to my feet.

Jagun swings himself on top of Bisi, and when I begin to climb up, he doesn't offer me a hand this time, and I feel oddly bereft at the absence. I don't look at him as I seat myself, holding myself stiffly.

Zaye rides beside me as the night grows around us.

"Let's begin, then."

I hold a hand up to my brow and squint at her. "What do you mean? We can't pray on the guiamalas."

"I know. But we can go over the prayers that you can do now that you've been chosen. Specifically, the ones that might be more helpful." Zaye brushes a small glitter of green butterflies from her shoulder. They leave behind a crush of emerald glow. "I mean, there's no point in teaching you how to ease the constipation of an elder, or how to rejuvenate a crop of maize or purple yams."

She's right. I let Bisi's long stride rock me gently while we discuss a litany of prayers that could be used for more than their original purpose, bouncing ideas back and forth. An air of easiness forms, fragile but there nonetheless.

"Why do you hate me so much?" The question is out before I can even really think about it.

Zaye straightens up as her face closes. I think she won't answer, but then she shrugs, facing forward, not looking at me when she says, "You've always had . . . more than me. A mother who is the principal iyalawo. Kakra is besotted with you, like she's your other mother. It's like you have two when I don't even have one."

I open my mouth but she waves me quiet.

"You're clever. And you can use most herbs to help heal." Zaye looks at me and her own eyes are glassy. "You can also sense idan as easily as breathing, and now both gods have chosen you."

My mind reels. *Zaye* is the one who has always been the best, the lucky one. Always chosen in public displays of prayers and used as an example by Iya for me over the years. *Why can't you pray like Zaye? See the turn of her ankle and the arch of her foot?* Is it any wonder I began to hate her as much as she seemed to hate me? "But I can't dance! I can only do the basic prayers through sheer panic."

She shakes her head. "You let your feelings block you. The way you broke apart the earth, and the idan you channeled so quickly with water? That takes other priestesses and priests months to master. And you did it in days."

I let her words sit. Zaye seemed to have it all, but perhaps it was just what *I* wanted, not what she needed. Attention, family. Love.

"Look," I say, picking my words carefully. "You're right. I know that I've always had a place in the temple, that my mother's position has made my life easier in ways. That Kakra took me under her wing. But I also struggled."

Zaye's mouth sets at my words.

"Wait, let me finish. I know people speak about my herbs, but that was all I had to prove myself. When I didn't learn any prayers easily, which you *never* let me forget, I had to find another way." I take a breath. "My father was banished, and I don't even know whether he's alive or dead. I miss him every day. *Every day.*"

I'm close to crying now and I hate it.

"The pressure has been all on me. How could I let Iya down when her husband is known as mad? Do you know how hard it is to be a disappointment? My mother is the principal iyalawo, *the principal iyalawo*. And she has a daughter who can only just about master the basic prayers. I bring her shame and I never forget it."

My words hang between us in the warm air. Zaye picks at a loose thread of her reins.

"And furthermore, Panyin hates me!" I let out a frustrated sigh. "I can't remember a time she didn't. And I swear I've never done anything to deserve that!"

"Panyin hates most people."

"Not you."

"Yes, not me." Zaye shrugs. "Although she did look at me funny the other week."

"No, she didn't. You're just trying to make me feel better."

"You're right. I am." She smirks.

I take another deep breath. "I just want to say, to learn from you would be almost as good as from the higher iyalawos."

"Almost?" scoffs Zaye, but she's smiling, and her eyes are bright. "You know you're downplaying my strengths."

I laugh and the sound surprises me, but not as much as when the girl joins in.

Jagun's deep voice rumbles from behind me. "We're close to the borders of the Anyoto. I suggest we stay as quiet as we can."

Zaye shoots him a nod, her face softening at his voice. She urges her guiamala into a trot and moves away, catching up to Nox, and a quiet settles over Jagun and me.

He remains silent as we head deeper into the grasslands, and I shift in my seat. For some reason, the air between us seems tight, and I find myself missing the excuse of Zaye's conversation.

"Are you all right?" I murmur, without turning around.

He doesn't speak right away, and I wait, giving him time.

"I was just thinking about what Baba has done." The prince moves behind me, his knee catching my side. I feel a quick press of his hand to my waist as a brief apology. "It is . . . unforgivable."

I say nothing, feeling out the sincerity in his tone.

"My iya would have done something, I know she would,"

says Jagun, leaning forward. Heat radiates from his body, his breath warm on the back of my right shoulder. "She would have made it right. But now it is up to me."

A quiet righteousness hardens his words, adding to the ever-evolving idea I have of him. That he cares so much means I've been right to trust him.

"It's up to *us*. Besides, it's not just about your father now. Addaf will follow, and the emi buburu are eating at the world as we speak." I pick my words carefully. "Our parents are not going to save us. They can't." I twist to look him. His eyes are wide, ringed with thick lashes and luminous with the moon. There's a small dimple in his chin, hidden by the beginnings of a beard.

I face ahead, watching the stars lace the sky. "It's up to us now," I say.

CHAPTER SEVENTEEN

The night deepens and no one speaks.

So far, we've taken a slightly longer route to trek around the territories of the Anyoto, and now, with time running short, I wonder if we should have just risked going straight through.

But after the eloko and the Nefu, with Addaf and the emi buburu on our tail . . . the last thing we need is to endanger ourselves further. Still, the unease returns, and I find myself glancing desperately at the sky.

"Can we rest for a moment?" Zaye asks quietly.

Nox glances back at her. He's flipping the leather stopper of the waterskin on and off as he continually scans our surroundings. The trees have grown more lush, turning into the pale green of the Kakum Forest. Here and there, copper circles dangle from random branches of marula trees, said to be favored by the Anyoto. There are piles of bones beneath two that we pass, and I shudder as I catch a gleam of what look like lime-colored eyes before I blink and they disappear.

"Only for a bit," he says, voice tight. "I don't like being so close to the forest when it's nighttime."

And so close to the Anyoto's territory, I think but don't say.

When I slide from Bisi, my legs shake and I drop into a crouch with a groan, and there's a thud next to me. I look up, my gaze raking over muscled thighs and the blaze of Jagun's agbada. The gold bands on his wrist are not solid bangles but thin twists that coil together to give the appearance of one thick band, while still being light enough to enable sparring. He makes his way over to Zaye and helps her down from her guiamala. At the sight of the prince, the girl's face lights up.

I look away and sit in the tall grass, head tipped up to a velvet sky. I have no right to feel any way about whether there is something between them, and certainly not after the kiss with Nox. A coil of anger at myself stirs. Why am I even feeling this way? Jagun is the ọba's son and not someone I could be with even without what has happened. If anyone is a match for me, it is Nox. Our families are equal in position, and he knows me, he understands me. All I've been thinking about for months is him kissing me. So why am I thinking of Jagun?

You feel nothing, I tell myself. *Nothing.*

If I say it enough times, then perhaps it'll feel true.

A tired ache washes over me as more stars break through the dark, and I wonder if Dam is already at his monastery, with Yida tucked tight in the earth beneath him. For a moment, hope lights up my chest. Perhaps when we arrive, he'll be fully healed by the prayers of the pious babalawos. I pat Yida's tear, reassured by its outline.

My thighs hurt and my tailbone aches in a way that makes me yearn for the hot baths in the temple and their soothing steam. I think of the scooped-out hollow of my chamber, the tapestry I sewed that depicts my father's favorite constellations, and the crystals set in the walls. They glowed even when the torches were not lit and always made me feel safe.

When Nox comes jogging toward me, I stand up quickly, my muscles screaming in protest.

"What is it?" I ask as he clasps both my hands, his palms sliding into mine.

"We need to leave. Now." His voice is tense but low and a line sits between his eyebrows. "There's signs of the Anyoto watching us."

I think of the glimpse of glowing eyes. "But we're not on their territory." The tall grass sways in a small breeze, and I shiver. "What do we do?"

"We keep moving. But don't let them know that we've seen them. Maybe they'll just watch and make sure we respect their village boundaries."

I nod as Jagun moves toward us at what appears to be a leisurely pace. The only sign of his tenseness is the muscles in his jaw, pulsing.

"Come," he says, holding his hand out to me. "Quickly."

Nox stands still for a moment, his eyes darkening. And then he nods at me, knowing there is no time to argue.

I step toward Jagun as he climbs Bisi. He helps me up into the saddle with a bump, his hands resting on either side of me, holding the leather straps. "Just keep your eyes ahead," he murmurs.

Bisi lurches forward, moving faster than she ever has. Maybe she senses something too. I keep my head straight, strangely glad for the press of Jagun behind me. His warmth is a comfort as my heart hammers in my chest.

While still a forest, the land shifts. Large bushes spiked with small bright orange fruit populate the tall grass. A hoot from our left startles me, and I snatch a look on instinct, meeting the glare of a silver owl, its beak sharp like a freshly forged sword.

I scan the rippling thickets as we gallop faster, night clouds pressing down on us, their bodies full of storm. Ahead of me, Zaye and Nox keep level, but I see them checking back, making sure we're close.

And then something launches toward us from the thickness of low bushes. Fur shines in the moonlight, but it is the glint of claws that makes me call out in fear.

The creature lands just short of Zaye's guiamala, raking across the animal's side, eliciting a bellow of pain.

"Keep going!" Nox screams as the girl wobbles on her mount. She yanks on the reins, but the guiamala only manages to stagger forward another few steps, blood gushing from its side.

I kick my feet against Bisi. Jagun's arms clamp tighter around me as we move faster, the guiamala either rushing to escape or rushing to help. But we don't reach Nox and Zaye quick enough, and I watch in horror as the creature rises from the ground, shaking its great feline head, flank dappled with the marks of a leopard. The monster stands on two legs, claws held out like vicious hands, head jutting forward, shoulder muscles abnormally thick. Its eyes flicker, the lime green of them momentarily eclipsed by black.

The Anyoto. Leopard beings. The only creations of Yida that do not heed her teachings in the way her other worshippers do. Their fierce protectiveness of their territory and their inclination for indiscriminate violence are said to be flares of idan, which affects them differently than it does the dragon's other creations.

Zaye rights herself on her guiamala as it limps onward, keeling to the side. Even Bisi bleats to the animal, her call strangled with panic. The reins slip in my hands as we catch up, the scent of blood heavy in the air. We reach them just as the creature's skinny legs buckle, and Zaye is thrown from its back as the guiamala crashes to the ground.

Nox jumps down and scoops up Zaye as more Anyoto flood the clearing. I blink away tears as I stare at the injured beast. It gives one last groan before it is silent, head lowered for the final time to the earth.

"There was no need for this death. We were passing around you!" I shout as Nox frantically pushes Zaye up to the saddle of his guiamala and climbs back himself. "*Around* you!"

"There was no need for death if you had only listened." The voice floats out from the forest as Addaf steps from the trees, and my heart plummets. Shadows wrap around his body, like twists of a second skin. The breeze carries a sudden wave of burnt bones and rot, and I fight the need to retch.

He bares his red teeth in a mockery of a smile. "There is a natural balance of our world. If you take, you must seek to give. And you have taken something that I need."

The sky crackles with the storm that is building, and more heavy purple clouds drift across the bright moon. He signals to the Anyoto, a simple flutter of his fingers, and my hand goes to Yida's tear, swaddled in the folds of my wrapper. I'm tired. I'm tired of running.

And I'm tired of guessing at Addaf's motives. My anger rises, sharp enough to cut. "Why?" I call out. "Why do you want the destruction of our world? Because you must know that is the only option when you let the emi buburu free."

Addaf creeps closer, moonlight illuminating his face. I flinch at his hollowed cheeks and grayed skin. His reddish-gold hair no longer shines, hanging in greasy hanks.

"Would you like a story?" The man tilts his head, skull sharp underneath a thin scalp. "All children love a story."

"I'm not a child," I snap back, even though my voice wavers.

"I'm sure that's what you think, but your parents know otherwise."

I stay quiet at that mention of Iya and Bannu as Addaf comes to a stop in front of me. The Anyoto snarl behind him, but with one look from him, they stay where they are.

"When the dragon gods created our world, they created seven kingdoms, but they blessed the Kingdom of Kwa. They gave you the ability to use their magic, their power. And they gave the rest of us *nothing*." Addaf leans forward, and I flinch as some of his spittle flies through the air. "We have been left to fend for ourselves while still worshipping the dragons lest they forsake us."

"But the gods created us all."

"Yes, but not equally," he says, stroking his chin. His faded blue and brown eyes are feverish. "We have had to watch your lands prosper while ours withered. A blight manifested in Carew this last year." His voice cracks, but he tightens his mouth and continues. "A rot took hold of our crops, then our animals, and then our people. Many died, including my wife and my daughter."

I think of the brief sadness in his eyes when he came to our temple with the ọba, and I swallow past the lump in my throat. Jagun said his father had refused to help Carew. "The iyalawos didn't know," I start. "And although some can use idan to heal—"

"A chance," Addaf hisses as thunder booms above us, the sky crackling with the coming storm. "That's all they needed. As did hundreds who lost their lives." He taps long yellowed nails on the stain of his teeth as he looks down at me. "If we had been given the chance that Kwa was, the chance to use the dragon's powers, then more could have been saved."

I shake my head, trying to wrap my thoughts around what he is saying, all who have died.

"It was not us who made things this way," says Jagun, his voice strong.

"No. But it was your kingdom's decision not to let your priests and priestesses help anyone but your people. And it was the gods who chose to only give their power to you."

My mind reels. There was never enough of our pious to truly make a difference anywhere other than Kwa. That's what we'd always been told. But now, hearing of the sickness in Carew . . .

I wonder how much of this is true, wonder how naïve I might have been.

Addaf lifts a finger to me as clouds thicken above him. "That tear you hide away," he grits out, "is important in ways you don't even understand. Your route has been predictable, following Dam's favored flight ways." Addaf swivels his gaze to take in the other remaining guiamalas, Nox, and Zaye. "But I spent quite a long time separating the gods and freeing the emi buburu, and I will not have you meddling in any of this."

The dark shadows swirl around him as he lifts bone-thin

fingers. Darkness oozes from his pale palms as the air fills with faint moans. For a horrifying moment, I think I hear my name.

"The shadow spirits are the guardians of the underworld. We call their power—your idan—*hud,* and it can be gained from the dragons or the shadow spirits. Since Yida and Dam chose Kwa, I have no other choice but to call on the *tywyll duw,* the dark gods. They alone have offered to help me after Kwa would not." His voice falters. "They are the only way that I can bring my wife and daughter back."

"So you help the emi buburu reclaim the world," I try, the quaver in my voice strong. "And then what? Will you bring your family back to a place where the shadow spirits roam? Look at how much they are taking from you. They thrive on the idan in your soul, in anything living. They will only do the same to everything and everyone else. Consuming it all until there is nothing left."

But Addaf keeps smiling, flicking his left hand once, a guttural laugh escaping when the Anyoto leap forward, snarling through wide jaws as the spirits wrap them in their influence.

"I have already been consumed, but make no mistake, I am still in control. And with this hud, Carew will be restored. What happens in Kwa is none of my concern." He lifts his chin, paperlike skin draped on the bones of his face. "Just like we were none of yours."

The guiamalas jerk, prancing nervously as the Anyoto creep forward. Addaf lets both hands fall, and the shadow spirits stream toward the leopard creatures, seeping into them.

I cry out. Their limbs spasm in shock and panic, but it doesn't matter. Soon the spirits consume their souls until they have control of their bodies.

Nox's guiamala whinnies loudly, large hooves peppering the

earth in stamps as all around us the trees and bushes lose their color, crackling to an ash-dark charcoal. We can do nothing but watch as the forest rots and the Anyoto are possessed by the emi buburu. The creature that killed one of our mounts bares its teeth now, snarling as it rushes past Addaf, joining its brethren as the man stands still.

I watch as Zaye clutches at the saddle, Nox reaching behind him, fingers on her arm. I press a hand to Yida's tear and the daggers on my chest. Perhaps I could use the blades again, but I'd only be saving myself. Frustration spikes through me. I clench my teeth, a scream bubbling up my throat.

"You need to take the tear and go!" calls Nox. "We'll try and hold them off!"

I shake my head at his words. I won't leave them. I won't.

The rest of the Anyoto encircle us, gnashing their fangs, wrapped in the darkness that streams from Addaf's palms. One lunges at Bisi, great claws scraping her side. She lurches and moans, and Jagun and I scramble for the reins. My head pounds—I can hardly comprehend what is happening. Panic sears through my veins and I reach for the feel of Dam—

Until suddenly, I am drenched by the now-familiar cold sting of the dragon's idan pressing down from above. The iciness grows, chilling my skin. I let Jagun hold the reins alone, raising my palms to the shiver of the sky. Jagged power flows from the storm that has been building, and it calls to me . . .

I call to it.

In this moment, somehow I do not need Nox to show me how, and I reach for the flex of the tempest that is full of idan. I feel the water that is vapor, the thickness of the air, it all sings to me, and pulling it toward me is as natural as breathing. Sweat beads on my forehead, running in cold rivulets down my chest.

More Anyoto gather, crouched behind Addaf. Their eyes glow green before blackening with the dark gods' hud. They stand, triangular heads pointed at the sky.

Taking a breath, I strain harder, visualizing the clouds descending, imagining the idan cleaving through the creatures. As if in response, lightning strikes nearby, and I feel the energy pulsing, coursing through me. Despite the Anyoto and Addaf, a smile stretches across my face, open and wild.

One leopard being jumps up, snapping at Zaye's feet, before it pins its curved eyes on me, thin black lips lifting in a snarl. Its muscles tense. The rest of the Anyoto keep circling as Addaf watches.

Rather than fear now, I feel a calm flood me. A cold burn streaks across my palms as I raise them to the heavy sky again, feeling an arctic frisson reach back toward me. A glint of silver makes me look up at the dragon wrapped around my wrist. The tiny scales are glowing the color of an iced moon.

Dam chose me.

With that thought, I point my fingers, nails slashing at the sky as I scream to the storm. There is no doubt, no wondering if I am good enough.

Not this time.

Not now.

The tang of iron floods my mouth as the clouds descend. Fog swirls around us, and I bring my hands down, pulling with them the power of the sky. Another scream builds in my throat as idan courses through me, setting every nerve alight in cold fire. Sparks of lightning rain down by the guiamalas.

"Keep going!" I hear Jagun call out.

Ice weaves its way along the bones of my hands and arms,

but I continue to tug and pull at the breaking storm. Thunder presses down from above, the rumble reverberating in my bones.

And when it explodes, the sound pulsing around us, I feel the last of Dam's essence leave me. I gasp as my body collapses, and the trees and bushes burn, creating a tunnel of fire.

CHAPTER EIGHTEEN

"Mo? Moremi?"

Arms snake tighter around my waist, holding me in place on the saddle. I open my eyes to flaming, blackened branches, a crown of spent lightning that anoints the land. The smell of burning and blood fills my nostrils, and I retch once before a waterskin is pressed to my cracked lips.

"Drink."

I tip my head back, resting it against Jagun's chest as he pours more water into my mouth. A trickle escapes and I bring my hand up to wipe it away, the silver dragon on my wrist catching in the moon's radiance. Faint cold idan lingers in my veins, a memory of the power that coursed through me.

I shiver and push away from the warm arms holding me. "Where are the others?"

"There. See?" Jagun shifts away now, pointing to our left, where Nox and Zaye ride on the same guiamala. Suddenly, grief for Zaye's guiamala knocks me silent, and the gush of blood flashes through my mind. My stomach roils again.

"Addaf and the Anyoto?" The words are a rough scrape, but I manage them. "What happened?"

"You brought the storm to earth. The lightning set the land on fire, and we were able to get away." Jagun tucks the waterskin in a saddle pocket and eases me back against his chest. "Rest now."

I don't remember passing out again.

I wake to a sky sprayed with stars and a large, bulbous moon.

I'm no longer on the back of Bisi but lying in the folds of a blanket that smells of hay and guiamala. Dam's constellation is bright, hovering to the north, over the temples.

Immediately, I think of home and brace myself for the tears, my throat aching from screaming earlier.

Instead, anger fills me. Hot as coals. Cold as ice. It winds through me, overwhelming. I wonder if the Anyoto escaped the storm.

They don't deserve to. The thought comes to me in a whisper. *Didn't they allow Addaf to give them to the emi buburu? In that, they made their choice.*

Then I try to sit up but only manage to prop myself on my elbows. The muscles in my arms and shoulders shout in protest, the tips of my fingers still numb.

"You're awake, then," comes Zaye's voice, and I turn to find her and Nox looking down at me, frowning.

"I told you she'd be fine," Nox says.

I shut my eyes and let the anger seep away. There's a moment before I can bring myself to respond. "Where are we?"

"On the edges of the Great Plains," Nox says, his eyes skating over me. "A day from the sky monastery. Stay lying down."

"I'm fine." I get up, muscles screaming, white flashing at the corners of my vision.

"You channeled a storm." Nox clucks his tongue in annoyance. "Even my baba would need to recover from that."

Always telling me what to do, thinking he knows more than me. I ignore his pursed lips and flex my hands, looking round for Jagun. When I see him rooting around in Bisi's saddlebags, I relax slightly. He's not hovering over me; instead, he's showing his belief in my strength rather than doubt. Behind the prince, a small fire burns, and I can smell meat roasting. The flames draw me in, reminding me of Yida, of the promise I made in pledging myself to her, of the prayers I spent weeks and sometimes months learning. Of the temple and the lessons from Kakra and Panyin. That is what I need to focus on. The purity and intent for idan.

"I told you, I'm fine."

"You see this girl?" Zaye throws a hand up in a parody of annoyance, but I don't miss the tinge of relief in her tone.

"You need to rest a little more," says Nox.

I take a steadying breath. "We're off track, and we don't have time. I don't need to rest anymore, so stop trying to coddle me."

The smile slips from the boy's lips. "Better off track than dead," he retorts.

The anger roils in my chest, dark and righteous. "For you, maybe. Because Addaf might be willing to live in a world ruled by the emi buburu, but I am not." I frown at my own words, but I can't ignore the fact that time is slipping away. Glancing up at the god's stars again, I feel determination bubbling up in me. I can channel idan, really use it. First the way I opened the ground in the forest, and now controlling the storm. And once Dam sees Yida's tear, I can remind him of her grief, of their bond, of their need to be together.

Zaye sits back as Nox stomps away. "Look who woke up with joy in her heart and honeyed words on her tongue." But she's smiling at me. "We are not the Anyoto's dinner, and for that I give thanks to Yida. And to Moremi."

Her comment catches me off guard, and as I stare at her, I realize my mouth is open.

"I know." Zaye shifts closer to me. "I know we didn't really get on—"

I snort, unable to help myself. "What an understatement."

"But what you did back there, to save us, it was . . ." She pauses. "It was amazing. You channeled idan like it was nothing."

"Thank you. I think."

She laughs and I join her, enjoying the slight easing between us.

"Moremi . . ."

I take a deep breath. *Here we go.*

"While I think what you did was blessed by the gods, I want you to be careful. I . . . I'm worried."

"What?" Zaye, worried?

"You know I came to the temple an orphan. But you don't know why. Only your iya does." Zaye looks down at me through a glint of tears. "My father died when I was a baby. He was a trader, and he was set upon by robbers in a northern village."

"I—"

She holds a hand up. "Wait, I'm not done. And this isn't so you can feel sorry for me, by the way. I just want you to understand."

"I'm listening."

"My mother was a talented iyalawo, chosen by Yida."

"She wasn't in the temple? I would have known her," I croak.

"Will you ever shut up? You don't know everything."

I purse my lips. Good thing I am still weak from using idan. I lie back down and keep quiet.

"Thank you. As I was saying, she was a talented iyalawo and was placed in the village I was born in to see off a pestilence that took hold. She was strong. Strong enough to keep the people healthy. But her confidence and hunger for idan grew. She could not resist the call of the dragon, and so she used more and more of Yida's essence. Until her mind could no longer take it."

"Is that even possible?" I whisper. But deep down, I know she's right. Iya always said that learning to channel idan takes a toll. And the feel of the storm was something I have never felt before. Pure power. Iya never spoke of this, though, and I wonder why.

"Idan broke her, Moremi." Zaye hugs her knees now, looking away from me into the dark and the shadows that crouch around us. "It scorched her mind so that she did not want to live anymore. She killed herself when I was six. I . . . I wasn't there, and the villagers made sure that I didn't see." Zaye inhales deeply. "I was taken to the temple, and I knew that I wanted to continue her legacy in the right way, to follow in her footsteps but not make the same mistakes."

"Zaye, I am so sorry."

The girl looks down at me now, her face flickering in shadows and fire.

"I don't want you to make the same mistakes either. The dragons' idan is felt differently by people. It flows in you like no one else I've seen. And it scares me." She lays a hand on my arm, and I don't move. "Be careful. I know you're strong, but stay you; don't let the gods consume you."

"I won't. I—" But I don't get a chance to finish. The taste of metal fades from my mouth as a sudden wave of nausea rolls over me. "I think I might—"

I manage to turn my head to the left as vomit surges up. A hand rubs hard at my back while another keeps my braids from swinging into my face. I spit. And then suck in a deep breath as shame sweeps through me. I can feel Zaye's worried gaze, but I can't bring myself to look at her.

Her concern touches me, but idan whispers inside me that she doesn't know how it feels to wield this power. None of them do. I can control it. "Thank you." I wipe my mouth and spit again.

I don't say anything else, twisting my fingers so I won't have to see them shaking.

And I realize, as the nausea passes, that I'm no longer trembling from weakness; I'm not sick with fear or feeling spent. Because Iya didn't tell me about this other feeling. And Zaye didn't describe this part either.

I want more.

Looking up at the sky, I find myself disappointed to see just the spread of stars. I want the surge of power, the jolt of Dam's energy wound through the clouds, clear and razor-edged in lightning. I want the heat and burn of Yida. I want to feel the earth rip open underneath me.

But I keep this to myself. I press my lips together hard, trying to quell the ache in me. The need that winds through my bones...

It doesn't feel quite right.

There's a rustle from my other side as Jagun approaches. "How are you?" he says gently.

Nox glares at us, hands in fists. Jagun comes to a stop, the ends of his two plaits glinting in gold and silver. He has some star apples, their purple skins tight and shining.

"Eating might help settle your stomach."

I push the selfish need for the feel of power to the back of my thoughts.

"We're all hungry," says Zaye, plucking one from his hand and taking a huge bite.

Jagun says nothing, holding out the fruit to me. As I take it, our fingers brush, and my cheeks warm at the way he watches me. There is that tenderness he showed as he cradled me on the back of Bisi. I find it hard to look him in the face.

Focus on what you need right now, I tell myself. I lift the star apple to my mouth, biting into the sour flesh. We eat in silence for a moment, the night wrapped around us.

"So what do we do?" Zaye's eyes are large in the gloom, the fire flickering on her skin.

"We regroup," says Jagun, stretching out his arms as he finishes his fruit.

"And work out the quickest way to the sky monastery," Nox adds as he wanders over, as if not to be outdone.

"Well, the food should be cooked now." Jagun's gaze lingers on me. "I'm glad you're feeling better."

"I don't need to be told twice." Zaye stands, throwing a glance at the prince, an eyebrow raised. "Come, lazy girl."

"Are you just annoyed that you couldn't command a storm?" I brush down my wrapper and try a small smile. "I'm sure I can explain how."

She laughs at me, eyes crinkling into a real smile. I don't think I've taunted her back before, but it feels different now.

I feel different now.

Zaye links her arm through mine, and I let her, a little stiff with the shock of her actions. I bend my elbow as she settles her hand in the crook. She runs her fingers over the dragon scales seared into my skin.

"How did it feel?" Her voice is quiet for once, her tone reverent. "Channeling Dam's idan?"

I take my time to think of an answer, reliving the feel of the storm. "Like the sky pressed down on the earth because I told it to. Like the strength of the lightning lit up my blood. I felt like Dam was with me. Right there." I pause, struggling with how to explain the difference between the gods' idan.

Her grip on me tightens, and quickly I regret my words. Did I go too far?

But that was exactly how it felt. And now it feels as if some of that power is still in me. Shards of light and pressure and idan all mixed up in my blood, in my bones.

"I am happy"—Zaye glances at me before focusing on the fire ahead—"that one of us has been chosen. If not for you, today would have ended very differently." She squeezes my arm and I feel my shoulders relax.

"Thank you." I take her words for what I think they are, an apology. For the doubt she had. For the doubt she created about me, and in me.

Jagun makes his way past us, back toward the fire. "Here, Moremi, Zaye." He places some steaming meat on two large banana leaves.

"What is it?" I say.

"Rock rabbit." He grimaces. "It was all I could catch."

Zaye nudges me and I ignore her, my face heating as I disentangle my arm from hers and accept the food from the prince. He nods as he hides a smile, and I turn away quickly as I head toward a nearby tree stump.

Nox sits next to me and I offer him a strip of meat, but he shakes his head. He touches my chin, tipping my gaze up to his. "Are you all right?" His pupils dilate and I see him glance at my mouth.

I nod but grip the leaf, nearly dropping the food. Our kiss in the whirl of water seems so long ago. I'm not even sure if I'm the same person.

He lets go of me and stands. "Once we've caught our breath, we'll be able to work out a route."

I look around. The trees that ring us feel unfamiliar, and I realize I don't recognize the lay of the land at all.

We are hopelessly lost.

"We need to leave now," I say, familiar panic rising.

He looks down at me, eyes hooded in shadows. "I'm going to check on Zaye." His mouth opens and then he closes it as he scans the makeshift camp, eyes going to Jagun. "We need a bit of time, Mo. We can't all go at your pace."

I wince as he walks away. The dark seems deeper somehow, the shadows pressing against us. Even the flicker of flames fights against it, the moon above us a pale sickly yellow. I pause and listen. There are none of the usual sounds of night birds and animals waking or settling into the night, just an aching silence. Every living thing has fled or has been taken. I don't want to wait around either, even though I know Nox is right.

I watch as he collects some roasted meat before he reaches Zaye. She's staring into the fire, hands loosely held in her lap. Even from here I can see the weariness in her face. I pick at my food, guilt plucking at me, but the uneasy restlessness remains. The need to move, to do something.

Perhaps it's the remnants of idan in me. I take some deep breaths, trying to center myself.

Jagun approaches me with a waterskin as I finally begin to eat. He sits down next to me and rests his elbows on his knees. "Are you not tired?"

I shake my head, my braids swaying, then look up at the stars again.

Stars.

I sit up straighter, scanning the black blue of the sky, the whispers of my baba's teaching curling into my mind.

"We're not lost," I say, craning my neck to catch sight of the Stars' Path, the pathway made by the girl trying to get home when she was lost in the bush. I follow the bright spray right until I come to the herd of guiamala and two bulls chasing them. And there it is.

I point, my finger shaking with excitement. "There. The Crux. Those stars point south. Baba told me it was the reason the sky monastery had been built in that location, directly under the brightest one. We just have to follow it."

"So it is." Jagun sits close, almost too close, his arm touching mine as he gazes up at the silken expanse of a cloudless sky. "There are only a few hours left. We should tell the others."

I glance at the lump of sleeping guiamalas and Nox and Zaye, who have their eyes closed. "Let them rest a little longer," I say, my voice quiet.

I think about lying down, but my mind will not let up, full of dragons and shadows and idan. The earth feels warm beneath my feet as I stand. Too much energy twists in my blood. I want space. And I want to move. I caress the straps that hold the daggers, watching Jagun watch me. When I take out Yida's, his eyes gleam.

I feel"—I take out Dam's blade too, liking the way they both feel in my hands—"as if I need to do something or I'll burst."

Jagun chuckles and stands with me, the heat of his skin radiating from his chest. I swallow and look into his eyes. He doesn't move, returning my gaze before gesturing to the daggers.

"Would you let me show you how to use them?" the prince asks.

"Who says I don't already know how?"

We stare at each other for a beat and then I relax my shoulders. I can't afford to be proud, not now.

"Iyalawos learn how to heal . . . not this," I concede.

"You should know how to protect yourself. It's important." Jagun steps closer to me, half of his face in darkness, the rest a golden orange from the fire. "But I know that channeling the gods' essence can be hard on your mind and body. I don't want to push you more than you are comfortable with."

I step back and place both forefingers on the dagger hilts. His words are gentle, so different from Nox's forceful, confident tone. Fresh energy thrums through me, flowing to the blades in my hands. The dragon scales gleam in the moonlight as I lift them.

I pause, thinking, and then I flip Yida's dagger, holding it out to Jagun. He kept me safe when I burned the world around us. If that doesn't deserve some trust, then I don't know what does.

The boy stares at the blade, eyes widening. "You would give it to me?"

"For now. How can I truly learn if you don't have one?"

Jagun reaches out to take the dagger. "Thank you. For trusting me. Let's start with the parts of the weapon first, yes?"

I nod, Dam's cold dagger clutched in my hand.

"All right, then. Here, the top of the blade is the spine, which is the thickest part." Jagun slides his finger down Yida's dagger; his voice is soft. He has a scar on the top of his thumb, as if the end had been cut deep. I find myself wondering how he did it, who healed him. "All the way to the tip. This is important for stabbing at close quarters."

His finger trails down the blade, his voice low. "Just below the tip is the belly, used for slashing. The edge is underneath and is usually less sharp, which can help with blocking or catching an enemy's blade." His hand comes around the handle, closing around it firmly. I watch, my eyes never straying. "Both weapons have a full guard integrated into the handle so your grip won't move to the blade."

"Spine. Tip. Belly. Edge." I nod, concentrating on the shimmer of the scale fashioned into a deadly weapon. I *will* learn this. Just as I learned how to wield idan. Just as I will learn anything that helps me stop the emi buburu.

Jagun moves closer, musk and vanilla washing over me as

he taps the pommel. A smile steals across his lips. "This can be used as a blunt striking point."

"Got it." I force some firmness into my tone, hoping it will give me confidence.

"Knowing the names is only the beginning. Now it's all about teaching you to use the weapons. You want the blades to be level with your bent elbows." He touches my arms, carefully adjusting them as I tighten my grip on the hilt.

I tense as Jagun guides me through defensive stances and the angles and directions to launch an attack. He is patient and doesn't raise his voice once. The night still holds heat, but it is his next words that make me sweat.

"Now attack me."

I lift the blade and try to bounce on the balls of my feet in the way he just showed me.

"Now?"

"Now."

"But what if I hurt you?"

Jagun laughs. I glare at him, letting indignation fuel me as I lunge forward, bringing the blade through the humid air. The ọmọ ọba jumps backward, and I stagger, trying to find my balance as I whirl to face him.

When I strike again, I am met with the whoosh of his scent and the feel of him holding me from behind. He keeps my arms pinned by my sides as I pant, my back flush against the slick heat of his chest. The vibrations of Jagun's laugh reverberate against my spine as I bring Dam's dagger up and then down, slamming the pommel into the top of his right knee.

The boy grunts as he loosens his grip, and I wrench myself away, a huge grin splitting my face.

"Again," he says.

I relax into the crouch he showed me, Dam's scale in my right hand. Already the chill of idan seeps through the bone handle, and I twist my neck from side to side, feeling the cold spread up my arms. My feet are planted in the earth, toes tingling hot from a slice of Yida's idan. I smile. It's like I can feel the gods all the time now.

"Come at me," says the ọmọ ọba. And before he can finish speaking, I am lunging forward and bringing the blade up, its tip slashing at the still night air.

Jagun widens his eyes and then smiles back at me. "I can see you've learned quickly."

I don't answer. Yida's idan flows through my steps, tugging me in the direction of her blade, so that even when the moon is obscured, I can sense where the prince is. We whirl through the cooling night, trading blows where the daggers clash against one another, fire against ice. But this time, I feel the strength of them both.

Even though I rely on the basics he taught me, I hold my own. The steps feel easier, my feet guided by Yida's idan and my hands by Dam's. I leap away from a low slash from Jagun and then make the mistake of raising the dagger in triumph.

And then Jagun is in front of me, Yida's blade held against my throat, his other arm tight around my waist. I'm out of breath, my chest tight, sweat pooling against the folds of my wrapper.

"At least I lasted longer than before." I try to laugh, but Jagun's eyes are dark. Doubt splits me as I freeze in place. Have I been stupid to think that he would so easily join us? Has he waited for the others to be asleep before he takes what he wants and leaves?

I lift my chin. "Do it, then," I dare him.

Jagun shifts, pressing me against him as he lowers the dagger, still looking down at me. He could have run by now, but he hasn't. The shadows ripple over his face, but I watch his lips part just as he brings his face closer to mine.

"You are stronger than you realize," he whispers, his fingertips digging deeper into my waist.

Idan leaps in me at his words, its embers and glaze still in my bones. The power calls to me, pulling and tugging, willing me to give in.

I am stronger than I realize.

Jagun leans down, grazing his lips lightly across my mouth, and I stop breathing.

For a moment, I don't move, my head reeling as I realize that *this* was his intention instead, not slitting my throat. Then, slowly, I tip my head back, curving into his arm as his hands slide to the dip of my spine. My pulse is a thunder of blood, and madly, I wonder if he can feel the way my heart is beating, as if it will burst from my chest. If I hold myself carefully, I can also feel his, the frenetic pace of it.

He smells of musk and the faint tang of meat from dinner. I push against him, one hand clutching Dam's dagger, the other bunching the edge of his agbada into a tight knot. I can see the quick pulse of his heart in his neck, and I lose myself in the press and swirl of hot skin.

Maybe it would have been better if he tried to stab me, because this is a different kind of pain that I hadn't expected.

You can kiss him. The thought is there, pulsing with the idan. *You can do whatever you want. What is the point of so much power if you do not claim all you want?*

"Mo?"

At Nox's voice, I wrench back from Jagun. I veer toward the sound, a hand to my lips.

The night is still dark, wrapping the boy in the silk of shadows. But I don't need to see his face; I can tell what he's thinking by the way his shoulders angle forward, his silhouette hard.

CHAPTER NINETEEN

My mind goes back to the way Nox held me, the spin of water around us and the softness of his lips as they slid from mine. But then why did getting close to Jagun make me feel as if my blood was on fire?

"I only wanted to say that we should head out now." Nox steps into the dying light of the fire, turning his back. I see the swing of his tight fists and my stomach clenches with guilt. I ache to explain, even though I'm not sure what I would say. That I don't know whether I would have let Jagun kiss me? That my heart feels like it stutters whenever he looks at me? I don't know the answers myself. Besides, Nox is my friend. I am not betrothed to him. And I know he has kissed other people, the trader from the Kingdom of Alkebulan he told me about last year.

Nox goes to his guiamala, strapping the folded blanket on its back, tightening the padded leather buckles. He hears me behind him and stills.

"It's fine, Mo." But his voice is tight, breaking on my name, and I feel my eyes blur.

"You're my best friend," I say softly, and he scoffs, but I grab his hand and squeeze his fingers tightly. "You always have been, and you always will be."

"I know." Nox stares at me, his eyes flash across my face.

"Nothing has changed," I say, and the words are not a lie. I still feel the same about him. He's still the person I want to tell everything to, the person I trust above all others. Jagun makes me feel like someone brand-new, someone stronger and more capable, but I am still me too. "Nothing has changed between us."

"But it has. Back at the stream . . ." He lifts his hand to graze my cheek, and I blink. "What does it mean to you?"

I know that things have been shifting between us. The way my blood would almost sing when Nox was close to me, the small touches that felt as if they seared my skin. I know I've thought about him a lot for a while now. But I don't know how to put all of that into words that won't lock me into something that I'm not completely sure about yet.

"We kissed."

"And?" Nox steps back now, one eyebrow cocked. "Did it mean nothing?"

"Of course not!" I move with him now, wanting to touch him. "It meant something. But I don't know what you want from me. And now is not the time to find out." My words are whispered, the weight of them dragging my voice.

Nox opens his mouth to answer and then looks over my shoulder, snapping his mouth shut. There's the sound of someone clearing their throat.

A hand touches my arm briefly and I flinch.

"Don't," I tell Jagun, only looking at him long enough to snatch Yida's dagger, stuffing both weapons into their leather holders.

The prince holds his empty hands up. "You did well," he murmurs.

Something shifts in Nox's gaze. "She needs to learn how to channel Yida's idan." He moves toward me, his nostrils flaring. "She needs to learn prayers."

The ọmọ ọba looks down at the dragon coiled around my wrist. "It should be her choice what knowledge she chooses to pursue. Not yours. Granted, learning to channel idan will help. But that's twice the effort. And that takes years, right?" He looks from me to Nox. "Look, I'm not saying she's not strong enough to do that, but we all saw how she merged idan with the daggers with little effort. It is up to Moremi to decide what she wants and needs."

"What would you know about what Moremi needs? You've sat behind the gilded walls of the palace for your whole life, and now you're playing at being a soldier."

"I am here." I cross my arms and mutter, "Not that it seems to matter." They've been working their way toward this for days now.

"I know more than you, someone who has known her for years. What does that say?"

Nox narrows his eyes and lunges toward Jagun. There's a shove, and then the boys are grappling with one another in the glow of the fading fire, the last flames painting them in shades of red and orange.

"Stop!" I shout as a punch is thrown and Jagun's head rocks

sideways. He twists, bringing his own fist up, catching Nox in his stomach.

I push forward, planting myself between them, and a stray blow lands against my temple.

I crumple, palm pressed against the burst of pain, knees in the rough grass, head ringing. Hands are reaching for me—

When the burst of idan pulses from me in one jolt of power. Chest heaving, I try to control my breathing, to get the feel of idan under control. With a howl, I get to my feet, hands swinging in fists, the dragons on my ankle and arm flashing. Idan bubbles against my skin, snaking into my mind, straightening my spine so that I feel even taller, even stronger.

I will not have anyone telling me what I should and should not be doing.

"Enough!" I roar, molten rage sliding into ice and then back into an intense heat, consuming me.

There is a scorched silence as I come back to myself, the idan within me retreating.

But where did it come from?

"Moremi?" Zaye's voice is small as she crouches between the boys, who watch me warily.

I shake my head at them both, annoyance running through me at the sight of their wide-open eyes. How dare they look at me as if I am the monster?

I turn toward Bisi and swing myself up. "We're leaving," I say. Without another word, Zaye helps Jagun to her guiamala instead.

"Moremi . . ." Nox begins, but I hold a hand out. We will have to ride together.

"Get on. The only thing that is important is getting to the gods. We don't have any more time to waste."

The night lifts in shades of black and blue. Nox has not stopped trying to get me to talk, but when I continue to ignore him, he eventually accepts my silence.

At dawn, we still can't see the peaks of the Adamawa Mountains that house Kwa's oldest monasteries, and the brightest star of the Crux has faded. Instead, we are surrounded by giant iroko trees. The creatures of the forest can be heard in a cacophony of yips and rustles, and it gives me hope that the land here is not yet spoiled. Although when I see two quaggas, their flanks covered in faint stripes, stumble through the fresh light, the hope snakes away. They should not be here; they're only found on the Great Plains. When I listen more carefully, the yelps and calls sound like screams, and I wonder if it is the emi buburu the creatures are running from. Or if the shadow spirits have possessed predators other than the Anyoto. Using them to take more life.

No one has spoken, but the tension is taut, broken by Zaye.

"We're lost, aren't we?" She keeps her voice quiet, but I look to Nox and Jagun anyway and see that their expressions mirror the question's tone. "The god's stars will fade soon and we don't know which way to go."

I don't answer, anger strangling my words. She's right and it makes me furious. I glare away, studying the low bushes, the black of their roots and the tiny birds and ferrets that feed them with their bones.

"Moremi."

Now I look closer and see the speckled rot on the leaves, smell the tang of dead things decomposing. The death and destruction is spreading.

"Moremi!"

Nox is louder now, and I whirl to face him. "What?!"

"We can't just keep going without knowing *where* we're going."

I open my mouth to shout back at him, and then I feel a twist of cold. Idan. Tugging me from what feels like the northeast. A plan begins to form in my mind, feverish and ambitious.

"We can't, you're right," I answer. "Didn't you say it was hard to sense Dam himself, but it's not impossible, right?"

"I mean, it has been done. But there are so many unknowns, even for those who have been channeling his idan their whole lives." He shifts behind me. "Mo, even my father hasn't managed to do it."

"But it's something that can be done?" I sit taller on the back of Bisi, looking at the dragon on my wrist.

"Idan is often stronger where the gods have recently been, you know this. It could be done . . . if you can separate your sense of his idan from his essence, if that makes sense. But it's like separating rivers and streams from him; even the moisture in the air before it rains can throw you off. It's not exact at all. It's confusing, which is why it's never been used to locate or track him." I can sense him lean forward, though he's careful not to touch me. "It could throw us off course even more."

"Are you saying that I can't do it?" *The gods chose me,* is all I can think.

"No, of course not. And if you have to ask that, then you're being silly. Listen, earlier—"

"Then it's settled." I turn away, shutting him down and gesturing to Zaye, who nudges her guiamala closer to ours. "We're going to end up wandering around, getting even more lost, if I don't do something."

"I know." Her voice is tiny, so different from her usual. She's tired, slumping to the left in her saddle, kept in place by the bulk of Jagun.

"I'm going to try and use Dam's idan to follow the route he took, maybe even sense the god himself. If I can get a hold on his essence as well as his idan, then it'll guide us in the right direction."

Zaye frowns. She moves her hair, placing the braids over the delicate blade of her shoulder. "You can do that?"

I nod, thinking of all I've already done and the way idan flickers and flows at each of my thoughts. "I think so, anyway. Besides, we need to try something."

"Is there a chance that we'll be even more lost?" Jagun's question forces me to finally look at him properly. His forearms are bunched with muscles as he grips the reins tightly.

"Perhaps," I say carefully. I hold my hands out, frustration spilling from me. "But isn't it worth taking the chance? We don't have any other choices."

The others are silent, and an acidic rush of annoyance rises up in me. Have I not shown that I can feel idan? I look at the dragons on my skin and twist my neck, stretching.

"You can all stay here if you want." Idan pulses within me. *I don't need you anyway,* it whispers. "I understand how far you've come. How much it has cost you." I look into Jagun's eyes. "Even when this wasn't your choice."

"We can't go back," says Nox, his eyes unreadable.

"Agreed." Zaye clucks at her guiamala and moves closer. "Let's hope the gods were right in choosing you, Moremi."

"And you?" I finally bring myself to look at the ọmọ ọba. His brown eyes appear greener at this time in the morning, and I force myself to hold his gaze.

"I go where you all go." Jagun stares back and I swallow, my hands tightening on Bisi's reins. "That was decided a while ago."

"No one would think any less of you if you decided to return home." Nox's voice is strong and clear behind me.

"I've come too far. Besides, none of you are fighters," the prince answers, and I feel Nox stiffen. "And Kwa will be the kingdom I rule one day. I'm not my father. I'll do what's best for everyone."

I nod and turn Bisi toward the last part of the dying night now pinkened by the new day. Nox's lesson returns to me, and I raise my hand, fingers outstretched and bent ever so slightly. For a moment, there's nothing, just the warming breeze that whispers across my skin. My nails shine in the shaft of sun that washes over us.

And then a touch of frost chills my fingertips, spreading to my palm even when I drop my hand.

I smile.

"This way," I say.

CHAPTER TWENTY

I follow the cold crackle of idan into the heat of the day. Dam's razor chill cuts through the humidity, freezing my skin as I aim my face to a burning sky. With my eyes closed, my lids are lit up in a dazzle of orange, the metal taste sharp in my mouth as I guide Bisi in the direction of the dragon's essence. The more I feel for it now, the more it comes, almost as if I've opened up the gates to it and now there's no shutting them.

We don't speak as we head north, tall mangroves signaling a change in the land. Although I can sense the water, Dam's idan is different. Sharper and always tugging at me.

Time passes, and finally, I open my eyes. On the other guiamala, Zaye seems to have perked up. She raises her eyebrows when she sees me watching and offers a nod. Jagun, meanwhile, avoids my gaze, keeping his arms rigid as he holds the reins behind Zaye.

"Is it getting stronger?" Nox asks me.

I fight the urge to ignore him, to only think of idan. The

power is all I need. Ice pinches at my crown, threading around my arms. I shiver in answer, pointing to a large cluster of mangroves and the swamp that begins just before us. The stagnant pools of water flash in shades of green, their surfaces laced with moss. A wave of damp rot washes over us, and I hold back a gag, breathing through my nose. "Can you see the land beginning to rise just beyond?"

Nox shifts behind me, craning to look over my shoulder. His breath tickles my neck. From this angle, the peak of the mountain can be seen, almost eclipsed by clouds.

"It's just through the grove?" Jagun's voice is deep. He takes a sip from his waterskin before handing it to Zaye.

She takes a sip and sits up straighter. "So a few more hours, then."

"By nightfall," I promise, the words leaving my lips wrapped in hope. There is only one more day that Dam's stars will be aligned with Yida's stones. And then it will all be too late.

I push the worry away and focus on the crisp, bright idan that flexes again when I reach for it. The flow of the god's essence comes so easily now that I bask in the feeling, allowing the cold to push out everything else.

Nox clears his throat and I feel him tense behind me. "Mo, do you see that there?" He points to the thickening treeline, the exposed roots steeped in a water that reflects the sky. For a moment, I don't notice anything wrong. And then I see it.

The tallest tree shimmers in the sun, its leaves gilded gold and silver. It looks as if the precious metals have been threaded into the trees, giving them an ethereal glow. And spun in the sparkling midst: a nest woven out of gold and silver.

The izulu's home.

The "bird of heaven" is famous in the two temples and is the only creature created by both gods. Linking the sky to the earth with their power to control lightning, the izulus lay their eggs where it strikes. Not many people get to see one; the last ọba declared the bird sacred, a representative of the royal line that should not be disturbed. They are not naturally aggressive and only attack if their nests are threatened. We will be fine.

"Moremi . . ."

I clench Bisi's reins and try to swallow, my dry throat burning. The sky flickers as clouds scroll rapidly across the sun. I wave my hand at Nox, fingers slicing the air. Scanning the vegetation ahead, finding solace in the bright of the day.

"There are tales in Yida's scriptures about the bird's affinity for her, with iyalawos said to be more tolerated by the izulu."

"But the izulu is—"

"Shy. And a creature that is protective of its nest, nothing more, like all mothers," I say. The feel of Dam's power is there, lapping at my mind, drawing me on. "If we're not a danger to its nest, and we aren't, it will be fine. Besides, it's the fastest way."

Zaye looks at me, unease sliding across her face. "There might be more."

I know that the god will guide me, and the feeling gives me a calm that inspires the confident smile on my lips. "Look, if we skirt the entire part of the land where it's nesting, we add at least a day, if not two. And we can't afford to lose that amount of time. Kakra said she safely traveled through a whole colony in the southern forests."

Jagun studies the sheen of the giant bird's nest. There is no sign of the creature, but its wings could easily be folded into the surrounding foliage. "I don't like it. There must be another way."

I sit back on Bisi, my face burning with annoyance. *What does he know?* The idan within me sizzles, and I find myself frowning.

What does he know, indeed.

Who is he to question me, when *I'm* the one chosen by the gods? My skin itches, and I scratch at the hot flesh of my arms. "There is another way, but it doesn't guarantee getting us to the monastery in time. And did you all not agree to carry on just this morning?" I bite out, voice louder and lower now. "Or was I imagining that?"

No one replies. My fingertips tingle with ice as I slide from Bisi, landing in the shallows of the swamp. The bitter smell of the brown, still water is pungent as it soaks my ankles, brushing against the dragon on my skin. I don't look at any of them, letting my toes sink deep into the drenched earth. A sudden roil of heat surges up from beneath me. My head rocks backward and I feel my eyes roll at the pulse of idan. Cold from above and heat from below, the two meeting in a clash of power that has me shuddering.

I can feel both gods.

I am of them both.

The thought settles itself on my skin, burrowing deep, slinking past muscle, grazing bone, until it blends with my very essence.

I can do this alone.

A calm envelops me, and I step forward, body tight and thrumming with idan. "Stay here if you don't trust me. You will only slow me down." I turn round to look at them, unable to mask the contempt in my eyes. "And don't think I've forgotten that you didn't think I was capable of even getting us this far."

Their voices rise behind me, but I don't stop to listen. Gliding forward into the swamp, I let the gods' magic call to me, its essence lining my veins and lighting me up from within. As I reach for the idan, my eyes flicker in pleasure at the magic that runs through me.

With this power, I can do anything.

The sun falls on my face and shoulders in slices of heat while the water cools my soles. Yida's idan pulses, flexing and waning, ghostly trails of where she must have been a long time ago, but Dam's only grows, glacial slithers that guide me in the direction of the dragon and the sky monastery. I can make it there alone, and I will be the one to align the gods. Who else but one marked by both could do this?

I don't look back. There are splashes behind me, but I don't feel any pleasure knowing that the others are following. I think about telling them to stay where they are, but I let the idan be all I need. Each footstep crackles, my joints on fire and my skin chilled. I know that Dam has been this way, and I move faster now, pushing past bushes with their sticky fruits of waterberries and their spiked leaves. I pant, excitement zigzagging through me. All I can think of is getting to the monastery and showing Yida's tear to Dam. I ache for the sudden swoop of his wings, the way he will surely take to the glides and trails in the sky as he makes his way back to his wife.

And then all will be well.

All will be well.

All will be well.

"Moremi!"

I ignore Nox's call. He flips the reins, urging the guiamala to walk next to me.

"Just get back on Bisi! You don't need to walk!"

But I can feel the dragon god better here, the water whispering to me of scales and teeth and the promise of wings that will obliterate the sky. I shake my head and continue to push through the shallows, mud sucking at my feet.

I step over the roots of mangrove trees, ignoring the flashes of snakes with their green backs and white bellies. They hiss before slithering away, all yellow eyes and forked tongues. Nothing can harm me, I know, and I push on, push deeper into the swamp as the trees grow closer together.

I pause for a moment, blinking, slowly aware of where I am, Dam's crisp idan now flowing through me.

There is a thickening silence that wraps around me like the coils of a python. My chest tightens as I listen to the wrongness of no noise. I have been following the frozen ribbon of Dam, not really paying attention to where I am, intent only on the snap of his power.

I look up, the leaves like knives of gold and silver, their tips pointing down, ready to slice the land. Sunlight glitters through the leaves that hold up a nest spanning at least four trees. There is no sign of the izulu, and I smile.

I was right.

And now I will get to the monasteries in good time. I let the drag of the water slow me down. Behind me, I hear the guiamalas do the same, but my focus remains ahead.

The nest is a sight to behold. Gold and silver chains, offered in tribute to the gods by villagers, are woven among the branches, with a glowing yellow moss that iyalawos ha-call dragon's gold. A splinter of icy idan catches at me, and I wrench my gaze away from the canopy, moving to the left of the nest.

A sudden swath of cloud gulps at the blue of the sky. The heat rises, sucked above me as the hairs on my arms prickle. It is said the izulu's wings bring thunder, and as a rumble creeps in from the west, I know it is not a coincidence.

Ahead of us, I can see the marsh turning to grass and the gentle slopes of the green hills that will eventually lead to the Adamawa Mountains. The sight brings a flood of relief that mixes with the idan.

Then a distant screech stills me, my stomach clenching. I pick up my pace, the water eddying around my shins in brown swirls.

"Stay calm," I call to the others. "Remember, it is nothing more than a bird. A bird that will not attack unless provoked. It will sense we mean it no harm."

A groan comes from behind me, breaking me from my idan-soaked stupor. Dazed, I look back to see that the guiamalas have frozen in fear. Their black eyes roll, long jointed limbs now stationary stalks. Nox and Jagun jiggle the reins and kick against their great sides, but still the creatures do not move. Cannot move. I see Bisi thrash her head as the guiamalas plant their hooves firmly in the thick mud of the swamp.

I sigh, annoyed. I can't leave them behind even though the idan sings to me, calling me to keep going. Shaking my head, I wade back to them, grab Bisi's leather reins, and tug.

"Come." The creature lowers her head as I stroke her side. She moans quietly. "Come, Bisi."

I tug again, pleased when the guiamala takes a tiny step, her companion copying her. I snatch a look up and find Nox frowning and Zaye with her eyes shining. I know they're wary, can see it in the lines of their hunched shoulders and in the set of their mouths. Jagun glowers behind the girl, scanning the skies through the treetops. *Why do they not trust me?* The question makes me angry, and I yank Bisi along as I lead the guiamalas forward, the swamp stirring around us.

Another thud of thunder shakes the earth and sky as the izulu cries out somewhere above us.

"It is fine. We're moving away from the nest. It won't attack," I say over my shoulder.

I heave myself from the muddy shallows, clumps of grass soft under my soles. I reach out, calling for more of Dam's idan, needing to feel its ice to reassure myself that I have made the correct decision, aching to feel the flow of power. And then the sky pulses, as if it is the flexing skin of a drum. Thunder sounds again, closer now, almost right on top of us.

A feathered belly zips over the trees, red legs matching a curved beak that blazes crimson. Behind it streams a long tail the green-blue color of the ocean, its tip a burn of orange. The izulu opens its bill to screech again, black eyes on us as it lands on its gilded nest.

"Keep going," I say as calmly as possible. "Remember, we're not a threat, so don't act like it, and everything will be fine."

I edge backward, fluttering my hands at the others. But something in the stance of the bird, the dip of its head, makes me uneasy. The lightning bird continues to watch us, but now it unfurls its white wings, sparks of silver lining the edges, and as it tips forward, I see the ignition of its tail. The very last feather lights up the color of a vicious sunset as the bird lets out a screech.

We're on solid ground now, grass growing taller, but the izulu is still clearly agitated. With another loud shriek, it takes flight, swooping down toward us, trailing sparks of red. A few embers land on the grass, the dry stalks turning into small fires immediately even as the bird wheels away.

"What do we do?" asks Zaye.

Perched on her guiamala, she looks smaller and more vulnerable than I've ever seen her.

"It's just warning us," I say as the izulu soars back over its nest, black eyes shining as it splits open its beak.

"It's a warning because it's getting ready to attack," says Jagun.

I want to snap at him, but there's no mistaking the bird's intent as it rains down sparks of fire that float toward us. We're nowhere near it, so what's wrong with it? And then I see the black rot on the trunk of the tree next to the nest. I'd been right about the lightning bird and its behavior—it does only attack when it's threatened. I remember the cries of different animals, the quaggas as they slipped through the forest. There was a reason they were leaving. Somewhere, the forest is changing, and it must be spreading.

Guilt washes through me. I have been so focused on the power I've felt, I've only been thinking about what I believed I knew. I should have been paying more attention to the land and the creatures. I haven't because I've lost myself in the idan.

The dragon's essence has grown in a way that I both want and fear. When it flares through me, I can feel the yank of it, the way it changes me from the inside out. Iya often said that you can't seek to take without giving. Perhaps giving part of yourself to the gods is the price of using their magic. Perhaps once you give yourself over to the gods, you are never truly the same.

"Mo?" asks Zaye, her voice little. "What do we do?"

"We move. Now!" I turn and begin to run, hearing the pounding of hooves as Nox and Jagun urge the guiamalas to follow me. The fire spreads as the izulu circles us, more flames falling through the sky like red-hot rain, forcing the docile creatures to rush in a way that I can't.

I sprint now, putting my head down and pumping my arms and legs, dodging past the trunks of mangrove trees, leaping over roots that loop up and around before burrowing into the earth. Smoke rolls through the spaces between the trees as the foliage begins to burn. I cough, hacking with a wrist pressed against my mouth, teeth sliding on warm skin as I continue to run.

"Mo!" Nox leans down, his hand held out to me.

I shake my head. I know that he wants me to stop so that he can lift me onto Bisi, but it will only slow them down. The smoke creates a gloom, banishing the sun from the grove, but I still run, thinking of just the other night when I was blindfolded, speeding through the dark to find my way to Yida's stone henge. If I could do that, then I can do this.

And all at once the world explodes in silver, a loud crack splitting the air. I clap my hands to my ears, skidding to a stop in front of a giant mangrove tree cleaved in two shards. The ragged edges are wreathed in smoke from the lightning that has destroyed it. A deafening caw comes from above, and I look up, fear crashing in my chest, to see the izulu bearing down on us, its beak and large red claws sharp and sparking.

The bright white of lightning lines the bird's feathers as it soars back up, each beat of its wings generating bolts of pure energy that strike at the forest around us. More of the grass ignites, small fires that bloom like red-and-orange flowers. The sheer heat has me squinting, my chest heaving when I struggle to suck in air. In the thickening gloom, I don't see the fallen branch and it sends me sprawling. Stunned for a moment, I cough, fresh ashes at the back of my throat, as Nox and Bisi loom over me. His curls, once a frosted white, are now dark gray with soot, and he moves to get down, but I shake my head, struggling to my feet. Zaye and Jagun pause next to him, their eyes watering in the acrid air as they survey the ruin of the trees around us. Sparks dance in a slight breeze, spinning bright, and some land on the crown of the girl's braids. Jagun brushes them from her hair, the muscles in his jaw tensing.

"Follow me!" I shout.

The sooner we're away from the nest, the safer I hope we'll be. Surely the spooked izulu won't leave its territory?

I thrash through the forest, the need to get away growing stronger as I notice now that there are no animals, not even insects. Silence blankets the land and fills me with more unease. We have left the spitting fire of the izulu behind, but now I see more of what made it so aggressive. Withered bushes and tree trunks rotting from the inside out mar the green of our surroundings. The sky pushes down, heavy with bulbous clouds that look as if they are bloated with something worse than rain.

I keep running, with the thud of guiamala hooves behind

me, panic lacing my steps. I follow a ridge of land filled with dead bushes and the dry sway of grass, focused only on getting back to idan, back on track. And then I feel it. The icy course of Dam's magic. It plucks and then pulls at me, guiding me forward, urging me on. This is the way he came, the way we need to go.

Panting, I push through the spike of dead leaves and tall bushes, running so fast that I don't stop to think. My heartbeat is a steady thump in my ears, blood screaming as I take a giant leap forward and then stop, sole hovering over nothing but a crumble of land and air. I stare down at the sudden cliff and the twist of a fast river at the bottom. My foot slips on the lip of earth. I gulp and shuffle backward.

The land looks as if it has been shorn away, carved out and dropped into the water that rushes below. The drop feels unnatural to the landscape, like something has just reached up to claw the forest apart. As I teeter on the rim of loose soil and black tree roots, I look for Addaf. There is no sign of him, but what's happening must be because of the emi buburu. They are unpicking the very earth itself.

I draw in a hot breath just as the gallop of guiamala hooves grows louder behind me. Spinning around, I lift my hands up, a warning ready to spill from my mouth. But before I can release it, the guiamala carrying Zaye and Jagun is upon me. The creature hits me with a fling of its leg, and I am tossed to the side as it charges forward, plunging over the crag. A strangled scream rings out, and then nothing.

I roll away from the edge, dirt in my mouth and a scream in my throat, just as Nox throws himself from his guiamala as it charges on ahead blindly. And then he's rolling, leaning over the side, pulling at something, and shouting, but his words are only fuzzy blocks of sound as a dizziness smothers me. I should have been more careful. Instead, I stormed ahead, not properly reading the land, only intent on the feel of idan.

"... Mo. Mo? Help me!"

Crawling, I make my way closer, acid-sharp tears stinging my eyes. Hope is something I have always had, in my thoughts of mastering prayers, of my baba, of making Iya proud. I keep it close now, trying to calm the kick in my chest and the fear that coils tight deep in my belly. Nox is hanging over the precipice, grasping Jagun's hands, the muscles of their forearms bulging and tight. Below him, the river glistens cruelly between sheer black rocks.

As their grunts fill the air, Jagun locks eyes with me, and I lean over Nox, pulling at his arm to lift the prince. I can't help looking down, though, and a moan escapes me. The river is so far away that I know a fall is not survivable.

"Zaye?" I manage.

Nox shakes his head, and I bite the side of my mouth, tasting the sudden rush of blood.

"Pull!" he says through the grit of his teeth.

But even though I lean back, trying to use my weight, I see Jagun's hands slipping. I let go and move around Nox to hold the prince's arm from a different angle. Cold sweat slides down my forehead and into my eyes. It's only as I blink it away that I realize that Yida's tear is slipping from my wrapper. I look at the crystal orb, but still I don't let go.

Jagun sees too. And as the tear tumbles from the loosened fabric, he lets go of one of Nox's hands, snatching the pink crystal from the air as it falls free. My relief lasts for only a split second before Nox is pulled forward, the weight and unevenness dragging him closer to the edge. I reach down for Jagun's arm but it's too late. He holds the dragon's tear in a tight fist but his grip on Nox is compromised, and I watch in horror as the twist of their fingers slips and Jagun falls.

CHAPTER TWENTY-ONE

"We can still get to them," I rasp, tasting blood as my lips crack. "Somehow."

Nox pulls me away from the cliff's dark edges, half lifting me when I struggle.

"There's no way, Mo. They're gone." His words are split and ragged, and I shake my head, not wanting them even though I know they are true.

I press a hand to the sob that wants to be a scream. Swallow it despite its bitterness. Zaye warned me, and I didn't listen, bloated as I was on the gods' magic and confidence. I think of the idan crashing through my veins, the pulse of it in my bones, and the guilt washes over me. The gods' power made me feel that I could do anything, be anything. With their idan I could split the earth or call a storm, but the others were not me. I let my tears drip onto my chest. I've failed them. The old Moremi would never have dragged her friends through something so dangerous, risked their lives for the sake of being right, for the sake of magic and power and the feeling they bring. And now Zaye and Jagun are dead.

A cold lick of idan laps at my mind and anger explodes when I can't even push it away. It's a part of me now, always there. I sink back to the ground, lift my arms, and curl them around my head. Iyalawos heal; they do not kill.

Nox is speaking, and I feel the tug of his hands as he tries to get me to sit up. I ignore him, only trying to keep the idan out. But as it snakes through me in hot and cold pulses, the earth cooling around me, I know that I can't stop it. It's a part of me and there is no changing that. But if this is truly who I am now, then I will use it any way I have to.

When I finally sit up, Nox is watching me, his back against a speckled tree trunk.

He leans forward, taking my hand.

"I know you think this is all your fault, but it's not." His eyes are piercing as he squeezes my fingers. "Don't let this make you doubt yourself. I am here and I promise I always will be."

I try to smile through the blur of tears. His words are a balm to my mind and the thoughts that endlessly tumble around. My friends are gone and the shadow spirits are only growing stronger as they set about reclaiming the world. I gulp at the air, trying to get myself together. I can't change what has happened, and I can't change the idan that flows to and through me. But I can change what has damaged our lives. At least I can try. *Deal with what needs to be done first.* My mother's voice seeps into my mind.

"We don't have Yida's tear, but we will find a way." My voice is stronger than I feel. "But first, we need to honor Zaye and Jagun."

I brush my feet in a wide arc, clearing leaves and small

branches. When I start to move, I close my eyes and imagine the spin of Zaye when she danced, the determined flare in her eyes and the sharpness of her smile, softer recently as I got to know her. While we had only just begun to become friends, I feel the loss of the future, of what we might have become.

I pray for Jagun and I think of his kindness, his courage. The way he was so very gentle with me. I think of him reuniting with his iya, and I refuse to cry, to try to take that as a comfort. I summon all the good memories I have of them and send those down into the earth after their souls. We are born and we live and then we die. I sway and move, my feet patting the floor in repeating circles that mimic the cycle of life. And as I dance, Nox slow claps Dam's death prayer in the air above us, murmuring words of comfort for their souls.

The funeral prayers are always done this way, and when they are complete, my shoulders drop. Nox tugs on my arm, pulling me to him, my back tight against his chest. I feel his chin shake, bony on the top of my head, as I cry, the shiver of his own grief mixing with mine. I let my spine curve, head hanging, tears landing on the bunched muscle of my thighs and my stained wrapper. I trace a finger over the gold thread, the frayed ends catching on the ragged tip of my nail. Just a short while ago, I was only worried about Zaye saying something annoying to me, and whether I could keep up with night prayers. And now . . . I feel more furious tears gather, but I don't let them fall, not yet, not until this is all done.

"We follow Dam's idan still." I pull away from Nox now, scanning the forest behind us. "There will be a way through. The god will guide me, I trust in that. And once we get to the monastery, the babalawos may know what to do."

"I hope so," answers Nox as he takes my hand again and squeezes. "But we need to get there to find out."

"We'll have to risk the izulu again to pick up idan." I move back into the forest now, leaving the cliff and river behind us.

"Then that's what we'll do," Nox says, following me as I lead him from the dead trees wreathed in smoke. Images flicker on a loop in my mind, the roar of the fire, the chasm, Zaye as she disappeared, Jagun's eyes. *They are dead. They are dead.* I let the anger mix with idan, let it all keep me going, and as I walk, my nails ease between the strands of one of my braids, picking it apart. The crinkle of my hair tickles the side of my face as I move on to the next. I repeat the action over and over, letting the repetition carry me forward, letting a cloud of black settle over my shoulders and down to the dip of my back. The traditional way of letting down our hair after an iyalawo passes.

Nox catches my eye, and his hands rise to his own curls, hovering over the tips he so carefully whitened on the day of our initiations. He ruffles his hands through the coils, sending a scatter of ash and gray flakes onto his shoulders, removing his once-white tips the way that babalawos do after a death of anyone pious.

It does not ease the grief, but there is a certain peace in being able to show this respect.

We skirt the edges of the burnt and dying forest, and once we're nearly clear of its ruined canopy, the snowy peaks of the Adamawa Mountains emerge. The range edges the Kwa Kingdom, giving way only to the ocean. The tall ridges rise high into the sky, and I feel an ache for home. If I close my eyes and imagine, I can smell the gowé seeds, the fresh rice, and the salted eggs placed on Yida's altar. I can see Iya's smile as she prepares for evening prayer and hear the beat of women's soles on the warm stone of the hall.

The idan is thick now, glacial and raw as it lines my veins. We walk until the sun slides down the sky, until we reach the beginning of a stone path, only pausing to eat some waterberries. The sour tang of their juice is a welcome relief for my dry throat, and I palm the rest into my mouth, not caring when they slightly sting my cracked lips.

"We'll be there by nightfall," I say.

Nox nods and I don't speak again. As we head up the pass, I give in to the guilt that chases round and round my mind, wondering what would have happened if I had been paying attention to more than Dam's idan. I scratch at my arms and try to push the thoughts out of my head. There will be plenty of time to pick my actions apart, to grieve, after.

As we climb up the mountain pass, the air quickly cools around us.

What's more, Dam's idan grows with every step. Frosted needles and keen strands of ice drape my head and shoulders, pulling me on.

I look at Nox as my hands grow colder from both the altitude and the dragon's essence. And I break our silence. "Can you feel it?"

He nods, not able to hold back the relief that softens his expression. "I can. Dam must be there."

We both look up at the path as it coils higher. There are no trees or bushes now, only the occasional scrub of grass that stubbornly reaches for a dark blue sky shot through with ruby and orange. In the distance, a few white-speckled nundá cubs scuttle back into their rocky den. We are in the thick of the mountains, with the peaks rising to stab at the sun, and I shiver once, rubbing the tops of my arms.

As the track rounds the harsh slopes of the mountain, we are suddenly met with a sheer rise of rough rock. I stop, cold stone digging underfoot. "It ends here?" I ask, twisting back to look at Nox.

He steps around me and reaches up with a large hand, palming it across the cliff face. And I realize that what look like jagged cuts of stone are actually giant overlapping scales.

Now I can make out the stretch of colossal wings etched in stone. The gates rise into the sky, slabs of rock that look as if they've been hewn from the mountains themselves. Deep grooves line either side of the gates, swoops and swirls mimicking the clouds in the sky.

I reach out, nails clicking on the stone wall. The sky monastery was founded by the first babalawo, Baba Seun, and only accepts priests with exceptional gifts for sensing and channeling Dam's idan. They are often called upon by the ọba when needed for emergencies or important tasks, like when the flood of ten years ago threatened the central grassland villages. A fortress to protect the assets of Kwa. I wonder if Addaf would be able to penetrate such a place. With the emi buburu, he could.

Nox steps away from the gates. When he stands next to me, I move closer to his heat.

"They'll already know we're here," he says, almost to himself.

I don't ask how. Standing still next to each other, we wait.

I shiver again and Nox wraps his arm around me, pulling me to his side. Any lingering anger from earlier melts away, and I lean into him.

And then I see the sky.

Where the clouds just were, a riotous blush now creeps across the sky. Ripe mango, soft peach, deep blue, and a crisp emerald spiral above us. We crane our necks up, following the lazy turn of the bright cast as it curves round the mountain peaks.

Dam's sign.

Idan spills over me and ices my blood, snapping in keen ribbons through my veins. I step forward, pulled by the essence of the god. Hope blooms in the tightness of my chest. The dragon is here. We were *right*. I try not to think about Yida's tear. If we can get to him, there must be a way.

A sudden, loud crack rings through the air, and I freeze. The scrape of stone on stone shrieks, and we jump back as the gates shudder. Nox tightens his grip on my shoulders. My hands go to the daggers on my chest.

"Halt."

The words emanate from the gap in the gates. A figure drifts forward, wearing gray-and-blue robes mirroring a twilight sky. The priest holds his hands out toward us, diamond rings glittering, and as silver sparks flicker between his dark fingers, my mind flashes to the lightning in the forest.

"I've heard about such pious and powerful babalawos," whispers Nox. "They can hold the power from a storm in their very body."

I think of the split in the earth I created when we came across Addaf, and the squall I brought to earth to escape the Anyoto, and I still myself. I am powerful too. We wait as the man steps out from the gates. A white-tipped beard spreads down his chest, swaying from side to side as he strides toward us.

"The monastery is off-limits."

"We need to speak with someone immediately," Nox says, his words nearly running into one another.

The man laughs, full of scorn. "Return to your village and stop wasting my time." He turns, one broad shoulder draped in white fur with faint cream dots. The snow nundá is found only in the remotest parts of the mountains, and though slaying one is forbidden, once they are dead, their pelts can be worn by Dam's most worthy. You must be powerful to earn that right.

"We know Dam is here," I say quietly, ignoring Nox's cutting look. "We can feel him."

The man laughs again, a sour sound. Disgust unfurls in my belly, and I can still taste the ashes from the forest fire on my tongue. I don't care how much authority he holds—how dare he mock us? Idan crackles along the bones of my spine as I straighten.

He flutters a hand at me, his palms pale. "What would *you* know of the god? Him, maybe, but not you."

I take a step forward, anger flickering like the flames that nearly destroyed us. I've had too many people expect little from me. Idan swells inside me and I flex my fingers, swallowing the metal taste. Nox sees the flash in my eyes and steps in front of me before I can open my mouth.

"We need to speak to Baba Yaa. It's important. Can you tell him that my father, Baba Bannu, sent us?"

The monk doesn't smile. He takes a step back, arms stretching wide, holding on to both of the gates. The dismissive look on his face adds to my growing fury.

"Impossible. As I said, the monastery is currently off-limits."

Dam's idan courses through me like a cold blaze, and I crick my neck, welcoming the icy burn of it. My hands go to the daggers. As soon as my fingertips touch the scales from the dragon gods, a roaring fills my ears and a fire slides through me. I slip the blades free, calling on the jagged frisson of heat as well as the coil of frost. The blades' edges spark blue and red, and the monk's eyes widen.

I bare my teeth, my body ready. Reveling in the power bubbling up, fully taking hold.

We did not come here for this, lose Zaye and Jagun for this. To be turned away and treated like this. Too much has happened. Our world is at stake. Grief rises in me, the hot bitterness of it spilling over into outrage edged with a swelling pulse of idan. My hands curve around the hilts of the weapons, fingers tight. The gods' essence roars inside me.

I step forward. I could use the gods' blades to slice into this man's belly, teach him a lesson for his disrespect. I could cut the ears from his head. I could—

Nox wraps his arms around me and spins me to face him.

"What are you doing?" he hisses. "Put them away."

But the dragons' magic flows through me, and I feel it, heat and cold, fire and ice. I taste the now-familiar tang of cold water, metallic and fresh, the ashes that are sharp on the back of my tongue. "He doesn't deserve our respect," I seethe. "How dare he tell us who we can and can't see?"

"Mo, this is the monastery." Nox's tone is calm, but his eyes flicker over my face, as if he doesn't recognize me. "They are the most reverent and powerful of the babalawos. You know this." He pushes at my wrists, trying to lower my hands, but I don't move.

"He's daring to question us!" I spit, choking on the words when all I want to do is slit the priest wide open. "When we've done so much. Been through..."

And then I'm remembering everything all over again. The feeling of despair when Iya revealed what needed to be done, the eloko and their teeth, the fire and how it ate the forest. I swear I can feel the softness of Bisi's ears and see the smile on Zaye's face when I mastered the healing prayer. The chasm. Jagun and Zaye... gone. The idan calls to me and I grasp it, letting it burn, before I remember what happened the last time I gave in to the complete feel of it.

I don't want to lose myself again.

I sag, letting my stance weaken. I can't change any of it, but I can try to make some things right. My veins snap with idan, but it dies to a shimmer as tears spill down my cheeks. Nox is right. I sheathe the daggers, but my hands stay in fists, shoulders tight.

"What is this?" The monk's eyes are on my weapons. "You dare to threaten a pious babalawo of the monastery? We have more than enough to deal with without insolent children!"

I say nothing, power still rumbling within my veins, when he pulls at the gates. A slick of guilt spills inside me, and I hang my head, shoulders rounding. The gates shriek, stone on stone.

"No, don't! Wait, I can explain."

But the man snaps his fingers, summoning a gust of wind powerful enough to close the gates, before—

"Keep them open." The voice is deep, echoing through the pass.

Something in the bass of it speaks to me, but I can't see the babalawo who speaks. A shadowy figure approaches the slit of the open gates.

"Apologies," the first priest says, bowing his head. "I was about to come and inform you that they—"

"Enough, Baba Olu. Move so that I might see them for myself."

The monk who sneered at us backs away into the gloom, and a new man steps forward. His wrapper is the purple of a strong mountain storm, and both shoulders are draped in the white fur of snow nundás. As the man walks toward us, I see the wide planes of his cheekbones, a high forehead that gives way to thick frosted curls, and a strong chin dimpled in the center. The man emerges fully from the gates and stops, eyes widening as we stare at one another.

"Moremi?"

I blink, tears rippling my vision as I stumble forward. Nox grabs at my elbow, but he can't catch the swoop of joy and hope that spins through me.

"Baba?"

CHAPTER TWENTY-TWO

I have a favorite memory of my father. I must have been about five years old, just tall enough to reach his hip. In the recollection, he hoists me high into the night sky, my feet kicking against the breeze. Baba has taken me for a walk, a chance to be separate from the temples, where we are only father and daughter. A chance to be just . . . us.

"You see them? You see the stars?"

I laugh, joy bubbling up within me as I gaze at the glitter above us. "I do, Baba."

"Look carefully, little one. The spread of the sky always tells us a story. Whether it is when to plant our crops or how to navigate, they hold so much information. Information we can never ignore."

I remember lifting a pudgy hand, grasping at the soft folds of the night. "Which one is the most important, Baba?"

"Dam's stars," he answers straightaway. "Their appearance is the most celebrated because of what they mean to our kingdom."

The dragon's constellation. A symbol in the sky, for as long as the gods may be united to bless our lands.

Now Baba takes hold of my arms, gaze raking over me. His stare lingers on the mark on my ankle, and then the one that wraps about my wrist, a perfect match to his. For a moment, his spine straightens . . .

And then he is enfolding me in his arms, pressing my face against the fur on his shoulder. I can't help the sobs that spill out of me as I cling to Baba, feeling him drop a kiss on my head.

"What . . . ?" He looks down at me, frowning when he runs a hand over my freed curls. I see the worry flash across his face.

"It's not Iya," I say quickly, and he sighs, shoulders relaxing.

"I knew you would be here at some point. Come. Come inside, we have a lot to discuss."

We follow my father as he leads us through the stone gates before they scrape shut behind us. I shiver, taking in the monastery's central courtyard.

Open to the sky, the space stretches ahead, frost clinging to the rock walls that rise around us. Clouds drift across the dusk, turning from white to gray. Cold lights in iron sconces flicker, dispelling some of the gathering shadows, highlighting serpentine scales carved into the walls. Two enormous corridors stretch to the right and left, and I wonder which one leads to Dam. With each step, idan sings deep in my bones, chilling me from the outside in. My shoulders tremble at the force of it.

"Fetch them some furs," Baba says, and the monk who opened the gates to us scurries off. "And tell the Assembly I'll be there shortly."

I look up at Baba, questions blooming and dying on my

tongue. There are so many that I'm not sure where to start. But as I open my mouth to speak, I burst into tears once again.

"I'm sorry," I manage to gasp as Nox stands close. "It's just . . . I didn't think . . ."

"I know." Baba's voice is soft and deep as he drapes a fur of plush gray around my shoulders. "It is a lot to take in." He turns to the boy beside me and claps him on his back. "And you, Noxolo. Look how you have grown!"

The young priest holds his left wrist to show his respect.

"We . . . I . . . did not expect to see you again."

Baba throws his arms around our shoulders and steers us down the covered corridor. A tall archway opens on our right and my father leads us through it, heading toward a fire cradled in an enormous grate made of black stone. There are several chairs carved from bleached ash wood and arranged in a semicircle, gleaming in the firelight. At the end of the room, a large table takes up the space, scrolls spilling across its circular expanse. Everything else is bare and stark, plain stone walls and large floor tiles arranged in interlocking hexagons.

"Sit, sit." My father presses me into the chair and kneels beside me. Even then he must stoop to look in my eyes. I forgot just how tall he is. "I know you have questions, Moremi. And I will answer them. But after I attend the Assembly meeting. We've heard what happened with Ojaja and there have been reports of many changes. Even Dam's appearance here, though blessed, is concerning us all. The others will want to meet you, to see who has been allowed within our walls at such a crucial moment. I cannot put them off. This is already a grave breach of protocol."

"No," I say, tears rising despite the loudness of my tone. The ceiling stretches up high, and I feel small, swallowed in confusion and hurt and the expanse of this place. At times, I thought Baba was dead, and no one would talk to me about him. It's all too much. The failed Dírágónì ceremony, losing Zaye and Jagun, seeing my father.

I wipe at my wet cheeks roughly. "I've waited for years; surely they can wait a few minutes."

My father tries to put his arms around my shoulders, but I push him away, idan surging in me. I want to make the ground shake, crack the mountain open, and bring every storm down from the sky. The last threads of control threaten to unravel.

"Where have you even been? Here? Why didn't you send me any kind of message?" My voice rises to a wail as my vision blurs. Idan scribbles bright in my blood. "I want to know. Before anything else, I want to know why you left Iya. Why you left *me*."

There is silence as my father strokes his beard and measures his words.

"Moremi, you know that Ọba Ojaja banished me." Baba's words are soft with sadness. His tone calms the idan in me.

"I do. But I never knew if you were dead or not." I look up at him through the veil of black curls and tears. "How could you not let me know that you were alive?"

My father bends again so that he can look me in my eyes. "I am sorry, daughter. I am truly sorry. The Assembly let me stay here, but only if it was kept quiet in case the ọba would interfere. And your iya . . . I decided that it was best that I keep away. I didn't want her position to be compromised."

His arms wrap around me, but I can't stop the tears.

"I knew that you would be special, Moremi. And I knew that you would find me here." Baba pulls away now, his eyes shining as they skitter over my face. "I had visions all those years ago. Ones the ọba did not approve of. Ones in which the gods are brought together in one person—not in one kingdom and one people, as we are all taught to believe. But a new way of uniting the dragons, even though it would demand sacrifice and struggle."

Whose sacrifice? Whose struggle? I think of this new surge of idan but keep quiet, wanting to hear all he has to say first.

He turns over my wrist, running his forefinger over the dragon's scales. We both look down at my ankle, taking in the matching dragon seared into the skin there.

"The visions didn't show you, but it is beginning to make sense now. Dam arriving here only adds to the alignment."

"We know," says Nox.

"We both felt him. Is he still hurt?"

Baba holds my gaze for a moment, one corner of his lips rising in a half smile. "No. He took a little while to heal and now he's mostly angry. He still comes at dawn and accepts our prayers. He will do so until his constellations fade. And I knew that you would sense him. I will answer any other questions you have later, for now I need to let the monks know what I've always known—how special you truly are. They've been waiting." He squeezes my hand in his large grip and then stands, knees cracking. At the doorway, my father looks back for a long, stretched moment, something passing over his face, and then he sweeps from the room.

"Mo?" asks Nox, placing a hand on my back.

I don't say anything for a few moments, still turning over

in my mind the fact that Baba is here. "I'm all right. It's just . . . a lot."

He opens his mouth to say something else but thinks better of it and we sit in silence. We don't wait long before the door is thrown open, though, and monks pour into the room in a sudden rush of wrappers the shades of every kind of sky, all with ivory furs strewn across their shoulders. Baba stands in front of them, and it's now that I notice his beard has streaks of white amid the black, mirroring the curls at his temple.

"Moremi, Noxolo. This is the Assembly of the monastery."

The men behind him are even taller than the villagers of Akyem, and white swirling marks adorn the varying browns of their skin. All regard us with hopeful expressions before they nod, almost as one, grasping their wrists. Nox returns the gesture, nudging me slightly with his elbow. After a pause, I do the same, and pleasure floods through me at the shock in the men's faces. I see them look at Dam's mark on my wrist, his tail flicking at the crook of my elbow.

"So it is true. You were right." A monk as tall as my father makes his way to Baba's side. His eyes are dark, his lids heavy. "I don't know how this is possible, but the girl is one of Dam's chosen."

There's something in the way he says this, and the others' reactions, that irks me. Did they expect less of me because I am a girl? I lift my chin. Let them be even more scandalized, then. I shift my leg so the mark on the joint between my calf and foot can be seen. "And Yida's."

I feel their gazes crawl over me and then several audible gasps as the dragon that twines around my ankle is sighted. There's an explosion of raised voices as the men turn to my father, questions layered over shouts of indignation, awe, and anger. I take a step back as Nox places his hand on my spine.

"Stay close to me," he murmurs.

But my hands go to the daggers on my chest, more than a flex of idan, there if I need. They comfort me, and for a moment, I think of Jagun, the dance of blades and balance that he taught me, and then I force it away. I glance at my father. Baba lets the Assembly shout, his eyes only on mine, a smile curving his lips. He steps forward.

"Enough!" The voices die immediately as he swivels slowly to face them all, but indignation still stains the air. "When I first sought refuge here, I told you the gods would become one and be worshipped accordingly. And you listened. When I promised you the answers to your questions, you were patient in my belief. And now my daughter has arrived, proof of all I have been preaching. Chosen by both gods."

"Really?" I can't see who asked the question and it doesn't matter, I know they're all thinking the same thing. "How is this even possible?"

"I do not know why you are so shocked. This is what I prophesied. What we have been waiting for."

"You did not say that it would be through a child! And a girl child at that."

I bristle, standing taller, trying to catch the glare on my face before it turns into a scowl and proves the disbelieving monks right in their scorn.

"That aside, what about today?" a man calls from the back. "All that we have learned?"

I glance at Nox. Is it the same as what we came to tell them? He widens his eyes but says nothing.

"Dam has spoken in our communion with him," the man

continues, his eyes like beetles, his stare as cold as the wind that escapes through the slitted windows above. "He is . . . angry and agitated. That the ọba would disrespect the gods has changed everything. Why still remains to be seen, but we have sent messengers to the villages and the palace to ascertain—"

"Ọba Ojaja did more than attempt to unite the gods at the Dírágóni ceremony," I interrupt, my words carrying around the room. "He released the emi buburu."

"Rumors, surely?"

"There were signs from the villagers, and we have felt this in our prayers."

"The god was injured; this must be why."

The cries echo around us until my father shushes them once again, allowing me to explain Addaf's manipulation of the king. There is a brittle silence as the men swallow my words. I can tell by their lined and creased faces that they are finally taking me seriously.

As they mutter furiously, I know they're thinking about how they will lose the gods' essence, and the chaos the shadow spirits will bring, the dark thoughts, the wars, the death. A swirl of nausea makes me lightheaded, and I press a finger to my temple.

I clear my throat and step forward, standing before the Assembly. I've never been in front of so many people of a higher rank than me, but now I let my gaze swing over them, lifting my chin and keeping my shoulders back.

"I hope you all realize that it's not just idan that we will lose," I say, my voice growing so that it can be heard over the grumbles and exclamations of the men. "The ọba was tricked. He said the prayer he thought would unite them, but instead it has invited in the emi buburu. They've been taking life from the people and the land and infecting minds ever since."

"The shadow spirits?" scoffs a man with tiny eyes, his short eyebrows knitted tightly. "How do we know that the girl speaks the truth? They have not been seen in our world since the gods remade it."

"We cannot ignore the signs we have been receiving," says Baba. "I've relayed to you the pleas from the farmers outside the Kakum Forest."

"A blight—"

"More than a blight!" roars my father. "And you know it!"

"An ambassador from Carew convinced Ojaja." My voice grows now, as does my impatience. The ins and outs do not matter. "And he will not stop until the gods cannot reunite, and the emi buburu will be unstoppable."

"But why?" cries out a babalawo at the front. "Why would he be so foolish?"

I glance at the windows set high in the stone walls. The monastery is a fortress, but it doesn't make me rest any easier. "You need to post guards."

The room is thick with silence as the monks gape at me. And then they explode in riotous anger and fear. Baba steps between us, holding his large hands with pale palms up, his eyes shaded with sadness.

"She is right. It is not just idan. Unless the gods are brought together as they should be, the emi buburu will finish what they have already started and bring an end to everything we know, everything we hold dear, everything we hold sacred."

The room erupts in murmurs and hisses about the shadow spirits.

"There is a way," I say, but my voice is swallowed by the cacophony of voices that continues to rise. I clear my throat and try again. "I said, there is a way."

Baba comes to stand by my side, his arm around my waist. "Let my daughter speak."

The men quiet, faces tight with anger and panic, and my heart flips with nerves. But I push them away, taking strength in the two dragons etched into my skin and the relics strapped across my chest.

"We must send Dam to Yida." My voice quavers but I force it louder. "The gods do not need us in the way we need them, but they created us. Let us rely on their love for us. Let us remind them of why they share their idan. Let us prove ourselves. There is still time to unite them, and then they will be able to fulfill their cleansing at the Dírágóni ceremony like they've always done, ridding the lands of the emi buburu."

The monk who had opened the gates steps forward, his lip curling. "And how would you do that? You can't force a god to do anything. No one can. Perhaps they will decide to leave us, after such disrespect. The signs are there, they know what is happening, and still they do not intervene."

"I have been informed that Yida is in her inner sanctum at the monastery," Baba reassures them. "It can be done."

His words bring me relief, and I find that I am missing the strength of the goddess's idan, the burn of it.

"We need to remind them of what they created; we need to remind them of what they promised to do as our gods." My voice cracks on the last word. "We need to find a way to bring them together as they should be, to bear witness to our worship and cleanse the world."

Nerves jangle as I think of Yida's tear. I look down at my feet quickly, heat flushing across my chest. There is a way, *was* a way, but the tear is gone. Eneh said they can be united by one who symbolizes them both. There *must* be a way for me to do it.

Baba raises a hand to my shoulder and squeezes. "I know how that can be done." Every gaze snaps to him. "But first, I need to speak with Nox and my daughter. Alone."

The Assembly members begin to talk again, their voices overlapping, but my father raises his hands, and they fall silent. "You have placed your trust in me before. All I ask of you is to do it once more."

There are grumbles, but the complaints die down and the men slowly back out of the room. My father moves to stand in front of the fire, the glow licking at his back as he says nothing, his brow furrowed.

"Everything will become clear," Baba says, breathing in deeply as he turns to face Nox. "There is another way to take Dam back to Yida. And it involves you."

The boy's eyebrows fly up as his hands go to his chest. "Me?"

"Yes. Legendary scriptures say that a new priest is still connected to Dam for a few days after being marked. Because of this, he can offer himself to the god, and if Dam accepts, then the priest can communicate directly with him."

Nox frowns. "But how?"

"The new priest must show his mark to Dam and press it against his scales. It's just a matter of getting you to the dragon so that you can attempt the bonding."

"Attempt?" I ask as my father grasps Nox's arm. "What do you mean?"

Baba looks up at the ceiling and strokes his beard, and we follow his gaze. Clouds and swirls of sky adorn the highest part of the room. I imagine flashes of silver scales, the slink of a tail. I shiver as a flash of want for the dragon's idan streaks through me.

"The scriptures warn of a risk to the new babalawo, which is why it has never been attempted. And there is a chance the dragon god may refuse the priest. Most think this will happen if the period between initiation and bonding is too long. Which means there is only a short space of time to influence Dam. And if he does accept, it is believed that being bonded—though one of holiest things a priest can do—may cause a . . . severing of the young man."

"What do you mean, a severing? What happens to the babalawo afterward?" My voice is quiet. I think about Zaye's mother. My father's face is drawn, and he looks at Nox apologetically. "Say it," I whisper.

"To join your mind with a god is something that doesn't just change you. It can swallow you whole." Baba looks between us, his mouth turned down and his hands twined together in front of him. "You might not truly return to the person you were beforehand. The mind of a god is so much greater than ours. And it's thought that its base instinct is to consume."

"No," I say, anger rising as Nox squares his shoulders. I hold one finger in the air before he can open his mouth. "There must be another way."

"Mo . . ."

"No. No. Just . . . no." I'm not losing anyone else. I blink furiously and wipe at my cheeks.

Baba bows his head at Nox. "Regardless, you must come to

your decision by morning. There is only one day left with the stars in alignment with the stones." My father gathers himself, adjusting one of the white furs on his shoulders. "I must tell the Assembly what needs to be done." His face softens. "Moremi, I will find you after."

But I don't watch him leave. Right now, I only have eyes for Nox.

"I'm going to do it." Nox bobs his head, nodding to himself. "I am. We've come all this way, and my baba, and Zaye . . ." The boy shuts his eyes and stops speaking for a moment. He takes a deep breath. "If it's the only way to get Dam back to Yida, then I'll do it."

"No, you won't." I grab his hands, idan sparking in our grip. "I'm not letting you."

"You can't tell me what to do, Mo." Nox links his fingers through mine. "I know you're scared—"

"I'm not scared. It's stupid," I spit, my chest heaving. "There must be another way."

"There's no time. You know this."

I stare up at Nox, the boy I have known all my life. He was the only one to listen to me speak about my baba when I was little, the only one to not judge him. Nox sneaked me the sky temple's sweet honey cakes and comforted me when I couldn't get my prayers right. He tested my herbal mixtures and oils, sang my praises when they were effective.

I think of his face when Jagun held me. And still, he has not given up on me. Nox has always wanted what's best for me. There's no one who knows me better, not even my mother. He's always been there. And I trust that he always will be.

In the firelight, I let my gaze drift to his lips, remembering how soft they were when he kissed me in the whirl of water, the way Dam's idan sparkled between us when we channeled it together. What if he bonds with the god and he is never the same?

When Nox brings his face down to mine, I stand on tiptoes to meet him.

"Please . . ." I whisper as his lips brush over mine.

"Please what?" he murmurs.

"Don't do this." My stomach clenches at the thought of him giving himself to Dam. My mind spins, searching for another way, but it comes up empty.

There must be another way. There may be no other way. I swallow. "Nox, I—"

He stops my words with his mouth.

The kiss is different from our first. There's no tentativeness, just the press of urgency as our teeth clash and we wrap our arms around one another. I lean my head back, caught in the cushion of his mouth as Nox pulls away a little, feathering kisses on the edge of my mouth.

I think of the promise he made to be there with me no matter what. I can do the same for him. I *will* do the same for him.

"I'm not going to ignore the fact that Dam chose me." The boy looks down at me and gives me a tiny smile. "But remember, I choose you too, and I'm not going anywhere."

CHAPTER TWENTY-THREE

Baba gathers us to eat with the Assembly, leading us deeper into the monastery to a hall that is filled with tables of cod fish, rice, fufu, and pale boiled corn. Moonlight falls through the slice of windows set high in the ceiling, while fires burn in four grates around the room, lending a strange mix of white and orange to the light. I can't help twisting my hands in my lap, fingertips sharp with idan.

Dam burns through me, an icy scald, constant since we arrived at the gates. He chills my veins and clears my mind, even as frustration beats in my chest. What is the point of this power if I can't use it to get what I want?

Baba sits to my right, Nox to my left, with three other members of the Assembly at our table. My father leads a short prayer of thanks before any of the food is touched, his large hands clapping in a familiar pattern.

There are only small murmurs as the monks eat, scooping the yam into open mouths and stripping the fillets of their bones with nimble fingers. I look away from the man who opened the gate for us as he pops a milky fish eye into his mouth. I've only managed to eat a small bowl of rice and a few spoonfuls of white bean stew. At Baba's urging, I pick up some corn and nibble, but the same thought goes through my mind.

I won't lose Nox.

I place the corn back onto my platter as pale light splashes on the skin of my wrist. Dam's scales flash in the night glow as another tug of idan pulses through my chest. And then I think back to what my father said before, about a fresh babalawo being bound with the dragon.

I twist my wrist, watching the miniature scales gleam. It wasn't through the initiation, but Dam did choose me. What if I can do it? What if I can bind myself to him and take him to Yida?

The idea grows in my mind. I remember the flex of Yida's and Dam's idan, and a slither of hunger in me grows. If it felt so magnificent just to channel their essence, what must it be like to connect fully with a god?

I cast a glance at Nox. I don't need to sacrifice anyone else I care for.

Water is poured into small silver cups until the food has been eaten, and then flagons of palm wine are brought out. As I pick at my bowl of plain rice, the monks visibly relax around us as they sip at the wine. They believe Nox will attempt to offer himself to Dam. No one would even think to stop me.

None of them assume I have what it takes.

As the dinner comes to an end, the men file out of the hall, each moving past Nox and offering him their slapped prayers, palms brought together to show their respect.

"I'll return as soon as our invocations are done," Baba says, guiding me from my chair. "You will sleep in my rooms.

Rest. Nox and I will take the collective dormitory. We can rise with the day and help him prepare. Let me show you the way."

"Thank you, Baba," I murmur, my yawn only slightly feigned.

Nox leans down so that he can look into my eyes, one hand on my waist while my father's back is turned. "We can end this. *I* can end this," he says quietly. "I'll see you before the ceremony?"

"I'll be there," I answer. Technically, I am not lying.

"Come, Moremi." Baba opens his arms wide as he walks backward, his leather sandals scuffing the cold stone. "Tell me as much as you can of what I have missed in the last few years."

"Over ten years," I correct him as he leads me through the wide hallways of rough-hewn stone.

I tell him of life in the temple, leaving out some parts that I'm not quite ready to speak about, but Baba's face still looks downcast by the time we reach his rooms.

"We will have more time to spend together when all this is done," he says, as if reading my mind. "But tell me, how is your mother?"

I think of Iya's pain at his leaving, the way it stayed in the quietness of her words and the lines in her face for years. "She's led the temple well and steered the ọba in ways only she can."

Baba smiles at the words, but I know he's noticing that I do not tell him how sad she was, how much shame she felt. We step inside his rooms, and I'm quiet as I take in the surroundings that my father has called home for so many years without his family. A fire is burning in the grate, and the walls are adorned with silk hangings. On them, images of Dam and Yida swoop and open their great jaws in silent roars, their scales in rich threads that sparkle in the hues of the earth and sky.

"The sky monastery lets you have both gods here?" Before

Baba left, he had struggled with splitting his time between duties at the sky temple and visiting me and my mother. At least here, he has a home where he can be himself.

"They know what I believe. Now look up," says Baba.

I gasp when I do. There is no ceiling, only an open expanse of sky flooded with stars. Baba puts his arm around my shoulders, and I lean into the comfort of him, tears prickling at my eyes. He even smells the same, of the herbs from his pipe and the strong mint tea he favors. Again, I am overwhelmed as we stare up at the night sky together.

After some time, my father sits down by the fire, gesturing for me to join him. "I may have left the temple, but I have not given up my devotion to Dam." When he reaches for my hand, I see the flash of his own mark. "I would never forsake being chosen. But I know there is more. And this too is something you feel."

I don't need to answer. The marks on my wrist and ankle do it for me.

"I wanted to reach out to you and your iya," Baba says quietly. "But I didn't want Ojaja to take anything out on either of you. Moremi, I am so glad you found me. I knew you would." His eyes slide to the daggers against my chest and he smiles. "I had a vision of Dam telling me to leave the blade in Akyem. And I was right. It was obviously meant for you. How did you come by the other one?"

I think of Jagun, and the words are dry in my throat. I cough, unable to help patting Yida's dagger.

"Nox took it from the ọmọ ọba."

Baba nods. "Be careful with the power they will give you. It needs to be used wisely."

I think back to the eloko's crunch of teeth and reel with a pitch of nausea. "I will."

"Have you been able to channel idan? I know you won't have had the teachings yet, but—"

"I have." My words are abrupt, and briefly, I think of telling Baba what the gods' essence does to me . . .

But being able to wield so much idan still feels unnatural. Wrong. I keep the knowledge to myself.

"I want to hear more about it when all this is done." My father smiles, proud, and then yawns. "Perhaps I can even teach you a few prayers?"

"I'd like that," I answer as I take hold of his hand, brushing his knuckles, slightly swollen now, the veins thick and soft. He is older than I remember him being, and my heart pulses with another wave of grief over time lost.

"We should both get some sleep," Baba says, and gestures to his sleeping mat arranged on goatskins, piled high with blue woven blankets and gray n'dama furs. "I will come and fetch you just before dawn."

I think of what I'm about to do, and my heart rises in my throat.

He bends down to kiss my forehead, and I reach up, closing my eyes and inhaling deeply. I want to remember all of him.

Just in case, something whispers in my mind as I watch him leave me once more.

When the moon disappears from above me and I'm sure that enough time has passed, I push the blankets from my lap and creep toward the door of Baba's rooms. The floor is freezing, and I wrap a pale gray n'dama fur around my shoulders. When I reach the wide corridor, I turn right, drawn by a slash of frosty idan.

My heart is pounding in my ears, so I pause to calm myself before carrying on, my fingers trailing along the corridor wall; the stone is damp, almost as if the mountain is crying. The sconces flicker, the scent of oil heavy in the thinning night as I look around to make sure that I'm alone.

I walk quickly to the prayer hall, the corridor sloping upward and ending at a set of doors of bleached wood that shines brightly in the gloom. They are heavy, as tall as the high ceiling, and I'm forced to yank and tug at them. I flinch as they scape open, my nerves fizzing along with idan at the resounding screech.

I'm standing on the threshold of a room ablaze with light from the moon, the marble floor glistening like a sky cleansed by a powerful storm. The prayer space is phosphorescent in its beauty, open to a star-studded night.

Although it is different from Yida's temple, burrowed deep in the earth, the hall brings forth evocations of peace and hope, all gifts offered to the god. In the center is an altar of luminous marble. Silver bowls of rice and corn are placed around the base, a quiet dazzle of pale food.

The doors close behind me, and I swing my gaze around, looking for something that shows how I can reach the heavens. The space is vast and there are no shadow-filled recesses hiding anything. And then I realize a ladder is in plain sight.

The altar. Stretching up like a bone-white spine, it's centered on the marble dais, and as I draw closer, I can see the notches on the dragon statue's vertebrae. Hand- and footholds.

I press my lips together, unable to stop the quickening of my pulse.

It's so high.

I take a deep breath, weaving my hair into a hasty plait. I'm going to show the monks of the Assembly that I am chosen by Dam. That my father's visions are true. That I am worthy.

The altar steps are a smooth cold, the grooves larger than my hands, made for the tall babalawos. When I get halfway up, the fur slips from my shoulders, and I instinctively grab for it. My grip slides, my nerves prickle, and sweat streams from my temples as the pelt drops to the altar.

The strong snap of idan pushes me on, sparks radiating across my crown and shoulders. Dam is here, I know it, his essence so palpable that my tongue feels as if it is coated in iron, every swallow a reminder of the god. My arms shake from the effort and icy air, but I keep going, keep moving without looking down.

I reach the sky as it begins to snow, blotting my face with ice as delicate as lace. I pull myself over the lip of the prayer hall ceiling and lie on my back. All I can do for a while is breathe, my chest rising and falling in high crests, as I try to relax the shaking of my muscles. When I feel like my heart has stopped pounding as much, I sit up and look around me.

The peak of the mountain rises just above a ring of clouds. The crag I am on is the tallest in the Adamawa range, charcoal rock blanketed with snow. I know that somewhere below us is the smallest peak, which houses Yida's monastery, but I can't see it through the snow and clouds.

No matter. Dam will find it.

I roll onto my knees and stand as the wind throws my curls across my face. Pink and peach seep into the sky, the promise of the approaching morning. I snatch a glance behind me, trying to calculate how long I have before the babalawos make the same climb to give their prayers and witness Nox offer himself to Dam.

The plinth is just ahead of me. A large rock with gouges that matches the god's claws. The perch is on the edge of the peak, rising from a bank of snow. Clouds wrap around it, giving it the appearance of floating in the sky. It is massive.

I lick my cold lips nervously as the sun continues to creep up from behind the rock, turning the blue black a lighter hue. Where is Dam? Baba said the dragon god makes his way here at dawn, but he is nowhere in sight.

Shivering, bile rising, I spin around in a panic. Until a beating in the air makes me freeze.

Gusts of snow billow around me as I blink away the small ice crystals forming on my eyelashes. My body shakes as idan flows through me like cold lava.

The god descends from clouds, and I try to stay still, hands stinging with the intense wind, my lips quivering as the dragon's wings stretch across the fading moon. He swoops toward the plinth, claws extended, and when he lands, it is with a shudder that shifts snow, revealing more of the mountain beneath us.

His beauty is still a shock, and I can't take my eyes from the iridescent gleam of his scales. Dam flexes his head to the sky, spines glittering like a crown made from ice as he folds his enormous wings against his sides.

He swings his great head toward me, and I hold my breath as silvered eyes lock onto mine. The god tilts his head to one side, and I know this is when I need to make my plea.

As I walk across the snow, I'm unable to feel my feet. The

rush of idan numbs my nerves, and I know I am meant to be here in this moment.

I know.

The dragon regards me, nostrils flaring in great plumes that dissipate into the fading night. When I stand before him, the mark on my wrist glows.

I raise my arm, hand trembling, fingers fluttering in the thin light. There's a shout from behind me, but I don't turn. Dam does not move, and I'm close enough to see the slivers of teeth that protrude from his lips. Close enough to see the sheen of his scales, each one a different gradation of white, silver, and faint pale blue. There is no fear now, no worries, just a cold void. Idan washes through me, taking it all away, leaving me with a certainty of what I am about to do. A flick in the corner of my eye, and I see his tail twist before it wraps around him and encircles me.

Baba's warning fills my mind, of how the babalawo might lose who they are. But after everything that has happened, the girl I was before is already lost.

There is no other choice.

I lift the mark of Dam up as the god bends down, offering me the porcelain gleam of chest. I swallow, hope and fear flickering together, and then press my mark against the great dragon.

CHAPTER TWENTY-FOUR

There is an explosion of white.

My mouth fills with saliva as my head is thrown back, my arm yanked forward. Bursts of silver slice through my vision as I blink, trying to see past the energy. The mark on my inner arm burns with a cold fire. I want to open my mouth to scream, but I can't move my lips, can't muster any sound. Wind screams around us, picking up the snow that falls faster and heavier now as the dawn burns brighter. The dragon bends his head to mine and splits open his jaws. Teeth graze the curls that have escaped from my rough braid, and for a moment, I think that he will reach down and swallow me in one bite.

Iya, I tried, I think, hoping that even though she is far away, my thoughts will somehow find her. *I love you.* I think of Zaye and Jagun and Nox. Of Baba. If it is my time now, then I am grateful for all I have had.

I close my eyes.

But Dam's teeth do not clamp around my flesh. Instead, he releases a delicate stream of idan that wraps around me, and I open my eyes as sounds and clicks invade my mind. I jerk my head in the smallest of movements, the taste of iron fresh on my tongue. *Breathe,* I think, and as I calm, the sounds twist and separate, turning into words that reverberate in my thoughts.

I marked you the other day. You spoke to me in a way no other has. The god pauses, blinking silver eyes at me, his voice thundering and clear. *If you are bound to me, this will be forever. Do you agree to this?*

I think of my father's warning. The mention of a person losing their sanity to a dragon. He also said any binding would be temporary, but my mind is made up. Better me than Nox. And better this than the destruction of our world by the emi buburu.

"Yes," I whisper, thinking of Yida and my pledge to her as one of her new iyalawos. What if the binding affects my sense of her idan? *The goddess will understand,* I tell myself. I hope.

Then so be it.

Lightning splits a thunder-broken sky as Dam opens his mouth and roars. The snow thickens and my spine jerks straight as the dragon's essence falls on me, a crackle that sinks into my skin and hair until all I can feel is a stinging bite of cold. The world opens in a way I didn't think possible.

The whirl of snow slows so that each flake is a delicate filigree, dancing slowly around us. My eyelids flutter as the wind scrapes at my skin. The blades of the dragon scales press against my chest, strapped tight, their hilts digging into my flesh. Behind me, there are tiny thuds, people climbing the ladder, their small cries constricted with panic. The wind is a wild howl, but I can also hear the soft shift of snow and the way it scuffs over rock.

The dragon's breath spreads over me like clinging fog, his

idan filling me as a scream blooms once again at the back of my throat. I can feel everything, see everything, hear everything.

It's too much, everything is too much. My eyes roll up as my mind blacks.

Then, from behind closed eyes—a burst of stars, explosions of yellow and red and green. Two dragons swoop across it all, twining together as one before they plummet toward a small star—

The flicker of dark spirits as the gods claim the new world. They spew their god fire over the shadows—

Dam flies low over an ocean while his wife burrows through the earth, throwing up hills and mountains—

A stream of stars and stones arranged beneath them, signs from the gods that they need to be as one—

Figures that jerk to life as idan flows over them, eyes opening and mouths curving as they regard the gods that have given them life, given them souls—

The founding of the temples. Yida's deep in the mountain and her husband's at the very top. The first Dírágónì ceremony. The pounding of feet and the smack of hands as the gods are worshipped for their gift of life and idan. The dragons circling the world as they cleanse it each time they are united—

Rage at the summoning of the emi buburu and the incomplete ceremony. The separation of the gods in their hurt and fury. The dragons' distance stretching their bond. The seep of shadow spirits from Addaf—

Yida's tear glowing the same shade as a summer dawn. Brown hands cradling the crystal, and inside—

Dam snaps his jaws shut, and my wrist is released from his chest as I cry out at the last image, sucking in air and scrabbling at my stomach. The god closes his eyes and turns his head from me as a swell of nausea rises, and I heave onto the rock beneath me. How could I have not known, not guessed? Wonder and horror cut across the image the god has shown me.

"Yida needs you," I gasp. "We need you both together."

Your kind did not need me when it suited them to try and change the way of things. To call on those that we banished.

I cringe as I think of Ojaja's selfish act, one that has endangered us all. And then I think of why Addaf has been following us, wanting the tear, and now I think I know why.

We are not the most important ones.

I am not the most important one.

"I understand your anger, your fury. But please, come with me to Yida and let me help repair what has been done."

You will make this right?

"I will," I promise. "I will."

Dam snorts once, plumes of white air spiraling into the newly born day.

We shall see. You are weakened from the bonding. We will leave when you are rested and ready. But do not be long.

The god closes his silver eyes and tucks his great head beneath a large pale wing, and I am left in a world blanketed in white that cannot keep out the angry shouts echoing behind me.

Turning my head, I see Nox and Baba charging toward me and, behind them, the monks of the Assembly scrambling from the altar ladder one by one.

"Mo?" Nox's hands slide underneath my armpits, lifting me up, his glare sharp. "What have you done?"

I don't have the energy to answer. Isn't it obvious? But then I see my father's gaze as he studies me, his eyes wide with wonder and knowing.

"You are bound to Dam," says Baba. He holds my face in

his hands and kisses my forehead. "I knew you would take your own path."

My shivering wanes and I lean backward, the idan still spiking inside me, and decline the furs Nox offers. Though I can still feel Dam's essence, I am not cold.

"I did what needed to be done." I look up into the anger that thins Nox's lips into a line, but I don't let his hurt stop me from pushing my shoulders back. "And you know that I wouldn't have risked you."

I look at the dragon crouched before us, at the spines on his great head. There are no words for what he showed me, the birth of our world, of us, and what is to come if we are to keep the emi buburu at bay.

"I need to eat for my strength. And then we leave."

Baba rushes into his rooms carrying a platter of rice and shredded roasted chicken, with several of the Assembly members behind him.

Nox hasn't spoken to me, and his hunched shoulders as he angles away from me tell me all I need to know. But I'm not sure how much I truly care. Even now, I can sense Dam. It's like more idan than I've ever felt, a constant humming sharpness inside me. A calmness has replaced the panic.

I will make things right.

There is no going back.

Being bound to a god has not changed the fact that my body is still mortal, and I am ravenous. I scoop up the rice and chicken with my right hand, cram the food into my mouth, and barely chew before swallowing.

Baba stands with the monks, talking quietly, but I can hear their hissed questions. They wanted it to be Nox. I sense it in their tones, can feel the weight of their stares. I finish the last of my food before turning to face them all fully.

The men suddenly hush, gripping their cups of water, but they don't soften their gazes, and a burst of fury at their disrespect rips through me. How many of them would risk losing themselves to a god? And how many of them would be accepted by Dam?

I flick my hands upward. Their cups jump, jerking in the air as I pull the water from them, directing it into each of the men's faces. Their mouths work as they splutter and try to speak.

"Say anything else and it will not be only your water that is thrown around." I take a step toward them, my hands curled, idan prickling the tips. "Dam accepted me, allowed me to be bound to him. You chose to give my father refuge and listen to his prophecies, yet you won't recognize them when they are fulfilled. Why? Because it is not a way you would have chosen?" I throw my head back, my laugh deep and rough. "I will not ask you for your respect. You will give it."

My gaze sears the hall, and the Assembly members lower their heads almost as one. Baba nods at me once before he ushers the men from the room, leaving me with Nox.

The boy's face is flat, mouth a disappointed slash. But whether that feeling is for me or him, I can't tell. I suck in a deep breath, pick up a bowl, and fill it with food.

"Eat."

Nox takes it but doesn't look at me directly. His shoulders are rounded, and the slouched line of his body speaks of displeasure. "Will you use your idan on me if I don't do as you say?"

I sag at his words, the sudden rage of earlier fading. "I . . ."

But I can't quite think of what to say to make any of this all right. I'm not sorry for binding myself to the dragon.

Nox puts the bowl down on the table with a crack. "You don't get to make decisions for me, Mo. It was my choice to make. Not yours."

"So you can make decisions for me, but I can't do the same? You've always looked out for me; why can't it be the other way around for once?"

He growls in frustration, throwing up his hands. "Because I've always been there for you. For whatever you needed, even if it was only help with finding your herbs. I was there for you when you struggled. With your father gone, with prayers and the expectations of your iya. But I never made choices for you. And I don't need you to do that for me."

I recoil, his words a slap. Because he's right. I did what I did because I wanted to look after him, but he doesn't need it. He doesn't need me.

I curl one hand around my stomach as I step through a shaft of light that beams into the room from the opening above. There are no more words. Not right now. I can feel the pull of Dam from above, but I don't give in to it, my emotions swirling over the power. "I only did what I thought . . ."

"This is exactly the problem. *You* thought. Why didn't you discuss this with me?"

I open my mouth and then shut it, teeth clicking. *I don't need to discuss this with anyone.* The stubborn thought spins and flares in my mind, but I don't want to antagonize Nox any more than my actions already have.

I throw my hands up and a whirl of papers rises. I can feel

my chest hitching as I take deep breaths to calm myself. "What was I supposed to do? Let you give yourself to Dam?"

"Yes!"

"But what if you'd been consumed?" I pause. "What if . . . what if I had lost you?"

"And what if I had lost *you*?" Nox lifts his hands to his curls, tugging on them. "Why would it be all right for me to experience that and not you?"

I deflate, my annoyance melting away. My hands uncurl as I reach out to him, fingertips skimming air when I lose my courage and let them drop. I look at my feet, still the same, still big. Nox brings me back to the girl I used to be. The girl who got excited over lemon balm, the girl who would sit up all night to see the stars just to be reminded of her baba. I thought if I became more powerful, people would be proud of me, but all I've done is take that feeling away from myself.

So much for being bound to a god.

"I'm sorry," I say quietly.

Silence stretches until Nox sighs. "It's done now."

I stare at him, hope creeping in as he looks at me with new eyes. The glare is gone, but in its place is a mix of something else. Some sadness. But also some of the boy's light that I've always known. The force of the god dragon's essence has filled me with more than I've ever felt, but I don't want it to ever dilute the feeling I have for those important to me.

Nox cocks his head to one side as he stares at me. "How do you feel? What did Dam . . . do to you?"

I think of the force of the dragon's power, the power that Nox craves, that he feels I have stolen from him. Yet still, I can't bring myself to feel regret.

"It feels... like when we wielded the idan for the first time, but magnify that by... by..." I throw my arms out, thinking of the snow falling, its delicate crush-petal sound when it floated down and settled on the rock. "As if I'm about to explode from it. Everything is sharper, clearer. *More.*"

I close my eyes briefly, remembering the images Dam showed me. I linger on the last one, the one of Yida's tear, my throat tightening. I'm not mentioning it to anyone until I know what should be done.

"Did it hurt?"

"No." But I wonder what it means for the goddess's idan. Will I still be able to sense her? Will I still be able to wield her heat? The thought of its absence hollows me out, leaving uncertainty.

We need to find Yida by this evening. My chest tightens when I realize that I've been so focused on getting Dam to his wife that I haven't fully considered what our plan will be. I know I need to unite them with the ceremonial prayer, and the best way to do that is for the god to coax Yida from the earth. I can only think of one way to get us there in time, and even then, I'm not sure if the dragon will listen.

But I will soon find out.

CHAPTER TWENTY-FIVE

When I go back to the ladder, I think only of the dragon, waiting.

I don't bother to look at the Assembly members' faces as I glide through their ranks. I hear murmurs and the smacking of hands as the emi buburu's name is hissed. Nox told me the Kakum Forest is dead now, that great cracks in the land have opened, taking animals and people with them. The monks have seen it from their perch, and they are truly scared. Scared enough to finally trust me and bless me with their prayers as the world is eaten around them.

Baba stands at the foot of the ladder, his arms laden with furs and wraps of leather. "You might not need this, Moremi, but Nox will freeze otherwise. We will make our way down with the monastery's n'damas. Not as fast as Dam, but we'll be there."

"Thank you, Baba."

The sight of Nox wrapping the leathers around his exposed skin is strange, and I blink as he then drapes himself with fur.

Or perhaps it is strange that I can no longer feel the frost of the mountain.

"You aren't cold?" Nox asks.

I pause, trying to find the right words. "I feel it, but it doesn't affect me, if that makes sense. I only feel the idan. Like . . . it's part of me."

Baba backs away, his eyes shining as he looks at me. "Remember, daughter, it is all in you. All of it."

The sky grows as I emerge from the temple roof, and my pulse eases at the giant body of Dam still crouched on the edge of the mountain peak. A veil of snow dusts the rise and fall of his great body, and I take a step, ice crunching under my bare feet as the world around us shimmers. The dragon flexes, shaking himself and uncurling his neck so that he stands tall above the peak, stretching out his wings, and the opalescent beauty of his scales snatches away my breath.

Dam lowers his head toward me in greeting, rippling in shades of ice and snow and cloud.

"We're ready," I say, my breath a plume of white smoke. Beside me, Nox doesn't speak, blinking rapidly.

We are bound and therefore I said I would take you to make things right. Not anyone else.

I reach behind me to hold the boy's hand, pulling him alongside me so that we climb the last steps to the god together. "You did. And just like you are pledged to Yida, we are pledged to one another."

Dam rears over us, the spines on his head fanning around him as he glares. He snorts once, blowing my hair around my shoulders as I hold still and do not give in to the temptation of flinching. Nox squeezes my fingers.

I can sense it in you. But he is not the only one you are pledged to.

I narrow my eyes.

You may lie to yourself, little iyalawo, but you cannot lie to me.

I say nothing. Jagun's face floats into my mind, his plaits, the dimple in his chin. But then I remember that he is gone. As well as Zaye. And a curl of anger unfurls inside me, blooming along with the idan there.

"That is not for me to explain to you. Will you carry us both?"

The god unclenches his claws from the plinth and drags them along the rock as he takes a giant step closer. I swallow hard, not letting my gaze leave his even though my hands shake.

I will. Just as I promised. Him too. But whether he survives the journey is your concern, not mine.

The dragon lowers himself so that his belly scrapes at the snow and rock, flattening his wings out and tilting them backward.

Gods are not made to be ridden like some of the creatures we created, but I will make an exception for you, little iyalawo. Where my spine and neck meet, there is a natural dip that will cradle you. Make your way there now.

Tentatively, I reach forward, my fingers sliding on the scales of the dragon. Another rush of idan, and I let the essence sink inside me as I climb up the joints of his leg.

"How will we stay on?"

You will see.

I hoist myself closer to the ridges of the dragon's thick spine, spotting the large hollow he described. Trembling, I slide into it. Nox swings himself up behind me more easily. The opening of the prayer hall looks tiny from the back of Dam, and I force myself to breathe evenly.

Then the dragon shifts, and the mark on my arm flares a brilliant silver, matching the god's back, locking against his scales.

I look back and the same has happened to Nox, his arm clamped to Dam's side, keeping him in place. He wraps his other arm around my waist.

"Just hold on!" I say, panic lifting my words as I squeeze my knees tighter around the massive vertebra, its sharpness digging into my thighs. But I'm still not prepared. Dam rises from his crouch, milky wings flexing wide on either side of us. I close my eyes briefly as the dragon's body jolts beneath us. The god lifts his wings up, and on their first downward stroke, he jumps, claws scraping on rock, and we are launched into the air.

I let out a shrill scream of sudden joy as Dam undulates his body, beating his wings faster to find the currents that will carry his weight. The skies around us are plaited with his symbol, coils of lemon and purple, twists of green, and ribbons of orange as the dragon swoops through them all, leaving behind a riot of color that hangs over the monastery. Nox's fingers pinch at my waist as he clamps his legs around me.

Below, the peak falls away, and as we skim to our right, I look over my shoulder at the brown grassland that yields to the now-desiccated Kakum Forest. I think of Zaye and Jagun again. Grief cuts into me like a blade.

"They've returned to the gods," says Nox, his voice firm behind me.

I don't answer, feeling the tear that escapes turn to ice on my cheek.

Cold wind whistles past us as Dam flies over the Adamawa Mountains. All we can do is to cling onto Dam's spine, our marks helping to keep us in place. I dare to dip my head, scanning the canopy for signs of Addaf, but I can't see any dead rot from the emi buburu. Yet.

Before long, the mountain that holds the earth monastery comes into view, the sky only just tipping into blush and coral. I scan the peak as we bank to our left, flying closer. Perhaps Yida will sense Dam and emerge herself. I don't let myself worry about the invocation; I know that it will come.

Though there is still the lingering question of the tear. At this thought, my stomach spasms. What if Addaf somehow found it? The images Dam showed me flash through my mind, and I have to force the panic away, my hands going to the familiar lines of the daggers. The flow of idan from the blades pulses hot and cold, and I take a shaky, steadying breath.

The dragon points his giant head downward, flattening his silver wings, and picks up speed as he rushes to the earth. I think that we will crash into the jagged rocks, but the god jerks to the side at the last moment and lands on the rough plateau that stretches across the lower peak.

Dam's colors stain the sky above, a natural announcement for anyone to see. I sit still, gathering myself, but there is neither the red gold of Addaf's hair nor the slink of shadows. The dragon mark on my arm dulls, releasing me from the god's back, and I slip down the side of his body as he crouches. A moment later, Nox lands next to me with a thump, blinking rapidly. I take his icy hands in mine. Sun glistens on the scattering of snow, throwing reflected rays as I massage his fingers gently. Though there is no movement around us, unease remains in my stomach.

"I need to get inside the earth monastery," I say, recalling

Baba's assurance that the goddess is in there. But I can't feel anything.

A flash of anxiety ripples through me. What if being bound to Dam has changed my ability to sense Yida?

"I'm going to ask your wife to come," I say to the dragon, turning to face the silver slits in his black eyes. "Please don't go anywhere. I need her to feel your presence. To come to you."

The dragon snorts once, plumes of steam with a shimmer of idan. *I will wait.*

I clap twice in a pattern of thanks that I've always seen Nox and his father do, cold palms brought together in hesitant smacks. Even though I've grown up with Dam's worshippers, I can only hope I've done it right.

The dragon lowers his head once and lets out a gentler breath. His crown of ice-colored spines glints as he opens his jaws in what looks like a semblance of a grin.

A twist of sudden breeze whips my hair across my face, and I pull Nox toward a crooked pathway that curls around the side of the peak to the base. We run, our feet skimming over dark rock and stones.

A wide-open space surrounds the base of the peak, with an archway carved into the rock. Coils of scales are etched carefully into the stone, their ripple catching the light. The earth monastery. I exhale in relief, running my eyes over the small gray doors of ash wood bound with scrambling vines, before I sense it around us.

A storm is coming.

Dark purple clouds scud across the sun, enveloping the morning in an unnatural gloom.

We hear them before we see them. The hard slap of sandals echoing around the mountain as the guards run up the pass.

Nox looks behind us, back up to the plateau, but I know that we don't have enough time to make it.

"We're not running," I say, placing my hands on the hilts of the dragon daggers, drawing them from their soft leather sheaths. The blades hum as I hold them by my sides, legs apart as I fall into a shallow crouch.

Then the ọba's men run into sight and skid to a stop behind us. The guard in the lead is taller than the rest, his double plaits snaking over both shoulders, brown eyes rimmed with green raking across my face.

"Moremi," says Jagun, as if my name is both a blessing and a curse.

CHAPTER TWENTY-SIX

I stare at the prince, and my first thought is, *He's alive.*

I want to rush to him, throw my arms around his neck, but I stop myself. Jagun may be alive, but he also had Yida's tear. And now he's here with the ọba's guards.

"Stay back," I snarl, daggers raised.

The soldiers behind him swarm, filling the narrow path. Snow swirls through the air, topping the white curls of Dam's followers and settling on the braids of Yida's, and again, I feel fury rise up. To see those who pledge allegiance to the gods turning against those who worship them too . . .

"Wait!" Jagun's order stops the men in their tracks.

"Moremi, I can explain." The boy moves away from the guards behind him, both hands held out. "The fall injured me. I was in shock when I hit the river. I tried to find a way back to you. But . . . I was hurt and you were gone."

I remember the steep cliff, the choking black smoke, and the haze of trees obscuring direction as well as vision.

The terror coiling alongside the burn and chill of the gods' idan.

"I swear, I tried to find you." Jagun's eyes latch onto mine as he lifts a hand toward me, and I remember how he held my waist when we rode Bisi. How he kept me safe after the Anyoto.

"Not very hard." Nox steps closer to me, a sneer on his face. He curls his hand into mine. "You thought only of yourself. Just like your father."

Jagun's lips press together as he shakes his head. "I'm nothing like him—"

"Yet here you are," I say quietly. I step back closer to Nox, shaking my head.

"The river . . . I nearly drowned." The ọmọ ọba's shoulders slump a little as his gaze leaves me. "Baba's men were there. They dragged me from the water. What was I supposed to do?"

"Zaye is dead," I say, my voice cracking. "She's dead."

"I know. I found her." Jagun's mouth loosens. He rubs a hand over his face. "I had hoped that because Bisi survived, perhaps Zaye might have too . . ."

Bisi. My heart blooms at the thought of the guiamala and I know my face softens.

"You ran. You thought *nothing*," snaps Nox.

His reply anchors me back in the present. It doesn't matter what happened before, what I thought I might have felt. Jagun chose his father and Addaf, even if it wasn't his first choice.

"Where is Yida's tear?" I ask, my voice firmer now. The ọmọ ọba looks up and the shadows in his eyes tell me all I need to know.

My lip curls. "You *gave* it to him?"

"Addaf took it! I was injured. What could I do? I thought that when I found you, we could work out a plan."

My breath stretches taut. Addaf has the tear. That's why he didn't follow us to the sky monastery. He didn't need to.

"Moremi, please."

But I've heard enough, even though the sight of Jagun still pulls at me. His pleas harden my heart.

He made his decision when he gave away Yida's tear. "You left us. Even after you knew what would happen if we didn't succeed. You left us."

"I didn't have a choice!" Jagun hangs his head. "It was not my intention to do anything to hurt you. You know me, you know what I want for Kwa—"

"I thought I did," I interrupt, moving closer to him, his familiar scent of sandalwood and vanilla rushing over me, and before he realizes, I press Yida's dagger against his throat. Behind him, the guards surge forward, but he holds a hand out to stop them. "You don't know what you've done."

"Mo, I promise, I was going to make things right." His whisper is close to my ear, the same deep velvet tones. The same soft sincerity. "I still can. Just give me a chance to prove it to you."

I waver, the blade aching to bite into skin, to feel hot blood sizzle against the burn of its power. "You left me with nothing."

We both understand the spaces between my words. He left me too. My visions blurs and my throat burns with tears as I pull the dagger between us.

"Mo, listen to me." He presses against the blade, even when a bead of blood breaks from his skin. "I came with them so I could find you and explain. But you need to go *now*. Addaf is coming with the rest of the guard. We were sent to scout ahead."

"Detain them!" calls a burly man barreling through the ranks. "You know the orders we have been given."

"No!" Jagun shouts, but the men do not listen to him. "I said *no*!"

I shove the prince away from me as the men come closer. The guard who called the order steps up to Jagun.

"I'm fine," says the prince, holding a hand to his neck, wiping the blood away. "Stand down."

"The ọba said you might behave like this. That you do not know your place. Our orders are to override you and secure the girl."

The soldiers push past Jagun as he frowns, spinning from side to side as the men crowd him, rushing forward.

Nox swings at a guard, his fist cracking a cheekbone, and the man's head snaps to the left, blood spraying the rock.

My breath comes heavy, my pulse a skitter of nerves as the guards close in on us. I leap forward with both daggers, blocking a hard hit from a man nearly as tall as Baba Bannu, the bones in my wrists jarring at the strength of his attack. Two men move to flank him, and I fall back next to Nox. Jagun's face twists, his shoulders sagging briefly as he draws his sword. Will he prove his allegiance to his father after all? Raw fear floods through me at the thought of fighting him.

He watches me, a frown darkening his eyes as he stalks forward. "I didn't want it to come to this, but I always knew that I wouldn't really have a choice. Serving Kwa is about more than taking what you want, doing what you want."

I still can't feel Yida, and so I reach for Dam's idan, cleaving to the crispness of it in my veins as it crackles just underneath my skin like a cold fire. Jagun steps toward me but there's a wisp of a smile on his lips that makes me pause. "I would always choose you, Moremi. Always."

And then he spins around to face the swell of the guard, using the thick hilt of his sword to bash the closest one in the face. As the man falls to the floor, the prince looks back over his shoulder at me.

"Run!"

The monastery doors draw closer and I lunge toward them. I only skid to a stop when Nox yanks me back. His face is stony as he changes his stance and squares his shoulders.

As I turn in the direction he's facing, I somehow know what I will find. A narrow path to the side of the monastery entrance is filled with men in the palace armor surging forward, cutting off the doors. Jagun is still managing to keep the other guards at bay, his skin splattered with blood and sweat, but now we are sandwiched between both.

Ojaja stands in the middle of the trail with palace guards around him, his face set in grim lines even as he clutches at his sword. Next to him, Addaf is gaunt, his eyes glittering black, skin now gray. Only a few wisps of hair remain on his head, the strands as white as bone. The shadow spirits are taking their toll.

"Traitor." He points his skeletal fingers at me as dense shadows billow up around him. The veil of smoke and curls of darkness form their semblance of human shape, red eyes and black jaws that stretch wide with charcoal teeth as they scream into the coming storm.

I blink at the first drops of rain, daggers in my hands again as the idan of both dragon gods blazes through the blades. The emi buburu take their monstrous shape and, as one, swarm toward us, blackened feet skimming over the stone path. Addaf grins, teeth rotten spines, and it's only as I see the curve of a smug smile that I spot what he cradles under his free arm.

Yida's tear is a pale pink, nestled in the folds of his gray and tattered tunic.

The rain spills from the sky in a deluge that gouges at the land. A rough fury fills me as I step forward, but the emi buburu attack in a whirlwind of black. I slash, the daggers sparking idan, blades slicing through shadowy flesh, but even though I parry and thrust, each one is replaced with another. My arms are shaking from anger, and I step back, chest heaving.

The guards follow the spirits, drawing swords and hoisting spears. I see the panicked whites of their eyes, but they still take their positions alongside the emi buburu.

We need to fight back. Now. There is no time to work out if the bonding has changed my use of the gods' essence. I know I can still feel Dam's and so I reach up into the metal sheet of sky.

Come. Come to me.

And his power does, in a rush of glittering frost so strong that it feels as if my very core is being turned inside out.

I breathe in ice and my chest blazes, feeling Dam's idan in a way I never have. I can do this, the god is in me. The rain whips faster and I snatch at the air, fingers sharp and stark in the sleek downpour. I bring them back and then forward again, hurling the rain with such force that each drop is like a pointed needle, and smile as the guards shriek in pain. Blood peppers the earth as they fall to their knees, hands scrabbling over their torn skin.

Nox watches me with horror and admiration, lifting his hands and doing the same, throwing the shards of rain as if they are tiny, vicious blades.

The water doesn't affect the emi buburu, though. "Keep going!" I shout at Nox as he braces himself, hands splayed, jaw tight, and continues to throw more of the torrent at the ọba's guards.

It gives me space and time to slash at the mass of spirits with my daggers, the blades slicing through shadow flesh. The air fills with hisses from the emi buburu as they try to re-form. I let the screams slide past me, not caring in a way that I would have before. The idan and the weapons keep me up, keep me moving, blades swinging in wild arcs.

"We need to get Yida's tear," I say to Nox.

But there remains a glut of emi buburu flocking close to Addaf, wrapping him in a protective black veil.

My heart pounds, and another slash from my dagger has the mass of spirits rearing back. More guards advance, surrounding Addaf, and I feel desperation claw at me.

Nox pants, "I can't keep this up."

Anger flares in my chest. We are so close to Yida and her tear. All to fail now? I join him, homing the rain again in between jabbing at the shadow spirits, but I feel the ache in my muscles, the crash and burn of Dam's idan that has me trembling under the force of it. We can't do this on our own for much longer. And then a solid wave of water roils through the air, smashing into the men and knocking the weapons from their hands. In the distance behind them ride Baba and a handful of the other babalawos, loping down the mountain path on the backs of giant n'damas. They're still not close enough to physically attack but make up for this by pulling at the sky as we have done, using the storm to batter at the soldiers.

Baba came. A wild grin steals over my lips, only to falter when a guard throws a spear their way and a babalawo cries out. He's knocked to the ground, blood turning the puddles beneath him a reddish pink.

"*No!*" I scream. But my cry is lost lost in the shouts of the men all around us as wrappers flash in the same violent shades of the storm above.

And then the air vibrates with the sudden deep scrape of the wooden monastery doors, and a gust of heat rolls from the open doorway. Iyalawos pour from the entrance, and for a moment, I am overcome with emotion, chest heaving as the doors shut behind them.

The women are small, with rounded shoulders and deep brown wrappers, and their feet pound, almost matching the thunder overhead. I see braids full of white and skin lined with lives that have seen laughter and hope and compassion. The iyalawos are stamping the same prayer as they move to form a line in front of the temple, glaring at Addaf and his warriors of dark and shadow. Next to him, the ọba cowers.

As the priests continue to manipulate the rain into watery barbs and pulses of waves, the priestesses focus on the earth. It's a prayer I recognize, one for preparing the land for crops, but I stare open-mouthed as the rocky ground begins to ripple beneath us. It's not like I haven't seen Kakra clear a fallow field of useless rocks, but this looks as if the whole layer of soil is being manipulated. The women pause, and then, as the doors shut behind them, they jump with both feet.

The earth lifts like the edge of a wrapper in the whirl of a dance. As the layer of land rises into the air, the iyalawos begin another fast-paced dance and the ground shakes. Addaf withdraws closer to the side of the mountain, edging toward the doorway, leaving the ọba and his men stumbling on the shifting dirt.

The ground flips again like a shaken rug, but it is not enough. The soldiers regain their balance as the earth settles. A woman steps forward, great long braids of black and white hanging down to her thighs, and I recognize her. Iya Bolu, who left the temple last year for the earth monastery. She nods at me once, her smile a gentle cradle for hope, and then she begins another complicated step. The same one I lucked out on with the eloko.

With the turn of her ankles, she releases a power that cracks the earth. Another woman with broad shoulders joins her, pulling the ground apart with the idan they channel. A wide black seam opens, swallowing a large clutch of guards. Their fading screams raise the hairs on my arms, but I force myself to think only of Yida's tear as I fight my way closer.

The ground trembles, the edge a giant quivering lip and the maw a hungry black mouth. Addaf looks down at the split of the earth and the pious fighters surrounding him. The emi buburu coil around his body still, and I see him calculate his chances. The spirits pulse as he flexes his control, sending their black monstrous arms to push at the iyalawos. I scream as the women tumble away from the temple entrance, teetering on the edge of the chasm they created. A rush of water from our left pushes them back, and I follow the stream to see Baba Seun controlling its flow.

But more palace guards run up the pass, and one swats Iya Bolu to the ground. We are outnumbered.

This is all my fault.

I'm still full of Dam's idan, but the storm is being pulled in so many directions by the pious that my use of it wanes. I squeeze my eyes shut against the panic, thinking of the god above us. Of the bond he accepted. I didn't think it would come to this, but we cannot lose now. I need to try something else. My hands press together as I reach out to him through prayer and the link that he told me is forever.

Please. We need you.

I have no way of knowing if it will work, if Dam will answer me, but I try anyway, pressing the words into energy. For a moment, there is nothing.

And then there is no mistaking the essence of the dragon, a cut of power that strikes me all at once.

My eyes roll back with the force of his presence just as the dragon drops from the sky. Translucent wings filter the sky in white and blue and silver, paling the sun and creating a reprieve from the rain.

I am coming, little iyalawo, but I will not intervene directly. Let my creations see me and think on their actions. Pray that their essence is connected enough for them to make the right choices.

The dragon blots out the last of the sun as he darts through banks of clouds. Only a few of the men catch sight of him at first, their mouths hanging open, swords dangling by their sides. When Dam cracks open his jaws to roar, everyone else sees the god. Those aligned with him straighten immediately, clapping in greeting, while the rest drop to the ground lest they displease him. All eyes are on the dragon that dips across the sky like slow-moving lightning.

Dam is beautiful.

The moonlike glimmer of his body slips in front of the sun, a sparkling juxtaposition that shows his magnificence.

"You will not displease the gods again!" I shout, counting on their worship, counting on their allegiance to the dragon they can see. "You have been lied to. Dam and Yida will bless us all. Just lay down your weapons."

When I manage to tear my eyes from the god, it is to Addaf edging toward the monastery entrance. The shadow spirits rip at the gray doors and vines with their smoke-colored hands, and the man crawls through the gap they have made.

The dragon skims the clouds one last time, gazing down on the people he helped create, before heading back to the peak of the mountain. I push my way closer to Ojaja, breaking through the ranks of the soldiers, whose weapons dangle by their sides, heads dipped in deference.

"Mo!" Nox runs past the men, who still stare at the sky, which is now streaked with Dam's sign in mango, blood red, and emerald.

I don't answer him, my gaze on the ọba, my daggers out, sizzling with blood and idan. The blades sing to me, wanting to please. Ojaja stares. I see the ticking of his jaw and the twitch of his left eye.

"This is none of your business, girl. Why must your kind inflate their importance? Just like your mother."

My kind. I let the words sit. The fact that he is still siding with Addaf, still hoping to gain some power, and now turning on his own people disgusts me. I think of how he has risked everyone. How he banished my baba and imprisoned my mother. How he sent Jagun after us, trusted Addaf with his only son.

What we have all faced.

All that we have lost.

My heart hardens as the idan burns inside me, cold and hot, furious and true. My palms itch, wanting to call the whole of the storm to me, to take all of its water and drown him in it.

But then I remember Addaf. He's in the temple with Yida's tear. I can't afford to waste any more time. I don't speak, just stalk forward, the daggers drawing me on. Ojaja opens his mouth to say something else, but I bring a hilt down on his nose, relishing the crunch of his bones as he falls to the ground.

CHAPTER TWENTY-SEVEN

The remnants of the wooden doors open at my touch, bringing a rush of gowé seeds mixed with the faint glimmer of iron. The familiar scents wash over me as I move past the entrance, fingers skimming over the coils carved in the surface of the doors. Our temple was the first to be officially declared, but the monastery's structure is older. Hewn from a giant ancient burrow of Yida's, it slinks through the base of the small peak and is said to hold massive amounts of the goddess's idan.

As I step into the hollowed tunnel, I feel a flicker of the dragon, and my eyelids flutter. Yida is still with me, despite the bond to Dam, and the relief rushes through every part of me.

I think of my mother being dragged out of our own temple, and with the image comes the vision of my daggers cutting deep into Addaf's desiccated flesh.

My blood churns at the vision.

I hurry through the dark corridor, small torches bright, showing the slant of the floor as the corridor dips down. The walls are carved with portraits of the goddess. The gloom and my pace only allow snatches of the images: Yida coiling above the world, the swoop of her as she settles on the land, the fire of her idan as she did her part in cleansing the world.

The murkiness shifts, growing darker as the corridor bends left before opening into a large oval dominated by the outline of Yida. Even larger than the one in our temple, this statue is a gleaming mass of red-and-gold-veined marble. Her wings are wide open, gossamer spreads of glass that shine with the sconces dotted around the warm chamber.

The moan stops me. It echoes around the oval, and I swing my head frantically, trying to work out where the sound is coming from. Around the base are the usual offerings, wooden bowls with spiced rice and red meat. Curved around the thick talons of the goddess's feet is a motionless body. Even from here, I can see the blackened peels of the woman's skin as she begins to claw softly at the dragon's feet, her brown wrapper a tattered wisp.

Once, my stomach would have turned, but now I just feel anger. I rush forward, hands outstretched. "What is it? Can I help?" My words are a whisper, but they still cause the iyalawo to flinch.

She moans again, a sound so low and wretched. "Go, find him!" the old woman hisses, and as she turns her face up to mine, I trip back, stumbling and falling to my knees. "He cannot be allowed in Yida's presence."

Her face is not a face anymore but a dark brown moon pockmarked with black pits where her eyes, nose, and mouth should be. Her skin hangs in folds, blood drying in the creases. I hold a hand over my mouth, tears springing at the ravaged priestess.

"He is taking idan to give it away, the gods for the shadow

spirits." The woman's voice is a cracked croak, as if she has screamed until her throat is swollen and sore. "He will not stop until he can properly free the emi buburu."

I scoot closer, fingers shaking as I reach out to take her hand. When I do, she grips it hard. "You must stop him." Her voice wavers now, her hold slipping. "He is heading to the goddess's inner sanctuary. He took the main tunnel."

The iyalawo's grip goes slack as her head lolls to one side. I stifle a cry as I fold her hand on the concave of her chest and look up at the statue of Yida. What god allows such death?

The question stops me for a moment, a chill stealing over me. Until I remember that these gods gave us our lives. There is only so much we can look to them for. The rest is up to us.

The daggers in my hands sing for Addaf's blood. They pull at the yearning in me. I let the rage consume me, powering me on, and I leave the oval space and its looming statue of Yida.

I promise to do the death prayer for the iyalawo when I have taken the life who took hers.

I follow the main tunnel that leads down and down, thinking only of getting to Addaf, getting to the tear. I run faster and faster.

So fast that when I charge around a corner blindly, I am forced to a stop, the blade of Addaf's sword flush against the hot column of my neck.

"I could cut your throat right now and watch you bleed out."

A trickle of warmth crawls down my skin as I pant. My heart skitters as I look up into his eyes. All their uneven color has gone now, and he sucks in deep breaths, his sunken chest rising and falling. A curl of blackness unwinds in his eyes. If there is any human left in him, it is not much.

"Let go of your daggers."

I reach for Dam's essence, but the mountain is like a weight above me, blocking his idan. Yida's is still an elusive twist, glimmering just beyond me, but at least I can feel her. The blade of the sword wavers against my neck as I squeeze the hilts of my weapons, fingernails to soft palms. Hissing, I let the pain bite, controlling my thoughts, replacing the anger that is telling me to try to flay the skin from his bones.

"I said, drop them. We both know that I don't need the spirits right now. Just one more push of this blade."

My gaze falls to Yida's tear, cradled in the crook of his arm. Just when I feel the sword press tighter against me, I let go of my weapons, my stomach sinking at the clatter when they hit the stone floor. Addaf kicks the daggers away from me and, without taking the sword from my throat, scoops them up and jams them under his belt.

"Your mother has been speaking of nothing but her fear." Addaf's cracked lips peel back as he sneers. I frown, my eyes narrowing even as I stay silent, trying not to stare at the tear. "For the gods and their idan. And for what the shadow spirits will bring to this world."

I scoff. "If you think the emi buburu can be controlled, then you—"

"Quiet." The man presses closer, the blade against my skin, and the trickle of blood thickens, spilling down my chest.

I swallow tightly. For the first time since we arrived, a true frisson of fear takes hold.

"They offer power unlike any other," Addaf continues, his breath a stream of gloat and rot, and his eyes gleam black, the whites now a dark yellow. "When all the spirits are truly free, the Kingdom of Carew will take Kwa's place in importance."

We both look at Yida's tear. The pearlescent pink glows in

the low lights of the hallway. Sweat slides down my back and fear into my heart as I remember what Dam showed me back at the monastery. Iya Eneh had assumed I was the one meant to unite the gods.

In this moment, nothing could feel further from the truth.

"Move." He gestures, dragging us closer to the golden door at the end of the tunnel. The sweetened scent of decay rolls over me. I retch once, twice, just barely holding the vomit in. "We will go to Yida's inner sanctuary together. The gods will soon no longer care about this world they have created, no longer care about cleansing your lands or imbuing your pious with idan. And thus, the spirits who have been banished to the underworld will be free to return and claim what is rightfully theirs."

"They won't bring your wife or your daughter back," I say quietly.

Addaf pauses, but I see his fingers tighten. "They will. They have promised," he croons, breath smelling of blood and blight as he prods me forward. "And with that, there will be power for our kingdom, so that no one in Carew will suffer again."

Addaf presses the sword between the blades of my shoulders, shoving me until I am tight against the raised scales of the door. The heat flushes against my skin, and I imagine the dragon below, wrapped around her offerings of gold in the warm dark.

"Do you truly know what you're doing? Calling on the emi buburu?" I ask, letting desperation clip my words, trying one last time to reason with him. "They will take from you until there is nothing left, and then they'll do the same to everyone else. Look at what they've already done to you. They have made you dark."

"They responded to the darkness inside me," seethes Addaf,

his black eyes burning. "And this darkness would not be here if not for Kwa's unwillingness to use idan for anything other than its own people."

I want to tell him that even in Kwa, idan cannot save everyone. But he is too far gone to listen.

"That doesn't matter, not when I have this." Addaf holds the tear up, just out of my reach, his lips curled. He turns it so the flames from the torches flicker over the crystallized surface. "People have taken Yida's tears as physical expressions of her sorrow when she first separated from Dam, but really, this is something else, something that symbolizes them both. The spirits have told me all. And when I destroy this in front of the dragon, her rage will be incandescent."

I still in horror.

He knows.

"Described as a tear, but really a promise of something new. Something even more powerful. The one thing that can unite the gods and stop the spirits."

My eyes go to the pale coral surface, to the beauty of the delicate gleam that hints of what hides within.

"Not a tear," says Addaf, showing the the rotting remains of his teeth in a wide grin. "But an egg."

CHAPTER TWENTY-EIGHT

Yida, red-bellied, love crushing her. A roar thick with pride, teeth bright sharp. Scorches of idan and a tear-shaped egg. The flicker of life within as the shell changes from scarlet to silver pink. A curl of a tiny tail, keen teeth, and the bead of black eyes. The gods' spawn cocooned, kept safe in the earth temple.

Once again, the images Dam flooded my mind with come back in powerful bursts, and I shudder at the wonder of them, the hope.

"Open the door." Addaf jabs the sword against my back as tears of anger burn in the corners of my eyes. "I said, *open it.*"

I reach for Dam, the memory of our binding close. Surely he will not forsake me? But the press of rock and earth is still too much, and there is nothing.

I take a deep breath and try to calm the writhing in my stomach as I grip for the handle covered in tiny scales, all overlapping in a metallic ripple. I remember the times just after my father left when I hated to be parted from my mother on the occasions she visited the inner sanctum with offerings of gold. And now I am about to descend into a similar place. But for a completely different reason.

I tug, and the door opens. Heat scented with the tang of metal rolls over me, and I stop, peering down into the blackness. The darkness seems to pulse like a slow heartbeat.

"You first," says Addaf, grabbing a torch from the wall and pushing me from behind so that I stumble, the stone hot and rough beneath my feet.

I slide my soles down over the lip of the first step, feeling my way through the dark warmth. The stairs are steep, leading straight down in an unending black, and despite just a flicker of light, Addaf keeps the sword point sharp against my spine. My breath comes heavy, the humid press of wet air feeling as if it is sticking to my chest.

Trying to calm myself, I think of the first prayer of thanks that I learned, remembering the stamps and steps that took me months to master. Kakra had shown me, taking the time to help and guide. I remember Iya's smile when she saw me dancing the prayer in the hall. I envision the herbs I collected, the people they helped, the pain eased. And then I think of the sense of pride and how at peace my mother was when she made her visits to Yida, to our goddess.

My goddess.

I push my shoulders back. My intentions are pure. I have nothing to fear.

After a while, the steps flatten out, leaving me to stand on the floor of a narrow corridor. The walls are still black rock, but here and there I can see a glitter of gold. I reach out, fingers skating over the metal veins that lighten the walls around us, the strands filling rough seams in the same way that wonder is seeping into me.

"Keep going." Behind me, Addaf's breathing is labored, but he's still close, weapon pushing me onward.

We walk into the growing heat, the mountain crouching above us. There's comfort in this for me, but I know that Addaf is not taking it the same way, the bursts of his panicked breathing giving him away.

A loud rumbling hiss stops us. I cock my head to one side. A surge of nerves rises and my breath quickens. The hiss comes again, and I move faster, almost stumbling as the floor dips. Ahead, there's a golden-red glow and a roiling heat that makes my knees shake. Sweat trickles down my forehead, snaking down my neck, and I tremble. The thought of the goddess is blinding. Fear is replaced by jittery excitement.

My soles feel as if they are being set alight by idan. The strength of it pours through me as we reach the archway, and I am forced to stifle a moan at the burning force. The room opens out into a chamber twice the size of the prayer hall, and I marvel at Yida's power. I think of how I can use it to rid Addaf of the weapon at my back, but I'm not sure how to make the idan do what I want without damaging the egg, even as idan now floods through me like molten fire.

Like a larger version of Iya Eneh's burrow, the space looks as if it were scooped out of the mountain and pressed into the shape of a curling dragon. Heaps of gold glitter everywhere, the black rock almost totally obscured by the precious metal: towering piles of gilded granules and nuggets, thick ropelike necklaces and chunky rings, slices of pure gold bars, and even statues of the dragon herself. The goddess is said to be pleased by the shine and glitter, pacified by the love of the people she created. I know that my mother is only one of the iyalawos who have been bringing the dragon tribute since the world began, each adding to the piles upon piles of treasure in different pockets of the earth.

We shouldn't be here, in this sacred place.

Addaf gnashes his teeth. "This is more wealth than the Kingdom of Carew has ever had. We might as well be like chickens scratching in the dirt."

But I do not listen, craning my neck, trying to see the dragon. The burn of idan is strong enough to feel as if it is searing my skin, sizzling along my spine, scorching me from the inside out. Yida must be here.

A movement to my left catches my eye, but when I turn, there's nothing but the glisten of gold. I stand still, something telling me not to turn away. And then I see it. The shifting of what I thought was the wall covered with carvings, the gleam of a dark scarlet scale that makes it look as if the surface of the whole cavern is moving. The idan pulls at me with hot hooks inside my very bones. I take a step away from Addaf, not caring when he shouts behind me, not wincing when the sword grazes the skin of my back.

Staggering, I fall to one knee, eyes still on the shifting piles around us. Gold cascades from serpentine sides as the dragon rises out of the offerings of pious worshippers. Yida flexes slowly, uncurling within her chamber, her body as large as the walls, tail coiling around and cutting off the way we had entered. The goddess lifts her head and turns her black gaze on us, the slits in her eyes regarding us with a torrid intensity that only adds to the heat of her lair.

At my back, I hear Addaf babbling something as he tries to yank at me. I spin. The goddess is here, and with her, the holy weight of idán that blazes through me. I don't care when I feel the scrape of his blade as I dart away and turn to face him, the dragon at my back.

I feel the moment Yida sees the egg.

Her sudden roar echoes through the chamber. But before she can strike, Addaf lifts both hands and grins as darkness pours from around him. The emi buburu form fast, larger this time, looming over Addaf like unholy babalawos. There are more than ever before, dozens lining the sanctum behind their conduit.

My heart knocks, but I plant my feet, the fire of idán surging from beneath. Yida hisses behind me. I feel the press of her scales against my sweat-slicked back, and all I know is that I can't let Addaf destroy the egg in front of her. I know he's right, that this one thing will be what sends her over the edge. She will care for no one if she loses her spawn.

Narrowing my eyes, I gauge the distance needed to take the egg, even as the shadow spirits swarm forward. The air cools with the whirl of them, bringing the stench of decaying flesh.

There's no time for the panic that tightens my chest. I feel the goddess's great inhale and know it's time to move. When I lunge, I sense the blast of the dragon's idán as she aims it at a spirit that reaches for me, clawed hands grabbing at my hair. Yida's magic cuts through the shadowy form, and I drop to slide along the rocky ground, the slip of scattered gold bars saving my skin.

The emi buburu's screeches fill the air as they rush at the dragon, but I must trust that Yida is healed enough now to cleanse them, although I'm not sure she can do this entirely without Dam. I scramble to my feet, eyes on the egg. I throw myself on Addaf, fingertips skimming the pink curve of it, even as he snatches it away.

"You should never have thought that you would be able to change anything," he breathes, seizing my wrists, his fingers crushing the delicate bones. I try to twist, to get away, but he pulls me closer, the power of the emi buburu in him. "The time of your gods is over."

He smiles at me, his teeth shattered red splinters, his blackened tongue flicking as he licks his cracked lips. I close my hands into fists and force deep breaths, letting the flow of idan rise through me. I move my feet, trying a prayer to shift the rock, but Addaf only lurches once before he cackles, turning me around.

"Behold your goddess."

The shadow spirits leap and claw at the dragon even as she spews idan through the air. I sob, watching as they push toward her, a flash in her gaze as her eyes roll in almost panic. The emi buburu twirl and flex, and Yida's stream of idan cuts one of them down, leaving curls of smoke and the smell of charred bones. She bellows, striking down another and another as she slinks forward, cracking the rock with her weight. The spirits do not have time to re-form before the dragon strikes again and again, until even the wisps of darkness have been burned from the air as Yida destroys the emi buburu. Around us the walls of the sanctum shift, rocks sliding in an uneasy groan, as if the mountain has borne her pain.

Addaf stiffens and I use his shock to turn. All I can see is the egg, and I lunge for it now, hope burning through me the same way Yida's idan cuts through the shadow spirits.

I don't feel the steel blade. Just a punching feeling.

When I look down, it's to Addaf pulling his sword free. Before I can move, he slices into my stomach again, the blade parting my already bloodied wrapper.

My legs don't listen to me. I crumple on the ground, a hand against my wounds. Blood flows over my fingers as I take shallow breaths of air.

And in this moment, I feel true dread. I try to swallow, to catch my breath. If I don't stop Addaf from destroying the egg, he will turn Yida mad with grief and even Dam will not be enough. Addaf drops his sword and moves closer to the goddess, cupping the egg in his large hands. His eyes are fixed on her, his grin feral.

I drag myself up and move, staggering behind him, blood-drenched fingers clawing the air.

I think of Iya and Bannu imprisoned, my father and all his years in exile. And then I think of Zaye.

With a surge of anger, I lunge, snatching my blades from Addaf's belt and slamming them into his back. I twist the daggers once. Twice. When I yank them free, a scream spills from my mouth.

He stands still a moment before he drops to his knees. I shove the blades in their holster, then lean around him to grasp for the gods' legacy, but I'm not quick enough and the egg slides from the crook of his arm to the stone floor. A crack splits the air and with it my heart jumps. Failure blooms and spreads as I turn to the goddess behind me, words bubbling up in a throat filling with fear.

I reach for the egg but fall to the ground, pressing a hand to my side. Crawling, I run bloodied fingers over the satin curve. It is whole as far as I can tell, and that small fact gives me some relief when I fold at the waist. I can feel the pump of my pulse crashing, even as my heartbeat grows fainter.

Slowly, I peel my fingers away from my side. Blood gushes over my wrapper as my throat fills with it too. My vision blackens at the edges. I close my eyes.

There is no one to perform a healing prayer for me. Perhaps this is the best way to die, with the goddess next to me.

A moan bubbles from my lips, and pain begins to filter through. I don't want to die. I want to see Baba and Iya. I want to learn all the ways to channel idan.

I want to live.

There is another way, my mind whispers as magic licks at my soul and blood still seeps from my wound.

With that, I heave myself up, groaning and lightheaded as I stagger toward the dragon.

Yida watches me without moving, and I have to believe she doesn't fault me for the theft of her egg. As my vision slides, I raise a red wet hand to the goddess, even though I'm not sure if what I am asking for can be granted. Until I look down at the dragon that encircles my ankle.

Yida chose me before.

She can again.

The heat of the dragon's power yanks me toward her. I shuffle close enough to see the shifting overlap of her scales, each one the size of my face. Yida lowers herself, lying supine in the hot hollow, and I am able to lift my leg despite the intense pain in my side. The goddess does not move as I press the scales on my ankle against the beat of her heart.

A scorch of heat wraps around me, cradling me in flames of idan. The dragon opens her jaws and roars, more red gold pouring from between the spines of her teeth. Her snarl changes, growls and clicks reverberating until I can finally make out words.

Who are you to offer yourself to me? You arrive with this oyinbo who dared to try to control us?

I can't speak; the pain has spread now, and I gasp, ashes and blood on my tongue. The only thing I can think to do, as my vision narrows, is to show her my ankle and then my wrist.

What is this? How did this come to be?

I open my mind to her, showing her the images of what has passed, unable to speak. Dam marking me in the gathering space, then the god on the frost and ice of the mountain, the swirl of snow wreathing his spines. The press of my mark against his body and the cold spread of his idan.

The goddess bends closer to me, her golden pupils unblinking. *You are bound to Dam, but you would ask this of me also?*

"Yes," I croak. My eyes flutter even as I hold both hands to the cut ribbons of my stomach. "It's . . ." I want to say its the only way I can live, the only way we can make sure that all of the emi buburu are truly cleansed, but no more words will come. She must know. Whether she will help me or not is another thing.

I slump forward, my body pressed against the dragon. Her scales are hard but warm, rising and falling with each one of her giant breaths.

And then comes the heat. I close my eyes to the red and orange of it as a stinging fever blazes through me. My mouth opens in a scream that builds in the tightness of my throat, but all sound is swallowed as the molten waves of idan consume me.

The world is on fire as the dragons circle it. The ships that arrive on our shores. A flash of the sky temple toppled, of the earth temple buried beneath rubble. And the palace on fire, homes lost in licks of violent scarlet.

I try to speak, to beg, but Yida shows me more of what could come, just as her husband showed me what had passed.

The palace jutting from the land like rotten teeth, all the fields and forests charred to blackened stumps. There is sorrow-lined fury as they spin around the ashes of their creations and then—

I feel her pain, and as the dragon howls, my mouth opens too, a ragged scream joining hers.

The goddess rears up, her head crowning the ceiling.

What you are asking comes with a weight. To change all I have shown you. Can you bear it?

I want to nod my head, but I feel so weak. "Yes," I croak.

To have both of our bonds means you will share in our burden. And the responsibility of the true unification that has been shown to humans in your visions.

Yida shows me her egg, the life within cracking and pulsing with an idan I have never seen before. Not fire or ice, but something different. A new power. A new magic for a new kingdom and a—

I think of how Dam showed me the creation of this world, and now Yida is showing me its end . . .

But what is an end if not a new beginning?

I know the goddess means that I will have to be a part of it all, good or bad.

Blood bubbles on my lips and I lick it away, using the metal tang to keep me tethered, to stop the blackness from pulling me under.

"Yes."

The dragon opens her mouth once again and releases more idan. I close my eyes as the red and gold takes me, freeing me from the pain in my stomach and the fear of what is to come. Yida shows me worshippers who pray to her, to Dam, and now to—

My fingers bend to claws as idan cracks through every bone, devouring and melting until I can no longer feel any part of my body. A growling fills my ears, but I can't tell if it is me or the dragon. And then a collar of fevered heat climbs from inside my chest, rising to my neck, where it flares and sears. I scream, my throat on fire, and when my eyes spring open, it is to the burnished gaze of the dragon.

Yida agreed.

We are bound.

CHAPTER TWENTY-NINE

I gently scoop up the egg, my hands shaking when I see the crooked line in its shell. As I hold it carefully, a tear rolling down my cheek, landing on the pink surface.

"I'm sorry," I say, turning to the goddess.

Yida watches me as I approach her, eyes flashing a dark gold before I place the egg between her talons. The dragon dips her head, nudging it with her great snout, nostrils gaping flares of black. She makes a keening sound that cuts deep inside me. The egg tilts to one side, and I reach to straighten it, in case it rolls.

And then it jerks again.

I gasp, jumping back as it moves once more, the shell shivering, cracking again. I thought the drop had damaged the egg, but what if it has caused something else?

I creep backward. Yida breathes out, the heat of her idan rolling over the spawn as it continues to shake. The shell breaks in more tiny fissures, and a sudden thin mewl splits the warm air. I fall to my knees, breath held tight in my chest. Yida releases a gentle stream of idan again in ribbons of red and gold, and the rest of the egg flakes away to reveal what is coiled inside.

A dragon the size of my fist crouches in the wreckage of the shell. Its scales are an iridescent blur, and as I lean closer, small wings unfurl, purple membranes stretching as it stares up at me with unblinking eyes of gold and silver. It lets out another sound, this time more like a miniature echo of its mother. I know my eyes are round, my mouth working to say something, but I can't find the words. The newborn dragon gnashes its needle-like teeth, snapping at the air.

One who symbolizes them both. Iya Eneh's words come back to me. It was not just one kingdom, one people, one . . . me. It was about the god spawn all along. And Addaf knew.

The young dragon opens its wings and hops toward me, tiny claws scraping on the rock. Small black horns tipped in purple sprout from its head like a miniature coronet. Night-blue scales line its back, but even as it shifts, they change to a pale blue and then an emerald green. Panicked, I push myself backward, not knowing what it will do.

You will look after Maha. She is part of Kwa's past, and a key to its future. Her power is ours, but is also unlike ours. Some will say better, and some will say worse. Which one will be determined by her guidance and the pious use of her idan.

I stare into Yida's large gold gaze, unblinking.

This was part of your choice in being bound. I cannot give Maha all that is needed. You will. Now you are of Dam and of me.

I blink at the dragon as she clambers onto my lap, hands hovering over her spine as she digs her claws into the fabric of my wrapper like a small nundá, turning until she makes herself comfortable. She looks up at me once before tucking her head under one wing. I lift my face to Yida, the heat of her idan wrapping around me and filling my mind with images.

Maha sleeping against my side, the people of Kwa and their changed worship, me standing at the palace walls—

I frown at what the goddess is showing me. "I don't understand."

We are united in you. And the ọba has ended his family line with his choices.

"But Jagun is his son. There is no end—"

Their line was severed by Ojaja's actions. A new one must begin.

Yida shows me another image, my mind pulsing with the enormity of it, one that has my hands folding around the gods' spawn, palms against her cool scales. Maha lets out a small growl.

"Dam is waiting for you," I manage.

I thank you for bringing my husband to me. Now I must tell him what has come to pass. I will heed your call. And together Dam and I will cleanse the lands and ensure that the rest of the shadow spirits who have dared to show themselves will be banished and the land healed.

She blinks slowly, almost like a gigantic nundá.

The rest is up to you.

With Yida's lair at my back, I pick my way past the piles of gold, soles crunching on rings and idan. I carry the young dragon in my arms, walking past the bloodied sprawl of Addaf. Though I feel pity, I don't feel guilt the same way I did when I ended the eloko's life. Maybe it is because of Addaf's insidious wants, or maybe I am no longer the girl I used to be. Or both.

The weight of the mountain and what the goddess has decreed presses down on me as I walk up the slant of corridor. Nothing feels the same as the soft dark swallows me. Can I really do all Yida has decided?

That will have to wait. The monastery is still empty as I hurry through the passage. Maha squirms in my arms as the breeze from outside finds us. Her opalescent wings open and close as I try to keep my hold on her.

"Wait, little one." I'm not sure that I should be calling a goddess "little one," but she is young. I make a clucking sound and the dragon quiets.

Shouts and the clash of metal can still be heard, and I run to the open entranceway. I should have known Ojaja would not give up. The spread of land surrounding the mountain is full of iyalawos, babalawos, and the palace guards. A blur of wind and storm, swords, and ripples of the earth under new moonlight. I spot Nox struggling against two soldiers, one of his eyes nearly swollen shut, and my anger rises hot and thick. Jagun is on the path, his sword flashing in the muted light as he parries against one of his own men. Baba whirls in the middle of the battle, chest gleaming with sweat and rain as he claps thunder from the sky.

Across from him, Ojaja snarls. "How dare you show your face?" He bares his teeth at Baba. "Was I not clear when I banished you? I should have never shown you mercy. Your prophecies have brought nothing but trouble."

My father laughs. "But have I not been proved right? Are you angry because I predicted what would happen, or because it was never destined to be you?"

The ọba roars, drawing back his weapon, preparing to strike.

"Leave him!" I shout, a dagger in one hand, Maha in the other. I already lost him once; I won't lose him again.

"Moremi, get back!" Baba says as he twists to face me just as the ọba jerks his sword.

Even as I'm pushing my way closer, I know that I'm too late.

Red blooms across Baba's white furs. He lifts a hand to his chest, his mouth opening and shutting. He looks down at me, his eyes widening.

"NO!" The scream is ripped from me as the tip of Ojaja's sword breaks my father's flesh.

The king's face falls apart as he stands behind Baba, but then he gathers himself. Ojaja tries to smooth the look on his face, tries to drape a haughty pride over his features as he yanks his sword free. When I reach my father, his knees weaken, and the priests on either side of him catch his elbows as he slides to the ground. I drop with him, knees stinging on the path.

For a moment, the dragons, the emi buburu, being chosen . . . all of it is far from my mind.

"Baba," I cry, my voice breaking. "Baba . . . please."

He tries to speak to me, but his words come only as whispers that I can't hear, and I shake with rough sobs. Baba widens his eyes once more before his sightless gaze falls on the mountain above me.

Someone keens. I don't realize the sound is coming from me until Maha's teeth nip at my arm.

The dragon climbs from under my arm to my lap, and together we look up at the ọba. He towers over us, flanked by his men, but it's his sword that holds my attention, the blade dripping with my father's blood.

"Baba?" comes Jagun's voice. "What happened? What did you do?"

Ojaja sniffs, but I see the uneasy shuffle of his feet. "I did not intend this. But he needed to be put in his place."

I only just got Baba back, and now he's been taken. Again. This time forever.

I bend down and splay my bloodstained fingers on the stillness of his chest. If he is dead, then why not the ọba? Why not everyone else? They do not matter.

Nothing but the idan that rips through me matters.

"What did you do?" Fury scorches my words as I stand now, Maha against my chest. *"What did you do?"* I scream, squeezing my eyes shut and releasing the fire and ice that have been building for days now, letting them twine together. The dragon against my chest throws her head back as she roars along with me, her small body vibrating against the grief that rattles through mine.

Loss and love and despair flood through me in a bitter rush. And then they tangle and roil, turning into something else, something new. The force licks at my mind and coils around my heart, squeezing hard. Idan, but like nothing I have felt before, a burst of black honey on the back of my tongue. Not fire or ice this time, but an endless thick seep that scorches, no, *invades* my skin and bones.

The power is beautiful, twisting and harsh like ripped satin, smelling like burning gold in a forge. It grows, swelling as if I am being consumed from the inside out. I don't need to wonder where it is coming from. I can feel it.

Maha.

The dragon in my arms continues to amplify my grief, somehow made tangible in her. And in return, she spews her idan, a shimmer of pearlescent energy with tendrils of onyx and gold in its center. I let it flow into me, and when I open my eyes, it is to a world I do not recognize.

The sky pulses in white and black, fractured by bursts of lightning. The priests, priestesses, and palace guards are all on their knees, heads tilted, spines bent back. But it is their eyes that catch me, blank white gazes that gleam from their faces, shining above mouths hung open.

Maha's jaws are wide as she crows over them all. It is said that our souls contain small shreds of idan, given to our ancestors when the gods first created us, and when one dies, their idan passes to another born. We are taught this when we are old enough to speak, but never did the elders mention what Maha is doing now. The tiny god is rigid as she inhales deeply, her body rippling. Slowly, small balls of metallic blue and red rise from the eyes of everyone around us, and with a crow, the dragon draws them to her.

Ojaja moans softly as his scrap of idan glistens, bobbing in the air as Maha calls it to her, to us. I watch, with a wicked glee, as his face draws in, hands curling as he slumps. His life is leaving him, and I am glad. Doesn't he deserve this?

I shudder as the idan flexes in me, flooding my heart so full that it feels as if it will burst. Throwing my head back, I let it fill every part of me, my hands shaking at the feel of it all.

The new god is taking their lives, their souls.

And offering them to me.

We could have them all, I think as the idan continues to flow, new and so raw. Priests and priestesses convulse as their energy is stolen, their eyes milky clouds. And then I see Jagun on his knees, a knot of idan leaving him. Nox is in the crowd, his eyes opaque as his soul leaves him. Iya Bolu is beside him, her hands clasped together in the dirt.

And then I remember Iya, my faltering steps in the temple as I learned the prayers. The worry about the initiation, my kiss with Nox. The way Zaye was proud of me, and how Jagun held me. I'm hurting them all.

"Stop!" I cry, fresh horror breaking the old.

The dragon lowers her head, my command stopping her. She looks back at me to see the crumple of my face and tears that glisten on my cheeks. I let her nuzzle my chin, her scales a dry rasp.

There are gasps as eyes open, idan drifting back like fresh smoke into everyone's gazes. Maha could have taken their essence, their lives. And then I think of how she only connected to me, to what I wanted.

I could have killed them all.

And I wanted to.

I fall to the ground, bile rising in my throat. My head is bowed as I press a hand to my heart. The temple gives, heals, and as an iyalawo, I am responsible for that too. Not this.

"Mo?" Nox bends down over me, a hand sliding against my spine as I push myself onto my knees. "Come."

When I get to my feet, it is to a silence so thick that it wraps around us all. There is no need to wonder if they recognize what I can do; I can see it as they bow their heads now, shoulders curved with respect and fear.

I look at my father's body, and again, the knifing grief nearly has me folded in two. Two priests are bent over, layering him with wrappers. For a moment, all I can do is keep breathing. I tilt my head to the sky as loss swirls inside me, threatening to drag me under. And then I see the stars that still slash the sky.

The Dírágónì ceremony.

But first, there is something I need to do. I can't let go yet.

I pick my way through the palace guards until I get to Ojaja. The ọba bows, his broad shoulders quivering at the sight of my feet, and a part of me revels in it. Maha climbs to my shoulder, curling her tail around my neck like a necklace of scales. I bend down to the king so that my mouth is close to his ear.

"I should let our new god take your life."

The ọba shakes his head, jowls swinging. "I only did what was good for Kwa."

"You did what was good for you!" I snarl, fists bunched.

He wrings his dimpled hands, rubies flashing like the blood splashed in the earth around us. "No, no, do you not see? What is good for me is good for Kwa."

I bark a rough laugh. "The fact that you still can't see the fault in your actions is why the gods are right. Your line has ended."

"The gods chose my ancestors. They chose me," tries Ojaja, his tone heavy with his plea.

"No, not anymore."

The dragon around my neck growls, the ebb and flow of her idan stretching through me, but I do not reach for it. There is no space for those who would see us fall, who would desecrate our holy places and take power only for themselves.

"You are no longer welcome in the Kingdom of Kwa," I say, my voice even despite the shaking of my hands and the anger in my heart. "But I will not stoop to what you have resorted to. Therefore, I banish you."

Ojaja frowns, getting to his feet now, his eyes hardening. "You do not have the authority in you to decree such a thing."

I smile. Maha responds to my thoughts, reaching out her idan to gently pull at the ọba's. We watch as he buckles, falling to one knee.

"Moremi, enough." Jagun winds his way through the men he fought against. "He should be tried by the council."

"No," I growl. "What he has done is unforgivable. He doesn't even deserve the mercy I'm showing him."

I glare at his father, enjoying the tilt of his eyes as they begin to cloud over and the spiral of his soul is drawn from his body. Perhaps I should just take it. It's what he deserves, after all. A life for a life.

Jagun steps between us, hands on my shoulders as he looks into my eyes. "This is not you."

I stop, panting, as Maha's idan seeps back into her. She settles down, gripping her tiny talons into my shoulder.

"This is me now," I hiss, and immediately, the turn and twist of my feelings for him returns. I ignore it. There is pain in his voice, but I can't listen to it. "The royal line has no place in Kwa. Not after all that has been done."

"If you banish him, then I will have to leave too." Jagun's hazel-ringed eyes flicker. "Is that what you want?"

No, an old part of me cries . . . My heart pulses, and I instinctively want to reach for him.

But the new burn of my soul roars and steels, bringing an icy cold. I turn to the guard. "The ọba and his son are to leave Kwa immediately. Make sure you see them on the first ship available." I gesture to Baba Seun. "Go. I want witnesses that this has been done."

Nox comes to Jagun's side, his gaze raking across mine. Whatever he finds in my eyes, whether it is the me he has always known or the new version that he accepts—either way, he is here with me, and that is what matters.

"You heard her," he says to those around us. "Kwa has an oloorì now. Recognize this, or leave."

One by one, the priestesses and priests lower themselves to

the ground, foreheads pressed against the path. And then the palace guards do the same, laying down their swords and spears, the ends pointed away.

At their deference, my shoulders soften, and I rub a thumb over the delicate scales of Maha's side. Above us, Dam's stars glitter in the early night, their brilliance sweeping across the sky.

"There is still time," I say, my voice loud and clear, "for the dragons to finish what they have started, to cleanse the land and heal it from the emi buburu. Join me in the Dírágónì ceremony, and with the gods' grace, the Kingdom of Kwa will forever flourish."

When I begin to dance, it is to the stamp and slaps of those around me as we celebrate the gods who created us. My movements are not the ones of my mother and Bannu, but something different. The sway and turn of my hips blends with the way my toes tap the ground, connecting to the earth, calling Yida's idan to me and sending my prayer to the goddess deep within. I twist my hands and wrists, palms brought together with Dam's magic, all in a rhythm that speaks of the heavens and the powerful currents they hold.

My head stays thrown back when I finish, eyes pinned on a clear sky, the slick crescent of the moon hanging over the peaks of the Adamawa Mountains. The ground splits open just as Dam's roar comes from above. When the dragon swoops down through the night, it is to his wife as she claws from the base of the mountain, her great head smashing through the broken doors. Yida's golden eyes fix only on her husband as she flexes free, standing at the base of the peak as we scramble backward, giving the gods space.

Dam lands next to her, spines resplendent with moonlight

as he bows to his wife. The gods bend their heads together as they greet one another. When they turn to us, it is as one.

Steer your new god. Together you will both lead in the way that is needed.

I nod at Yida's words to me, clutching the small dragon in my arms. The burn and destruction of Maha's power flares through me, and I exhale, knowing I will need to make choices for us all.

We will circle the world we have made and cleanse any remnants of the emi buburu. Maha is part of our legacy and the god you must all worship. Bring the worshippers together and spread our word.

Then the gods launch into the sky, leaving me with the metallic gaze of Maha as she turns in my arms.

CHAPTER THIRTY

I let myself sink into the deep water of the bathing chamber at the temple, calling on idan to make it even hotter. I don't even need to think about reaching for the gods' magic now; it's there. Always. My blood humming with power that I can feel deep in my bones.

Steam billows around me, and the sharp scent of marjoram gives the waters a delicate scent that soothes my muscles. Using a bathing sponge, I scrub at my body, trying to wash away the emotions that stain me. Grief has settled deep inside, but I find that I can't deal with it, not yet.

A small growl from my left, and I turn my head to see Maha, her head with two tiny horns tipped to one side, silver eyes with gold pupils watching me intently. She hops closer, pecking at my wet curls with her sharp beaklike jaws, separating me from my thoughts.

"I'm fine," I say.

The gods' spawn only looks at me, waiting. I know what she wants, and I flick a wrist, sprinkling the dragon's body with water. Maha purrs, spine shivering as she shakes herself like a small nundá before hopping onto a pile of clean linens, sprawling across them to dry. That such a tiny creature can hold so much power is something I am still struggling to comprehend.

When I emerge from the bathing chambers, it is to my mother with a sparkling wrapper draped over her arms. Kakra and Panyin flank her, eyeing my wet curls.

"There is not time to dress your hair in the way we should, but we can do our best," says Iya, steering me toward a small, polished stool. She allowed herself to cry when I told her about Baba but is determined to see out Maha's introduction to the people.

I sit, the satin wood smooth beneath me, as the women gather the weight of my damp curls. Maha sits in my lap, watching everyone carefully. She reaches forward, grabbing a strand of my hair in her jaws and tugging. I pull it from her teeth, running both hands over the scales of her back so that she stretches across my knees, her head down. She's already grown bigger. Baba would have been amazed by her, and the thought makes me blink against the tears.

While Kakra and Panyin oil my hair, detangling it with combs, Iya gathers gold pins adorned with rubies, laying them out next to us on a small copper table.

"Remember, none of this hunching. You need to stand up straight," says Panyin. I can tell she is braiding the left side of my head since her fingernails are sharp and she pulls the hair just that little bit harder than her sister.

"Yes, Moremi. Show them your strength and your beauty." I can hear the pride in Kakra's words as she gently twists my curls. Iya steps closer, musk oil and saffron washing over me.

"You will be yourself. Let the kingdom see what the gods

have chosen, and do not let doubt seep into any part of your mind. The people will sense the slightest weakness in how you speak or stand. You need to be strong." Iya leans over me, and I feel the cold slide of a gold pin pushed into my hair. "You have always been strong, even when you did not believe it. And now it is time for everyone to see it."

Kakra smudges kohl around my eyes before dusting my skin with golden powder. When the women step away from me, I raise a hand to my hair, fingers hovering over the tight coils they have created. I stand and let them wind the wrapper around me, its swaths of diaphanous fabric glittering with gold and silver. Once Iya finishes tightening the folds, I face the polished copper mirror, watching as my own eyes widen at what they see. The wrapper is a cloud of red and blue shot through with violet, the perfect combination of both gods, but it is my hair that stuns me. Broad plaits have been wound round the top of my head, studded with bulbous red jewels, giving me the appearance of wearing a black-and-ruby crown. Maha climbs onto my shoulders, wrapping herself around me.

Kakra and Panyin stand before me, and for once there is the same smile mirrored on their faces. As one, they each remove a single wide gold bracelet, offering them to me. I point my right foot, sole arched, in respect and take them without question, knowing they are showing me how much they trust in me. I slip the bangles over my fingers, where they sit perfectly at the joints of my wrists.

"Here." My mother takes my hands, rubbing in the rest of the oil, thumbs pressing against my palms and then at the pulse at my wrists. She wipes her hands and then looks down at the rings fashioned into dragons' jaws on her fingers.

"Iya, no. They belong to you . . ." I've never seen her

without them, and even the thought of her bare hands feels completely unnatural. Her calm is reflected in her eyes and in the way she touches me on the arm softly.

"And now they belong to you. You have earned them."

She slides each ring off and then waits for me to hold out my right hand. I do so, watching as my mother cradles the gold before easing the rings onto my fingers. The dragons bite at my knuckles, ruby for blood and gold for respect.

"Thank you," I whisper, holding my mother close. She lets me squeeze her tightly before pulling away and pushing back her shoulders.

"Come now. It is time."

We leave the temple and step into the muted sheen of early evening. I pause on the pathway when I see the line of priests. Maha raises her head to look around and then snuggles against me, her tail curled around my neck. The babalawos wait for us, skin adorned with silver chains shining in the moon. Nox stands at the front, next to his father. They're speaking together quietly but fall silent when we approach. I want to run to him straightaway, craving the comfort only he can give. But I know that I can't. Not now as oloorì.

Nox's eyes widen when they see me, lips parting as his gaze skims me from head to toe. Before I can say anything, the boy darts away, leaving me to swallow disappointment. Perhaps I have changed too much for even him.

Iya leads me straight to Baba Bannu and I move to greet him, but before I can arch my heel, the principal priest holds his left wrist with his right hand and then points his toes. The combination of greeting, not seen before, flusters me, and I do not respond, not even sure how.

I try to smile at Bannu as he cups my cheek. "I'm looking forward to your counsel."

"Thank you, Moremi." The priest's hands go to the thick twists of his silver necklace. Lifting it from his throat, he pulls it over his white curls. "May I?"

I take Maha from my shoulders and cradle her instead. She growls lightly but soon relaxes when I rub the soft scales of her belly. Bannu places the large silver chain over my head, settling its broad links around my neck. I touch the cold metal and take a deep breath. Gold from the priestesses and silver from the priests. It's a clear sign to send to the people of our kingdom before I even open my mouth.

The small thud of hooves and a moan draw me from my overthinking just before a long tongue licks my ear from behind. I flinch but I'm smiling already. I'd know that stinking breath anywhere.

"Bisi!" Throwing my arms around the guiamala's neck, I try not to cry, breathing in the scent of hay and her musk. Maha squawks in my ear as she's jostled.

"I thought that I'd save you from walking," says Nox, holding the creature's reins lightly. "She's fully healed and has had a wash. I've even arranged for a new saddle. One fit for the new leader of Kwa."

I ignore his last words, focusing on the guiamala. Her back legs were broken in the fall, and although she can walk, it is in a slow, crooked amble. A soft leather seat embroidered with gold and silver is perched on Bisi's back. I laugh and I swear she smiles at me, thin black lips drawn back to show all her large yellow teeth.

I climb the joints of the guiamala, kicking my wrapper from

around my legs so that it doesn't get caught. Once I'm seated with Maha on my lap, I look down at Nox.

"Are you coming?" I ask, watching as he grins at me, eyes lighting up.

"I'm not sure that this is appropriate, but after what happened at the monasteries, no one is going to argue with you when you're so powerful," he says as he swings himself up behind me.

I know Nox is trying to lighten the situation, but I press my lips together. "Don't. I . . . I hate it that I nearly lost control like that. The dragon's idan is sacred. I need to learn how to use it properly—"

"Shh, Mo. I'm joking." Nox slips his arms around my waist. "Never be ashamed of who you are. I've been telling you this for years now."

He squeezes my shoulders, and I settle back against him, feeling grateful that he doesn't see me any differently. *At least not yet*, says a little voice. I ignore it.

The winding path around Mandara Mountain takes us closer to the gathering place as the moon hangs low, its pocked surface tinged with a faint orange.

The drum announces me as Bisi makes her way to the gathering place. The councils of all the villages have been summoned over the last few days, and now they are waiting. Many others join them, all eager for news. I've never been good at speaking to lots of people, and my stomach knots.

The royal musician has his back to me, great slabs of muscles rippling as he strikes at the iya ilu, producing a deep beat. I place Maha in Nox's lap and climb down from Bisi. Pushing my shoulders back, I walk into the center of the crowd, a space ringed by iyalawos and babalawos, the people of Kwa gathered behind them. My heart thumps and I clear my throat twice, wishing I had water.

"I stand here in the colors of both Yida and Dam to announce a new beginning . . ." I try, but my words waver and are eventually swallowed by the growing cacophony of voices. "I stand here . . ."

I know I need to do something else, something to get their attention and hold it. Taking a deep breath, I pull at the clouds, fingers twitching as I wrap them around the moon, bringing darkness. And then I stamp once, soles hard against the earth, channeling enough idan to shake the ground the crowd stands on.

"Silence!" I shout. "You will listen." I scan the people of Kwa, seeing frowns and gazes lined with caution. I wait until they settle. "Over a week ago, Ojaja tried to alter the Dírágónì ceremony in order to gain the gods' idan." I pause to look around, steeling myself. "In doing so, he imprisoned our principal priest and priestess, and more importantly, he angered Yida and Dam, and invited in the emi buburu. His mistake meant the gods were hurt, and they were furious. And in this fury, the dragons abandoned the Dírágónì ceremony, ready to abandon us to the shadow spirits. Released by Ojaja and Addaf, the emi buburu took life and began to destroy our world."

There are moans from the people of Kwa. Two men at the front of the crowd fall to their knees, grasping at the earth, while a woman with long braids bound in blue clutches at her throat, wailing loudly. I don't like the fear I feel sweep through them all, but I know that it's needed if they are to understand and support the changes I'm about to announce.

"I searched for Dam to reunite him with Yida, along with Noxolo, son of Baba Bannu, and Zaye, an iyalawo . . ." My voice peters out, and I clear my throat, pushing the tears down.

"Dam and Yida listened to our pleas, forgave us the sins of Ojaja, and completed the Dírágónì ceremony, cleansing the world."

Cheers rip through the crowd, but I hold a hand up, wanting to make sure that I get this last part right.

"But something else happened along with this. The gods have chosen their pious, as they do in every initiation, but this year both Dam and Yida entrusted their idan, their power, in one person." I pause and take a deep breath, letting go of the clouds that cloak the moon as I step into a shaft of bright light. I wait a beat, my heart hammering. "The dragons gave me their marks and bound themselves to me, and per their wishes, there will be no separation. We will all worship together, as one."

There is a silence, and then shouts of denial and outrage. I stop myself from flinching as the people call out.

A large man, nearly as tall as the babalawos, steps forward, mouth downturned. "What does this mean? We have never done this before—it is not right!"

"How do we know you even speak for the gods?" shouts another, his hair white, as he leans on a gnarled walking stick.

Their angry questions pepper the air as the people clap and stamp prayers to their gods, seeking reassurance they are not getting from me. And I don't blame them. Who am I? A daughter of Yida. But that is not enough.

I roll my shoulders back, turn around, and stride up to Nox. Maha is watching, her small head snapping from side to side. I scoop her up, crooning to calm the rapid beat of her heart I feel as I press the small dragon to me.

"You will be loved," I whisper as I approach the crowd again.

Maha shivers in my arms as the calls of people swell up into the warm night. I lift her high and she cries out, her thin howl growing loud enough to be heard over the din. She opens her wings, their pearlescent gleam bright under the moon.

"Yida and Dam have given us proof of their decision for us to come together. They sent us their child to worship as one." I bring the small dragon back to the safety of my arms. "To be looked after by me as oloorì. There is balance in the two but now we worship one god, under one leader."

I hold my breath as Maha's tail lashes against my side.

Silence drapes over the crowd, thick and sudden. The stunned faces are mimicked across the gathering space until a small girl toddles forward and reaches up toward Maha. The dragon crows, opening her translucent wings again and gazing down at the child. A sweet smile spreads across the girl's face, cheeks full and round like star apples, as she stamps her feet and claps at the same time. Her mother runs forward to scoop her up even as the people copy the child, filling the gathering space with the dance and rhythm of their prayers as they roar their approval.

EPILOGUE

I stand at the balcony of the main palace, the marble floor cold beneath my feet, Maha draped across my shoulders. Even the sky cannot be fully seen amid the tall ceilings and awnings designed for shade. The weeks spent here have been long and tedious, but Iya wants me to send a message to the kingdom. If I am oloorì, then I need to act like it. Iya says the people need more reassurance, more guidance. And that needs to come from me.

I sigh and return inside. The palace receiving rooms are lit up with torches, sandy golden walls glowing on floors scattered with crushed petals in shades of the coming dawn. A celebration in the guise of seeking favor with Kwa's most influential. I would rather be in the archives or with my herbs, but I square my shoulders and make myself smile.

Small groups lounge on crimson-and-blue silk cushions, while the priests and priestesses favor hard, carved stools and the royal guards lurk at the edges of the room, backs straight, alert even when off duty. Clouds of Aziza swarm around, serving honeyed wine so strong it can only be drunk from small golden thimbles, and palace nundás slink about, reluctantly allowing themselves to be petted. Several low tables are laden with platters of fried fish and groundnut soup, the bowls glowing with the idan used to keep them warm. The alliance between all is still uneasy.

I wander through the throngs of people, passing some plates of chicken yassa. Maha curls her tail tighter around my neck and opens her mouth to yowl.

"The problem will not be in worship, but in the next Dírágónì ceremony."

The conversation winds through the chatter and I turn my head to see a group of council leaders. The largest man, wrapped in deep blue, is holding forth, golden chicken leg in one hand and palm wine in the other. He has yet to adopt the style of both gods' colors and the sight irritates me.

"What will happen when Dam's stars are next in alignment with Yida's stones? Where are the gods now? Will this new dragon take over the cleansing? It is just not clear."

"And if not? Will the emi buburu come back?" adds a short man as he reaches for his wine, bald head shining in the lights. "I heard entire farms and villages were consumed."

"And the Kakum Forest is nothing but rot. Nothing grows there now, not even weeds."

My pulse races at their words. These are the ones I had been afraid of. The questions that I do not have all the answers to yet, but they do not need to know this.

"That's not the biggest concern." The new voice is low and sure. The lone woman gazes around the small group, a hand on the rope of her golden necklace, a fat ruby hanging from its center. She clears her throat before continuing. "I have heard that the ọmọ ọba is betrothed. To a daughter of the Kingdom of Carew."

The news punches me in the gut and I press a hand to my stomach. Jagun betrothed? So soon? My breath comes shallow, and for a moment, there are bursts of red and orange at the edges of my vision.

"Ojaja knows how to make a situation work for him, I'll give him that."

"Rumors are that he is planning to use them."

"Whatever for?"

"His rightful crown, their land. The dragons... Who knows? After all, what will Yida and Dam do? The gods do not meddle in everything their creations get up to."

I drop my hand slowly, taking deep breaths even as the anger rises, sharp and spiked. How dare they talk like this? Where is their loyalty, their devoutness? I expected some... resistance, but not this gossip.

If it is just gossip, a small voice in my head says.

"The dragons will still be called on," I say loudly as I slip into the circle of men and one woman. I use a little idan to jostle and spill their drinks to fully gain their attention, and they startle, gold and silver flashing on arms and fingers. "I can feel the gods idan, even as they are cleansing the lands. And you have all seen but a snippet of Maha's power. One that I think needs not be used unless it is necessary." I pause, and Maha hisses. "Who knows what else she is capable of," I say simply.

There's a chilled silence at this as people avert their gazes and take quick swallows of their wine. Expressions change as fear shimmers across gazes.

"And as for Jagun..." I blink slowly as my voice cracks

on his name. "As for *Jagun,* I trust his father has chosen his betrothment in a way that will benefit them. He is always thinking of himself, after all. You would do well to remember that and his treason."

I stare at each of them in turn, Maha growling softly from my neck, her body vibrating with my anger. I feel her push her idan, flexing. I could use it to warn them, put them in their place...

But I don't. This is not the time and place to be using such power.

"Kwa will not stand for threats," I say calmly. "And if there are any, wherever they may come from, we will quash them. In ways they have never dreamed of." I make myself smile, showing my teeth. "I hope this has allayed your concerns. And if not, speak with me directly. Maha does not like tittle-tattle."

I lift my chin and stride away, needing space more than ever, needing to be alone. The room is wavy now as I manage to keep the tears at bay, but I gasp in shallow breaths. This place is too big, too far away from the earth and not close enough to the sky.

I need to get out.

I slip into the corridors that lead to the kitchens. The serving boys and girls bow their heads at me, but I don't miss the way they hold themselves carefully, their eyes flickering nervously, as if I would steal their souls without a second thought. I wonder what stories the people are telling, how they speak of me.

Jagun is to be married. Banishing him was hard, but this...
I breathe in deeply and try to be logical. Married, yes. But why Carew? And why so soon? I force myself to turn the thought over logically in my head. If the gossip has some truth in it,

we will need to prepare. What matters now more than ever is continuing to unite and strengthen the Kingdom of Kwa. Not Jagun. Not how hearing about his betrothal has made me feel as if I have been eviscerated.

Maha mewls in my ear, and I stroke the dragon still draped over my shoulders, sighing when I reach the outdoor palace kitchens and the silence of the night. The dark is softening now, and I can make out cassava and cowpea growing under the low moon. The sadness that has been crouched inside me continues to leap, and as I pass the herbs, I inhale deeply. I follow my nose to rosemary, hoping for calm. Hoping for comfort. I pick a sprig of the plant. I try to focus on the bright scent, and not the idan from Maha that swirls inside me, promising retribution.

ACKNOWLEDGMENTS

Writing a book requires a very complicated alchemy. It can't be done just on your own, and it involves many factors, one of the most important being the people around you. I wouldn't be able to create any of the stories I do without the people I have in my life.

Thank you to my children, for always being willing to bounce ideas around with me. Kareem, you give me such honest feedback, even if sometimes it's harsh! Jennah, you take care of me when I don't stop for breaks. And, Jamil, your affirmations and insights into plot are always spot on.

Thank you to my friends who tirelessly cheer me on. Clare, for constantly reminding me that I get to a panic stage with each draft and I can push through. Penny, for being my unofficial therapist, willing to listen to me waffle about random facts and to validate my obsessive thoughts. Atem, for dragging me out for dinner and indulging in long rambling talks. Nina, I think I'd be lost without our muay thai boxing. And, Adole, festivals and nights out... all are important motivation when it's deadline time.

Thank you, Emmanuel, for Kakra and Panyin. And for your support and excitement whenever I have any kind of idea. You're always willing to listen to me for hours (a privilege, to be fair) and entertain me as my mind shoots off in a million directions. When I'm stressed, you calm me down, and your confidence in me only pushes me to do better.

Thank you, Danielle, for the shared talks about writing and the affirmations you constantly shower me with. Your advice is always amazing.

Holly and Gytha, thank you for the Cambridge writing sessions, which are also much needed after days on my own.

Thank you to my agent, Jodi, who sees the good in my weird ideas and doesn't moan about my short emails.

Thank you to Tricia. Three books and counting. Your vision and guidance are the reason this book sparkles.

Thank you to the Random House Children's Books team for helping me write yet another book, especially Lauren Stewart, Caroline Abbey, Mallory Loehr, Ray Shappell, Ken Crossland, Rebecca Vitkus, Clare Perret, Liz Sutton, Cynthia Lliguichuzhca, Michael Caiati, Natalie Capogrossi, and Stephania Villar.

Thank you to India for your insights and support, and to the Penguin Random House UK team: Jess Mackay, Naomi Green, Jan Bielecki, and Chessanie Vincent.